PRIDE AND PREJUDICE

JANE AUSTEN

Modern English Version

Modernized Translation by

Harvest Research LLC

Tanya Johnson, Editor

Copyright © 2023 by Tanya Johnson

All rights reserved

No part of this publication may be reproduced, distributed, or transmitted in any form or by any means, including photocopying, recording, or other electronic or mechanical methods, without the publisher's prior written permission, except as permitted by U.S. copyright law.

The story, all names, characters, and incidents portrayed in this production are fictitious. No identification with actual persons (living or deceased), places, buildings, and products is intended or should be inferred.

Modernized by Harvest Research LLC

ISBN: 9798387338953

FORWARD

Jane Austen's classic novel Pride and Prejudice is a beloved tale of love, marriage, and social class set in Regency England. Since its publication in 1813, it has captured the hearts and imaginations of generations of readers, and has been adapted countless times for film, television, and stage.

As with many classic works, the language and style of Pride and Prejudice can be challenging for modern readers. The novel is written in a formal style, with complex sentence structures and archaic vocabulary that can be difficult to parse. This can make it challenging for readers to fully appreciate the wit, humor, and depth of Austen's characters and the world they inhabit.

In this modern English version of Pride and Prejudice, we have sought to make Austen's story accessible to contemporary readers while staying true to the spirit and intent of the original. We have updated the language and grammar to make the text more readable and easier to understand, while preserving the unique voice and perspective of the author.

We believe that this version of Pride and Prejudice will allow readers to fully appreciate Austen's timeless tale of love, misunderstanding, and societal norms, and to connect with the characters and themes in a way that would be more difficult with the original text alone.

We hope that this modern English version of Pride and Prejudice will bring new life and enjoyment to this beloved classic, and that it will introduce the story to new generations of readers who might not otherwise have the chance to experience it.

Harvest Research LLC

Table of Contents

Introduction 10

CHAPTER 1 14

CHAPTER 2 17

CHAPTER 3 20

CHAPTER 4 25

CHAPTER 5 28

CHAPTER 6 31

CHAPTER 7 38

CHAPTER 8 44

CHAPTER 9 50

CHAPTER 10 55

CHAPTER 11 62

CHAPTER 12 67

CHAPTER 13 69

CHAPTER 14 74

CHAPTER 15 78

CHAPTER 16 82

CHAPTER 17 92

CHAPTER 18 96

CHAPTER 19 109

CHAPTER 20 114

CHAPTER 21 119

CHAPTER 22 124

CHAPTER 23 129

CHAPTER 24 134

CHAPTER 25 140

CHAPTER 26 144

CHAPTER 27 150

CHAPTER 28 154

CHAPTER 29 158

CHAPTER 30 165

CHAPTER 31 169

CHAPTER 32 174

CHAPTER 33 179

CHAPTER 34 184

CHAPTER 35 189

CHAPTER 36 195

CHAPTER 37 200

CHAPTER 38 204

CHAPTER 39 207

CHAPTER 40 212

CHAPTER 41 217

CHAPTER 42 223

CHAPTER 43 228

CHAPTER 44	241
CHAPTER 45	247
CHAPTER 46	252
CHAPTER 47	259
CHAPTER 48	269
CHAPTER 49	275
CHAPTER 50	281
CHAPTER 51	287
CHAPTER 52	293
CHAPTER 53	300
CHAPTER 54	308
CHAPTER 55	313
CHAPTER 56	319
CHAPTER 57	327
CHAPTER 58	332
CHAPTER 59	339
CHAPTER 60	346
CHAPTER 61	351
Primary Character Summary	355
Secondary Character Summary	358

INTRODUCTION

Pride and Prejudice, published by Jane Austen in 1813, is widely regarded as one of the greatest works of English literature. Set in the late 18th and early 19th centuries in England, the novel is a commentary on the social, cultural, and economic norms of the Regency period. The story follows the Bennet family, particularly the second daughter, Elizabeth, as she navigates the intricacies of courtship, class, and society.

During the Regency period, England was undergoing a significant transformation. The Industrial Revolution was in full swing, and the country was becoming more urbanized and commercialized. Meanwhile, the landed gentry and aristocracy still held a great deal of power and influence, and the rigid social hierarchy of the time meant that one's class and status were of utmost importance. The Regency period is often associated with the reign of King George IV, who ascended to the throne in 1820 after a period of political instability and unrest.

Against this backdrop, Jane Austen's novel provides a vivid and insightful portrayal of life in the period. She explores the themes of marriage, love, and social class, showing how these concepts intersected and influenced each other. Austen's characters are both entertaining and poignant, with their strengths and weaknesses laid bare for all to see. Her writing is noted for its wit, humor, and incisive observations on human behavior.

In many ways, Pride and Prejudice is a product of its time, reflecting the attitudes and beliefs of the society in which it was written. However, its enduring popularity speaks to its timeless qualities as well. Austen's portrayal of the human heart and its desires, as well as her insights into the workings of society, continue to resonate with readers today.

In this modern English version of Pride and Prejudice, we have sought to make the story more accessible to contemporary readers while staying true to the spirit and intent of the original. We hope that this updated version will introduce the novel to a new generation of readers, and allow them to appreciate the timeless themes and insights that Austen has to offer.

Tanya Johnson
Harvest Research LLC

PRIDE AND PREJUDICE

Modern English Version

CHAPTER 1

It is a truth universally acknowledged, that a single man in possession of a good fortune, must be in want of a wife.

Though his feelings and opinions may be unknown upon his arrival in a new neighborhood, this truth is so deeply ingrained in the minds of the surrounding families that they consider him the rightful property of one of their daughters.

One day, Mrs. Bennet asked her husband, "My dear Mr. Bennet, have you heard that Netherfield Park is finally let?"

To which Mr. Bennet replied he had not.

"But it is," she retorted; "Mrs. Long has just informed me of it."

Mr. Bennet did not respond.

"Don't you wish to know who has taken it?" cried Mrs. Bennet impatiently.

"You want to tell me, and I have no objection to hearing it."

His invitation was enough.

"Well, my dear, you must know Mrs. Long says that a wealthy young man from the north of England has taken Netherfield; that he came down on Monday with a carriage and four horses to see the place, and he liked it so much that he agreed to rent it right away; that he will take possession before Michaelmas, and some of his servants will be in the house by the end of next week."

"What's his name?"

"Bingley."

"Is he married or single?"

"Oh, single, of course! A single man of enormous fortune; four or five thousand a year. What a great opportunity for our girls!"

"How so? How could it affect them?"

"My dear Mr. Bennet," his wife replied, "how can you be so dense? I'm thinking he might marry one of them."

"Is that why he's settling here, to marry?"

"Don't be ridiculous! But it's likely that he might fall in love with one of them, so you must visit him as soon as he arrives."

"I don't see why I should. You and the girls can go, or you can send them by themselves, which might be better, since you're as attractive as any of them; Mr. Bingley might like you the best of the group."

"My dear, you're flattering me. I used to be quite beautiful, but I don't pretend to be anything special now. When a woman has five grown-up daughters, she should stop thinking about her own beauty," said Mrs. Bennet.

"In that situation, a woman rarely has much beauty to think about," replied her husband.

"But, my dear, you must go and see Mr. Bingley when he comes to the neighborhood," said Mrs. Bennet.

"That's more than I can promise," said Mr. Bennet.

"But think about your daughters. Just imagine what an establishment it would be for one of them. Sir William and Lady Lucas are determined to go, just for that reason; because, in general, they don't visit new people. You really have to go first, because if you don't, we won't be able to visit him," Mrs. Bennet said.

"You're being overly meticulous, I must say. I believe Mr. Bingley will be pleased to see you. I'll give you a note to pass on to him, expressing my enthusiastic approval of whichever of the girls he chooses to marry. Though I must put in a good word for my dear Lizzy."

"I don't want you to do that. Lizzy is no better than the others, and she's not nearly as pretty as Jane or as good-natured as Lydia. But you always favor her."

"None of them have much to recommend them," he replied. "They're all silly and ignorant like other girls, but Lizzy is a bit smarter than her sisters."

"Mr. Bennet, how can you talk about your own children like that? You take pleasure in upsetting me and have no sympathy for my poor nerves."

"You're wrong, my dear. I have a lot of respect for your nerves. They're my old friends. I've heard you talk about them with great admiration for the last twenty years, at least."

"Ah, you don't know what I go through," she replied.

"But I hope you will get over it and live to see many young men of four thousand a year come into the neighborhood."

"It won't do us any good if twenty of them come, since you won't visit them."

"Trust me, my dear, when there are twenty, I will visit them all."

Mr. Bennet was such a strange mix of quick wit, sarcastic humor, reserve, and whim that his wife hadn't been able to understand him in the twenty-three years they'd been married. Her own mind was easier to understand. She had little understanding, knowledge, or temper. Whenever she was discontented, she would become anxious. Her life's purpose was to get her daughters married and her solace was visiting and gossip.

CHAPTER 2

Mr. Bennet was one of the first to visit Mr. Bingley. He had always intended to visit him, though he always assured his wife that he would not go; and until the evening after the visit, she did not know of it. It was then revealed in the following way. Seeing his second daughter decorating a hat, he suddenly said to her,

"I hope Mr. Bingley will like it, Lizzy.

"We don't know what Mr. Bingley likes," her mother said resentfully, "since we're not visiting."

"But you forget, Mom," Elizabeth said, "we'll meet him at the assemblies, and Mrs. Long has promised to introduce him."

"I don't think Mrs. Long will do that," Mrs. Bennet said. "She has two nieces of her own. She's a selfish, hypocritical woman, and I think little of her."

"Neither do I," Mr. Bennet said. "I'm glad you don't depend on her to help you."

Mrs. Bennet didn't respond, but, unable to contain herself, started scolding one of her daughters.

"Stop coughing so much, Kitty, for heaven's sake! Have some compassion for my nerves. You're tearing them apart."

"Kitty has no control over her coughing," said her father.

"I'm not coughing for fun," Kitty said, irritated. "When is your next ball, Lizzy?"

"It's two weeks from now," she replied.

"That's right!" exclaimed Mrs. Bennet. "And Mrs. Long won't be back until the day before, so she won't be able to introduce him to her."

"Then, my dear, you can take the advantage over your friend and introduce Mr. Bingley to her."

"Impossible, Mr. Bennet, I don't even know him myself. Why are you being so difficult?"

"I respect your caution. Two weeks isn't enough time to really know someone. But if we don't take a chance, someone else will. So Mrs. Long and her nieces will have to take their chances. Therefore, if you don't want to do it, I will."

The girls looked at their father in surprise. Mrs. Bennet only said, "That's ridiculous!"

"What could that emphatic exclamation mean?" he asked. "Do you think the rules of etiquette and the emphasis placed on them are ridiculous? I don't quite agree with you there. What do you think, Mary? You're a thoughtful young lady who reads a lot of books and takes notes."

Mary wanted to say something wise, but didn't know how.

"While Mary is thinking," he continued, "let's get back to Mr. Bingley."

"I'm so over Mr. Bingley!" his wife declared.

"I'm sorry to hear that; why didn't you tell me earlier? If I had known, I wouldn't have gone to visit him. It's too bad, but since I already went, we can't avoid the acquaintance now."

The ladies were astonished, which was exactly what he wanted – Mrs. Bennet's astonishment was even greater than the others. Once the initial joy had passed, she began to say that she had expected it all along.

"How kind of you, my dear Mr. Bennet! But I knew I could eventually convince you. I was sure you loved your daughters too much to ignore such an opportunity. How pleased I am! And it's so funny that you went out this morning saying nothing about it until now."

"Now, Kitty, you can cough as much as you want," said Mr. Bennet, and as he spoke he left the room, exhausted by his wife's enthusiasm.

"What an amazing father you have, girls," she said when the door was closed. "I don't know how you will ever repay him for his kindness, or me either for that matter. It's not so enjoyable for us at our age to be making new acquaintances every day; but we would do anything for you. Lydia, my love, I'm sure Mr. Bingley will dance with you at the next ball."

"Oh," said Lydia confidently, "I'm not worried; even though I'm the youngest, I'm the tallest."

They spent the rest of the evening discussing when Mr. Bingley would return Mr. Bennet's visit, and when they should invite him to dinner.

CHAPTER 3

Despite Mrs. Bennet and her five daughters' best efforts, they could not get any useful information from Mr. Bennet about Mr. Bingley. They tried everything from direct questions, to indirect guesses, but he managed to dodge them all; and in the end, they had to rely on their neighbor, Lady Lucas' account. She spoke very highly of him. Sir William had been charmed by him. He was young, incredibly handsome, very pleasant, and, to top it all, he was planning to come to the next assembly with a large group of people. It sounded perfect!

Nothing could be more delightful! Having an affinity for dancing was seen as a sign of potential romantic interest, and the Bennet family had high hopes that Mr. Bingley would be romantically interested in one of their daughters.

A few days later, Mr. Bingley paid a visit to Mr. Bennet, and was in the library with him for about ten minutes. Unfortunately, he only got to meet the father, and not the daughters, who were, however, able to observe from an upper window that he was wearing a blue coat and riding a black horse.

An invitation to dinner was soon sent, and Mrs. Bennet had already come up with the menu, when an answer arrived that put off the dinner. Mr. Bingley had to be in town the following day, and so could not accept the invitation. Mrs. Bennet was quite disconcerted. She couldn't understand why he would be in town so soon after arriving in Hertfordshire, and she started to worry that he would always run around from one place to another, instead of staying at Netherfield like he should. Lady Lucas tried to reassure her by suggesting he had gone to London to get a big group for the ball, and soon it was being said that Mr. Bingley was bringing twelve ladies and seven gentlemen to the assembly. The girls were upset at such a large number of ladies, but the day before the ball they heard he had only brought six - his five sisters and a cousin. When they arrived at the assembly, there were only five of them: Mr. Bingley, his two sisters, the husband of the eldest and another young man.

Mr. Bingley was attractive and well-mannered; he had a pleasant appearance and easy, natural behavior. His sisters were beautiful and had a very fashionable air about them.

His brother-in-law, Mr. Hurst merely looked like a gentleman, but it was Mr. Darcy who quickly caught everyone's attention with his tall stature, handsome features, and air of nobility, not to mention the rumor that he had an income of ten thousand pounds a year. The gentlemen commented that he was a fine-looking man, the ladies declared he was even better-looking than Mr. Bingley, and for about half the evening he was admired by all. However, his proud and unapproachable attitude soon caused people to turn away from him in disgust, and even his great wealth in Derbyshire couldn't save him from having an unpleasant expression and being unworthy to be compared to his friend.

On the other hand, Mr. Bingley quickly became acquainted with all the important people in the room. He remained cheerful and open, danced every dance, expressed his disappointment when the ball had to end so soon, and even suggested throwing one himself at Netherfield. His amiable qualities spoke for themselves. What a difference between him and his friend! Mr. Darcy only danced with Mrs. Hurst and Miss Bingley once each, refused to be introduced to any other lady and spent the rest of the evening wandering around the room, occasionally talking to his own group. His personality was clear. He was the most arrogant and unpleasant man in the world and everyone hoped he would never come back. Mrs. Bennet was one of the most hostile towards him, her dislike of his general behavior made worse by him ignoring one of her daughters.

Elizabeth Bennet had been forced, because of the lack of gentlemen, to sit out two dances; and during that time, Mr. Darcy was close enough for her to overhear a conversation between him and Mr. Bingley, who had come from the dance for a few minutes to urge his friend to join it.

"Come on Darcy," he said, "you have to dance. I can't stand seeing you standing around like this. You'd be much better off dancing."

"I won't. You know I hate it unless I'm really familiar with the person I'm dancing with. At a gathering like this it would be unbearable. Your sisters are already dancing and there's not a single other woman here that I'd want to dance with," said Darcy.

"I wouldn't be so picky as you," said Bingley. "I'd give anything to dance with these girls. I've never met so many pleasant girls in my life and some of them are really pretty."

"You're dancing with the only attractive girl in the room," said Darcy, looking at the oldest Miss Bennet.

"She's the most beautiful thing I've ever seen! But one of her sisters is sitting just behind you and she's very pretty. Can I ask my partner to introduce us?"

"Which one are you referring to?" he asked, turning to look at Elizabeth momentarily. When she met his gaze, he quickly looked away and responded in a distant and detached tone. "I suppose she's alright, but she's not attractive enough to tempt me. Besides, I'm not in the mood to elevate the social status of young ladies who have been rejected by other men. You should go back to your partner and enjoy her company, because you're wasting your time with me."

Mr. Bingley followed his advice and Mr. Darcy walked off. Elizabeth didn't feel kindly towards him. Nevertheless, she told the story to her friends with great enthusiasm as she had a lively, playful nature that enjoyed anything amusing.

The evening was a pleasant one for the whole family. Mrs. Bennet was delighted to see her eldest daughter admired by the Netherfield party. Mr. Bingley had danced with her twice and his sisters had paid her special attention. Jane was pleased, though in a more subdued manner, and Elizabeth was happy to share in her sister's joy. Mary had heard herself being talked about by Miss Bingley as the most talented girl in the neighborhood; and Catherine and Lydia had been lucky enough to never be without a dance partner, which was all they had been interested in at the ball. So they happily returned to Longbourn, the village where they lived and which was mainly populated by them. Mr. Bennet was still awake when they got back. He was engrossed in a book and had been curious to find out how the evening had gone. He had been hoping his wife's opinion of the stranger would not be fulfilled, but he soon realized he was wrong.

"Oh, my dear Mr. Bennet," she said as she walked into the room, "we had an amazing evening, a brilliant ball. I wish you had been there. Jane was so admired, it was incredible. Everyone said how good she looked; and Mr. Bingley thought she was gorgeous and danced with her twice. Can you imagine that, my dear? He actually danced with her twice; and she was the only one in the room he asked to dance a second time.

"At first, he asked Miss Lucas. I was so upset to see him stand up with her; but, he didn't seem to like her at all; nobody can, you know; and he seemed really taken with Jane as she was leaving the dance. So he asked who she was and got introduced, and asked her for the next two dances. Then, the third and fourth dances he danced with Miss King, and the fifth and sixth with Maria Lucas, and the seventh with Jane again, and the eighth with Lizzy, and the Boulanger ----"

"If he had had any sympathy for me ," cried her husband impatiently, "he wouldn't have danced so much! For God's sake, don't talk about his partners any more. I wish he had twisted his ankle in the first dance!"

"Oh, my dear," continued Mrs. Bennet, "I'm so pleased with him. He's so incredibly handsome! And his sisters are delightful. I've never seen anything more elegant than their outfits. "I dare say the lace on Mrs. Hurst's dress..."

Here she was interrupted again. Mr. Bennet objected to any description of her fancy clothing. She was therefore forced to find another topic and spoke bitterly and somewhat exaggeratedly about the rude behavior of Mr. Darcy.

"But I can tell you," she continued, "that Lizzy doesn't miss out on much by not catching his eye; he's a horrible, disagreeable man, not worth pleasing at all. So arrogant and conceited, it was unbearable! He was walking around here and there, thinking he was so great! Not even good-looking enough to dance with! I wish you had been there, my dear, to give him one of your put-downs. I can't stand the man."

CHAPTER 4

When Jane and Elizabeth were alone, the former, who had been careful in her praise of Mr. Bingley before, told her sister how much she admired him.

"He's exactly what a young man should be," she said. "He's sensible, good-natured, and lively, and I've never encountered such pleasant manners! So much ease, with perfect etiquette!"

"He's good-looking too," Elizabeth replied. "A young man should also strive to be attractive if he can. That completes his character."

"I was really flattered when he asked me to dance a second time. I didn't expect that kind of compliment."

"Didn't you? I did for you. But that's one of the big differences between us. Compliments always surprise you, but never me. What could be more natural than him asking you again? He couldn't help seeing that you were five times as pretty as any other woman in the room. No thanks to his chivalry for that. Well, he certainly is very pleasant, and I give you permission to like him. You've liked plenty of dumber people."

"Dear Lizzy!"

"Oh, you're much too quick, you know, to like people in general. You never see a fault in anyone. Everyone is good and agreeable in your eyes. You have never said a bad word about anyone in your life."

"I try not to be too quick to judge, but I always say what I think."

"I know you do, and that's what makes it so amazing. With your good sense, you're so blind to the foolishness and nonsense of others! It's common enough to pretend to be open-minded, but to be genuinely honest with no show or agenda - to take the good from everyone's character and make it even better, and never mention the bad - that's something only you can do. So, you like this man's sisters too, huh? Their manners don't match his."

"Not really, not at first glance anyway, but they're quite pleasant to talk to once you get to know them. Miss Bingley will live with her brother and taking care of his household, and I'd be surprised if we don't end up with a very delightful neighbor in her."

Elizabeth stayed quiet but she thought little them; they had not made a good impression at the assembly. The sisters were really quite lovely, they had been to a top private school, had a fortune of twenty thousand pounds and liked to spend more than they should and associate with people of high standing, so they thought highly of themselves and looked down on others. They were from a distinguished family in the north of England and had made their fortune through trade.

Mr. Bingley inherited almost one hundred thousand pounds from his father, who had intended to buy a property but passed away before he could. Mr. Bingley had the same intention, and he sometimes chose a place in the county, but since he had a nice house and the freedom of a manor, many people who knew how easy-going he was, weren't sure if he would spend the rest of his life at Netherfield and leave it to the next generation to buy.

His sisters were very eager for him to get his own estate, but even though he was only renting, Miss Bingley was not unwilling to be the hostess at his table, and Mrs. Hurst, who had married a man with more status than money, was also happy to consider his house her home when it suited her. When Mr. Bingley had been of age for two years, he was encouraged to look at Netherfield House due to an unexpected recommendation. He examined it for half an hour, liking the location and the main rooms, and believing what the owner said about it, so he took it right away.

Despite the fact that their personalities were very different, there was a strong bond of friendship between him and Darcy.

Bingley was drawn to Darcy because of his easy-going, open, and flexible nature, and he never seemed unhappy with Darcy's personality. Bingley had the utmost trust in Darcy's judgement and respected his intelligence. Darcy was haughty, reserved, and picky, and his manners, though polite, were not inviting. In that regard, Bingley had the upper hand. Bingley was sure to be liked wherever he went, whereas Darcy often caused offence.

The way they spoke about the Meryton assembly was a perfect example of their personalities. Bingley had never met nicer people or prettier girls in his life; everyone had been really kind and attentive to him; there was no formality or stiffness; he soon felt like he knew everyone in the room; and as for Miss Bennet, he couldn't imagine an angel more beautiful. Whereas, Darcy had seen a group of people who weren't very attractive and he had no interest in any of them and he didn't receive any attention or pleasure from them. Miss Bennet, he admitted was pretty, but she smiled too much.

Mrs. Hurst and her sister acknowledged that Miss Bennet was a sweet girl, and they admired and liked her. They even expressed a desire to get to know her better, and their brother felt justified in considering her a potential romantic interest.

CHAPTER 5

Not far from Longbourn lived a family who were very close with the Bennet's. Sir William Lucas had formerly been in business in Meryton, where he had made a decent amount of money and been honored with a knighthood for an address he had made to the king during his time as mayor. This honor may have had too strong an effect on him, as it made him dislike his business and residence in the small town, so he moved his family to a house about a mile away called Lucas Lodge. Here, he could take pleasure in his own importance without the restraints of work and be courteous to everyone he met. Although he was proud of his social status, it didn't make him haughty; in fact, he treated everyone with great respect and consideration. He was naturally kind, affable, and helpful, and his time at St. James's had taught him good manners and courteous behavior.

Lady Lucas was a kind woman who was a valuable neighbor to Mrs. Bennet. They had several children, the eldest of whom was around twenty-seven, and was Elizabeth's close friend.

It was necessary for the Miss Lucases and Miss Bennets to get together to discuss the ball. The day after the assembly, Miss Lucas came to Longbourn.

Mrs. Bennet said to her, "Charlotte, you started the evening off well; you were Mr. Bingley's first choice."

"Yes, but it seemed like he liked his second choice better."

"Oh, you mean Jane, since he danced with her twice. It seems like he was admiring her; I heard something about it, but I'm not sure - Something about Mr. Robinson?"

"Maybe you mean what I heard between him and Mr. Robinson. Didn't I tell you about it? Mr. Robinson asked him how he liked the assemblies in Meryton and if he thought there were many pretty women in the room and which one he thought was the prettiest. And he immediately answered the last question with 'Oh, the eldest Miss Bennet without a doubt. There can't be two opinions on that'," said Elizabeth.

"My eavesdropping was more useful than yours, Eliza," said Charlotte. "Mr. Darcy isn't as interesting to listen to as his friend. Poor Eliza, to only be just okay."

"I hope you don't put it in Lizzy's head to be upset by his bad behavior," said Charlotte. "He's such an unpleasant person that it would be a real shame to be liked by him. Mrs. Long told me last night that he sat close to her for half an hour without saying a word."

"Without saying a word?" said Jane. "Are you sure, ma'am? Is there a mistake? I definitely saw Mr. Darcy talking to her."

"Yes, because she asked him how he liked Netherfield and he couldn't help responding to her, but she said he seemed really angry about being spoken to."

"Miss Bingley told me," said Jane, "that he doesn't talk much unless he's with people he knows well. He's really friendly with them."

"I don't believe a word of it, my dear. If he was so pleasant, he would have chatted with Mrs. Long. But I can guess what happened; everyone says he's full of himself, and I bet he heard that Mrs. Long doesn't have a carriage and had to come to the ball in a hack chaise."

"I don't mind him not talking to Mrs. Long," said Miss Lucas, "but I wish he had danced with Eliza."

"Maybe next time, Lizzy," said her mother, "I wouldn't dance with him if I were you."

"I believe, ma'am, I can safely promise never to dance with him," said Lizzy.

"His pride," said Miss Lucas, "doesn't bother me as much as it usually does because there's an explanation for it. It's not surprising that such a handsome, well-off young man would think highly of himself. If I can put it this way, he's allowed to be proud."

"That's absolutely correct," Elizabeth replied. "I would be willing to overlook his pride, if he hadn't hurt my own feelings."

"Pride is a very common flaw," Mary replied, her thoughts taking a more serious tone. "Everything I've ever read suggests that it's extremely widespread and that very few of us don't have some degree of self-importance, whether it's based on something real or not. Pride and vanity are two different things, though the words are often used interchangeably. Pride has more to do with our opinion of ourselves, while vanity is more about what we want others to think of us."

"If I was as rich as Mr. Darcy," chimed in young Lucas, who had joined his sisters, "I wouldn't care how proud I was. I'd keep a pack of foxhounds and drink a bottle of wine a day."

"Then you would drink a lot more than you should," Mrs. Bennet replied. "If I saw you doing that, I would take away your bottle right away."

The boy argued that she shouldn't, but she kept insisting that she would and the conversation ended when the visit was over.

CHAPTER 6

The women of Longbourn paid a visit to those at Netherfield, which was then returned in due form. Miss Bennet's charming demeanor won over the good opinion of Mrs. Hurst and Miss Bingley, despite their disdain for the mother and younger sisters. They expressed a desire to get better acquainted with the two eldest Bennet sisters. Jane was delighted with the attention, but Elizabeth noticed that they still behaved superciliously towards everyone, even her sister, and she did not like them. However, their kindness towards Jane had some value, as it likely stemmed from their admiration for their brother. It was clear to everyone whenever they met that he admired Jane, and to Jane it was equally clear that she was developing feelings for him. Despite her strong emotions, Jane's calm demeanor and cheerful personality would prevent any unwanted attention from the impertinent. Elizabeth confided in her friend, Miss Lucas, about her observations.

"It may be pleasing," replied Charlotte, "to deceive others in matters of the heart, but it can also be a disadvantage to be too guarded. If a woman conceals her feelings too well from the person she cares for, she may miss the opportunity to win their heart. It's not much comfort to think that others are in the dark about your feelings. Gratitude and vanity often play a role in our attachments, so it's not wise to leave anything to chance. It's natural to begin with a slight preference, but few of us have the courage to truly love someone without some encouragement. In nine cases out of ten, a woman is better off showing more affection than she feels. Bingley undoubtedly likes your sister, but he may never move beyond that if she doesn't help him along."

"But she does help him along, as much as she can given her nature. If I can see her regard for him, he must be a simpleton not to see it too."

"Remember, Eliza, that Bingley doesn't know Jane's personality as well as you do."

"But if a woman likes a man and doesn't try to hide it, he will surely figure it out."

"Perhaps he will, if he spends enough time with her. However, Bingley and Jane only meet for short periods of time at mixed social gatherings, and they don't have the opportunity to talk privately very often. Jane should therefore make the most of every moment in which she can engage his attention. Once she has his attention, there will be plenty of time for her to fall in love as much as she likes."

"Your plan is a good one," Elizabeth replied, "when all that matters is wanting to be married; if I was determined to get a rich husband, or any husband, I'm sure I would follow it. But that's not how Jane feels; she's not doing this on purpose. She can't even be sure of the intensity of her own feelings, or if they're reasonable. She has only known him for two weeks. At Meryton, she danced with him four times. she saw him one morning at his own house, and has since had dinner with him four times. That's not enough for her to understand his character."

"Not as you describe it. If she had only had dinner with him, she may have only seen if he had a good appetite; but you must remember that four evenings were spent together as well – and four evenings can do a lot."

"Yes," replied her friend. "These four evenings have let them know that they both prefer the card game 'Vingt-un' to 'Commerce', but I don't think they've discovered much else about each other's personalities."

"Well," Charlotte said, "I wish Jane all the best. If she got married to him tomorrow, I think she'd have as good a chance of being happy as if she spent a year getting to know him. When it comes to marriage, happiness is all down to luck. Even if you know each other's personalities very well before, or if they're very similar, it doesn't make any difference. You always end up being different enough to have your share of arguments. It's better to know as little as possible about the flaws of the person you're going to spend your life with."

"You're making me laugh, Charlotte," her friend replied, "but it's not sensible. You know it's not sensible, and you'd never do this yourself."

Elizabeth was too busy watching Mr. Bingley's attention on her sister to realize that she was becoming an object of interest to his friend. At first, Mr. Darcy had barely thought Elizabeth was pretty. He had looked at her without admiration at the ball, and when they next met, he only looked at her to criticize. But soon, he realized that her dark eyes were intelligent and expressive. He then had to admit that her figure was light and pleasing, and even though he had said her manners weren't fashionable, he was charmed by their playfulness. She had no idea about this; to her, he was just the man who didn't mingle with anyone and hadn't thought her attractive enough to dance with.

He wanted to know more about her and, as a way to start a conversation with her; he paid attention to her conversations with others. This caught her attention. It happened at Sir William Lucas's, where there was a large gathering.

"What is Mr. Darcy doing," she asked Charlotte, "listening to my conversation with Colonel Forster?"

"That's something only Mr. Darcy can answer," Charlotte replied.

"But if he does it again, I'll definitely let him know that I know what he's up to. He has a very sarcastic eye and if I don't start by being rude to him, I'll soon be scared of him."

On his approaching them soon afterwards, though without seeming to have any intention of speaking, Miss Lucas challenged her friend to mention the topic of the ball to him, which immediately prompted Elizabeth to do it. She looked at him and said,

"Don't you think I did really well just now when I was trying to get Colonel Forster to give us a ball in Meryton?"

"You were very enthusiastic," he replied. "But it is a subject that always makes a lady passionate."

"You're being a bit harsh on us," Elizabeth said.

"It'll soon be her turn to be pestered," Miss Lucas added. "I'm going to open the instrument, Eliza, and you know what that means."

"You're a very strange friend! Always wanting me to play and sing in front of everyone! If I was musically inclined, you'd be invaluable, but as it is, I'd rather not perform in front of people who are used to hearing the best of the best," Eliza replied. But when Miss Lucas persisted, she added, "Okay, if it must be, it must." She then glanced at Mr. Darcy and said, "There's an old saying that everyone here is probably familiar with: 'Keep your breath to cool your porridge, I'll keep mine to swell my song.'"

Her performance was good, but not great. After a couple of songs, and before she could respond to the requests from the crowd for her to sing again, her sister Mary took her place at the instrument. Mary, who was the only plain one in the family, had worked hard to gain knowledge and accomplishments, and was always enthusiastic to display them.

Mary had neither genius nor taste, and although vanity had given her determination, it had also given her a pedantic attitude and a conceited manner, which would have ruined any higher level of accomplishment than she had achieved. Elizabeth, who was easy and natural, was listened to with much more pleasure, even though she wasn't playing nearly as well; and Mary, at the end of a long concerto, was glad to gain praise and gratitude by playing Scotch and Irish tunes, at the request of her younger sisters, who, along with some of the Lucases and two or three officers, eagerly joined in the dancing at one end of the room.

Mr. Darcy stood near them in silent disapproval of such a way of spending the evening, with no conversation, and was so caught up in his own thoughts that he didn't notice Sir William Lucas was nearby until Sir William said:

"What a delightful pastime for young people this is, Mr. Darcy! Nothing beats dancing, really. I see it as one of the finest accomplishments of civilized societies."

"I consider it to be one of the first signs of a sophisticated society," Sir William said. "It's also popular among less refined societies; everyone can dance." Sir William smiled. "Your friend dances very well," he said, looking at Bingley who had just joined them. "I'm sure you are an expert in the art yourself, Mr. Darcy."

"You saw me dance at Meryton, I believe, sir," Darcy replied.

"Yes, and I enjoyed it very much," Sir William said. "Do you often dance at St. James's?"

"Never, sir," Darcy said.

"Wouldn't it be a sign of respect to the place?" Sir William asked.

"I try to avoid it if I can," Darcy answered. "I assume you have a house in town?"

Darcy nodded in response.

"I had thought of settling in town myself since I enjoy the company of people of high social rank; however, I was not sure that Lady Lucas would be able to tolerate the air of London."

He paused, waiting for a response, but his companion stayed silent. At that moment, Elizabeth came close to them and he had an idea.

"My dear Miss Eliza, why aren't you dancing? Mr. Darcy, I must introduce this young lady to you as a very desirable partner. You can't refuse to dance when there is so much beauty in front of you." He took her hand and tried to give it to Mr. Darcy, who, though taken aback, was not unwilling to accept it. But Elizabeth quickly stepped back and said to Sir William:

"I have no intention of dancing, sir. Please don't assume that I came here to ask for a partner.

Mr. Darcy, with great politeness, asked if he could have the honor of her hand, but she refused. Elizabeth was determined and Sir William's attempts to persuade her did not change her mind.

"You are so skilled at dancing, Miss Eliza, it would be a shame to deny me the pleasure of seeing you. Though this gentleman may not like the activity in general, I'm sure he will be happy to oblige us for a half hour."

"Mr. Darcy is very polite," Elizabeth answered with a smile.

"He certainly is charming," said Miss Bingley. "But given the opportunity, my dear Miss Elizabeth, we can hardly blame him for being agreeable. After all, who would object to having such a partner?"

Elizabeth looked slyly at Miss Bingley and turned away. Her earlier refusal had not diminished the gentleman's opinion of her, and he was thinking fondly of her when he was approached by Miss Bingley who said, "I can guess what you are thinking about."

"I don't think you can."

"You must be thinking about how terrible it would be to spend many evenings in this company. I could not agree more. The dullness and yet the noise, the emptiness and yet the self-importance of everyone here! I would give anything to hear your thoughts about them!"

"You are wrong. I was actually thinking about how much pleasure a pair of beautiful eyes on a pretty woman's face can bring."

Miss Bingley immediately looked at his face and asked who this woman was. Mr. Darcy answered bravely, "Miss Elizabeth Bennet."

Miss Bingley repeated, "Miss Elizabeth Bennet! I'm astonished. How long has she been your favorite? When can I congratulate you?"

"That's the exact question I expected you to ask. A woman's imagination is very quick; it goes from admiration to love, and from love to marriage in no time. I knew you would be congratulating me."

"Well, if you're so serious about it, I'll consider it done. You'll have a lovely mother-in-law, and of course she'll always be at Pemberley with you."

He listened to her with no emotion, while she kept talking; and as his calmness showed her that everything was alright, she kept going.

CHAPTER 7

Mr. Bennet's wealth was almost entirely made up of an annual income of two thousand pounds, which unfortunately for his daughters, was inherited by a distant relative in the absence of male heirs. His wife's fortune, although it was sufficient for her lifestyle, was inadequate to make up for the shortfall. Her father had been a lawyer in Meryton and had left her four thousand pounds.

She had a sister who was married to a Mr. Philips, who had been a clerk for their father and had taken over the business, and a brother who had settled in London in a respectable profession.

The village of Longbourn was only a mile away from Meryton, which was a very convenient distance for the young ladies, who usually visited there three or four times a week to pay their respects to their aunt, and to visit the milliner's shop right across the street. The two youngest members of the family, Catherine and Lydia, were especially thrilled by these activities. They were more empty-headed than their sisters and so, when nothing else was available, they'd take a walk to Meryton to pass the morning and have something to talk about in the evening.

Mrs. Philips was usually able to provide them with interesting news. Recently, the arrival of a militia regiment in the area had made them even happier as it was to stay for the whole winter and Meryton was the headquarters. Visiting Mrs. Philips now brought them the most exciting information. Every day, they learnt more about the officers' names and family backgrounds. Soon, they knew where they were staying and even started to meet the officers. Mr. Philips visited them all and his nieces were suddenly filled with joy they'd never experienced before. All they could talk about was the officers and Mr.

Bingley's wealth, which thrilled their mother, was nothing compared to the uniforms of an ensign.

After hearing them talk at length on this topic one morning, Mr. Bennet calmly remarked,--"Based on how you two are talking, it seems like you must be two of the most silly girls in the country. I've been thinking that for a while, but now I'm sure of it."

Catherine was embarrassed and didn't say anything, but Lydia, completely unfazed, kept talking about how much she liked Captain Carter and how she hoped to see him that day before he left for London the next morning.

Mrs. Bennet said, "I'm surprised you would think your own children are silly. If I wanted to think badly of someone's children, it shouldn't be my own."

"If my children are silly, I hope I'll always be aware of it"

"But luckily, they're all very clever."

"That's the only thing we don't agree on. I was hoping we'd have the same opinion on everything, but I have to disagree with you and think our two youngest daughters are especially foolish."

"My dear Mr. Bennet, you can't expect young girls to have the same sense as us. When they get to our age, I'm sure they won't be so interested in army officers like we were. I remember when I used to like a red coat very much - and I still do - and if a wealthy colonel with five or six thousand a year wanted to marry one of my girls, I wouldn't say no. I thought Colonel Forster looked very handsome the other night at Sir William's in his uniform."

"Mamma," said Lydia, "my aunt says that Colonel Forster and Captain Carter don't go to Miss Watson's as often as when they first arrived; she often sees them standing in Clarke's library."

Mrs. Bennet was about to answer when the footman arrived with a note for Miss Bennet; it was from Netherfield and the servant was waiting for a reply. Mrs. Bennet's eyes lit up with joy and she eagerly asked, while her daughter read:

"Well Jane, who is it from? What is it about? What does he say? Come on Jane, tell us quickly, my love."

Jane replied, "It is from Miss Bingley" and then read it aloud:

"My dear friend,
if you are not so compassionate as to dine today with Louisa and me, we shall be in danger of hating each other for the rest of our lives; for a whole day's tête-à-tête between two women can never end without a quarrel. Come as soon as you can on the receipt of this. My brother and the gentlemen are to dine with the officers.
Yours ever, Caroline Bingley."

Lydia exclaimed, "With the officers! I wonder why my aunt did not tell us of that."

Mrs. Bennet said, "Dining out, that is very unlucky."

Jane asked, "Can I have the carriage?"

"No, my dear, it looks like it's going to rain so you'd better go on horseback and stay overnight," said Elizabeth's father.

"That would be a good idea," said Elizabeth, "if you're sure they won't offer to send her home."

"Oh, the gentlemen will have Mr. Bingley's carriage to go to Meryton and the Hursts don't have any horses," her father replied.

"I'd much rather go in the coach," said Elizabeth.

"But I'm sure your father can't spare the horses, can you, Mr. Bennet?" her mother asked.

"I need them on the farm more often than I can get them," he said.

"But if you have them today," Elizabeth said, "my mother's plan will be fulfilled."

Finally, her father admitted that the horses were already taken and Jane had to go on horseback. Her mother saw her off with many cheerful predictions of bad weather. Sure enough, Jane had only been gone a short time before it started raining heavily. Her sisters were worried for her, but her mother was delighted. The rain kept going all night without stopping; Jane obviously couldn't come back.

"This was a great idea of mine," Mrs. Bennet said more than once, as if she was taking all the credit for making it rain. She didn't realize how successful her plan was until the next morning. Just after breakfast, a servant from Netherfield brought a note for Elizabeth:

"My dearest Lizzie,

"I'm feeling really sick this morning, which I guess is from getting soaked yesterday. My kind friends won't let me go home until I'm better. They also want me to see Mr. Jones, so don't be alarmed if you hear he's been to see me. Except for a sore throat and a headache, I'm not too bad. The distance is nothing when one has a motive; only three miles. I shall be back by dinner."

"Yours, etc."

"Well, my dear," said Mr. Bennet, when Elizabeth had read the note aloud, "if your daughter were to become seriously ill—if she were to die—it would be a comfort to know that it was all in pursuit of Mr. Bingley and under your orders."

"Oh, I'm not at all afraid of her dying. People don't die from a little cold. She'll be taken good care of. As long as she's there, all will be good. I would go and see her if I had the carriage."

Elizabeth, feeling very anxious, decided to go to her, although the carriage wasn't available. Since she wasn't a horsewoman, walking was her only option. She announced her decision.

"How can you be so silly," cried her mother, "as to think of such a thing, in all this mud! You won't be fit to be seen when you get there."

"I'll be perfectly fit to see Jane—which is all I want."

"Is this a hint to me, Lizzy," said her father, "to send for the horses?"

"No, indeed. I don't wish to avoid the walk. The distance is nothing when you have a motive; it's only three miles. I'll be back by dinner."

Mary replied, "I admire your enthusiasm, but you should always make sure your feelings are guided by reason and that your efforts match the task at hand."

Catherine and Lydia then offered, "We'll go as far as Meryton with you." Elizabeth accepted and the three of them set off.

Lydia said as they walked, "If we hurry, maybe we can see Captain Carter before he leaves."

Once they reached Meryton, the two youngest went to the lodgings of one of the officers' wives, and Elizabeth continued her walk alone, rushing through fields, jumping over stiles and puddles, until she finally arrived at the house, her ankles aching, her stockings dirty, and her face flushed from the exercise.

She was taken to the breakfast parlor, where everyone except Jane was gathered, and her arrival caused quite a stir. Mrs. Hurst and Miss Bingley were astonished that Elizabeth had walked three miles in such dirty weather and by herself. They seemed to think less of her for it. However, they welcomed her politely. Mr. Darcy was impressed with how the exercise had improved her complexion, but he was also skeptical if the situation justified her coming so far alone. Mr. Hurst was only thinking about his breakfast.

When Elizabeth asked about her sister, she was not given a very positive response. Miss Bennet had slept badly and was very feverish, so she was not well enough to leave her room. Elizabeth was glad to be taken to her immediately, and Jane was delighted at her arrival since she had wanted to see Elizabeth but was afraid of alarming or inconveniencing her. She wasn't able to talk much, so when Miss Bingley left them alone, Elizabeth just sat there with her.

After breakfast, Jane's sisters joined them and Elizabeth began to like them when she saw how much love and care they showed for Jane. The doctor came and said, as expected, that she had caught a bad cold and that they needed to get her better. He told her to go back to bed and gave her some medicine. Elizabeth stayed in the room the whole time and the other ladies weren't often away either, since the men were out.

When it was 3 o'clock, Elizabeth realized she had to go, and said so reluctantly. Miss Bingley offered her the carriage, and it only took a bit of persuading for Elizabeth to accept it. Jane showed such distress at the thought of them parting that Miss Bingley had to change the offer of the chaise into an invitation for Elizabeth to stay at Netherfield. Elizabeth was very grateful and a servant was sent to Longbourn to inform the family of her stay and to bring back some clothes.

CHAPTER 8

At five o'clock, the two ladies went to their rooms to get ready, and at half-past six, Elizabeth was called to dinner. She was asked many polite questions at the table, and Mr. Bingley showed a greater interest in her than anyone else. However, she had to give an unfavorable answer. Jane was still very ill. When the sisters heard this, they expressed their sympathy several times, saying how sorry they were and how unpleasant it is to have a bad cold, and how much they disliked being ill themselves. But then they stopped talking about it and didn't seem to care much about Jane anymore. Their indifference towards Jane when she wasn't right in front of them brought back all of Elizabeth's original dislike of them.

Their brother, indeed, was the only one of the party whom she could regard with any approval. His concern for Jane was obvious, and his attentions to her most pleasing; and they kept her from feeling as unwelcome as she believed the others thought she was. She got very little attention from anyone else. Miss Bingley was completely taken up with Mr. Darcy, and her sister was almost as devoted; and as for Mr. Hurst, who Elizabeth was sitting next to, he was an idle man who only cared about eating, drinking, and playing cards, and when he found out she preferred a simple dish to a fancy one he had nothing to say to her.

After dinner she went straight back to Jane, and as soon as she left the room Miss Bingley started criticizing her. Her manners were said to be very bad, a mixture of pride and rudeness; she had no conversation, no style, no taste, no beauty. Mrs. Hurst thought the same, and added:

"She has nothing, in short, to recommend her, except for being an excellent walker. I'll never forget how she looked this morning. She really looked almost mad."

"She did indeed, Louisa. I could hardly keep a straight face. It was very silly of her to come at all! Why did she have to go running around the countryside because her sister had a cold? Her hair was so untidy and wild looking!"

"Yes, and her petticoat; I hope you saw her petticoat, it was six inches deep in mud. I'm sure of it, and the dress she had let down to cover it wasn't doing its job."

"Your description is very accurate, Louisa," said Bingley; "but I didn't notice any of that when Miss Elizabeth Bennet came into the room this morning. Her dirty petticoat went right past me."

"I'm sure you noticed it, Mr. Darcy," said Miss Bingley; "and I'm sure you wouldn't want your sister to be seen like that."

"Of course not."

"To walk three miles, or four miles, or five miles, or however far it was, with her ankles in the dirt, and all alone! What was she thinking? It seems to me that it shows a horrible kind of arrogant independence, a complete disregard for propriety."

"It shows a very sweet affection for her sister," said Bingley.

"I'm afraid, Mr. Darcy," Miss Bingley said in a low voice, "that this experience has affected your appreciation of her beautiful eyes."

"Not at all," he replied, "they were made brighter by the activity."

After this, there was a short pause and then Mrs. Hurst started talking again:

"I have a great fondness for Jane Bennet, she is really a very sweet girl, and I wish with all my heart that she was in a better situation. But with parents like hers and such low connections, I'm afraid it's impossible."

"I believe I heard you say that their uncle is a lawyer in Meryton?"

"Yes, and they have another who lives somewhere near Cheapside."

Her sister added, "That's great!" and they both laughed heartily.

"If they had enough uncles to fill up all of Cheapside," Bingley exclaimed, "it wouldn't make them any more pleasant."

"But it would greatly reduce their chances of marrying men of any standing in the world," Darcy replied.

Bingley didn't answer, but his sisters agreed with him and laughed for a while at the expense of their dear friend's lowly family.

With renewed affection, they went to her room after leaving the dining room and stayed with her until they were called for coffee. She was still very ill and Elizabeth refused to leave her until late in the evening when she saw her asleep. When she went downstairs to the drawing room, she found everyone playing cards and was immediately invited to join them, but she suspected they were playing for high stakes and so made an excuse of her sister and said she would amuse herself with a book. Mr. Hurst looked at her in astonishment and said:

"Do you prefer reading to cards? That's rather unusual."

Miss Bingley added, "Miss Eliza Bennet despises cards. She's a great reader and has no pleasure in anything else."

"I don't deserve such high praise or criticism," Elizabeth replied. "I'm not a great reader and I do find pleasure in many things."

Bingley said taking care of your sister gives you pleasure. "I hope she gets better soon."

Elizabeth thanked him from the bottom of her heart and then walked to a table where a few books were lying. Bingley immediately offered to get her more from his library.

"I wish I had more books for your benefit and to make me look better, but I'm a lazy person. Even though I don't have many, I have more than I've ever read."

Elizabeth assured him that she could find something from the books in the room.

"I'm shocked that my father had such a small collection of books," Miss Bingley said. "You have such a great library at Pemberley, Mr. Darcy!"

"It should be good, it's been built up over many generations," he replied.

"And you've added to it yourself - you're always buying books."

"I can't understand why families don't make use of their library in this day and age."

"Neglect! I'm sure you don't neglect anything that can make Pemberley even more beautiful. Charles, when you build your house, I hope it's half as nice as Pemberley."

"I hope so too."

"I really recommend you buy a property in that area and use Pemberley as your inspiration. There isn't a better county in England than Derbyshire," said Charles.

"I'll buy Pemberley itself if Darcy will sell it."

"I'm just talking hypothetically, Charles," replied Caroline.

"Honestly, I think it would be easier to buy Pemberley than to imitate it."

Elizabeth was so intrigued by their conversation that she put her book down and moved closer to the card table, standing between Charles and his eldest sister.

"Has Miss Darcy grown since the spring?" asked Miss Bingley. "Will she be as tall as me?"

"I think she will be. She's around the same height as Elizabeth Bennet, or maybe a bit taller."

"I can't wait to see her again! She's so lovely and so talented for her age. Her piano playing is amazing."

"It's amazing to me," said Bingley, "how young ladies can have the patience to become so accomplished."

"All young ladies accomplished! My dear Charles, what do you mean?"

"Yes, all of them, I think. They all paint tables, cover screens, and net purses. I hardly know anyone who cannot do all this. And I'm sure I never heard a young lady spoken of for the first time without being informed that she was very accomplished."

"Your list of the common extent of accomplishments," said Darcy, "is too true. The word is applied to many women who deserve it no more than by netting a purse or covering a screen. But I am very far from agreeing with you in your estimation of ladies in general. I cannot boast of knowing more than half a dozen in the whole range of my acquaintance who are really accomplished."

"Neither do I," added Miss Bingley.

"So," Elizabeth continued, "you must have a very broad definition of an 'accomplished' woman."

"Yes, I do," he replied.

"Oh, absolutely," exclaimed Darcy's loyal assistant. "No one can truly be considered accomplished unless they surpass what is normally expected. A woman must have a thorough understanding of music, singing, drawing, dancing, and modern languages to deserve the label. And in addition to all of that, she must possess a certain something in the way she carries herself, walks, speaks, and expresses herself, or the label will only be half-earned."

"She must possess all of these qualities," added Darcy, "and in addition, she must also continually improve her mind through extensive reading."

"I'm not surprised you only know six accomplished women," Elizabeth replied. "I'm surprised you know any."

"Are you so hard on your own sex that you doubt this is possible?"

"I've never beheld such a woman - with so much capacity, taste, application, and elegance all in one."

Mrs. Hurst and Miss Bingley both objected to Elizabeth's implied doubt, claiming they knew many women who fit the description. But Mr. Hurst cut them off with complaints about their lack of attention. With the conversation at an end, Elizabeth soon left the room.

"Eliza Bennet," said Miss Bingley, after the door was shut, "is one of those women who try to make themselves attractive to the opposite sex by putting themselves down. I'm sure it works for some men, but I think it's a cheap trick, a really low tactic."

"Undoubtedly," replied Darcy, to whom this comment was directed, "there is something base in all of the tactics that women sometimes resort to in order to captivate. Anything that has an affinity to cunning is contemptible."

Miss Bingley wasn't very pleased with this response, so she dropped the subject.

Elizabeth joined them again just to say that her sister was worse, and she couldn't leave her. Bingley suggested they get Mr. Jones to come right away, while his sisters said that local advice wouldn't be of any help and they should get an express to town for a famous doctor. Elizabeth wasn't keen on that, but she was willing to accept Bingley's suggestion, and it was decided that Mr. Jones should be sent for in the morning if Miss Bennet wasn't better. Bingley was feeling very awkward; his sisters said they were miserable. To cheer themselves up they sang duets after dinner while Bingley tried to make the sick lady and her sister as comfortable as possible.

CHAPTER 9

Elizabeth spent the night in her sister's room and in the morning was able to give a satisfactory answer to Mr. Bingley's inquiries. Even so, she asked for a note to be sent to Longbourn to inform her mother of Jane's condition. The note was sent and Mrs. Bennet, along with her two youngest daughters, arrived at Netherfield soon after breakfast.

If Jane had been in any immediate danger, Mrs. Bennet would have been very unhappy, but upon seeing that her daughter's illness was not serious, she did not want her to recover immediately, as that would mean leaving Netherfield. She refused to listen to her daughter's suggestion of being taken home, and the apothecary who arrived around the same time did not think it was a good idea either. After spending some time with Jane, the mother and three daughters joined Miss Bingley in the breakfast room upon her invitation. Bingley greeted them with the hope that Mrs. Bennet had not found Miss Bennet worse than expected.

"Indeed I have, sir," she replied. "She is far too ill to be moved. Mr. Jones says we must not think of moving her. We must stay here a little longer and depend on your kindness."

"Removed!" exclaimed Bingley. "It must not be thought of. My sister, I'm sure, will not hear of her being removed."

"You can be certain, madam," Miss Bingley said politely, "that Miss Bennet will receive every possible attention while she stays with us."

Mrs. Bennet was very thankful.

"I am sure," she added, "if it wasn't for such good friends, I don't know what would become of her, because she's very sick and suffers a lot, even though she does it with the greatest patience in the world. That's always the way with her, she has the sweetest temper I've ever encountered. I often tell my other girls they can't compare. You have a nice room here, Mr. Bingley, and a beautiful view from that gravel walk. I don't know of any other place in the countryside that's as nice as Netherfield. I hope you won't be leaving soon, even though you only have a short lease."

"Whatever I do, I do in a hurry," he replied. "So, if I decided to leave Netherfield, I'd probably be gone in five minutes. Right now, though, I think I'm staying here."

"That's exactly what I would have expected of you," Elizabeth said.

"Are you starting to understand me?" he said, turning to her.

"Oh yes, I understand you perfectly."

"I wish I could take that as a compliment, but being so easily seen through is kind of embarrassing."

"It doesn't mean that a complex character is necessarily more admirable than a simpler one."

"Lizzy," Mrs. Bennet interjected, "remember where you are and don't talk like you would at home."

"I didn't know before," Bingley continued, "that you were so good at reading people. That must be a fun hobby."

"Yes, but complex characters are the most entertaining. They have that advantage, at least."

"In the countryside," Darcy said, "there aren't many people to study. In a small town, you're always surrounded by the same people."

"But people change so much, so there's always something new to observe in them."

"Yes, there's just as much of that going on in the country as in the city," Mrs. Bennet said, offended by Darcy's comment.

Everyone was surprised and Darcy, after looking at her for a moment, turned away without saying anything. Mrs. Bennet, thinking she had won the argument, continued:

"I don't think London has any great advantage over the countryside, apart from the shops and public places. The countryside is much nicer, isn't it Mr. Bingley?"

"When I'm in the country I never want to leave, and when I'm in the city it's much the same," he replied. "They both have their advantages and I can be equally happy in either."

"Ah, that's because you have the right attitude," said Mrs. Bennet, looking at Darcy.

Elizabeth blushed for her mother, "No, mama, you're mistaken," she said. "Mr. Darcy only meant that there aren't as many people to meet in the countryside as in the city, which you must agree is true."

"Of course, nobody said there was. But I don't think there are many neighborhoods bigger than this one. I know we dine with twenty-four families," said his sister.

Bingley had to maintain his composure due to his concern for Elizabeth. However, his sister was less tactful and looked at Mr. Darcy with a suggestive smile. Elizabeth, in an attempt to divert her mother's attention, asked if Charlotte Lucas had visited Longbourn since her departure.

"Yes, she came by with her father yesterday. Sir William is such an agreeable man, isn't he, Mr. Bingley? He's so fashionable and polite. He always has something to say to everyone. That's my definition of good manners. Those people who think they're very important and never talk are getting it all wrong."

"Did Charlotte dine with you?"

"No, she went home. I think she was needed for the mince pies. For my part, Mr. Bingley, I always make sure to hire servants who can do their own work; my daughters are raised differently. But everyone is entitled to their own opinion, and the Lucases are a very nice family, I can assure you. It's a shame they're not more attractive! Not that I think Charlotte is so very plain; but she is a close friend of ours."

"She seems like a very pleasant young woman," said Bingley.

"Oh yes, but you must admit she's not very good looking. Lady Lucas has said so herself, and she's even been envious of Jane's beauty. I don't like to brag about my own daughter, but it's true that Jane is really attractive. That's what everyone says. I don't trust my own judgement. When Jane was only fifteen there was a man at my brother Gardiner's in town who was so in love with her that my sister-in-law was sure he would propose before we left. But he didn't. Maybe he thought she was too young. But he did write some poems about her, and they were really nice."

"And that's the end of his love," said Elizabeth, impatiently. "I think many people have experienced the same thing. I wonder who first discovered that poetry could be used to drive away love!"

"I have always thought of poetry as the nourishment of love," said Darcy.

"It may nourish a strong and healthy love. Everything strengthens what is already strong. But if it is only a slight and weak affection, I am convinced that one good sonnet will completely starve it away."

Darcy only smiled, and the ensuing silence made Elizabeth worry that her mother might embarrass herself again. She wanted to speak but couldn't find anything to say, and after a short pause, Mrs. Bennet began thanking Mr. Bingley for his kindness to Jane and apologizing for troubling him with Lizzy. Mr. Bingley was polite in his response, and even forced his younger sister to be polite too. She performed her part without much enthusiasm, but Mrs. Bennet was satisfied and soon afterwards called for her carriage. At this signal, the youngest daughter stepped forward. The two girls had been whispering to each other during the entire visit and had decided that the youngest one should ask Mr. Bingley about the ball he had promised to give at Netherfield when he first arrived in the country.

Lydia was a robust, well-grown girl of fifteen years old, with a fine complexion and a good-natured expression. She was a favorite of her mother, who had brought her into society at an early age. Lydia had high levels of energy and a natural self-importance that the attention of the officers, who were invited to her uncle's dinners and impressed by her easy manners, had increased to confidence. Therefore, she was quite capable of addressing Mr. Bingley about the promised ball and abruptly reminded him of his promise, adding that it would be the most disgraceful thing in the world if he did not keep it. His response to this sudden attack was pleasing to her mother's ears.

"I am completely prepared, I assure you, to keep my promise. And, when your sister has recovered, you can name the exact day of the ball if you wish. But you wouldn't want to be dancing while she is still unwell?"

Lydia declared herself satisfied. "Oh yes, it would be much better to wait until Jane was well, and by then, most likely, Captain Carter would be in Meryton again. And when you have given *your* ball," she added, "I shall insist on their giving one too. I'll tell Colonel Forster that it will be a shame if he doesn't."

Mrs. Bennet and her daughters then left, and Elizabeth immediately returned to Jane, leaving her own and her family's behavior to the remarks of the two ladies and Mr. Darcy, the latter of whom, however, could not be persuaded to join in their criticism of her, in spite of all Miss Bingley's witticisms about her "fine eyes."

CHAPTER 10

The day was much like the day before. Mrs. Hurst and Miss Bingley had spent some time with the sick woman in the morning. She was slowly improving. In the evening, Elizabeth joined them in the drawing room. However, the loo table did not appear. Mr. Darcy was writing, and Miss Bingley, who was seated close to him, watched as he wrote his letter. She repeatedly interrupted him with messages for his sister. Mr. Hurst and Mr. Bingley were playing piquet, while Mrs. Hurst was watching their game.

Elizabeth took up some needlework and was entertained by the conversation between Darcy and Miss Bingley. The lady's constant praises, whether of his handwriting or the evenness of his lines, or the length of his letter, and the complete indifference with which her praises were received, created a peculiar dialogue, which was completely in line with her opinion of each thing she praised.

"I am sure Miss Darcy will be very happy to receive such a letter!" said one person.

The other did not respond.

"You write very quickly," said the first person.

"You are mistaken. I write quite slowly," replied the other.

"You must have to write a great many letters throughout the year! And business letters too! I would find them so tedious."

"Fortunately, they fall to my lot instead of yours," responded the other.

"Please let your sister know that I am eager to see her."

"I have already conveyed your desire to her."

"I am afraid you do not like your pen. Allow me to fix it for you. I am very good at fixing pens."

"Thank you, but I always fix my own."

"How do you manage to write so neatly?"

The other remained silent.

"Tell your sister I'm thrilled to hear about her progress with the harp and that I absolutely love her design for a table - it's way better than Miss Grantley's."

"Can I postpone your enthusiasm until I write back? I don't have enough room to do it justice right now."

"Oh, it's fine. I'll see her in January. But do you always write such long, charming letters to her, Mr. Darcy?"

"They are usually long, but whether they are always charming is not for me to say."

"I have a rule that anyone who can write a long letter easily can't write badly."

"That would not be a compliment to Darcy, Caroline," exclaimed her brother, "because he does not write with ease. He studies too much for words with four syllables. Isn't that right, Darcy?"

"My writing style is very different from yours," replied Darcy.

"Oh," exclaimed Miss Bingley, "Charles writes in the most careless manner imaginable. He leaves out half of his words and blots the rest."

"My ideas flow so quickly that I do not have time to express them, which means that my letters sometimes do not convey any ideas at all to my correspondents," explained Charles.

"Your modesty, Mr. Bingley," said Elizabeth, "should prevent criticism."

"Nothing is more deceiving than the appearance of modesty," remarked Darcy. "It is often simply carelessness of opinion and sometimes an indirect boast."

"And which of the two do you call *my* little recent piece of modesty?" asked Charles.

"The indirect boast. You are truly proud of your writing flaws because you believe they come from quick thinking and careless execution, which, if not admirable, you believe is at least highly interesting. The ability to do anything quickly is always highly valued by the possessor, often without any attention to the imperfect performance. When you told Mrs. Bennet this morning that you could leave Netherfield in five minutes if you ever decided to, you meant it to be a kind of praise or compliment to yourself. Yet, what is so commendable about haste that leaves necessary business unfinished and cannot benefit you or anyone else?" replied Darcy.

"No," objected Bingley, "this is too much, to remember all the foolish things that were said in the morning at night. However, I honestly believed what I said about myself, and I still believe it. At least, I did not pretend to be needlessly hasty just to impress the ladies."

"I'm sure you believed it, but I'm not convinced that you would actually leave so quickly. Your actions would be just as susceptible to chance as those of any other man I know. If, as you were getting on your horse, a friend suggested, 'Bingley, you might want to stay until next week,' you would probably do it - you probably wouldn't leave - and with another word, you might stay for a month."

"You've only shown," Elizabeth said, "that Mr. Bingley didn't do justice to himself. You've shown him off much better than he did himself."

"I'm very pleased," Bingley said, "that you're interpreting what my friend said as a compliment to my good nature. But I'm afraid you're giving it a different meaning than he intended; for he would certainly think better of me if, in such a situation, I flat out refused and rode away as fast as I could."

"So, Mr. Darcy, would you say that my initial rashness was atoned for by my stubbornness?"

"I cannot explain the matter exactly - Darcy must explain for himself," said Bingley.

"You expect me to account for opinions that you choose to attribute to me, but which I have never admitted. Even if we accept your version of events, Miss Bennet, you must remember that the friend who supposedly requested Bingley's return to the house and the delay of his plans did so without offering any arguments in favor of their correctness," replied Darcy.

"To give in easily to a friend's persuasion is no virtue in your eyes," retorted Miss Bennet.

"To give in without being convinced is no compliment to the intelligence of either person involved," concluded Darcy.

"Mr. Darcy, it seems to me that you do not take into account the influence of friendship and affection. A fondness for the person making the request often causes one to comply readily, without needing arguments to persuade them. I am not specifically referring to the situation you have described with Mr. Bingley. Perhaps we should wait until such an event occurs before discussing the wisdom of his actions. But in general, when one friend asks another to change a relatively insignificant decision, would you condemn that person for complying without requiring persuasion?" asked Miss Bennet.

"Wouldn't it be a good idea, before we continue this conversation, to be more precise about how important the request is, as well as the level of friendship between the people involved?"

"Definitely," said Bingley. "Let's hear all the details, including their heights and sizes, as that will have more of an effect on the argument than you might think, Miss Bennet. I assure you that if Darcy wasn't so tall compared to me, I wouldn't be so respectful to him. I don't know of anything more intimidating than Darcy in certain situations, especially when he's in his own house and it's a Sunday evening and he has nothing to do."

Mr. Darcy smiled but Elizabeth thought he was a bit offended so she stopped her laugh. Miss Bingley was angry at the disrespect he received and argued with her brother for saying such things.

"I see what you're doing, Bingley," said his friend. "You don't like arguments and want to stop this one."

"Maybe I do. Arguments are too much like disputes. If you and Miss Bennet wait until I'm out of the room I'd be very grateful and then you can say whatever you want about me."

"What you're asking for," said Elizabeth, "is no trouble for me and Mr. Darcy should finish his letter."

Mr. Darcy followed Elizabeth's advice and finished his letter.

When that task was completed, he asked Miss Bingley and Elizabeth if they would like to listen to some music. Miss Bingley eagerly went to the piano and, after politely asking Elizabeth to go first, which Elizabeth politely refused, she sat down.

Mrs. Hurst sang with her sister; and while they were singing, Elizabeth noticed that Mr. Darcy kept looking at her. She was surprised that such an important man would be interested in her and even more puzzled that he would look at her if he didn't like her. She eventually concluded that he was looking at her because he thought she was more wrong or immoral than anyone else in the room. This didn't bother her as she didn't care for his opinion.

After playing some Italian songs, Miss Bingley changed the atmosphere by playing a lively Scottish air; and then Mr. Darcy, coming close to Elizabeth, said to her,--

"Don't you feel like dancing a reel right now, Miss Bennet?"

She smiled, but didn't answer. He was surprised by her silence and repeated the question.

"Oh," she replied, "I heard you before, but I couldn't decide what to say in response. You wanted me to say 'Yes' so that you could have the pleasure of despising my taste, but I always take pleasure in thwarting those types of plans and depriving someone of their premeditated contempt. Therefore, I have decided to tell you that I don't want to dance a reel at all. Now, if you dare, you may despise me."

"Actually, I do not dare," he replied.

Elizabeth had anticipated offending him and was surprised by his gallantry. However, there was a combination of sweetness and playfulness in her demeanor that made it difficult for her to offend anyone, and Darcy had never been as enchanted by any woman as he was by her. He truly believed that if it were not for her inferior social connections, he might be in some danger of falling in love with her.

Miss Bingley saw or suspected enough to become jealous, and her strong desire to help her dear friend Jane recover from her illness was augmented by her wish to get rid of Elizabeth. She frequently attempted to incite Darcy's dislike for her guest by mentioning their supposed engagement and planning his happiness in such an alliance.

"I hope," she said, as they walked together in the shrubbery the following day, "that when this desirable event takes place, you will offer your mother-in-law some suggestions about the benefits of keeping her thoughts to herself. Additionally, if possible, try to prevent the younger girls from chasing after the officers. And, if I may bring up such a delicate matter, please try to temper your wife's tendencies towards conceit and impertinence."

"Do you have anything else to suggest for my domestic happiness?"

"Oh yes. Do put the portraits of your uncle and aunt Philips in the gallery at Pemberley. Put them next to your great-uncle the judge. They are both in the same job, you know, just in different areas. As for the portrait of your Elizabeth, you must not try to have it taken, for how could any painter do justice to those beautiful eyes?"

"It would be hard to capture their expression; but their color, shape and those incredibly fine eyelashes could be copied."

At that moment they were met from another walk by Mrs. Hurst and Elizabeth herself.

"I didn't know you were planning to take a walk," said Miss Bingley, a bit embarrassed, in case they had been overheard.

"You treated us terribly," Mrs. Hurst replied, "running off without telling us you were going out."

Then she took the free arm of Mr. Darcy and left Elizabeth to walk by herself. The path was just wide enough for three. Mr. Darcy felt their rudeness and quickly said:

"This path isn't wide enough for our group. We should go into the avenue."

But Elizabeth, who had no desire to stay with them, laughed and said,

"No, no, stay where you are. You're nicely arranged and look very attractive. Adding a fourth would ruin the picture. Goodbye!"

She then ran off happily, rejoicing as she wandered around, in the hope of being back home in a day or two. Jane had already recovered enough to plan on leaving her room for a couple of hours that evening.

CHAPTER 11

After the ladies left after dinner, Elizabeth ran up to her sister and, making sure she was well protected from the cold, accompanied her to the drawing room where she was greeted by her two friends with many expressions of joy. Elizabeth had never seen them as pleasant as they were during the hour before the gentlemen arrived. They were able to describe an event with precision, tell a story with humor, and laugh at their acquaintances with enthusiasm.

But when the gentlemen came in, Jane was no longer the main focus; Miss Bingley's eyes immediately went to Darcy and she had something to say to him before he had taken many steps. He directly spoke to Miss Bennet with a polite congratulations; Mr. Hurst also gave her a slight bow and said he was "very glad"; but Bingley's greeting was full of joy and attention. He was filled with joy and enthusiasm. The first half hour was spent stoking the fire, so she wouldn't be cold in the new room; and at his request, she moved to the other side of the fireplace, farther away from the door. He then sat down next to her and barely spoke to anyone else. Elizabeth, working in the opposite corner, watched it all with great pleasure.

When tea was over, Mr. Hurst reminded his sister-in-law of the card-table, but to no avail. She had gotten word that Mr. Darcy didn't want to play cards, and Mr. Hurst's open invitation was quickly refused. She assured him that no one was going to play, and the silence of the whole party seemed to back her up. Mr. Hurst had no choice but to lie down on one of the sofas and go to sleep. Darcy picked up a book and Miss Bingley did the same; and Mrs. Hurst, mostly preoccupied with playing with her bracelets and rings, occasionally joined her brother's conversation with Miss Bennet.

Miss Bingley was paying more attention to watching Mr. Darcy read than to her own book. She kept asking him questions and he would just answer and continue reading. Eventually, she gave a big yawn and said, "What a nice way to spend an evening! I think reading is the best way to pass the time. When I have my own house, I'll be so unhappy if I don't have a great library."

No one responded. She yawned again, put down her book, and looked around the room for something to do. Then, when she heard her brother talking to Miss Bennet about a ball at Netherfield, she quickly turned to him and said:

"Oh, Charles, are you really thinking of having a dance at Netherfield? I suggested to you to consult the wishes of the people here before making a decision, I'm sure some of us would find a ball more of a punishment than a pleasure."

"If you're referring to Darcy," her brother exclaimed, "he can go to bed before it starts if he wants to, but the ball is a definite thing, I'll send out my invitations as soon as Nicholls has made enough white soup."

"I'd much prefer balls if they were run differently," she replied, "the normal way of doing it is unbearably dull. It would be much more sensible if conversation was the main event rather than dancing."

"That would certainly be more sensible, Caroline," he said, "but it wouldn't be anything like a ball."

Miss Bingley didn't answer and soon after she got up and walked around the room. She had a graceful figure and walked well, but Darcy was still intently studying and didn't notice. In desperation, she decided to try one more thing and turning to Elizabeth she said:

"Miss Eliza Bennet, let me persuade you to take a turn around the room with me. I assure you it will be very refreshing after sitting for so long."

Elizabeth was surprised, but agreed. Miss Bingley had achieved her goal; Mr. Darcy looked up. He was as interested in the unusual attention from that side as Elizabeth was and, without thinking, he closed his book. He was asked to join them but he declined, saying he could think of two reasons why they were walking around the room together and his joining them would interfere with either of them. Elizabeth was dying to know what he meant and asked her if she could understand him.

"No, not at all," she replied. "But I'm sure he's going to be tough on us, and the best way to disappoint him is to not ask about it."

Miss Bingley, however, was unable to disappoint Mr. Darcy in anything and kept pressing him for an explanation of his two motives.

"I have no problem explaining them," he said as soon as she gave him a chance to speak. "Either you two are out here because you share secrets and have things to talk about, or because you know you look better walking than sitting. If it's the first, I'll be in the way; if it's the second, I can admire you better from here by the fire."

"Oh, how horrible!" Miss Bingley exclaimed. "I've never heard anything so awful. How should we punish him for saying that?"

"It's easy if you want to," Elizabeth said. "We can all make fun of and tease each other. You two know how it's done."

"I swear I don't," Miss Bingley said. "My friendship with him hasn't taught me that. Tease him for his calmness and presence of mind? No, no; I think he can withstand that."

"Mr. Darcy is not to be laughed at!" Elizabeth exclaimed. "That's an uncommon advantage and I hope it stays that way, because I would hate to have many such acquaintances. I truly love to laugh."

"Miss Bingley," he said, "has given me more credit than I deserve. Even the wisest and best of men, and their best actions, can be made to look foolish by someone whose main goal in life is to joke around."

"Of course," Elizabeth replied, "there are such people, but I hope I'm not one of them. I hope I never make fun of what is wise or good. I do find foolishness and nonsense amusing, and I laugh at them when I can. But I assume that's something you don't have."

"Maybe it's not achievable by anyone, but I've made it my life's mission to steer clear of weaknesses that can make even the most intelligent person look foolish."

"Such as vanity and pride."

"Yes, vanity is a real weakness. But pride - when there is a real superiority of mind - pride should be kept in check."

Elizabeth said, turning away to hide a smile.

"I presume your assessment of Mr. Darcy is done," Miss Bingley said.

"I am completely certain that Mr. Darcy has no flaws. He admits it himself without trying to hide it," Elizabeth replied.

"No," Darcy said. "I haven't claimed to have no flaws. I have enough flaws, but I don't think they are in my understanding. I can't control my temper and it is probably too unyielding for the world. I can't forget the foolishness and wrongdoings of others as quickly as I should, nor can I forget the wrongs that have been done to me. My emotions don't get easily swayed. My temper could be called resentful and when I lose my good opinion of someone, it's gone for good."

"That really is a fault," Elizabeth exclaimed. "An unforgiving temper is a dark mark on someone's character. But you have chosen your flaw well. I can't make fun of it. You are safe from me," she said.

"I believe that everyone has a tendency towards some particular evil, a natural defect, which even the best education cannot overcome."

"And your defect is a propensity to hate everybody,"

"And yours," he replied with a smile, "is to willfully misunderstand them."

Miss Bingley, bored by the conversation in which she had no part, exclaimed, "Do let us have a little music! Louisa, you will not mind my waking Mr. Hurst."

Her sister made no objection and the pianoforte was opened. Darcy, after a few moments' reflection, was glad for the distraction. He began to feel the danger of paying Elizabeth too much attention.

CHAPTER 12

In accordance with an agreement between the sisters, Elizabeth wrote to her mother the next morning requesting that the carriage be sent for them that day. However, Mrs. Bennet, who had expected her daughters to remain at Netherfield until the following Tuesday, which would mark the end of Jane's week, was not pleased by the request. Her answer, therefore, was not positive, at least not what Elizabeth wanted, as she was eager to get home. Mrs. Bennet sent them word that they could not have the carriage until Tuesday; and in her postscript it was added that if Mr. Bingley and his sister asked them to stay longer, she would be fine with it. Elizabeth, however, was determined not to stay any longer - she didn't think they would even ask - and, worried that they would be seen as imposing on the Bingleys, she encouraged Jane to ask for their carriage right away. It was finally decided that they would mention their intention to leave that morning and make the request.

Everyone expressed their concern and said they should stay at least until the next day, which swayed Jane. Miss Bingley was then regretful that she had suggested the delay; for her dislike of one sister far exceeded her love for the other.

The master of the house was filled with sorrow when he heard they were leaving so soon and repeatedly tried to convince Miss Bennet that it was not safe for her yet, as she was not completely recovered. Jane was adamant that she was doing the right thing, and Mr. Darcy was relieved by the news.

Elizabeth had been at Netherfield for too long and he was attracted to her more than he liked, and Miss Bingley was treating her unkindly and teasing him even more than usual. He decided to be extra careful not to show any signs of admiration for her, as he was aware that his behavior the previous day would have an effect on her opinion of him. Keeping to his resolution, he hardly said a word to her throughout Saturday and even when they were left alone for half an hour, he stayed focused on his book and refused to look at her.

After Sunday morning service, the separation, which was pleasing to almost everyone, occurred. Miss Bingley's politeness to Elizabeth improved very quickly, as did her fondness for Jane. When they said goodbye, Miss Bingley assured Jane that it would always give her pleasure to see her either at Longbourn or Netherfield, and she even hugged her affectionately. She even shook hands with Elizabeth. Elizabeth said goodbye to the entire group in high spirits.

Their mother did not welcome them home warmly. Mrs. Bennet was surprised by their return and thought it was very wrong of them to cause so much trouble. She was sure that Jane would catch a cold again. However, their father, while very brief in his expressions of joy, was genuinely pleased to see them. He had felt their importance in the family circle. When they were all gathered for evening conversation, it had lost much of its liveliness and nearly all of its sense due to the absence of Jane and Elizabeth.

They found Mary, as usual, deep in the study of music and human nature; and they had some new quotes to admire and some old moral lessons to listen to. Catherine and Lydia had news of a different kind. A lot had happened and been said in the regiment since the Wednesday before; several of the officers had dined with their uncle recently, a private had been flogged, and it was even suggested that Colonel Forster was going to get married.

CHAPTER 13

Mr. Bennet said to his wife at breakfast the next morning, "I hope you have ordered a good dinner today, because I'm expecting an addition to our family party."

"Who are you referring to, my dear? I don't know of anyone who is coming, unless Charlotte Lucas happens to visit. And I hope my dinners are good enough for her. I don't think she often has such meals at home."

"The person I'm referring to is a gentleman and a stranger."

"Mrs. Bennet's eyes lit up. 'A gentleman and a stranger! It must be Mr. Bingley. Why, Jane, you never mentioned a word of this, you sly thing! Well, I'll certainly be extremely pleased to see Mr. Bingley. But, good Lord! How unlucky! There isn't a bit of fish to be had today. Lydia, my dear, ring the bell. I must speak to Hill this very moment.'"

"It's not Mr. Bingley," he added. "It's someone I've never seen in my life."

This caused a lot of surprise and everyone started asking him questions.

After having fun with their curiosity, he explained: "About a month ago I got this letter and I answered it about two weeks ago because I thought it was a delicate matter that needed to be dealt with quickly. It's from my cousin, Mr. Collins, who, when I'm gone, could kick you all out of this house whenever he wants."

"Oh, my dear," his wife exclaimed, "I can't bear to hear that. Please don't talk about that horrible man. I really think it's the worst thing in the world that your estate has to be passed down to someone else's children and if I were you, I would have done something about it a long time ago."

Jane and Elizabeth tried to explain to her the concept of entailment. They had tried to do so in the past, but it was a topic that Mrs. Bennet was not receptive to reason about. She continued to bitterly complain about the unfairness of an estate being passed on to a man who no one cared about, rather than to a family of five daughters.

"It's absolutely unfair," Mr. Bennet said, "and Mr. Collins cannot be cleared of the blame of inheriting Longbourn. But if you read his letter, you might be somewhat moved by his way of expressing himself."

"No, I'm certain that I won't. I think it was very rude of him to write to you at all, and it's so hypocritical. I detest such false friends. Why couldn't he continue quarreling with you, just like his father did before him?"

"Well, it seems he did have some reservations about that, as you'll see:"

"Hunsford, near Westerham, Kent, 15th October.
Dear Sir,
I have always been troubled by the disagreement between you and my late beloved father. Since his passing, I have often wished to mend the rift, but I hesitated, afraid that it may seem disrespectful to his memory for me to be on good terms with someone he had always been at odds with. But now I have made up my mind; I was ordained at Easter and have been blessed with the patronage of the Right Honorable Lady Catherine de Bourgh, widow of Sir Lewis de Bourgh, who has appointed me to the valuable rectory of this parish. I will strive to show her Ladyship the utmost respect and will faithfully carry out the rites and ceremonies of the Church of England. As a clergyman, I feel it is my duty to promote peace in all families I am close to; therefore, I believe my offer of goodwill is commendable and I hope you will overlook the fact that I am next in line for the Longbourn estate. I am sorry to have caused distress to your daughters and I apologize for it. I am willing to make them amends. If you don't mind, I would like to come to your house on Monday, November 18th at four o'clock to visit you and your family. I plan to stay with you until the following Saturday week, and I hope that this won't be an inconvenience.

Lady Catherine has no objections to my absence on Sundays, as long as another clergyman is available to do the church service. Please give my regards to your wife and daughters. I remain your friend and well-wisher.
 William Collins"

"At four o'clock, then, we can expect this gentleman who seeks to make peace," said Mr. Bennet as he folded the letter. "He appears to be a very conscientious and polite young man, in all honesty, and I have no doubt that he will prove to be a valuable acquaintance, particularly if Lady Catherine should be kind enough to permit him to visit us again."

"There is some sense in what he says about the girls," Jane said. "If he is willing to make amends, I won't stop him."

Jane said, "It is hard to guess how he plans to make up for what he thinks is due to us, but at least he wishes to do so, and that is commendable."

Elizabeth was particularly impressed by his great respect for Lady Catherine and his intention to baptize, marry, and bury his parishioners when necessary.

"He must be strange," she said. "His style is very pompous. What does he mean by apologizing for being next in the entail? We can't assume he would help it if he could. Is he a reasonable man, sir?"

"No, my dear; I don't think so. I'm optimistic that I'll find him to be quite the opposite. His letter has a combination of servility and arrogance that looks promising. I'm eager to meet him."

"Regarding the writing itself," Mary said, "his letter doesn't seem to have any flaws. The metaphor of the olive branch may not be original, but I think it's well put."

Catherine and Lydia were not at all interested in the letter or its writer. They had no hope that their cousin would arrive in a scarlet coat, and it had been weeks since they had enjoyed the company of a man in any other color. As for their mother, Mr. Collins's letter had removed much of her hostility towards him, and she was getting ready to see him with a level of calmness that surprised her husband and daughters.

Mr. Collins arrived at the appointed time and was welcomed with great politeness by the entire family. Mr. Bennet, however, remained mostly silent, while the ladies were eager to engage in conversation, and Mr. Collins needed no encouragement to speak. He was a tall and heavy-looking young man, around twenty-five years old. His demeanor was serious and dignified, and his manners were very formal. He had not been seated for long before he praised Mrs. Bennet for having such a fine family of daughters. He said that he had heard a lot about their beauty, but that, in this case, fame had fallen short of the truth. He added that he had no doubt that she would see all of them well married in due time. This flattery was not to the liking of some of the listeners, but Mrs. Bennet, who never turned down a compliment, readily answered him.

"You are very kind, sir, I am sure; and I wish from the bottom of my heart that it will be so, otherwise they will be in a very difficult position. Things are so strange."

"Perhaps you are referring to the entailment of this estate?"

"I do indeed, sir. It is a terrible matter for my poor girls, you must admit. Not that I intend to blame you, for such things, I know, are all a matter of chance in this world. There is no telling how estates will be passed down once they become entailed."

"I am fully aware, ma'am, of the difficult situation faced by my dear cousins, and although I could speak at length on the matter, I must be careful not to seem presumptuous. However, I can assure the young ladies that I have come with the intention of admiring them. For now, I will say no more, but perhaps when we are better acquainted..."

He was called to dinner, and the girls smiled at each other. They were not the only objects of Mr. Collins's admiration. He examined and praised the hall, dining-room, and all of their furniture. His commendation of everything would have touched Mrs. Bennet's heart, but for the mortifying thought that he viewed it all as his future property. The dinner, too, was highly praised, and he asked which of his fair cousins was responsible for its excellent cooking. Mrs. Bennet set him straight and told him that they were perfectly capable of keeping a good cook, and that her daughters had nothing to do in the kitchen. He apologized for having displeased her and she said she was not offended. He continued to apologize for about a quarter of an hour.

CHAPTER 14

During dinner, Mr. Bennet said very little. But once the servants had left, he thought it was time to talk to his guest and so he brought up a topic he thought Mr. Collins would be sure to know a lot about. He remarked that Mr. Collins seemed to have a very generous patroness in Lady Catherine de Bourgh. Mr. Collins was very enthusiastic in his praise of her. This made him much more serious than usual and he declared that he had never before seen someone of such high rank be so kind and gracious as Lady Catherine had been to him. She was very pleased with both of the sermons he had already had the honor of preaching in her presence. She had also invited him to dinner at Rosings twice and had even asked him to come the Saturday before just to make up her pool of quadrille for the evening. People thought Lady Catherine was proud, but he had never seen anything but kindness from her. She had always spoken to him like she would any other gentleman; she hadn't objected to him joining in with the other people in the neighborhood or leaving his parish for a week or two to visit his relatives. As long as he chose wisely, she had gone so far as to advise him to marry when he could. She had even gone to his humble parsonage and approved all the changes he had made and even suggested some, like shelves in the closets upstairs.

"That's all very polite and kind of her," said Mrs. Bennet, "and I'm sure she's a very pleasant woman. It's a shame that most ladies aren't more like her," Mrs. Bennet said. "Does she live near you, sir?"

"My house is only separated from Rosings Park, her Ladyship's home, by a lane," he replied.

"I believe you said she was a widow? Does she have any family?"

"She has only one daughter, who is the heiress of Rosings and has a great deal of money," he answered.

"Ah," Mrs. Bennet sighed, shaking her head, "then she's better off than many girls. What kind of young lady is she? Is she pretty?"

"She is a very charming young lady," he said. "Lady Catherine herself says that in terms of true beauty, Miss de Bourgh is far superior to the most beautiful women. Unfortunately, she has a weak constitution which has stopped her from making the progress in many areas she would have otherwise achieved, according to the lady who taught her and still lives with them. But she is very friendly and often takes the time to drive by my house in her small carriage and ponies," said Mr. Collins.

"Has she been formally introduced to the royal court? I don't recall hearing her name mentioned among the women who have been presented there."

"Unfortunately, her poor health prevents her from being in town and attending court, as I mentioned to Lady Catherine myself one day. It is a pity because she is the brightest ornament of the British court. Lady Catherine seemed to like the idea, and I am always happy to offer delicate compliments that ladies appreciate. I have mentioned to Lady Catherine more than once that her charming daughter seems destined to be a duchess. Even the highest rank would be adorned by her instead of giving her consequence. These are the little things that please her Ladyship, and it is a type of attention that I consider myself especially obligated to give."

"You are right," said Mr. Bennet. "You are lucky to have the talent to flatter so delicately. May I ask if these pleasing gestures come from the heart or have you practiced them?"

"They mainly come from what is happening in the moment, and although I sometimes enjoy coming up with and arranging flattering comments that are appropriate for the occasion, I always want them to seem as natural as possible."

Mr. Bennet's expectations were met. His cousin was as ridiculous as he had anticipated and he listened to him with great pleasure, keeping a composed expression and not needing a partner in his amusement, apart from the occasional glance at Elizabeth.

By the time tea was over, Mr. Bennet was happy to take his guest back to the drawing-room and after tea, he invited him to read aloud to the ladies. Mr. Collins agreed and a book was brought out, but upon seeing it and realizing it was from a circulating library, he recoiled and apologized, stating that he never read novels. Kitty looked at him in surprise, and Lydia exclaimed in shock. Other books were brought out, and after some consideration, he selected "Fordyce's Sermons." Lydia gaped as he opened the book, and before he could read more than three pages with tedious solemnity, she interrupted him with—

"Do you know, mamma, that my uncle Philips is thinking of sending Richard away? If he does, Colonel Forster will hire him. My aunt told me so herself on Saturday. I'm going to Meryton tomorrow to find out more and to see when Mr. Denny comes back from town."

Her two eldest sisters told her to be quiet but Mr. Collins, very offended, put down his book and said:

"I have noticed how little young ladies are interested by books that are written for their benefit. It amazes me, I must confess, because there is nothing more advantageous to them than instruction. But I won't bother my young cousin anymore."

He then turned to Mr. Bennet and offered to play backgammon with him. Mr. Bennet accepted the challenge and said he was wise to leave the girls to their own amusements. Mrs. Bennet and her daughters apologized very politely for Lydia's interruption, and promised it would not happen again if he would continue reading. Mr. Collins assured them he held no ill will towards his young cousin and would not take her behavior as an insult, so he sat down at another table with Mr. Bennet and they began to play backgammon.

CHAPTER 15

Mr. Collins was not a very intelligent man, and the lack of natural ability had not been improved much by education or society. Most of his life had been spent under the guidance of an uneducated and stingy father. Even though he had gone to one of the universities, he had just done what he had to do there and had not made any useful connections. The submissiveness which his father had instilled in him had originally made him very humble, but now it was mostly cancelled out by the vanity of a weak mind, living in isolation, and the feelings of early and unexpected prosperity. A fortunate opportunity had introduced him to Lady Catherine de Bourgh when the position of rector of Hunsford became available; and his respect for her high rank, combined with his admiration of himself, his authority as a clergyman, and his rights as a rector, made him a blend of pride and servility, self-importance and humility.

Now having a good house and a more than sufficient income, he had decided to marry; and in his attempt to reconcile with the Longbourn family, he had a wife in mind, as he intended to choose one of the daughters, if they were as attractive and pleasant as he had heard. This was his plan of reparation - of making amends - for inheriting their father's estate; and he thought it was an excellent one, full of advantages and suitability, and excessively generous and unselfish on his own part.

His intentions did not change upon seeing the Bennet sisters. Miss Bennet's beautiful face confirmed his ideas and established his strictest notions of respecting seniority, and for the first evening, she was his chosen partner. However, the next morning, a conversation with Mrs. Bennet before breakfast, which began with the discussion of his parsonage-house and naturally led to his hopes of finding a suitable wife at Longbourn, resulted in a change of heart. Mrs. Bennet, with smiles and encouragement, warned him against choosing Jane as she was likely to be engaged soon. While she could not speak for her younger daughters, she felt it necessary to mention her eldest daughter.

Mr. Collins just had to switch from Jane to Elizabeth and it was done in a flash, while Mrs. Bennet was stoking the fire. Elizabeth, who was the next oldest after Jane and just as beautiful, was the obvious choice.

Mrs. Bennet noted the suggestion and hoped that she would soon have two daughters married, and the man she had been so reluctant to talk about the day before was now in her good graces.

Lydia had not forgotten her intention to walk to Meryton and all of her sisters except Mary agreed to go with her. Mr. Collins was asked by Mr. Bennet to accompany them, as he was eager to have the library to himself. Mr. Collins followed Mr. Bennet to the library after breakfast and talked to him about his house and garden at Hunsford without much interruption. This disturbed Mr. Bennet greatly, as he usually found tranquility and leisure in the library and was used to being free from foolishness and vanity in that room. Therefore, he was quick to invite Mr. Collins to join the sisters on their walk and Mr. Collins, being better suited to walking than reading, was pleased to close his book and go.

They passed the time with Mr. Collins talking pompously and the cousins giving civil responses until they reached Meryton. The younger ones were no longer paying attention to him and their eyes were searching up the street for the officers. It took something really special, like a fancy hat or a new dress in a shop window, to get their attention back.

But the attention of every woman was soon caught by a young man they had never seen before, who walked with an officer on the other side of the street. The officer was the very

Mr. Denny whom Lydia had come to inquire about, and he bowed as they passed. Everyone was struck with the stranger's appearance and wondered who he could be. Kitty and Lydia were determined to find out and led the way across the street, pretending to want something in a shop on the other side. Luckily, they had just reached the pavement when the two gentlemen turned back and reached the same spot. Mr. Denny addressed them directly and asked if he could introduce his friend, Mr. Wickham, who had returned with him the day before from London and had accepted a commission in their regiment. This was exactly as it should be, for the young man only needed a military uniform to make him completely charming. His appearance was greatly in his favour; he had all the best parts of beauty, a handsome face, a good figure, and a very pleasing manner. The introduction was followed by a happy readiness of conversation, which was both perfectly correct and unassuming. The whole party was still standing and talking very agreeably when the sound of horses drew their attention, and Darcy and Bingley were seen riding down the street. When they recognized the ladies, the two gentlemen came directly towards them and began the usual pleasantries. Bingley was the principal speaker, and Miss Bennet was the main topic. He said that he was on his way to Longbourn to inquire about her. Mr. Darcy confirmed this with a bow and was beginning to determine not to fix his eyes on Elizabeth when they were suddenly arrested by the sight of the stranger. Elizabeth happened to see the countenance of both as they looked at each other and was astonished by the effect of the meeting. Both men changed color; one turned white, the other turned red. Mr. Wickham, after a few moments, touched his hat, which Mr. Darcy just deigned to return. What could be the meaning of it? It was impossible to imagine; it was impossible not too long to know.

A minute later, Mr. Bingley left without appearing to acknowledge the situation and rode away with his friend.

Mr. Denny and Mr. Wickham then walked the young ladies to the door of Mr. Philips's house, and bowed despite Miss

Lydia's insistence that they come in and Mrs. Philips shouting out of the window to invite them in.

Mrs. Philips was always happy to see her nieces, and particularly pleased to see the two eldest who had just returned home. She was expressing her surprise at their sudden return when Jane introduced Mr. Collins. Mrs. Philips received him with great politeness, and he apologized for intruding on her without any previous acquaintance, but justified it by his relationship to the young ladies who introduced him. Mrs. Philips was awed by his good manners, but the conversation soon turned to the other stranger in town. She could only tell her nieces what they already knew, that Mr. Denny had brought him from London and that he was to have a lieutenant's commission. Mrs. Philips had been watching him for the last hour as he walked up and down the street, and had Mr. Wickham appeared, Kitty and Lydia would have continued watching him. Mrs. Philips promised to invite Mr. Wickham to dinner if the family from Longbourn would come in the evening, and they agreed. They parted in good spirits, with Mr. Collins repeating his apologies and being assured that they were needless.

As Elizabeth and Jane walked home, Elizabeth told her sister what she had witnessed between the two men. Jane was unable to explain their behavior and could not defend or condemn either of them.

Upon his return, Mr. Collins greatly pleased Mrs. Bennet by complimenting Mrs. Philips on her manners and politeness. He stated that, apart from Lady Catherine and her daughter, he had never seen a more refined woman. Mrs. Philips not only received him with the utmost courtesy but also included him in her invitation for the following evening, despite being a stranger to her. He believed that his relationship with the Bennet sisters may have played a role, but he had never received such attention in his life.

CHAPTER 16

Since there were no objections to the young people spending time with their aunt and Mr. Collins had no issues leaving Mr. and Mrs. Bennet alone for one evening during his visit, he and his five cousins were taken by the coach to Meryton at an appropriate hour. Upon entering the drawing-room, the girls were delighted to hear that Mr. Wickham had accepted their uncle's invitation and was currently in the house.

When they were all seated, Mr. Collins had the chance to look around and admire the room. He was so impressed with its size and furniture that he claimed he could almost believe himself to be in the small summer breakfast parlor at Rosings. At first, this comparison did not seem to bring much pleasure, but Mrs. Philips was able to appreciate it once she learned what Rosings was and who its owner was. When Mr. Collins described just one of Lady Catherine's drawing rooms and revealed that the chimney-piece alone had cost eight hundred pounds, Mrs. Philips felt the full force of the compliment and would hardly have taken offense at being compared to the housekeeper's room.

Describing to her the grandeur of Lady Catherine and her mansion, with the occasional praise of his own humble abode and the improvements it was receiving, he was happily occupied until the gentlemen joined them. Mrs. Philips was a very attentive listener and her opinion of his status increased with what she heard. She was planning to share it all with her neighbors as soon as she could. The girls, who had nothing to do but to wish for an instrument and examine their own mediocre imitations of china on the mantelpiece, found the wait to be very long. Eventually, the gentlemen did approach. When Mr. Wickham walked into the room, Elizabeth realized that she had neither been seeing him before nor thinking of him since with the smallest degree of unreasonable admiration.

The officers were, in general, very respectable and gentlemanly, and the best of them were present. However, Mr. Wickham was more impressive than them all in his appearance, looks, and mannerisms. He was far more attractive than the port-wine-breathing, broad-faced, stuffy Uncle Philips who followed them into the room.

Mr. Wickham was the man who many of the female eyes were drawn to, and Elizabeth was the lucky woman who he eventually sat beside. The way he started talking, even about the mundane topic of the wet weather and the likelihood of a rainy season, was so agreeable that it made even the dullest conversation interesting.

With such competition for the attention of the ladies as Mr. Wickham and the officers, Mr. Collins seemed to fade into the background. The young ladies paid him no attention at all, but Mrs. Philips still occasionally listened to him, and she made sure he was well supplied with coffee and muffins.

When the tables for playing cards were arranged, he was able to return the favor by playing whist with her.

"I don't know much about the game right now," he said, "but I'd like to learn more; since I'm in my current situation in life..." Mrs. Philips was very grateful for his willingness, but didn't wait for him to finish his sentence.

Mr. Wickham wasn't playing whist, so he was welcomed with enthusiasm to the other table between Elizabeth and Lydia. At first it seemed like Lydia would monopolize him completely, since she was a very talkative person; but since she was also very passionate about lottery tickets, she quickly became so wrapped up in the game, making bets and shouting out when she won, that she didn't pay attention to anyone in particular. So, apart from the usual demands of the game, Mr. Wickham had some time to talk to Elizabeth, and she was happy to listen to him, even though what she wanted to hear most of all, the story of his relationship with Mr. Darcy, she knew she wouldn't be told.

She was too scared to even mention that gentleman. But her curiosity was surprisingly satisfied when Mr. Wickham started talking about it himself. He asked how far away Netherfield was from Meryton and, after she told him, he asked in a hesitant way how long Mr. Darcy had been staying there.

"About a month," Elizabeth said and, not wanting to drop the topic, added, "I understand he has a large estate in Derbyshire."

"Yes," Wickham replied. "It's a noble one. Clear ten thousand per annum. You couldn't have met someone more qualified to tell you about it than me – I've been connected to his family in a special way since I was a child."

Elizabeth couldn't help but look surprised.

"You must be surprised, Miss Bennet, at such a statement, after seeing how cold our meeting was yesterday. Are you well acquainted with Mr. Darcy?"

"As much as I ever want to be," Elizabeth said warmly. "I've spent four days in the same house with him and I think he's very unpleasant."

"I cannot give my opinion," said Wickham, "about whether he is agreeable or not. I am not qualified to make a judgment. I have known him for too long and too well to be an objective judge. It's impossible for me to be impartial. But I think your opinion of him would generally surprise people, and maybe you wouldn't express it so strongly anywhere else. Here, you're with your own family."

"Honestly, I'm not saying anything here that I wouldn't say in any other house in the neighborhood, except Netherfield. He's not popular in Hertfordshire. Everyone is put off by his arrogance. You won't find anyone who speaks of him favorably."

"I can't pretend to be sorry," said Wickham, pausing for a moment, "that he or anyone else isn't seen for who they really are; but with him it doesn't happen very often. People are blinded by his wealth and status, or intimidated by his grand demeanor, and only see him as he wants to be seen."

"Even from my brief interactions with him, I'd say he's bad-tempered." Wickham just shook his head.

"I wonder," he said, when he had the chance to speak again, "if he's likely to stay in this country for much longer."

"I don't know for sure, but I didn't hear anything about him leaving when I was at Netherfield. I hope his presence in the area won't affect your plans for the regiment."

"No, I won't be driven away by Mr. Darcy. If he wants to avoid seeing me, he'll have to go. We're not on good terms and it always hurts me to see him, but I have no other reason to avoid him than what I can tell anyone - I feel like I've been treated very badly and I'm filled with deep regret that he's the way he is. His father, Miss Bennet, the late Mr. Darcy, was one of the best people who ever lived and the truest friend I ever had; and I can't be in the same room as this Mr. Darcy without being filled with sadness from all the fond memories. His behavior towards me has been outrageous; but I truly believe I would forgive him anything and everything, except for him failing to meet the expectations and dishonoring the memory of his father."

Elizabeth found the topic interesting and listened intently; but the sensitivity of it prevented further questions.

Mr. Wickham started talking about more general topics, such as Meryton, the surrounding area, and the people, and seemed to be very pleased with everything he had seen so far. He spoke particularly charmingly about the people, making his gallantry evident but in a subtle way.

"I was mainly attracted to join the ----shire by the prospect of being in good and constant company," he said. "It is a highly respectable and pleasant regiment, and my friend Denny further tempted me with his account of their current quarters and the great attentions and excellent acquaintances they have made in Meryton. I admit that society is necessary for me. I have been a disappointed man, and I cannot bear solitude. I need employment and socializing. A military career was not my intended path, but circumstances have made it attractive. The church was supposed to be my profession; I was raised for it. At this moment, I would have possessed a valuable living had it not been for the gentleman we were just speaking of."

"Really?"

"Yes—the late Mr. Darcy left me the next position of the best living in his gift. He was my godfather and was very fond of me. I can't express his kindness adequately. He wanted to provide for me generously, and thought he had done it; but when the living became available, it was given to someone else."

"Goodness!" exclaimed Elizabeth; "but how could that be? How could his will be ignored? Why didn't you seek legal help?"

"There was an informal clause in the bequest that made it impossible for me to have any hope through legal means. A man of integrity could have no doubt as to the intention, but Mr. Darcy chose to doubt it or treated it as a mere conditional recommendation. He claimed that I had forfeited all my right to it due to my extravagance, imprudence, or in short, anything or nothing. It is certain that the living became available exactly two years ago when I was old enough to take it, and it was given to someone else. Also, it is certain that I cannot blame myself for doing anything that could justify losing it. I have a warm and unguarded temperament, and perhaps, I have sometimes expressed my opinion of him too freely, both to him and of him. I cannot remember anything worse than that. But the truth is, we are very different kinds of people, and he despises me."

"That's terrible! He should be publicly shamed."

"Someday he will be, but not by me. Until I can forget his father, I can't challenge or expose him."

Elizabeth respected him for these feelings and thought he was even more attractive as he expressed them.

"But what," she asked after a moment, "could have been his motive? What could have made him act so cruelly?"

"A deep-seated, strong dislike of me, which I can only attribute in part to jealousy. If the late Mr. Darcy had liked me less, his son might have been more tolerant of me, but I think his father's special attachment to me made him angry very early in life. He didn't have much love for his mother, and I've always thought he was selfish. His disposition must be dreadful."

"I didn't think Mr. Darcy was so terrible - although I never liked him, I didn't think he was capable of such cruelty, vindictiveness, and inhumanity," Elizabeth said.

After pondering for a few moments, she added, "I do recall him once boasting at Netherfield about how he is unforgiving and unyielding when it comes to holding a grudge. His temperament must be quite terrible."

"I cannot give an unbiased opinion about him," responded Wickham, "so I will refrain from commenting on that."

Elizabeth was once again lost in thought, and after some time, she exclaimed, "To treat the godson, friend, and favorite of his own father in such a manner! She could have added, "And a young man like you, whose very appearance indicates that you are amiable." However, she was satisfied with saying, "And one who, as you said, was probably his companion from childhood, connected to him in the closest manner."

"We were born in the same parish, within the same estate. We spent most of our youth together, living in the same house, enjoying the same amusements, and receiving the same parental care. My father began his career in the same profession as your uncle, Mr. Philips, who seems to be doing so well in it. However, my father gave up everything to be of service to the late Mr. Darcy and devoted all of his time to managing the Pemberley estate. Mr. Darcy held my father in the highest regard and considered him a close and trusted friend. Mr. Darcy often acknowledged that he was greatly indebted to my father for his active oversight, and just before my father's death, Mr. Darcy voluntarily promised to provide for me. I am convinced that he felt this promise was just as much a debt of gratitude to my father as an expression of affection for me."

Elizabeth exclaimed, "How strange! How abominable! I can't believe that Mr. Darcy's pride hasn't made him do the right thing by you. If nothing else, he should have been too proud to be dishonest."

"It's amazing," responded Wickham. "Almost all of his actions can be attributed to his pride, and pride has often been his closest ally. It has linked him more closely to virtue than any other emotion. However, none of us are entirely consistent, and in his treatment of me, there were even stronger motivations than pride."

"Could such detestable pride as his ever have benefited him?"

"Yes, it has often led him to be generous and charitable. He freely gives his money, shows hospitality, assists his tenants, and helps the poor. Family pride and pride in his father, whom he is very proud of, have motivated him to do this. To avoid bringing shame to his family, to not disappoint their expectations, or lose the influence of Pemberley House, is a powerful incentive. He also has pride in his sister and, along with some brotherly affection, makes him a very kind and attentive guardian. You will hear him praised as the most attentive and best of brothers."

"What kind of girl is Miss Darcy?"

He shook his head. "I wish I could describe her as amiable. It pains me to speak badly of a Darcy, but she is too much like her brother - very, very proud. As a child, she was loving and charming, and very fond of me. I spent hours and hours entertaining her. But now she means nothing to me. She is a beautiful girl, around fifteen or sixteen years old, and I understand she is highly skilled. Since her father's death, her home has been in London, where she lives with a lady who supervises her education."

After numerous pauses and attempts to discuss other topics, Elizabeth could not resist returning to the initial subject and said,

"I am amazed at Mr. Bingley's close friendship with Mr. Darcy. How can Mr. Bingley, who appears to be a good-humored and, I believe, genuinely kind person, be friends with someone like Mr. Darcy? How can they get along? Do you know Mr. Bingley?"

"Not at all."

"He is a sweet-tempered, kind, charming man. He cannot be aware of Mr. Darcy's true nature."

"Perhaps not, but Mr. Darcy can be charming when he chooses. He is not lacking in abilities. He can be a sociable companion if he deems it worthwhile. Among those who are of equal importance to him, he is quite a different man than he is to those who are less fortunate. His pride never abandons him, but he is open-minded, fair, honest, reasonable, honorable, and perhaps even pleasant in the company of the wealthy, taking into account their social status and appearance."

After the whist party broke up, the players gathered around the other table, and Mr. Collins took his place between his cousin Elizabeth and Mrs. Philips. The latter inquired about his success as usual. He had not done very well; he had lost every point. But when Mrs. Philips began to express her concern, he assured her with great seriousness that it was of no importance whatsoever; that he regarded the money as a trifling matter and asked her not to worry.

"I am well aware, madam," he said, "that when people sit down to a card table, they must be prepared for such outcomes. Fortunately, I am not in a position where five shillings would make any difference. Undoubtedly, many others could not say the same, but thanks to Lady Catherine de Bourgh, I am in a position where I do not have to worry about small matters."

Mr. Wickham's attention was drawn, and after observing Mr. Collins for a few moments, he asked Elizabeth in a quiet voice if her family was well acquainted with the De Bourgh family.

"Lady Catherine de Bourgh," she replied, "has recently given him a parish. I am not sure how Mr. Collins first came to her attention, but he certainly has not known her for very long."

"You are surely aware that Lady Catherine de Bourgh and Lady Anne Darcy were sisters, meaning that she is the aunt of the current Mr. Darcy."

"No, I did not know that at all. I knew nothing about Lady Catherine's family connections. I had never even heard of her until the day before yesterday."

"Her daughter, Miss de Bourgh, is expected to inherit a very large fortune, and it is believed that she and her cousin will join their estates."

This information made Elizabeth smile as she thought of poor Miss Bingley. All of her attention, affection for his sister, and compliments to him would be in vain if he was already betrothed to another.

"Mr. Collins," she said, "speaks highly of both Lady Catherine and her daughter, but from some of the details he has shared about her Ladyship, I suspect that his gratitude is misleading him. Despite being his patroness, she is an arrogant and conceited woman."

"I believe she is both to a great extent," replied Wickham. "I haven't seen her for many years, but I clearly remember that I never liked her and that her behavior was domineering and insolent. She is known for being remarkably intelligent and clever, but I think she owes some of her abilities to her social status and wealth, some to her authoritative demeanor, and the rest to the pride of her nephew, who demands that everyone connected with him has a first-class intellect."

Elizabeth agreed that he had provided a very logical explanation, and they continued to talk together with mutual satisfaction until supper ended the card game and gave Mr. Wickham a chance to pay attention to the other ladies. The noise of Mrs. Philips' supper party made conversation impossible, but his demeanor endeared him to everyone. Whatever he said was said well, and whatever he did was done gracefully. Elizabeth left with her mind full of him, unable to stop thinking of Mr. Wickham and what he had told her all the way home. However, there was no time for her to even mention his name during the trip since Lydia and Mr. Collins never stopped talking. Lydia incessantly talked about lottery tickets, the fish she had lost, and the fish she had won, while Mr.

Collins, in describing the politeness of Mr. and Mrs. Philips, protested that he did not care at all about losing at whist, listed all the dishes at supper, and repeatedly worried that he was crowding his cousins. He had more to say than he could manage before the carriage arrived at Longbourn House.

CHAPTER 17

In the following day, Elizabeth recounted to Jane the events that had transpired between herself and Mr. Wickham. Jane, taken aback and deeply troubled, struggled to reconcile her disbelief that Mr. Darcy could be capable of such dishonorable behavior towards Mr. Bingley with her inherent inclination to trust in the sincerity of a gentleman as amiable and well-mannered as Mr. Wickham.

The mere possibility of Mr. Wickham having truly suffered such unkind treatment was enough to stir up all of Jane's sympathetic feelings. As such, she resolved to regard both gentlemen in a favorable light, to champion the integrity of their respective actions, and to attribute any inconsistencies or misunderstandings to nothing more than the unforeseeable twists and turns of fate.

"Both of them," she said, "have surely been deceived but we cannot imagine how. It's possible that interested parties have misrepresented one to the other. In short, we cannot speculate about the reasons or circumstances that led to their separation, without unfairly blaming either of them."

"Indeed, that is very true," she agreed. "And now, my dear Jane, what do you have to say in defense of the interested parties who were likely involved in this matter? Please absolve them of any wrongdoing, or else we will have to think ill of someone."

"Laugh all you want, but I won't change my mind. It's disgraceful that Mr. Darcy is treating his father's favorite this way when his father had promised to take care of them. No man of decency or who values his reputation would do such a thing. Could his closest friends be so wrong about him? No!"

"I'd rather believe that Mr. Bingley was deceived than that Mr. Wickham made up the story he told me last night. Everything he said was so detailed and accurate. If it's not true, let Mr. Darcy deny it. Besides, there was truth in his eyes."

"It is difficult indeed - it is distressing - one doesn't know what to think."

"I beg your pardon; one knows exactly what to think."

But Jane could only be certain of one thing: if Mr. Bingley had been deceived, he would suffer greatly when the truth came out.

At that moment, they were interrupted by the arrival of some people they had been discussing: Mr. Bingley and his sisters had come to invite them to the long-awaited ball at Netherfield, which was scheduled for the following Tuesday. The two ladies were delighted to see their dear friend again and exclaimed that it had been ages since they had met. They asked Jane what she had been doing in the meantime. They paid little attention to the rest of the family, avoiding Mrs. Bennet as much as possible and barely speaking to Elizabeth and the others. Then, to their brother's surprise, they suddenly rose and hurried away, as if eager to escape Mrs. Bennet's hospitality.

The prospect of the Netherfield ball was extremely pleasing to all the women in the family. Mrs. Bennet believed it was given in honor of her eldest daughter, and she was especially pleased to receive the invitation from Mr. Bingley himself instead of a formal card. Jane imagined a wonderful evening with her two friends and their brother, and Elizabeth looked forward to dancing a lot with Mr. Wickham and seeing confirmation of Mr. Darcy's behavior. Catherine and Lydia's happiness was less dependent on any one thing or person, as they were both happy to dance with Mr. Wickham, but a ball was a ball. Even Mary said she had no objection to it.

"As long as I get my mornings to myself," she said, "that is enough. I think it is important for everyone to have some time for recreation and fun. Society has expectations of us all; and I consider myself among those who think it is beneficial to have times of relaxation and fun."

Elizabeth was so excited about the event that, even though she rarely talked to Mr. Collins much, she couldn't help but ask if he planned to accept Mr. Bingley's invitation and if he thought it was appropriate to join in the evening's entertainment. She was quite surprised to find that he had no qualms about it and was not worried about being reprimanded by the Archbishop or Lady Catherine de Bourgh for daring to dance.

"I can assure you," he said, "I'm not at all against a ball like this, held by a young man of good character, with respectable people. I'm not against dancing at all, so I hope all my fair cousins will honor me by dancing with me this evening, especially you, Miss Elizabeth, for the first two dances. I'm sure Jane will understand that I'm showing my preference for you, not disrespecting her."

Elizabeth realized she was tricked. She had been expecting to be asked to dance by Wickham, and now she had to accept Mr. Collins' proposal instead. There was nothing she could do. She accepted Mr. Collins' offer as graciously as she could and put off her own and Mr. Wickham's happiness for a little while longer. She was not pleased with his flattery, as it suggested something more was going on. It suddenly occurred to her that she had been chosen from among her sisters to become the mistress of Hunsford Parsonage and to help make up a card table at Rosings in the absence of more suitable guests. This idea soon became a certainty as she noticed his increasing politeness towards her and heard his frequent attempts to compliment her wit and vivacity. Although she was more astonished than pleased by this effect of her charms, it wasn't long before her mother made it clear that the possibility of their marriage was very pleasing to her. Elizabeth, however, did not want to respond to this hint, as she knew that a serious argument would be the result of any reply. Mr. Collins might never make the offer and until he did, it was pointless to argue about him.

If it hadn't been for the Netherfield ball to look forward to and talk about, the younger Miss Bennets would have been in a terrible state. From the day they got the invitation until the day of the ball, it rained so much they couldn't even go to Meryton. They couldn't get news from their aunt or the officers, and they had to get their shoe-roses for the ball from someone else. Even Elizabeth found the weather so bad that it stopped her from getting to know Mr. Wickham better. Nothing but the dance on Tuesday made the Friday, Saturday, Sunday, and Monday bearable for Kitty and Lydia.

CHAPTER 18

Until Elizabeth entered the drawing room at Netherfield and looked around for Mr. Wickham among all the red coats there, she hadn't even considered the possibility that he wouldn't be there. She hadn't been worried by any of the memories that might have made her anxious. She had taken extra care in getting dressed and was very excited to try to win the rest of his heart that hadn't been won yet, believing that it wouldn't take the entire evening to do it. But in an instant, a dreadful suspicion arose that Wickham had been purposely left out of the Bingleys' invitation to the officers; and though this wasn't exactly the case, Mr. Denny confirmed that he had been called away to town on business the day before and hadn't returned yet, adding with a significant smile,

"I don't think his business would have taken him away right now if he hadn't wanted to avoid a certain gentleman here."

Though Lydia hadn't heard this part, Elizabeth had, and it told her that Darcy was just as responsible for Wickham's absence as if her initial assumption had been correct. This made her so angry that she could barely respond civilly to Darcy's polite inquiries. Paying attention to, being patient with, and forbearing towards Darcy was an injustice to Wickham. She was determined not to have any kind of conversation with him, and she turned away with an expression of annoyance which she couldn't completely hide even when speaking to Mr. Bingley, whose blind favoritism was irritating her.

But Elizabeth was not the type to stay angry for long; even though her evening was ruined, she soon cheered up after talking to Charlotte Lucas, whom she hadn't seen in a week. The first two dances were embarrassing though, because she was partnered with Mr. Collins who was clumsy and serious, and kept apologizing instead of dancing. She was relieved their dances were over.

She then danced with an officer and was happy to talk about Wickham and to hear that he was well-liked. After that, Elizabeth returned to Charlotte and they were talking when suddenly Mr. Darcy addressed her, asking her to marry him. Elizabeth was so taken aback that she accepted without really knowing what she was doing. He then walked away and Elizabeth was left to regret her lack of composure. Charlotte tried to comfort her by saying,

"I'm sure you'll find him very agreeable."

Elizabeth replied, "Heaven forbid! That would be the worst thing of all - to find a man agreeable whom I'm determined to hate. Don't wish me such misfortune."

When the dancing started again and Darcy came to claim her hand, Charlotte whispered to Elizabeth not to be foolish and let her feelings for Wickham make her seem unpleasant to a man of much higher social standing than Wickham. Elizabeth said nothing and took her place in the set, amazed at the honor of being allowed to stand opposite Mr. Darcy, and seeing the same surprise in her neighbors. They stood for some time without saying a word; and she started to think that their silence would last through the two dances, and at first she decided not to break it; but then she thought that it would be more punishing for her partner if she made him talk, so she made some comment on the dance. He replied and then went back to being quiet. After a few minutes she said to him,

"It's your turn to say something now, Mr. Darcy. I talked about the dance and you should make a comment about the size of the room or the number of couples."

He smiled and told her that he would say whatever she wanted him to.

"That's good. That'll do for now. Maybe later I can say that private balls are better than public ones. But for now we can be quiet."

"Do you only talk when you're dancing because you have to?"

"Sometimes. You have to say something, you know. It would be strange to stay quiet for half an hour, but for the benefit of some, conversation should be arranged so that they don't have to say much."

"Are you thinking of your own feelings or do you think you're making me happy?"

"Both," Elizabeth said playfully; "I've always noticed that our minds are similar. We're both not very social, not wanting to talk unless we have something amazing to say that will be remembered forever."

"That doesn't sound like you at all," he said.

"I can't say if it's like me or not. You must be the judge of that."

He didn't answer and they were quiet until they finished the dance. Then he asked her if she and her sisters often walk to Meryton. She answered in the affirmative and, unable to resist the temptation, said, "When you saw us there the other day, we had just become acquainted."

This had an immediate effect. His features darkened with a look of haughtiness, but he didn't say anything. Elizabeth felt guilty for speaking out, but she couldn't keep going. Finally, Darcy spoke in a stiff tone,

"Mr. Wickham is blessed with such pleasant manners that he will make friends easily, but it's less certain if he will be able to keep them."

"He has been unfortunate enough to lose your friendship," Elizabeth said firmly, "in a way that he will feel for the rest of his life."

Darcy didn't reply and seemed to want to change the subject. At that moment, Sir William Lucas came up to them, intending to walk through the group to the other side of the room. When he saw Darcy, he stopped and bowed with great politeness, complimenting him on his dancing and his partner.

"I have been highly delighted, my dear Sir. Such excellent dancing is not often seen. It's clear that you are part of the highest circles. But let me say that your lovely partner does you credit and I hope to see this pleasure repeated often, especially when a certain desirable event, my dear Eliza, (glancing at her sister and Bingley) takes place. What congratulations will then come! You won't thank me for keeping you from the delightful conversation of that young lady, whose bright eyes are also scolding me."

The latter part of this speech was barely heard by Darcy, however, his eyes were focused intently on Bingley and Jane, who were dancing together. He soon collected himself and said,

"Sir William's interruption made me forget what we were talking about."

"I don't think we were talking at all. Sir William couldn't have interrupted any two people in the room who had less to say. We've tried a few topics already without success, and I can't imagine what we'll talk about next."

"What do you think of books?" Sir William asked, smiling.

"Books? Oh no, I'm sure we never read the same books or feel the same way about them."

"I'm sorry you think that, but at least there's no shortage of topics. We can compare our different opinions," Sir William said.

"No, I can't talk about books in a ballroom. My head is always full of something else."

"So, you're always thinking about the present in these situations, right?" Sir William asked, looking doubtful.

"Yes, always," she said without really thinking, as her thoughts had wandered far from the subject. Suddenly she exclaimed, "I remember you saying once, Mr. Darcy, that you hardly ever forgive and that your resentment, once created, is unappeasable. I suppose you're very careful about creating it."

"I am," he replied firmly.

"Will you never let yourself be influenced by prejudice?"

"I hope not."

"It is especially important for those who never change their minds to be sure of making the right judgement in the first place."

"Can I ask what these questions are leading to?"

"Just to get an idea of your character," she said, trying to appear less serious. "I'm trying to figure it out."

"And how's it going?"

She shook her head. "I'm not getting very far. I hear so many different things about you that it's very confusing."

"I can easily believe," he said seriously, "that people's opinions of me can vary greatly, and I would rather you didn't try to describe my character right now, as I fear it wouldn't do either of us any favors."

"But if I don't do it now, I might not get another chance."

"I wouldn't want to take away any of your pleasure," he said coldly. She said nothing more and they went down the other side of the dance floor and parted in silence. Both of them were dissatisfied, but for different reasons. Darcy had a strong feeling towards her which made him forgive her quickly and instead direct his anger at someone else.

Not long after they had separated, Miss Bingley came up to her and said with a look of disdain,

"So, Miss Eliza, I hear you are quite taken with George Wickham! Your sister has been telling me all about him and asking me a thousand questions. It seems he forgot to tell you that he is the son of old Wickham, the late Mr. Darcy's steward. Let me advise you, as a friend, not to take all of his words as truth. It's not true that Mr. Darcy treated him poorly; in fact, he has been very kind to him, even though George Wickham has been very disrespectful to Mr. Darcy. I don't know all the details, but I do know for certain that Mr. Darcy is not at fault. He can't stand to even hear the name George Wickham, and my brother, although he couldn't avoid inviting the officers to his gathering, was overjoyed to find out that Wickham had left town. Wickham's arrival in our town was a brazen and impudent move, and I'm amazed that he had the audacity to do so. Miss

Eliza, I feel sorry for you having discovered your favorite's wrongdoing, but given his background, we shouldn't expect anything better."

"His guilt and his background are the same thing, according to you," Elizabeth said angrily. "He told me himself that he's Mr. Darcy's steward's son."

"I apologize," Miss Bingley said with a sneer, turning away. "I meant well."

"To think that impudent girl imagines she can influence me with such a trifling attack!" Elizabeth thought to herself, indignantly. "She is sorely mistaken. I can see nothing in her words but her own stubborn ignorance and Mr. Darcy's malice." With that, she sought out her eldest sister, who had promised to gather information on the same topic from Bingley.

Jane greeted her with a smile of such serene contentment, such a radiant expression of joy, that it was abundantly clear how satisfied she was with the events of the evening. Elizabeth immediately sensed her sister's emotions, and in that moment, all her concerns for Wickham, her anger towards his enemies, and every other thought, yielded to the hope that Jane was on the path to happiness.

"I would like to inquire," she said, smiling just as radiantly as her sister, "what you have discovered about Mr. Wickham. But perhaps you have been too occupied with your own pleasure to consider a third person, in which case, you have my forgiveness."

"No," Jane replied, "I haven't forgotten him, but I don't have anything good to tell you. Mr. Bingley doesn't know the whole story, and he isn't aware of the things that made Mr. Darcy so angry. But he is sure that Mr. Wickham is an honorable man and has done nothing to deserve Mr. Darcy's bad opinion. I'm afraid he has been very foolish, and he has lost Mr. Darcy's respect."

"Mr. Bingley does not know Mr. Wickham himself?"

"No; he never saw him till the other morning at Meryton."

"So, this information is what he received from Mr. Darcy. I am completely content with that. But what did he say about the living?"

"He doesn't remember the exact details, although he has heard them from Mr. Darcy on more than one occasion. He believes that it was left to him only under certain conditions."

"I have no doubt about Mr. Bingley's sincerity," said Elizabeth, with conviction. "But please understand that I cannot be convinced by mere assurances. While Mr. Bingley's defense of his friend was undoubtedly eloquent, he is still unfamiliar with several aspects of the story and has learned the rest directly from his friend. Therefore, I shall continue to think of both gentlemen just as I did before."

She then shifted the conversation to a more agreeable topic that both of them could enjoy, and one in which there could be no difference of opinion. Elizabeth listened with pleasure as Jane shared her happy, yet unassuming hopes about Bingley's affection, and did everything she could to reinforce her sister's confidence in it. When Mr. Bingley himself joined them, Elizabeth withdrew and spoke with Miss Lucas. Before she could answer her partner's question about the pleasantness of her previous dance partner, Mr. Collins approached them with great excitement, announcing that he had just made a most important discovery.

I overheard the man telling the young woman who runs this house the names of his cousin Miss de Bourgh and her mother Lady Catherine. It's amazing how things like this happen! I would have never thought of running into Lady Catherine de Bourgh's nephew here! I'm so thankful I found out in time to greet him, which I'm about to do now. I hope he'll forgive me for not having done it earlier since I had no idea of the connection.

"You're not going to introduce yourself to Mr. Darcy?"

"Yes, I am. I'll ask him to forgive me for not doing it earlier. I believe he's Lady Catherine's nephew. I will be able to inform him that her ladyship was perfectly well the day before yesterday."

Elizabeth tried hard to get Mr. Collins to not go through with his plan, telling him that Mr. Darcy would see it as an intrusion rather than a compliment to his aunt and that there was no need for either of them to make contact. Mr. Collins listened to her with a determined look on his face, and when she finished he said,

"Elizabeth, I have a great deal of respect for your opinion, but you must understand that there is a difference between the etiquette of the clergy and the etiquette of the rest of society. I believe that the clergy are of equal importance to the highest ranking people in the kingdom, as long as they remain humble. You must therefore allow me to follow the dictates of my conscience on this occasion, which leads me to do what I think is my duty. Please forgive me for not taking your advice, which I will always follow in other matters, although in this case I believe I am more qualified to decide what is right due to my education and experience than yourself, a young lady." He then bowed low and left her to approach Mr. Darcy, whom she watched intently as he received her cousin's advances. Her cousin bowed solemnly before he spoke and though she couldn't hear what he said, she felt as if she was hearing it all and could see the words 'apology', 'Hunsford' and 'Lady Catherine de Bourgh' on his lips. It upset her to see him put himself in such an awkward position. Mr. Darcy was looking at him in amazement and when he finally gave him time to speak, he replied politely but coolly. Mr. Collins, however, was not deterred from speaking again and Mr. Darcy's disdain seemed to be growing with each word of his second speech. At the end of it, he just gave Mr. Collins a slight bow and moved away. Mr. Collins then returned to Elizabeth.

"I can assure you," he said, "I have no cause to be dissatisfied with my reception. Mr. Darcy seemed very pleased with my attention. He replied to me with the utmost politeness and even paid me a compliment by saying that he was so sure of

Lady Catherine's good judgement that he was certain she would never bestow a favor unwisely. It was a very kind thought. All in all, I am very pleased with him."

Since Elizabeth had no personal matters to attend to, she directed most of her attention towards her sister and Mr. Bingley. The train of pleasant thoughts that her observations inspired within her made her almost as happy as Jane. She imagined her sister settling into that very house, basking in all the joy that a marriage based on true affection could provide. She even felt capable, under such circumstances, of attempting to like Bingley's two sisters. She could clearly see that her mother's thoughts were likewise fixated on this subject, and she made up her mind to keep her distance, lest she hear too much.

Therefore, when they sat down to supper, Elizabeth regarded it as a most unfortunate coincidence that they were seated next to one another. She was deeply disappointed to discover that her mother was conversing freely and openly with Lady Lucas about nothing else but her expectation that Jane would soon be married to Mr. Bingley. It was an invigorating topic, and Mrs. Bennet appeared to be incapable of tiring while enumerating the advantages of the match. She enumerated his charm, wealth, and close proximity as the first reasons for self-congratulation, and then she reveled in the fact that Bingley's two sisters were so fond of Jane, and must surely desire the match as much as she did. Furthermore, Jane's promising marriage to such a wealthy man held such potential for her younger daughters, as it would bring them into contact with other affluent suitors. And lastly, it was so gratifying at her age to be able to entrust her unmarried daughters to the care of their elder sister, thus sparing herself from having to attend social gatherings more frequently than she preferred. It was necessary to express pleasure at this development, as it was expected in such circumstances, but no one was less inclined than Mrs. Bennet to find contentment in staying at home at any point in her life. She concluded with numerous good wishes that Lady Lucas might soon be similarly fortunate, even though it was evident from her triumphant tone that she believed there was no chance of it

Despite Elizabeth's attempts to slow down her mother's speech and encourage her to express her joy in a quieter voice, it was all in vain. To her immense frustration, Elizabeth noticed that Mr. Darcy, who was seated across from them, had overheard most of their conversation. Her mother only chided her for being foolish.

"What does Mr. Darcy matter to me, I ask you? Why should I be afraid of him? We certainly do not owe him any special courtesy that would require us to censor our speech according to his preferences."

"For goodness sake, Mother, please lower your voice. What could you possibly gain from offending Mr. Darcy? You will never win his friendship by behaving in such a way."

Despite Elizabeth's best efforts to intervene, nothing she said had any effect. Her mother persisted in speaking about her hopes in the same straightforward tone. Elizabeth blushed repeatedly with embarrassment and annoyance. She couldn't help but frequently glance over at Mr. Darcy, though each time she did, she was reminded of what she feared most: even though he wasn't always looking at her mother, she was certain that his focus was always fixed on her. The expression on his face gradually shifted from one of angry contempt to a calm and steady seriousness.

Finally, Mrs. Bennet had nothing more to say, and Lady Lucas, who had been yawning for some time at the repetition of joys she had no hope of experiencing, was left to enjoy her cold ham and chicken in peace. Elizabeth began to feel better, but the calm didn't last long. After supper, someone suggested singing, and Elizabeth was mortified to see Mary, with very little persuasion, getting ready to perform for the company. Despite Elizabeth's many significant looks and silent pleas, Mary refused to understand and began to sing. Elizabeth watched her progress through the various stanzas with great impatience and discomfort. When Mary finished, the table thanked her, but then she began another song after only a short pause, causing Elizabeth great agony. Mary's singing voice was weak, and her manner was affected. Elizabeth looked at Jane to see how she was coping, but Jane was calmly chatting with Bingley. Elizabeth also noticed Bingley's two sisters making mocking gestures at each other and at Darcy, who remained resolutely serious. She looked at her father, hoping he would intervene so Mary wouldn't keep singing all night. He got the hint and said,

"That's enough, Mary. Let the other ladies have a chance to show off their talents."

Mary pretended not to hear, but she was embarrassed and Elizabeth felt sorry for her and her father's comment.

Then Mr. Collins said, "If I could sing, I'd be happy to entertain the company. I think music is a harmless pastime, although I don't think it's right to spend too much time on it. The rector of a parish has a lot to do. He has to negotiate a good tithe agreement and write his own sermons. He also has to take care of his parish duties and his house. It's important that he's respectful and courteous to everyone, especially those who got him his job. I can't let him off that duty and I wouldn't think highly of someone who neglected to show respect to anyone connected to the family." With a bow to Mr. Darcy, he finished speaking, which was loud enough for half the room to hear. Many people were surprised, some smiled, but no one seemed more amused than Mr. Bennet himself, while his wife praised Mr. Collins for speaking so sensibly and quietly told Lady Lucas that he was a very clever and kind young man.

To Elizabeth, it seemed as if her family had made an agreement to embarrass themselves as much as possible during the evening. She thought it would have been impossible for them to have played their parts with more spirit or success. She felt happy for Bingley and her sister that some of the exhibition had escaped his notice and that his feelings were not the sort to be much distressed by the folly he must have witnessed. However, she found it bad enough that his two sisters and Mr. Darcy had such an opportunity to ridicule her family. She couldn't decide which was more intolerable: the silent contempt of the gentleman or the insolent smiles of the ladies.

The rest of the evening did not bring Elizabeth much amusement. Mr. Collins persisted in staying by her side, and even though she refused to dance with him again, he prevented her from dancing with others. She tried to convince him to stand up with someone else, and offered to introduce him to any young lady in the room, but he insisted that his chief aim was to recommend himself to her by being attentive and that he would remain close to her the entire evening. There was no reasoning with him on this matter. Elizabeth's greatest relief came from her friend Miss Lucas, who often joined them and kindly directed Mr. Collins's conversation towards herself.

She was glad that Mr. Darcy did not approach her or give her any further attention, even though he often stood very close to her without being engaged in conversation. She believed this was probably due to her allusions to Mr. Wickham, and she was happy about it.

The Longbourn party were the last to leave, and Mrs. Bennet's maneuver made them wait for their carriages a quarter of an hour after everyone else had gone. During this time, they observed how eagerly some members of the family wished them away. Mrs. Hurst and her sister barely spoke, except to complain about their tiredness and were clearly impatient to have the house to themselves. Their reluctance to engage in conversation cast a pall over the entire party. The situation was not improved by Mr. Collins, who gave long speeches complimenting Mr. Bingley and his sisters on the elegance of their entertainment and the hospitality and politeness they had shown their guests. Darcy said nothing. Mr. Bennet enjoyed the scene silently. Mr. Bingley and Jane stood a little apart from the rest and talked only to each other. Elizabeth maintained a steady silence, as did Mrs. Hurst and Miss Bingley. Even Lydia was too exhausted to do more than occasionally exclaim, "Lord, how tired I am!" followed by a loud yawn.

When they finally got up to say goodbye, Mrs. Bennet was extremely polite in expressing her hope to see the entire family soon at Longbourn. She spoke directly to Mr. Bingley, assuring him of how happy he would make them by simply joining them for a family dinner without the formality of a formal invitation. Bingley was full of grateful pleasure and readily agreed to take the earliest opportunity to visit them after his return from London, where he was obliged to go the next day for a short time.

Mrs. Bennet was very pleased and left the house with the delightful belief that her daughter would certainly be settled at Netherfield in three or four months, once the necessary preparations for settlements, new carriages, and wedding clothes were made. She also thought with equal certainty that another daughter would be married to Mr. Collins, which brought her some pleasure, though not as much as the prospect of Jane's marriage to Mr. Bingley. Elizabeth was her least favorite child, and even though the man and the match were good enough for her, they paled in comparison to Mr. Bingley and Netherfield.

CHAPTER 19

The following day, a new event took place at Longbourn. Mr. Collins made a formal declaration of his intentions. He had decided to do so quickly, as his leave of absence only extended until the following Saturday, and he did not feel nervous about it. He went about it in an orderly manner, following the customary procedures.

After breakfast, he found Mrs. Bennet, Elizabeth, and one of the younger girls together, and spoke to the mother, saying, "Madam, may I ask for your assistance in securing a private audience with your daughter Elizabeth this morning?"

Elizabeth was surprised and did not have time to react before Mrs. Bennet responded, "Oh dear! Yes, certainly! I'm sure Lizzy will be very happy. I'm sure she has no objections. Come, Kitty, let's go upstairs." Mrs. Bennet quickly gathered her work and was about to leave when Elizabeth called out, "Please, ma'am, don't go. I beg of you not to go. Mr. Collins can excuse me. There's nothing he needs to say to me that anyone else cannot hear. I will leave myself."

"No, no, nonsense, Lizzy," replied her mother. "I want you to stay here and listen to Mr. Collins."

Elizabeth didn't want to disobey, so she reluctantly sat back down and tried to distract herself from her distress and amusement. Mrs. Bennet and Kitty left the room and Mr. Collins began to speak.

"Trust me, my dear Miss Elizabeth, your modesty only makes you more endearing. I'm sure you can guess what I'm about to say, but I have your mother's permission to do so. My affections for you have been too obvious to be mistaken. As soon as I entered the house, I realized you were the person I wanted to spend the rest of my life with. But before I get too carried away, I should explain why I'm getting married - and why I came to Hertfordshire with the intention of finding a wife."

The idea of Mr. Collins, with all his seriousness, being swept away by his emotions, was so funny to Elizabeth that she couldn't use the short pause he gave her to stop him, so he continued:

"My reasons for getting married are first, that I think it's right for a clergyman in a comfortable situation like me to set a good example in his parish. Secondly, I'm sure it will make me much happier; and thirdly - which I should have mentioned earlier - it's the specific advice and recommendation of the very noble lady I'm honored to call my patroness. Twice she has given me her opinion (without me even asking!) about this topic; and it was only the Saturday night before I left Hunsford— while we were playing quadrille and Mrs. Jenkinson was arranging Miss de Bourgh's footstool—that she said, 'Mr. Collins, you must get married. A clergyman like you must get married. Choose carefully, choose a gentlewoman for my sake; and for your own, let her be someone who is practical and able to make a small income last a long time. This is my advice. Find someone like that as soon as you can, bring her to Hunsford, and I will visit her.' Allow me to point out, my fair cousin, that I do not consider Lady Catherine de Bourgh's attention and kindness as one of the least advantages I can offer you. You will find her manners to be beyond anything I can describe; and I think your wit and liveliness will be pleasing to her, especially when combined with the silence and respect her rank will undoubtedly inspire. Thus, I have explained the reason for my wanting to marry someone from Longbourn instead of my own neighborhood - that I, as the inheritor of this estate after your father's death (which may not be for many years yet), wanted to ensure that the loss to your family would be as little as possible when the time comes. I hope this explanation has not lessened my standing in your eyes. All that is left for me to do is to express the intensity of my affections. I am not concerned with wealth and will not ask for anything from your father, since I am aware that it cannot be granted - the only thing you will ever be entitled to is the one thousand pounds in the 4 per cents. that you will receive after your mother's passing. So, regarding that matter, I will keep quiet at all times. You can be certain that I will never say anything mean or critical about it once we are married."

It was absolutely necessary to interrupt him now.

"You are too quick, Sir," she said. "You seem to have forgotten that I haven't given you an answer. Please allow me to do so now. I appreciate the compliment you are giving me, and I am aware of the honor in your proposal, but I cannot accept."

"I am aware," replied Mr. Collins, gesturing formally with his hand, "that it is customary for young women to decline a man's proposal when they really mean to accept it, particularly when he first asks for their affection. Sometimes this refusal is repeated a second or even a third time. Therefore, I am not at all discouraged by what you have just said, and I hope to marry you soon."

"Honestly, that's an ambitious hope after what I said," Elizabeth replied. "I'm not one of those girls who would take a risk and hope to get asked a second time. I mean what I said. You can't make me happy and I'm sure I'm the last person who could make you happy. Even if Lady Catherine knew me, I'm sure she wouldn't think I'm suitable for the situation."

"If I knew for certain Lady Catherine would think that way," Mr. Collins said seriously, "but I can't imagine her disapproving of you. When I see her again, I'll be sure to tell her how modest, frugal, and all your other wonderful qualities you have."

"Actually, Mr. Collins, there is no need to compliment me. Please allow me to make my own judgment, and believe what I say. I genuinely wish you happiness and prosperity, and by refusing your proposal, I am doing my best to prevent you from being unhappy. By making this offer, you have shown your consideration for my family, and you can inherit the Longbourn estate without any remorse when it becomes available. So, this matter is now resolved."

Elizabeth got up to leave the room, but Mr. Collins stopped her with these words: "When I have the honor of speaking to you next about this matter, I hope to receive a more favorable response than the one you have given me now. However, I'm not accusing you of being cruel at the moment, because I know that it is customary for women to reject a man on his first attempt, and perhaps you have already given me enough encouragement to pursue you, which would be consistent with the true nature of a woman's delicacy."

"If what I have said so far sounds encouraging to you, I don't know how to make my refusal sound convincing."

"You must excuse me for thinking that your refusal of my proposal is just a formality. My reasons for believing this are these: I don't think my hand is unworthy of your acceptance or that the life I can offer you would be anything but desirable. My status in life, my connections to the De Bourgh family, and my relationship to your own are all in my favor; and you should also consider that, despite your many charms, it is not certain that you will ever receive another marriage proposal. Unfortunately, your dowry is so small that it will most likely cancel out your beauty and other attractive qualities. As a result, I must assume that you are not serious about rejecting me. Instead, I will choose to believe that you are trying to make me love you even more by keeping me in suspense, as is the customary practice of refined women."

"I can assure you, Sir, that I have no desire to be the kind of elegant woman who enjoys tormenting a decent man. I would rather be complimented by being believed sincere. I thank you once again for the honor of your proposal, but accepting it is completely out of the question. My feelings prevent me from doing so in every way. Can I be any clearer? Please do not think of me as an elegant woman intending to cause you trouble, but as a reasonable person speaking the truth from the heart."

"You're always so charming!" he replied, awkwardly trying to be gallant. "And I'm sure that if your parents approve, my proposal will be accepted."

Elizabeth did not respond to Mr. Collins' stubborn self-deception and immediately and silently left. She was determined that if he persisted in seeing her repeated refusals as encouragement, she would go to her father, who would give a definite and decisive negative answer. Her father's behavior could not be mistaken for the insincere actions of an elegant and coquettish woman.

CHAPTER 20

Mr. Collins did not have to contemplate his successful love for very long in silence. Mrs. Bennet had been waiting in the vestibule, and as soon as she saw Elizabeth open the door and quickly walk towards the staircase, she entered the breakfast room. She congratulated both Mr. Collins and herself enthusiastically on the happy prospect of their upcoming marriage. Mr. Collins received these congratulations with equal pleasure and then proceeded to recount the details of their conversation. He felt that he had every reason to be satisfied with the outcome, as his cousin's refusal was merely a result of her bashful modesty and genuine delicacy of character.

This news shocked Mrs. Bennet; she would have been pleased if her daughter had intended to encourage him by rejecting his offer, but she did not dare to believe it and had to say it.

"But I'm sure, Mr. Collins," she added, "that Lizzy will come to her senses. I will talk to her about it myself right away. She is very stubborn and foolish, and doesn't know what's good for her; but I will make her understand."

"Excuse me for interrupting you, Madam," Mr. Collins said, "but if she is really stubborn and foolish, I don't think she would be a suitable wife for a man in my position who looks for happiness in marriage. So if she insists on rejecting my offer, it might be better not to force her to accept me, because if she has such a temper, she won't be able to make me very happy."

"Sir, you are misunderstanding me," Mrs. Bennet said, alarmed. "Lizzy is only stubborn in matters like this. In all other ways, she is as good-natured a girl as ever lived. I will go talk to

Mr. Bennet right away and we will sort this out with her soon, I'm sure."

She didn't give him a chance to respond and hurried to her husband, calling out as she entered the library,

"Oh! Mr. Bennet, you are needed urgently; we are all in an uproar. You must come and make Lizzy marry Mr. Collins, for she says she won't have him, and if you don't hurry he will change his mind and not have her."

Mr. Bennet looked up from his book as she entered and fixed his eyes on her face with a calm unconcern which was not affected at all by her news. "I don't understand what you're saying," he said when she had finished. "What are you talking about?"

"I'm talking about Mr. Collins and Lizzy. Lizzy says she won't marry Mr. Collins and Mr. Collins is saying he won't marry Lizzy."

"What am I supposed to do about it? It looks like a hopeless situation."

"Talk to Lizzy about it. Tell her you insist she marry him."

"Have her come down here. She can hear my opinion."

Mrs. Bennet rang the bell and Elizabeth was called to the library.

"Come here, child," her father said when she appeared. "I asked you here to discuss something important. I hear Mr. Collins has proposed to you. Is that true?"

Elizabeth said it was.

"Very well. And you've refused his proposal?"

"Yes, Sir."

"Very well. Now we get to the point. Your mother wants you to accept it. Is that right, Mrs. Bennet?"

"Yes, or I won't see her again."

"Elizabeth, you have a difficult decision to make. If you don't marry Mr. Collins, your mother won't see you again, and if you do, I won't see you again."

Elizabeth couldn't help but smile at this strange demand, but Mrs. Bennet was extremely disappointed as she thought her husband wanted Elizabeth to marry Mr. Collins. Mr. Bennet then said,

"My dear, I have two requests. First, that you will allow me to use my own judgement in this matter, and secondly, that you let me have the library to myself."

Mrs. Bennet still did not give up and continued to try and persuade Elizabeth. She asked Jane to help her, but Jane politely declined. Elizabeth sometimes seriously and sometimes playfully replied to her mother's requests. Though her manner changed, her resolve never did.

Meanwhile, Mr. Collins was alone, reflecting on what had just happened. He thought too highly of himself to understand why his cousin had rejected him; and though his pride was wounded, he was not affected in any other way. His admiration for her was completely fabricated; and the possibility that she had done something to deserve her mother's criticism prevented him from feeling any remorse.

While the family was in turmoil, Charlotte Lucas arrived to spend the day with them. Lydia ran up to her, whispering excitedly, "I'm glad you're here, there's so much going on! Guess what happened this morning? Mr. Collins asked Lizzy to marry him, and she said no!"

Charlotte had hardly had a chance to respond before Kitty joined them, with the same news. As soon as they entered the breakfast room, where Mrs. Bennet was alone, she started talking about it too, asking Charlotte to use her influence to get Lizzy to do what the family wanted. "Please do, my dear Miss Lucas," she said sadly, "because no one is on my side, no one agrees with me, I'm treated terribly, no one cares about my poor nerves."

Charlotte didn't have to reply because Jane and Elizabeth came in.

"There she comes," Mrs. Bennet continued. "She looks completely unconcerned and doesn't care about us at all. It's as if we were in York, as long as she can have her own way. But let me tell you, Miss Lizzy, if you continue to refuse every marriage proposal like this, you'll never get a husband at all. And I don't know who will take care of you when your father dies. I won't be able to support you, and I'm warning you. I'm done with you from this day forward. I told you in the library that I would never speak to you again, and you will find that I keep my word. I don't enjoy talking to disobedient children. Not that I enjoy talking to anyone, really. People like me, who suffer from nervous complaints, have no great desire to talk. Nobody knows what I go through! But it's always like this. Those who don't complain are never pitied."

Her daughters listened to her sadly, knowing that any attempt to reason with her or soothe her would only make her more angry. She continued to talk without interruption until Mr. Collins arrived. Upon seeing him, she said to her daughters,

"Now, I insist that you all be quiet and let Mr. Collins and me have a conversation."

Elizabeth quietly left the room, Jane and Kitty followed, but Lydia stayed put, determined to hear as much as she could. Charlotte, however, was delayed first by Mr. Collins's politeness as he asked her a lot of questions about herself and her family, and then by curiosity. She satisfied herself by walking to the window and pretending not to hear. In a sorrowful voice, Mrs. Bennet began the conversation:

"Oh! Mr. Collins!"

"My dear Madam," he replied, "let us never speak of this again. It is far from me to resent your daughter's behavior. Resignation to inevitable misfortunes is the duty of all of us, especially a young man like me who has been fortunate enough to receive preferment at an early age. And I am resigned, even though I may have some doubts about my happiness if my cousin had accepted my proposal. I have often noticed that resignation is never more complete than when we begin to see the value of the denied blessing diminish in our estimation. I hope you won't think that I am showing disrespect to your family, my dear Madam, by withdrawing my proposal to your daughter without first asking for your help. I realize that it may be objectionable for me to have accepted your daughter's rejection rather than your own. However, we are all capable of making mistakes. My intentions have been good throughout the entire affair. My goal has been to find a suitable companion for myself while also considering the benefits to your entire family. And if my manner has been at all offensive, I humbly apologize."

CHAPTER 21

The discussion of Mr. Collins' offer was almost finished and Elizabeth had to put up with the uncomfortable feelings it brought. Mr. Collins himself showed his feelings through his stiff manner and resentful silence, rarely speaking to her. The attention he had previously shown her was now directed towards Miss Lucas, which was a relief for them all, especially for Elizabeth's friend.

The next day, Mrs. Bennet was still in a bad mood and Mr. Collins was still in a state of angry pride. Elizabeth had been hoping that his resentment might make his visit shorter, but it seemed that he was still planning to stay until Saturday.

After breakfast, the girls went to Meryton to see if Mr. Wickham had returned, and to express their disappointment that he had not attended the Netherfield ball. When they reached town, he joined them and went with them to their aunt's house, where everyone discussed his regret and frustration. He admitted to Elizabeth that he had chosen to be absent.

"I found," he said, "as the time drew near, that it would be better if I didn't meet Mr. Darcy; that being in the same room and at the same party with him for so many hours could be more than I could handle and that it could lead to awkward situations for more than just me."

She praised his restraint and they had plenty of time to talk about it as Wickham and another officer walked back with them to Longbourn. He paid special attention to her during the walk, which was a double benefit for her; she felt the compliment it offered to her and it was very useful in introducing him to her parents.

Shortly after they returned, Elizabeth saw her sister's face change as she read a letter that had been delivered to her from

Netherfield. The envelope contained a sheet of elegant, hot-pressed paper with a lady's neat handwriting. Elizabeth could tell her sister was focusing on certain parts of the letter. Jane quickly composed herself and, putting the letter away, tried to join in the conversation with her usual cheerfulness. But Elizabeth was so worried about the letter that she couldn't focus on anything else, not even Wickham. As soon as he and his companion left, Jane gave Elizabeth a look that told her to follow her upstairs. When they were in their room, Jane took out the letter and said, "Listen to what it says."

She read the first sentence aloud, which stated that they had just decided to follow their brother to town immediately and that they intended to dine that day in Grosvenor Street, where Mr. Hurst had a house. The next sentence read as follows: "I do not regret anything I will leave in Hertfordshire, except for your company, my dearest friend. However, we will hope to enjoy many returns of the delightful time we have spent together, and in the meantime we can reduce the pain of separation by frequently and candidly corresponding. I rely on you for that." Elizabeth listened to these exaggerated expressions with skepticism and although their sudden departure surprised her, she saw nothing to truly mourn. It was not to be expected that their absence from Netherfield would prevent Mr. Bingley from being there and as for the loss of their company, she was convinced that Jane would soon stop worrying about it once she started enjoying Mr. Bingley's company.

"It's a shame," she said after a brief pause, "that you won't be able to see your friends before they leave the country. But can we not hope that the time of future happiness that Miss Bingley is looking forward to will come sooner than she thinks, and that the wonderful friendship you have had as friends will be even better when you are sisters? Mr. Bingley won't be kept in London by them."

"Caroline definitely says that none of the group will go back to Hertfordshire this winter. I'll read it to you –

"When my brother left us yesterday, he thought that the job that took him to London might be done in three or four days, but as we know it won't be that quick, and also knowing that when Charles gets to the city, he won't be in a hurry to leave, we have decided to go after him so he won't have to spend his free time in an uncomfortable hotel. Many of my friends are already there for the winter; I wish I could hear that you, my dearest friend, had any plans to join them, but I don't think that will happen. I sincerely hope your Christmas in Hertfordshire will be filled with the joys that usually come with the season, and that you will have so many admirers that you won't miss the three of us who will be away."

Jane added, "It's clear that he won't be coming back this winter."

"It's obvious that Miss Bingley doesn't want him to," replied Elizabeth.

"Why would you think that? He's his own master. But you don't know the whole story. I'll read you the part that really upsets me. I won't hide anything from you."

"Mr. Darcy is eager to see his sister, and to be honest, we're just as keen to meet her again. I really don't think there's anyone as beautiful, graceful and talented as Georgiana Darcy, and Louisa and I are even more drawn to her because we hope she'll become our sister one day. I don't know if I ever told you how I feel about this, but I'm going to now. I don't think it's unreasonable. My brother already likes her a lot and he'll have plenty of chances to get to know her better. Her family is just as keen on the connection as his. I don't think my sisterly bias is misleading me when I say Charles is capable of winning any woman's heart. With all these things in favor of an attachment and nothing to stop it, am I wrong to hope for something that will make so many people happy?"

"What do you think of this, Lizzy?" Jane asked when she was done. "Is it clear enough? Does it mean Caroline doesn't want me to be her sister and she knows her brother isn't interested in me? Is she trying to warn me, in a nice way? Can there be any other interpretation?"

"Yes, there can; my opinion is completely different. Would you like to hear it?"

"I would love to."

"I can give it to you in a few words. Miss Bingley can see that her brother is in love with you and she wants him to marry Miss Darcy. She follows him to town in order to keep him there and she tries to convince you that he doesn't care for you."

Jane shook her head.

"Indeed, Jane, you should trust me on this. No one who has ever seen you two together could doubt his affection for you. Miss Bingley, I'm sure, does not doubt it either. She's not foolish enough to do so. If she had seen even half the love Mr. Darcy has for himself, she would have ordered her wedding clothes by now."

"But the fact is, we're not rich or grand enough for them, and Miss Bingley is even more determined to secure Miss Darcy for her brother. She thinks that once there has been one intermarriage, it will be easier to achieve a second. It's a clever plan, and it might even work if Miss de Bourgh were out of the way".

"However, my dearest Jane, you cannot seriously believe that just because Miss Bingley tells you her brother admires Miss Darcy, that he is any less aware of your own worth than when he last saw you on Tuesday. She cannot convince him that instead of being in love with you, he is in love with her friend."

"If we had the same opinion of Miss Bingley," Jane replied, "your explanation would make me feel much better. But I know it's not true. Caroline would never intentionally deceive anyone, so all I can hope is that she's been deceived herself."

"That's right. You couldn't have come up with a better idea, since you won't accept mine. Believe that she's been deceived, by all means. You've done everything you can for her now, so don't worry anymore," Elizabeth said.

Jane replied, "But how can I be happy if his sisters and friends all want him to marry someone else?"

Elizabeth replied, "You'll have to decide for yourself. If you think the unhappiness of upsetting his sisters is worse than the happiness of being his wife, then you should refuse him."

"How can you say that? Jane said with the faintest smile. "You know I'd be really upset if they didn't approve, but I wouldn't hesitate to accept him."

"I didn't think you would, so I don't feel very sorry for you."

"If he doesn't come back this winter, I won't have to make a decision. A lot can happen in six months!"

Elizabeth dismissed the idea, saying she didn't believe Caroline's wishes could influence such an independent man.

She strongly expressed to her sister how she felt about the situation and was soon delighted to see the positive effect it had. Jane was not pessimistic and was encouraged to think that Bingley would come back to Netherfield and fulfil her wishes.

They agreed that Mrs. Bennet should only be told that the family had left, so as not to worry about the behavior of the gentleman. Even this limited information caused her a lot of distress and she bemoaned the bad luck that the ladies had gone away just as they were getting close. After going on about it for a while, she was comforted by the thought that Bingley would soon be back and dining at Longbourn. To finish off, she determined that even though he had only been invited to a family dinner, she would make sure there were two courses.

CHAPTER 22

The Bennets had agreed to dine with the Lucases, and during most of the day, Miss Lucas kindly listened to Mr. Collins. Elizabeth took the opportunity to express her gratitude, "It keeps him in good humor," she said, "and I am more grateful to you than I can express." Charlotte assured her friend that she was happy to be of use, and that it was more than enough to repay her for the little sacrifice of her time. This was very amiable, but Charlotte's kindness extended much further than Elizabeth had imagined; its object was nothing less than to deflect Mr. Collins's attention from Elizabeth and towards herself. That was Miss Lucas's plan, and everything seemed to be going well. They would have almost certainly succeeded if Mr. Collins had not been leaving Hertfordshire so very soon.

Charlotte underestimated the fire and independence of Mr. Collins's character, which led him to escape from Longbourn House the next morning with admirable slyness, and rush to Lucas Lodge to throw himself at her feet. He was anxious to avoid the notice of his cousins, convinced that if they saw him depart, they would guess his plan. He was unwilling to have the attempt known until its success could also be known, for although he felt almost sure of success and had good reason to do so, since Charlotte had been moderately encouraging, he was somewhat hesitant since the incident of Wednesday.

However, his reception was very flattering. Miss Lucas saw him walking towards the house from an upstairs window and hurriedly set out to meet him accidentally on the lane. But she had not dared to hope for so much love and eloquence there.

They quickly settled everything to the satisfaction of both parties, although Mr. Collins's lengthy speeches made it take longer than necessary. As they entered the house, he implored her to name the day on which she would make him the happiest man alive. Although she knew she couldn't agree to that request at the moment, she had no desire to play games with his feelings. Mr. Collins's natural stupidity prevented him from having any qualities that might make a woman want to prolong their courtship, and Miss Lucas, who accepted his proposal solely for the purpose of securing a stable position, did not care how soon she achieved that goal.

Sir William and Lady Lucas were quickly asked for their permission, and they gave it with great enthusiasm. Mr. Collins' current situation made it an ideal match for their daughter, to whom they could give little money; and his prospects for future wealth looked very promising. Lady Lucas immediately began to calculate, with more excitement than the matter had ever caused before, how many more years Mr. Bennet was likely to live; and Sir William gave his opinion that when Mr. Collins was in control of the Longbourn estate, it would be very wise for him and his wife to appear at St. James' Court. In short, the whole family was overjoyed. The younger girls were hopeful that they could come out a couple of years earlier than they had anticipated and the boys were relieved that Charlotte wouldn't end up an old maid. Charlotte was fairly composed; she had achieved her goal and had time to think about it. Generally, she was content; Mr. Collins was neither sensible nor pleasant, his company was tedious and his affection for her was likely an illusion. But still, he would be her husband. She had always wanted to be married; it was the only respectable way for a well-educated woman of limited means to stay out of poverty. Now she had it and, at the age of twenty-seven and never having been attractive, she considered herself lucky. The least pleasant part of the situation was the surprise it would cause Elizabeth Bennet, whom Charlotte valued more than anyone else. Elizabeth wondered and blamed herself and, though she was determined not to change her mind, she felt hurt by her disapproval. She decided to tell her aunt the news herself and asked Mr. Collins, when he returned to Longbourn for dinner, to not tell any members of the family. He promised to keep it a secret, but it was difficult to do so since everyone was so curious about his long absence. He was also restraining himself, as he was eager to share his good news.

As he was leaving early the next day and wouldn't get to see any of his family members, they said their goodbyes when the ladies retired for the night. Mrs. Bennet was polite and friendly, saying they would be happy to see him again at Longbourn whenever his other engagements allowed.

"My dear Madam," he replied, "this invitation is particularly gratifying to me, as it is exactly what I have been hoping to receive. You can be sure that I will take advantage of it as soon as I can."

They were all astonished, and Mr. Bennet, who did not want him to return so quickly, said,

"But won't Lady Catherine disapprove of this, my good sir? You would be better off ignoring your relatives than risking offending your patroness."

"My dear sir," replied Mr. Collins, "I am particularly grateful for your friendly warning and you can trust me not to take such an important step without Lady Catherine's approval."

"You must be very careful. Risk anything rather than her displeasure; and if you find that she will be angry with your pursuit of happiness, which you rightly deserve, then look to us and be happy with us."

"I am very grateful for your affectionate attention; and you can be certain that I will soon write to thank you for this, as well as for all the other kindness you have shown me during my stay in Hertfordshire. As for my lovely cousins, even though I won't be away for long enough for it to be necessary, I will take the liberty of wishing them health and happiness, including my cousin Elizabeth."

The ladies then said their goodbyes with proper civilities and left the room, all equally surprised to learn that Mr. Collins was planning a quick return. Mrs. Bennet interpreted this as a sign that he was considering proposing to one of her younger daughters, and even Mary might have been convinced to accept him. Mary held his intellectual abilities in high regard, often impressed by the soundness of his reflections. Although she believed she was much cleverer than him, she thought that if he was encouraged to read and improve himself with an example such as hers, he might become a very agreeable companion. However, the next morning dashed all such hopes. Miss Lucas arrived soon after breakfast and had a private conversation with Elizabeth, sharing the events of the previous day.

Elizabeth had entertained the thought that Mr. Collins might fancy himself in love with her friend, within the last day or two. However, the idea that Charlotte could encourage him seemed almost as impossible as her encouraging him herself. Therefore, Elizabeth was greatly astonished when she first heard the news and could not help but cry out,

"Engaged to Mr. Collins! My dear Charlotte, impossible!"

Miss Lucas, who had been composed while telling her story, was momentarily taken aback upon receiving such a direct reproach, although she expected it. However, she soon regained her composure and calmly replied,

"Why are you surprised, my dear Elizabeth? Do you find it hard to believe that Mr. Collins could gain any woman's good opinion, simply because he was not successful in winning yours?"

Elizabeth had gathered herself and made a determined attempt to assure Charlotte, with a steady assurance, that she was greatly delighted with the potential of their relationship and wanted the best for her.

"I understand your surprise," Charlotte replied, "you must be very surprised, especially since Mr. Collins was recently seeking your hand in marriage. But once you've had time to think it all through, I hope you will be content with what I have chosen. You know I am not romantic, never have been. I only ask for a comfortable home. Considering Mr. Collins's character, connections, and position in life, I am convinced that my chance of happiness with him is as good as most people can hope for when entering the marriage state."

Elizabeth quietly responded, "Certainly," and after an awkward pause, they returned to the rest of the family. Charlotte did not stay for much longer, leaving Elizabeth to reflect on what she had just heard. It took a long time for Elizabeth to come to terms with the idea of such an unsuitable match. The fact that Mr. Collins had proposed twice within three days paled in comparison to the shock of Charlotte's acceptance. Elizabeth had always known that Charlotte's views on marriage differed from her own, but she never would have thought that her friend would sacrifice her principles for worldly gain. The thought of Charlotte as Mr. Collins's wife was humiliating, and Elizabeth was distressed not only by the idea of a friend disgracing herself and falling in her esteem, but also by the conviction that Charlotte had chosen a lot in life that would not bring her any real happiness.

CHAPTER 23

Elizabeth was sitting with her mother and sisters, pondering what she had just heard and wondering whether it was appropriate to mention it, when Sir William Lucas himself arrived. He had been sent by his daughter to announce her engagement to the family. Sir William complimented them and expressed his pleasure at the prospect of a connection between the two houses. He then explained the situation to an audience that was not only surprised but also skeptical. Mrs. Bennet, in her usual impoliteness, persisted that he must be mistaken, and Lydia, always careless and often rude, exclaimed loudly,

"Good heavens, Sir William, how can you tell such a story? Don't you know that Mr. Collins wants to marry Lizzy?"

Sir William's good breeding was the only thing that prevented him from becoming angry at their treatment of him, as nothing less than the complaisance of a courtier would have been enough to tolerate such behavior. Despite their impertinence, he politely begged to be allowed to remain positive about the truth of his information and listened patiently.

Elizabeth felt that it was her duty to relieve him of such an unpleasant situation, so she stepped forward to confirm his account by mentioning that she had prior knowledge of it from Charlotte herself. She then tried to put an end to her mother and sisters' exclamations by enthusiastically congratulating Sir William, and Jane joined in. Elizabeth also made various comments on the happiness that could be expected from the match, Mr. Collins's excellent character, and the convenient distance between Hunsford and London.

Mrs. Bennet was too overwhelmed to say much while Sir William was present. However, as soon as he left, she expressed her feelings without restraint. Firstly, she continued to disbelieve the entire matter. Secondly, she was convinced that Mr. Collins had been deceived. Thirdly, she was certain that they would never be happy together. Fourthly, she hoped that the engagement would be broken off. However, two conclusions were plainly evident from the situation. Firstly, that Elizabeth was the real cause of all the trouble. Secondly, that Mrs. Bennet herself had been treated cruelly by everyone. She focused on these two points for the remainder of the day, and nothing could console or appease her. Her resentment did not diminish over the course of the day. It took a week for her to be able to speak to Elizabeth without scolding her, a month before she could speak to Sir William or Lady Lucas without being rude, and many months before she could forgive their daughter.

Mr. Bennet was much more calm and composed than his wife, and he stated that his emotions were of a very agreeable kind. He found it satisfying to discover that Charlotte Lucas, whom he had thought to be quite sensible, was just as foolish as his wife, if not more so!

Jane was a bit surprised by the engagement, but she expressed her sincere desire for their happiness. Elizabeth could not convince her to believe that it was unlikely. Kitty and Lydia did not envy Miss Lucas, as Mr. Collins was only a clergyman. The news of the engagement was merely something to spread around Meryton.

Lady Lucas could not help feeling a sense of triumph as she was now able to retaliate against Mrs. Bennet and take comfort in the fact that her daughter had married well. She called on Longbourn more frequently than usual to express her joy, despite Mrs. Bennet's sour looks and unkind remarks that might have ruined the happiness.

Elizabeth and Charlotte had a tension between them which kept them both quiet about the topic; Elizabeth was sure that they could never be truly close again. She felt more affection for her sister, knowing that her opinion of her could never be damaged, and she became increasingly concerned for her happiness as Bingley had been gone for a week with no news of his return.

Jane had promptly replied to Caroline's letter and was eagerly waiting to hear back. The letter of thanks from Mr. Collins arrived on Tuesday, addressed to their father, and written with the gratefulness that a year of living with the family had inspired. After expressing his relief at having unburdened himself, Mr. Collins excitedly told them about his joy at having won the affections of their lovely neighbor, Miss Lucas. He explained that he had accepted their invitation to return to Longbourn so he could be close to her. He added that Lady Catherine was so pleased with their engagement that she wanted them to marry as soon as possible, which he hoped would convince his beloved Charlotte to set an early date.

Mr. Collins's return to Hertfordshire was no longer a source of pleasure for Mrs. Bennet. On the contrary, she was as inclined to complain about it as her husband. She found it very odd that he had come to Longbourn instead of Lucas Lodge. It was also very inconvenient and troublesome. She despised having visitors while her health was so poor, and lovers were the most unpleasant of all guests. These were Mrs. Bennet's gentle complaints, and they only subsided in the face of the greater distress caused by Mr. Bingley's continued absence.

Jane and Elizabeth were both uncomfortable with the subject. Day after day went by without any news of Mr. Bingley other than the report that had spread through Meryton that he would not return to Netherfield for the entire winter. This report greatly infuriated Mrs. Bennet, and she never failed to denounce it as a scandalous lie.

Even Elizabeth started to fear that Bingley's sisters would be successful in keeping him away, since the combined efforts of his sisters, his overpowering friend, the attractions of Miss Darcy, and the amusements of London, might be too much for his attachment to Jane. Jane was obviously more anxious than

Elizabeth, but she tried to hide her feelings, and the two sisters never talked about it.

Jane's anxiety under this uncertainty was naturally more distressing than Elizabeth's, but she was eager to conceal her feelings. Therefore, she and Elizabeth never spoke of the matter. However, Mrs. Bennet had no such reservations, and an hour rarely went by without her talking about Bingley, expressing her impatience for his return, or even demanding that Jane confess that if he did not come back, she would consider herself very poorly treated. Jane's constant calmness was needed to tolerate these attacks with some degree of tranquility.

Mr. Collins returned exactly two weeks later, but his welcome at Longbourn was not as warm as it had been on his first visit. Fortunately for the others, he spent most of his time at Lucas Lodge, and only returned to Longbourn in time to apologize for his absence before the family went to bed.

Mrs. Bennet was in a very pitiful state. The mere mention of anything related to the marriage would put her in a bad mood, and wherever she went she was sure to hear it discussed. She found the sight of Miss Lucas unbearable, as she saw her as a replacement for her in that house and hated her with jealousy. Whenever Charlotte and Mr. Collins spoke in low voices they were discussing the Longbourn estate and how Charlotte would take over once Mr. Bennet had passed away. Mrs. Bennet complained bitterly to her husband,

"It's so unfair that Charlotte Lucas will be the mistress of this house and that I'll have to make way for her and live to see her take my place in it!"

Mr. Bennet attempted to comfort her, "My dear, don't think like that. Let's hope for the best. Let's imagine that I will be the one to survive."

This did not provide much comfort to Mrs. Bennet, so instead of responding, she continued, "If it wasn't for the entail, I wouldn't mind it so much."

"What wouldn't you mind?"

"I wouldn't mind anything," she replied.

"Let's be thankful that you are not in a state of such indifference," said Mr. Bennet.

"I can never be thankful for anything regarding the entail. How could anyone have the conscience to take away an estate from their own daughters? And all for the sake of Mr. Collins too! Why should he have it more than anyone else?"

"You can decide that for yourself," said Mr. Bennet.

CHAPTER 24

Miss Bingley's letter arrived and put an end to any doubts. The first sentence assured them that they were all settled in London for the winter and concluded with her brother's regret for not having had time to pay his respects to his friends in Hertfordshire before he left the country.

Hope was gone, completely gone; and when Jane had the chance to read the rest of the letter, she found nothing that would bring her any joy, except the author's expressed affection. Most of the letter was dedicated to praising Miss Darcy and her many qualities, and Caroline was delighted to talk about their growing friendship and even made a prediction that her wishes in the previous letter would come true. She also wrote with great joy about her brother living in Mr. Darcy's house, and even mentioned some of Darcy's plans for new furniture with enthusiasm.

Elizabeth, who Jane told all this to, was silent with anger. She was both worried for her sister and angry with all the others. She didn't believe Caroline's claim that her brother was fond of Miss Darcy. She was no longer in doubt that he had a great fondness for Jane; she had never doubted it before. She had always liked him and now, despite her anger, she felt contempt for his lack of resolution which meant he was now a slave to his manipulative friends, sacrificing his own happiness for their whims. If it were only his own happiness at stake, she would have let him do what he wanted, but she knew Jane was also suffering. She thought about it for a long time but it was no use. She wondered if Bingley's feelings had really faded or if his friends had just convinced him to ignore them; either way, her opinion of him had changed but Jane's situation was still the same, her peace of mind was still wounded.

A couple of days passed before Jane had the courage to speak to Elizabeth about her feelings. However, when Mrs. Bennet left them alone after one of her usual rants about Netherfield and its owner, Jane couldn't help saying,

"Oh, I wish my dear mother had more control over herself. She has no idea of the pain she causes me with her constant remarks about him. But I won't complain. It won't last forever. He'll be forgotten and everything will go back to normal."

Elizabeth looked at her sister with disbelief but didn't say anything.

"You don't believe me," said Jane, blushing slightly. "You really have no reason to do so. He may remain in my memory as the most amiable man I've ever met, but that's all. I have neither hope nor fear, and I have nothing to blame him for. Thank God, I don't have that pain. So, in a little time, I'll certainly try to get over it."

She added, with a stronger voice, "I have the immediate comfort that it was just a fanciful mistake on my part, and that it has harmed no one but me."

"My dear Jane!" Elizabeth exclaimed. "You are too kind. Your goodness and selflessness are truly angelic. I don't know what to say to you. I feel like I haven't done you justice or loved you as much as you deserve."

Miss Bennet quickly denied any extraordinary virtue and gave the credit to her sister's strong affection.

"No," said Elizabeth, "this is not fair. You want to think the world is all respectable, and you're upset when I speak ill of anyone. I only want to think you're perfect, and you're against it. Don't worry about me going too far or infringing on your right to universal goodwill. You needn't. There are very few people I actually love, and even fewer whom I think well of. The more I see of the world, the more dissatisfied I become with it. Every day confirms my belief that all human characters are inconsistent and that one cannot rely on appearances of merit or sense. I've had two recent examples of this; I won't mention one, but the other is Charlotte's marriage. It's inexplicable! In every way, it's inexplicable!"

"My dear Lizzy, don't give in to such feelings as these. They'll ruin your happiness. You don't make enough allowances for differences in situation and temperament. Consider Mr. Collins's respectability and Charlotte's wise, stable character. Remember that she's part of a large family and that, in terms of fortune, it's a highly eligible match. Be prepared to believe, for everyone's sake, that she may have some feelings of regard and esteem for our cousin."

"To please you, I'd try to believe almost anything, but no one else would benefit from such a belief as this. If I were convinced that Charlotte had any regard for him, I'd think even less of her intelligence than I already do of her heart. My dear Jane, Mr. Collins is a conceited, pompous, narrow-minded, foolish man; you know it as well as I do. And you must feel, as I do, that any woman who marries him cannot be thinking properly. You must not defend her, even if it is Charlotte Lucas. You must not change the meaning of principles and integrity, or try to convince yourself or me that selfishness is prudence and insensitivity to danger is security for happiness, just for the sake of one person."

"I think you're speaking too harshly about both of them," Jane replied. "I hope you'll realize this by seeing how happy they are together. But let's talk about something else. You mentioned something else. You referred to two incidents. I understand what you mean, but please don't hurt me by blaming that person and saying your opinion of him has deteriorated. We should not be so quick to assume we have been intentionally harmed. We can't expect a young man to always be so careful and cautious. Often, it's just our own vanity that tricks us. Women tend to think admiration means more than it actually does."

"And men make sure to encourage that."

"If they do it deliberately, they cannot be justified. However, I don't think there's as much intention in the world as some people believe."

"I'm not suggesting that any part of Mr. Bingley's behavior is intentional," Elizabeth said, "but even without meaning to do wrong or make others unhappy, mistakes can be made and people can be hurt. Carelessness, not paying attention to other people's feelings, and a lack of determination can cause a lot of damage."

"Do you think that's what's happened here?"

"Yes, it's the last one. But if I keep talking, I'll offend you by saying what I think of people you respect. Stop me while you can."

"So, you still think his sisters are trying to influence him?"

"Yes, along with his friend."

"I can't believe it. Why would they want to do that? If he's attached to me, then no other woman can make him happy."

"Your initial argument is incorrect. It's possible for people to desire things beyond just his happiness. They might want many other things besides his happiness; they may wish him to become wealthier and more influential; or to marry a girl who has a lot of money, great connections, and pride."

"Without a doubt, they do want him to choose Miss Darcy," Jane replied. "But this could be because of better reasons than you are thinking. They have known her for much longer than they have known me; no wonder if they like her better. But, whatever their own wishes are, it is highly unlikely that they would go against their brother's. What sister would feel like she had the freedom to do that, unless there was something really bad about the situation? If they believed he was devoted to me, they wouldn't try to break us up; if he was, they wouldn't be able to succeed. By assuming such a strong emotion, you are making everyone act in an unnatural and wrong way, and making me very unhappy. Don't make me feel worse by suggesting this. I am not ashamed of having been mistaken – or, at least, it is a small thing, nothing compared to how I would feel if I thought badly of him or his sisters. Let me look at it in the best way possible, in the way that makes sense."

Elizabeth couldn't disagree with such a wish; and from that moment, Mr. Bingley's name was hardly ever mentioned between them.

Mrs. Bennet kept wondering and complaining about why he wasn't returning, and even though Elizabeth was able to explain it to her every day, she didn't seem to believe it. Her daughter tried to convince her that his attention to Jane had only been a passing fancy that had gone away when he stopped seeing her, but even though that seemed likely, she kept saying the same thing every day. Mrs. Bennet's only comfort was that Mr. Bingley would be back in the summer.

Mr. Bennet had a different take on the matter. "So, Lizzy," he said one day, "your sister has been rejected in love, I see. I congratulate her. Next to getting married, a girl likes to be rejected in love every once in a while. It's something to think about, and it gives her a kind of special status among her friends. When is it going to be your turn? There are plenty of officers here in Meryton to disappoint all the young ladies in the area. Let Wickham be your man. He's a nice guy and it would do you credit."

"Thank you, Sir, but I'd be happy with someone less agreeable."

"That's true," said Mr. Bennet, "but it's comforting to know that whatever happens to you, you have an affectionate mother who will always make the most of it."

Mr. Wickham's presence was helpful in lifting the spirits of the Longbourn family, who had been feeling down after recent events. They saw him frequently, and one of his appealing qualities was his willingness to speak openly. Elizabeth had already heard about his grievances against Mr. Darcy, and now these were openly discussed and debated by everyone. People were pleased to find out how much they had always disliked Mr. Darcy before they knew about these issues.

Miss Bennet was the only one who thought that there might be some mitigating circumstances in the case that were unknown to the people of Hertfordshire. She always tried to be fair and argued for the possibility of mistakes. However, everyone else condemned Mr. Darcy as the worst kind of person.

CHAPTER 25

After spending a week expressing love and discussing plans for their future happiness, Mr. Collins had to leave his beloved Charlotte when Saturday arrived. However, he tried to ease his pain of separation by preparing for the arrival of his bride, hoping that when he returned to Hertfordshire, they could soon set a wedding date. He bid farewell to his Longbourn relatives with the same solemnity as before, wished his cousins well, and promised to send their father another letter of thanks.

The following Monday, Mrs. Bennet was delighted to welcome her brother and his wife, who came as usual to spend Christmas at Longbourn. Mr. Gardiner was a sensible, gentlemanly man who was far superior to his sister in both nature and education. The ladies of Netherfield would have found it hard to believe that a man who worked in trade and had his warehouses in view could be so polite and charming. Mrs. Gardiner, who was several years younger than Mrs. Bennet and Mrs. Philips, was an amiable, intelligent, and elegant woman, and a great favorite of all her Longbourn nieces. There was a special bond between her and the two eldest nieces, as they had often stayed with her in town.

When she arrived, the first thing Mrs. Gardiner did was to give out her presents and tell them about the latest trends. After that, she had a less active role to play and it was her turn to listen. Mrs. Bennet had a lot of complaints and grievances to share. They had all been treated very badly since she last saw her sister. Two of her daughters had almost been married but it all fell through.

"I don't blame Jane," she went on, "Jane would have got Mr. Bingley if she could. But Lizzy! Oh, sister! It's so hard to think that she could have been Mrs. Collins by now if it wasn't for her own stubbornness. He proposed to her right here in this room and she refused him. The result is that Lady Lucas will have a daughter married before I do, and Longbourn estate is still entailed. The Lucases are very sly people, sister. They're all out for what they can get. I'm sorry to say it about them, but that's the truth. It makes me very anxious and unwell to be thwarted like this in my own family and to have neighbors who think of themselves before anyone else. However, your arrival just now is a great relief, and I'm very pleased to hear what you said about the long sleeves,"

Mrs. Gardiner gave a slight response to comfort her nieces, then changed the subject.

When they were alone later, she spoke more on the matter. "It seems like it would have been a great match for Jane," she said. "I'm sorry it didn't work out. But these things happen so often! A young man like you described Mr. Bingley can easily fall in love with a pretty girl for a few weeks, and when they're separated, he can easily forget her. These sorts of inconstancies are very common."

"That's a nice thought, I suppose," Elizabeth said, "but it doesn't apply to us. It doesn't often happen that the interference of friends can persuade a young man of independent fortune to forget a girl he was madly in love with just a few days ago."

"But 'madly in love' is such a cliché and so vague that it doesn't give me much of an idea. It's used to describe feelings that come from a half-hour's acquaintance just as much as real strong feelings. Tell me, how strong was Mr. Bingley's love?"

"I never saw a more promising inclination. He was paying no attention to anyone else and was completely taken by her. Every time they met, it was more obvious. He even offended a few young ladies at his own ball by not asking them to dance, and I spoke to him twice without getting an answer. Could there be better signs? Isn't being rude to everyone a sure sign of love?"

"Oh yes, of the kind of love I think he was feeling. Poor Jane! I feel sorry for her because, with her personality, she won't be able to get over it quickly. It would have been better if it had happened to you, Lizzy; you would have been able to laugh it off more quickly. Do you think she would be willing to come back with us? A change of scenery might do her some good, and a bit of a break from home might be as useful as anything."

Elizabeth was very pleased with this suggestion and was sure her sister would agree.

"I hope," Mrs. Gardiner continued, "that no thought of this young man will influence her. We live in such a different part of town, all our connections are so different, and, as you know, we go out so little, that it's very unlikely they'd meet at all, unless he actually came to visit her."

"And that's impossible; he's with his friend, and Mr. Darcy wouldn't let him come to Jane's in this part of London! My dear aunt, how could you think of it? Mr. Darcy might have heard of Gracechurch Street, but he would never think a month's worth of washing would be enough to cleanse him of its impurities if he ever went there; and you can be sure Mr. Bingley never goes anywhere without him."

"That's even better. I hope they won't meet at all. But does Jane write to her sister? She won't be able to help visiting."

"She'll cut off the friendship entirely."

Even though Elizabeth acted as if she was sure of this, and the even more important point of Bingley not seeing Jane, she still felt anxious about it. On closer inspection, she realized that she didn't think it was a completely hopeless situation. It was possible, and sometimes she thought it was likely, that his feelings would be rekindled and the influence of his friends would be overruled by the more natural influence of Jane's charm.

Miss Bennet was delighted to accept her aunt's invitation with pleasure; and she hoped that, with Caroline not living in the same house as her brother, she would be able to visit her occasionally without any risk of seeing him.

The Gardiners stayed at Longbourn for a week and, with the Philipses, the Lucases and the officers, there was never a day without something planned. Mrs. Bennet had made such careful arrangements for the entertainment of her brother and sister that they never once sat down to a family dinner. When the engagement was at home, some of the officers would always be present, and Mr. Wickham was almost always among them. Mrs. Gardiner, made suspicious by Elizabeth's enthusiastic praise of him, watched them both closely. She didn't think they were seriously in love, but it was clear that they preferred each other, which made her a bit uneasy. She decided to speak to Elizabeth before she left Hertfordshire and warn her of the imprudence of encouraging such a relationship.

Mr. Wickham had one way of giving Mrs. Bennet pleasure that had nothing to do with his general abilities. Gardiner and Wickham had one means of providing pleasure, not connected to his overall abilities. About ten or twelve years ago, before she married, she had spent a lot of time in the same part of Derbyshire he was from. They had a lot of acquaintances in common and, even though Wickham had not been there much since Mr. Darcy's father died five years before, he still had the ability to give her more recent news about her old friends than she could get on her own.

Mrs. Gardiner had seen Pemberley and was familiar with the late Mr. Darcy. So, they had an endless topic of conversation. As they compared her memories of Pemberley with the detailed description Wickham could give and praised the character of its late owner, they both enjoyed it. When Mrs. Gardiner found out about Mr. Darcy's current treatment of Wickham, she tried to remember something from when he was a kid that would fit that description and eventually recalled hearing that Mr. Fitzwilliam Darcy had been known as a very proud and mean-spirited boy.

CHAPTER 26

Gardiner gave Elizabeth a warning kindly and promptly when she had the first opportunity to speak to her alone. After being honest with her, she continued,

"You are too sensible of a girl, Lizzy, to fall in love just because you were warned against it. So, I'm not afraid to speak openly. Seriously, be careful. Don't get involved with him or try to get him involved in an affection that would be imprudent because of his lack of fortune. I have nothing bad to say about him - he's a very interesting young man. If he had the fortune he should have, I would say you couldn't do better. But as it is, use your common sense. Your father is counting on your good conduct and resolution. Don't let him down."

"My dear aunt, you're being serious," Elizabeth said.

"Yes, and I hope I can get you to be serious too."

"Okay then, you don't need to worry. I'll take care of myself and Mr. Darcy. I'll make sure he's not in love with me if I can help it."

"Elizabeth, you're not serious," her aunt replied.

"I'm sorry. Let me try again. Right now, I'm not in love with Mr. Wickham. No, definitely not. But he's by far the most pleasant man I've ever met. If he became really attached to me, I think it would be best if he didn't. I understand the risks. Oh, that awful Mr. Darcy! My father's opinion of me is so important to me, and I'd be devastated to lose it. But my father is partial to Mr. Wickham. In short, my dear aunt, I don't want to make anyone unhappy. But since we see all the time that when there's love, young people don't usually let money stand in their way, how can I promise to be wiser than so many others if I'm tempted? All I can promise you is that I won't rush into anything. I won't assume that I'm his first choice. When I'm with him, I won't be wishing things were different. In short, I'll do my best.

"It might be a good idea if you don't encourage him to come here so much. At least, you shouldn't remind your mother to invite him."

"Like I did the other day," Elizabeth said, blushing. "Yes, it's wise of me to not do that again. But don't think he's here all the time. It's because of you that he's been invited so often this week. You know my mother's thoughts on having her friends around her constantly. But I swear, I'll try to do what I think is smart. Are you happy with that?"

Her aunt said she was, and Elizabeth thanked her for the helpful advice. They said goodbye, which was a rare example of giving advice without it being taken the wrong way.

Mr. Collins returned to Hertfordshire shortly after the Gardiners and Jane had left. His stay with the Lucases was not a great inconvenience to Mrs. Bennet. His wedding was quickly approaching and she was resigned to the fact, even going so far as to say in a nasty way that she "wished them to be happy". Thursday was the wedding day and on Wednesday Miss Lucas said her farewell. As they went down the stairs together, Charlotte said,

"I shall expect to hear from you often, Eliza."

"That you certainly shall."

"And I have another request. Will you come and see me?"

"We shall often meet, I hope, in Hertfordshire."

"I'm not likely to leave Kent for a while. Promise me then to come to Hunsford."

Elizabeth could not refuse, though she knew the visit wouldn't be enjoyable.

"My father and Maria are coming to visit me in March," Charlotte added, "and I hope you will agree to join us. Eliza, you will be just as welcome to me as either of them."

The wedding took place and the newlyweds left for Kent from the church. Everyone had something to say or hear about it, as usual. Elizabeth soon heard from her friend and their correspondence continued as regularly as before, though it was not as open as it used to be. Elizabeth eagerly read Charlotte's first letters, curious to know how she felt about her new home, Lady Catherine and how happy she was. When she read them, Elizabeth found that Charlotte expressed herself on every point exactly as she had anticipated. She wrote cheerfully, seeming to be surrounded with comforts, and didn't mention anything that she couldn't praise. The house, furniture, neighborhood, and roads were all to her liking, and Lady Catherine was very friendly and obliging. It was Mr. Collins' description of Hunsford and Rosings, but toned down; and Elizabeth knew she'd have to wait until she visited there to find out the rest.

Jane had already written a few lines to her sister to tell her they'd arrived safely in London; and when she wrote again, Elizabeth was hoping she'd be able to say something about the Bingleys.

Her eagerness for the second letter was rewarded as it usually is. Jane had been in town for a week without seeing or hearing from Caroline. She explained it by thinking that her last letter to her friend from Longbourn had been lost by accident.

"My aunt," she continued, "is going to that part of town tomorrow and I'm going to take the opportunity to go to Grosvenor Street."

She wrote again after the visit, saying she'd seen Miss Bingley. "I didn't think Caroline seemed very cheerful," she said. "But she was really pleased to see me and scolded me for not letting her know I was coming to London. So I was right - my last letter hadn't reached her. I asked about their brother, obviously. He was fine, but he was so busy with Mr. Darcy that they hardly ever saw him. I heard that Miss Darcy was coming for dinner. I wish I could see her. I didn't stay long because Caroline and Mrs. Hurst were going out. I'm sure I'll see them soon."

Elizabeth shook her head when she read the letter. It made her realize that Mr. Bingley would only find out that Jane was in London by chance.

Four weeks went by and Jane didn't see him. She tried to convince herself that she didn't mind, but she couldn't ignore Miss Bingley's lack of interest anymore. After waiting at home for two weeks, expecting the visitor to appear, and inventing excuses for her every evening, the visitor finally showed up. However, the shortness of her stay, and the change in her manner made it impossible for Jane to deceive herself any longer. Jane wrote a letter to her sister expressing her feelings. She said,

"I know that my dear Lizzy will not take pleasure in my mistake about Miss Bingley's affection for me. But, my dear sister, although you were right, do not think me stubborn when I say that, based on her behavior, my trust in her was as natural as your suspicion. I do not understand why she wanted to be close to me, but if the same thing happened again, I am sure I would be fooled again. Caroline did not return my visit until yesterday, and during the meantime, I did not receive a note or a line from her. When she did come, it was very obvious that she was not happy about it. She made a brief, formal apology for not coming earlier, did not say a word about wanting to see me again, and was, in every way, a completely different person. When she left, I was completely resolved to end the friendship. I pity her, but I cannot help blaming her. She was wrong to single me out like that. Every step towards intimacy was initiated by her. But I feel sorry for her because she must realize that she was wrong, and I am very sure that her anxiety for her brother is the reason for it. I need not explain myself further, and although we know that her anxiety is completely unnecessary, if she feels it, it could easily explain her behavior towards me. And her brother is very dear to her, so any anxiety she may feel for him is natural and admirable. I cannot help wondering, however, why she has these fears now because if he really cared for me, we would have met a long time ago. I am certain that he knows I am in town because she mentioned it herself. Yet, it seems that she wants to convince herself that he truly favors Miss Darcy. I do not understand it. If I were not afraid of being too harsh, I would be almost tempted to say that there is a strong appearance of deceit in all this. But I will try to banish every painful thought and think only of what will make me happy: your affection and the unwavering kindness of

my dear uncle and aunt. Please write to me soon. Miss Bingley mentioned something about him never returning to Netherfield and giving up the house, but she was not certain. We had better not discuss it. I am so glad that you have heard pleasant things about our friends at Hunsford. Please go and visit them with Sir William and Maria. I am sure you will be very comfortable there."

"Your's, &c."

This letter caused Elizabeth some distress; however, her spirits lifted when she realized that Jane would no longer be taken advantage of by her sister. She no longer had any hope that her brother would renew his affections for her. Every time she thought about his character, it seemed to worsen, and she hoped that as a punishment for him, and as a possible benefit for Jane, he would soon marry Mr. Darcy's sister, as it seemed that would make him regret what he had given up.

Around this time, Mrs. Gardiner reminded Elizabeth of her promise to tell her about that gentleman, and Elizabeth had news to report that would make her aunt pleased, but not Elizabeth herself. His fondness for Elizabeth had faded, his attentions had ended, and he was now showing affection for someone else. Elizabeth was observant enough to see it all, but she could write about it without feeling much pain. Her heart had only been lightly affected, and she was content with the thought that she would have been his only choice if circumstances had been different.

The sudden acquisition of ten thousand pounds was the most remarkable feature of the young lady he was now trying to impress; but Elizabeth, less observant in his case than in Charlotte's, didn't criticize him for wanting to be independent. On the contrary, she thought it was a wise and desirable thing for both of them and she sincerely wished him well.

She told Mrs. Gardiner all this and then added: "I'm now convinced, my dear aunt, that I've never been in love because if I had truly experienced that pure and uplifting emotion, I would now hate his name and wish him all sorts of bad things. But my feelings towards him are not only friendly, I'm even neutral towards Miss King. I can't find that I hate her at all or that I'm even a little bit unwilling to think she's a nice enough girl. There's no love in this situation. My vigilance has been effective; and although I would definitely be more interesting to all my acquaintances if I was madly in love with him, I cannot say that I regret my relative lack of importance. Importance can sometimes be bought at too high a price. Kitty and Lydia are much more affected by his absence than I am. They are inexperienced in the ways of the world, and not yet able to accept the embarrassing truth that good-looking young men must have something to live on, just like the plain ones."

CHAPTER 27

With no more significant events in the Longbourn family, and nothing much to do besides taking walks to Meryton, sometimes muddy and sometimes cold, January and February passed by. March was when Elizabeth was to go to Hunsford. At first, she hadn't thought too seriously about it; but Charlotte was counting on it, and eventually Elizabeth began to look forward to it with greater pleasure and assurance. Being apart had increased her desire to see Charlotte again and lessened her aversion to Mr. Collins. The scheme was novel, and since home could not be faultless with such a mother and such unsociable sisters, a little change was not unwelcome for its own sake. The trip would also give her a chance to see Jane. As the time drew nearer, she would have been very unhappy with any delay. Everything, however, went smoothly, and the plan was ultimately settled according to Charlotte's initial proposal. She was to go with Sir William and his second daughter. Spending a night in London was later added as an improvement, and the plan became as perfect as a plan could be.

The only discomfort came from leaving her father, who would certainly miss her. When it came down to it, he disliked her leaving so much that he told her to write to him and almost promised to respond to her letter.

The parting between herself and Mr. Wickham was perfectly friendly, even more so on his side. His current pursuit could not make him forget that Elizabeth was the first to attract and deserve his attention, the first to listen and sympathize, the first to be admired. In his manner of bidding her farewell, wishing her every happiness, reminding her of what to expect with Lady Catherine de Bourgh, and trusting that their opinion of her, and of everyone, would always coincide, there was a concern, an interest which she felt would always make her sincerely attached to him. She parted from him convinced that whether married or single, he would always be her model of amiability and charm.

Her fellow travelers the next day were not the kind to make her think less of him. Sir William Lucas and his daughter Maria, a good-natured girl but as empty-headed as her father, had nothing to say that was worth hearing and were listened to with about as much pleasure as the sound of the carriage. Elizabeth loved absurdities, but she had known Sir William for too long. He could not tell her anything new about the wonders of his presentation and knighthood, and his courtesies were worn out like his information.

It was only a twenty-four mile journey and they left so early that they were in Gracechurch Street by noon. As they drove up to Mr. Gardiner's house, Jane was at a window watching their arrival and when they got inside Elizabeth was happy to see that she looked healthy and beautiful as ever. On the stairs were a bunch of little boys and girls who were too excited to wait in the drawing room and too shy to come down as they hadn't seen her for a year. Everyone was happy and the day passed quickly with them doing some shopping in the morning and then in the evening going to the theatre.

Elizabeth then arranged to sit next to her aunt. Their initial topic of conversation was Elizabeth's sister. Elizabeth was more sorrowful than surprised to learn, in response to her detailed inquiries, that Jane made an effort to maintain her spirits but experienced periods of sadness. However, it was reasonable to expect that these periods would be temporary. Mrs. Gardiner also provided details of Miss Bingley's visit to Gracechurch Street and recounted conversations that had taken place at various times between Jane and herself, confirming that Jane had genuinely ended the acquaintance from her heart.

Mrs. Gardiner then teased Elizabeth about Wickham's abandonment and congratulated her on dealing with it so well.

"But, my dear Elizabeth," she added, "what kind of girl is Miss King? I wouldn't want to think our friend is being motivated by money."

"Please, my dear aunt, what is the difference between a mercenary and a prudent motive in matters of marriage? Where does discretion end and greed begin? Last Christmas you were afraid of him marrying me because it would be imprudent and now, because he is trying to get a girl with only ten thousand pounds, you want to find out that he is being motivated by money."

"If you just tell me what kind of girl Miss King is, I'll know what to think."

"She seems like a very nice girl, I don't think she's done anything wrong," said Elizabeth.

"But he didn't pay her any attention until she inherited her grandfather's money."

"No, why would he? If it wasn't acceptable for him to court me because I had no money, why would he court a girl he didn't care about who was equally as poor?"

"But it seems inappropriate for him to pursue her so soon after she got the money."

"A person in a difficult financial situation doesn't have the luxury of being able to follow all the social rules that other people have to. If she doesn't mind, why should we?"

"Her not minding doesn't make it okay. It just shows that she's either not very sensible or not very sensitive."

"Well," Elizabeth said, "you can think what you want. He can be motivated by money and she can be foolish."

"No, Lizzy, that's not what I want to think. I would be sorry to think badly of someone who has lived in Derbyshire for so long."

"Well, if that's all, I have a very low opinion of young men from Derbyshire, and their close friends from Hertfordshire aren't much better. I'm tired of them all. Thank goodness I'm going tomorrow to meet someone who doesn't have one attractive quality, no manners or sense. Stupid men are the only ones worth knowing in the end."

"Be careful, Lizzy; that sounds like you're disappointed."

Before they said goodbye at the end of the play, she was delighted to receive an invitation to join her uncle and aunt on a summer vacation.

"We haven't decided where we're going yet," said Mrs. Gardiner, "but maybe to the Lakes."

Elizabeth was thrilled and accepted the invitation eagerly. "My dear, dear aunt," she exclaimed joyfully, "what a pleasure! What joy! You've given me a new lease on life. Goodbye to disappointment and gloom. What are men compared to rocks and mountains? Oh, what wonderful times we'll have! And when we come back, we won't be like other travelers, unable to accurately describe anything. We will know where we have been and remember what we have seen. Lakes, mountains and rivers won't be mixed up in our minds and when we try to describe a scene, we won't argue about its location. Let's make sure our first descriptions are better than those of other travelers."

CHAPTER 28

Elizabeth found every object on their journey the next day to be new and captivating, and her spirits were high as she had seen her sister looking healthy, eradicating all fear for her wellbeing. The idea of their upcoming trip to the north was a constant source of joy.

As they left the main road and turned onto the lane to Hunsford, everyone's eyes searched for the Parsonage, expecting to see it at every turn. The boundary of Rosings Park could be seen on one side, and Elizabeth smiled as she remembered everything she had heard about the inhabitants of the park

Finally, the Parsonage came into view. The garden sloping down to the road, the house standing in it, the green pales, and the laurel hedge all declared that they had arrived. Mr. Collins and Charlotte appeared at the door, and the carriage stopped at the small gate which led to the house via a short gravel walk, amid nods and smiles from the entire party. In a moment, they were all out of the carriage, rejoicing at the sight of each other. Mrs. Collins welcomed her friend with great enthusiasm, and Elizabeth was even more pleased with her decision to come when she saw how affectionately she was received. She immediately noticed that her cousin's manners had not changed after his marriage, and his formal courtesy was just as it had always been. He kept her and her family members at the gate for a few minutes to inquire about their well-being before pointing out the neatness of the entrance and taking them into the house with no further delay. As soon as they were in the parlor, he welcomed them once again with ostentatious formality to his humble abode and repeated all his wife's offers of refreshment with punctuality.

Elizabeth was prepared to see Mr. Collins show off his home and belongings, and she couldn't help but feel that in displaying the good proportion of the room, its aspect, and its furniture, he was addressing her specifically, as if he wanted to make her feel what she had lost by refusing him. Although everything seemed neat and comfortable, she couldn't please him by showing any sign of regret and instead looked with wonder at her friend for being able to maintain a cheerful demeanor with such a companion.

Whenever Mr. Collins said anything of which his wife might reasonably be ashamed, which was certainly not uncommon, Elizabeth involuntarily turned her eye to Charlotte. Once or twice, she could see a faint blush, but in general, Charlotte wisely pretended not to hear.

After sitting long enough to admire every piece of furniture in the room, from the sideboard to the fender, and to give an account of their journey and everything that had happened in London, Mr. Collins invited them to take a stroll in his large, well-laid-out garden, which he tended himself. Working in his garden was one of his most respectable pleasures, and Elizabeth admired the way Charlotte spoke of the healthfulness of the exercise and how she encouraged it as much as possible.

Mr. Collins led the way through every walk and crosswalk, barely allowing them a chance to praise the views he pointed out in detail. He could count the fields in every direction and tell how many trees there were in the most distant clump. But of all the views that his garden, or the country, or the kingdom could boast, none could compare with the prospect of Rosings, which could be seen through an opening in the trees that bordered the park nearly opposite the front of his house. It was a handsome, modern building, well-situated on rising ground.

From his garden, Mr. Collins would have led them around his two meadows, but the ladies didn't have appropriate shoes to walk on the frost-covered ground, so they turned back. While Sir William accompanied him, Charlotte took her sister and friend around the house, probably happy to have the opportunity to show it without her husband's help. It was rather small but well-built and convenient, and everything was fitted and arranged neatly and consistently, for which Elizabeth gave Charlotte all the credit. When Mr. Collins wasn't in the picture, there was genuinely an air of comfort throughout the house, and by Charlotte's evident enjoyment of it, Elizabeth assumed that he must be forgotten often.

She had already learnt that Lady Catherine was still in the area. At dinner, they spoke of it again and Mr. Collins said,

"Yes, Miss Elizabeth, you will have the honor of meeting Lady Catherine de Bourgh at church on Sunday and I'm sure you will be delighted. She is so gracious and kind. I have no doubt that she will invite you and my sister Maria to join us in any activities we have during your stay here. She is very kind to my dear Charlotte. We dine at Rosings twice a week and we are never allowed to walk home. Lady Catherine's carriage is always ready for us. I should say one of her carriages, since she has several."

"Lady Catherine is a very respectable and sensible woman and a very attentive neighbor, " added Charlotte.

"That's right, my dear. She is the kind of woman that one must treat with the utmost respect."

The evening was mostly spent discussing news from Hertfordshire and repeating what had already been written in letters. When the night ended, Elizabeth was alone in her chamber, reflecting on Charlotte's level of contentment, her ability to lead her husband, and her composure in dealing with him. Elizabeth also thought about how her visit would go, the peaceful routine of their activities, the annoying interruptions of Mr. Collins, and the fun times they would have with Rosings. Her active mind quickly figured it all out.

The next day, as she was in her room getting ready for a walk, a loud noise downstairs indicated that the whole house was in chaos. After listening for a moment, she heard someone running up the stairs in a rush and calling her name. She opened the door and saw Maria on the landing, who was out of breath and exclaimed,

"Oh, my dear Eliza! Please hurry and come into the dining room because there is such a sight to be seen! I won't tell you what it is. Hurry up and come down this instant."

Elizabeth asked questions in vain. Maria would not tell her anything more, and they both ran into the dining room which faced the lane to see what the fuss was about. It turned out to be two ladies in a low phaeton stopping at the garden gate.

"And is this all?" cried Elizabeth. "I expected at least that the pigs had gotten into the garden, and here is nothing but Lady Catherine and her daughter!"

"La! My dear," said Maria, quite shocked at the mistake, "it is not Lady Catherine. The old lady is Mrs. Jenkinson, who lives with them. The other is Miss De Bourgh. Only look at her. She is quite a little creature. Who would have thought she could be so thin and small!"

"She is terribly rude to keep Charlotte outside in all this wind. Why doesn't she come in?"

"Oh! Charlotte says she hardly ever does. It is a great favor when Miss De Bourgh comes in."

"I like her appearance," said Elizabeth, struck with other ideas. "She looks sickly and cross. Yes, she will do well for him. She will make him a very proper wife."

Mr. Collins and Charlotte were both standing at the gate talking to the ladies, and Sir William, to Elizabeth's amusement, was in the doorway, admiring the grandeur before him and bowing whenever Miss De Bourgh glanced his way. Eventually, there was nothing more to be said; the ladies drove off and the others went back inside. As soon as Mr. Collins saw the two girls, he started congratulating them on their luck, which Charlotte explained by letting them know that the whole group had been invited to dine at Rosings the following day.

CHAPTER 29

Mr. Collins was delighted at the prospect of showing off the grandeur of his patroness to his astonished visitors and was pleased to see her being so courteous to himself and his wife.

"I must say," he said, "I wasn't that surprised when Lady Catherine invited us to tea and to spend the evening at Rosings. I had a feeling that she would be so kind. But who could have imagined that we would receive an invitation to dine there, and for the whole party, so soon after our arrival?"

"I am not so surprised by what happened," Sir William replied, "as I am familiar with the manners of the elite from my position in life. Such displays of politeness are not uncommon around the court."

For the rest of the day and the following morning, all anyone could talk about was the visit to Rosings. Mr. Collins was carefully preparing them for the experience, making sure that the sight of such grandeur, the many servants and the lavish dinner would not be too overwhelming."

As the ladies were getting ready, he said to Elizabeth,

"Don't worry, my dear cousin, about your clothing. Lady Catherine doesn't expect us to dress as elegantly as she and her daughter do. I would suggest you just wear your nicest clothes, there's no need for anything else. Lady Catherine won't think less of you for being simply dressed. She likes to maintain the distinction of rank."

As they were getting dressed, he came to their doors a few times to urge them to hurry, since Lady Catherine didn't like to be kept waiting for her dinner. Maria Lucas, who was not used to company, was frightened by the descriptions of Lady Catherine and her lifestyle, and she was as apprehensive about her introduction at Rosings as her father had been about his presentation at St. James's.

As the weather was nice, they took a pleasant walk of about half a mile across the park. Every park has its own beauty and views and Elizabeth saw plenty to be pleased with, but she was not as excited as Mr. Collins had expected the scene to make her and she was only slightly affected by his description of the windows of the house and what the glazing had cost Sir Lewis De Bourgh.

When they reached the steps to the hall, Maria was getting more and more anxious and even Sir William was not looking very relaxed. Elizabeth stayed brave. She had heard nothing about Lady Catherine that made her seem extraordinary or miraculous, and she thought she could face the grandeur of her wealth and rank without trembling.

From the entrance hall, which Mr. Collins pointed out with an ecstatic expression on his face, and the fine proportions and decorations, they followed the servants through an antechamber to the room where Lady Catherine, her daughter, and Mrs. Jenkinson were sitting. Her Ladyship, very graciously, got up to welcome them and, as Mrs. Collins had arranged with her husband that she would do the introduction, it was done properly without any of the apologies and thanks that he would have thought necessary.

In spite of having been at St. James's, Sir William was so completely awed by the grandeur surrounding him that he had only enough courage to make a very low bow and take his seat without saying a word. His daughter, frightened almost out of her senses, sat on the edge of her chair, not knowing which way to look. Elizabeth found herself quite equal to the scene and could observe the three ladies before her composedly.

Lady Catherine was a tall, large woman with strongly marked features that might once have been handsome. Her air was not conciliating, nor was her manner of receiving them such as to make her visitors forget their inferior rank. She was not rendered formidable by silence; but whatever she said was spoken in so authoritative a tone as marked her self-importance and brought Mr. Wickham immediately to Elizabeth's mind. From the observation of the day altogether, she believed Lady Catherine to be exactly what he had represented.

After examining the mother, who bore some resemblance to Mr. Darcy, Maria was astonished to see the daughter was so thin and small. Miss De Bourgh and the mother had no similarities in either face or figure. Miss De Bourgh was pale and sickly and spoke very little, except to Mrs. Jenkinson who was entirely focused on listening to her and placing a screen in the proper direction before her eyes.

The group then went to a window to admire the view and Mr. Collins pointed out its beauty. Lady Catherine informed them that it was much better to look at in the summer.

The dinner was very luxurious and all the servants were present, as well as the silverware that Mr. Collins had promised. As he had predicted, he took his seat at the bottom of the table by her ladyship's request, looking as if he thought life couldn't offer anything better. He carved, ate and praised with enthusiasm, and every dish was applauded first by him and then by Sir William, who was now well enough to repeat whatever Mr. Collins said. Elizabeth was surprised that Lady Catherine could endure it. But Lady Catherine seemed pleased by their excessive admiration, and gave gracious smiles, especially when any dish on the table was new to them. The conversation wasn't very lively. Elizabeth was ready to talk whenever there was an opportunity, but she was sitting between Charlotte and Miss De Bourgh - the former was listening to Lady Catherine and the latter didn't say a word to her throughout the dinner. Mrs. Jenkinson was mainly concerned with how little Miss De Bourgh was eating, urging her to try something else, and worrying that she was unwell. Maria thought it would be inappropriate to speak, so the gentlemen just ate and admired.

When the ladies returned to the drawing-room, all they could do was listen to Lady Catherine talk without a break until coffee was served. She spoke with such authority that it was clear she wasn't used to anyone disagreeing with her. She asked Charlotte very personal and detailed questions about her domestic affairs and gave her a lot of advice on how to manage her small family, including the care of her cows and poultry. Elizabeth noticed that nothing was beneath Lady Catherine's notice if it gave her an opportunity to instruct others. During her conversations with Mrs. Collins, she asked Maria and Elizabeth a variety of questions, particularly Elizabeth, whose connections she knew the least about, and whom she commented to Mrs. Collins was a very polite and attractive girl. She asked Elizabeth at different times how many sisters she had, whether they were older or younger than herself, whether any of them were likely to be married, whether they were handsome, where they had been educated, what carriage her father kept, and what had been her mother's maiden name? Elizabeth felt the impertinence of the questions, but answered them calmly. Lady Catherine then said,

"Your father's estate is entailed on Mr. Collins, right? For Charlotte's sake, I'm glad, but otherwise I don't see why estates should be entailed from the female line. It wasn't necessary in Sir Lewis de Bourgh's family. Do you play and sing, Miss Bennet?"

"A little," Elizabeth replied.

"Oh, then, sometime or other we'll have to hear you. Our instrument is a great one, probably better than..." Lady Catherine continued, "Do your sisters play and sing?"

"One of them does," Elizabeth said.

"Why didn't you all learn? You all should have learned. The Miss Webbs all play and their father doesn't have as much money as yours. Do you draw?"

"No, not at all," Elizabeth answered.

"What, none of you?" Lady Catherine asked.

"Not one," Elizabeth replied.

"That's very strange. But I suppose you didn't have the opportunity. Your mom should have taken you to the city every spring for some extra lessons."

"My mom would have been okay with that, but my dad hates London," Elizabeth replied.

"Has your governess left you?"

"We never had a governess," said Elizabeth.

"No governess! How was that possible? Five daughters raised at home without a governess! I've never heard of such a thing. Your mom must have worked really hard on your education."

Elizabeth couldn't help but smile as she told the woman that wasn't the case.

"So then, who taught you? Who looked after you? Without a governess, you must have been neglected."

"Compared to some families, I guess we were," said Elizabeth. "But those of us who wanted to learn never lacked the resources. We were always encouraged to read, and had all the teachers we needed. Those who chose to be lazy, well, they could."

"Yes, of course," said the woman. "But that's something a teacher would have stopped. If I had known your mom, I would have strongly advised her to hire one. I always say that nothing can be accomplished in education without consistent and regular instruction, and only a governess can provide that. I'm always pleased when I'm able to find a good job for someone. Mrs. Jenkinson's four nieces were placed through my help, and recently I recommended another person who was mentioned to me, and the family was very pleased with her. Did I tell you that Lady Metcalfe came to thank me yesterday? She finds Miss Pope a treasure. 'Lady Catherine,' said she, 'you have given me a treasure.' Are any of your younger sisters out, Miss Bennet?"

"Yes, Ma'am, all."

"All!--What, all five out at once? Very odd!--And you only the second.—The younger ones out before the elder are married!--Your younger sisters must be very young?"

"Yes, my youngest sister isn't sixteen yet, she may be too young to be much in company. But really, Ma'am, I think it would be very unfair for younger sisters to not have the same opportunities for socializing and having fun because the elder may not have the means or desire to get married early. The last born has just as much of a right to the joys of youth as the first. And to be restricted for such a reason - I don't believe it would encourage sisterly love or sensitivity.

"Honestly," said her Ladyship, "you are quite confident in your opinion for someone so young. How old are you?"

"With three older sisters grown up," Elizabeth replied with a smile, "I don't think it would be appropriate for me to tell you." Lady Catherine seemed shocked that she didn't get a direct answer; Elizabeth thought she was the first person who had ever dared to playfully mess with such a dignifiedly haughty person.

"You can't be more than twenty, I'm sure - so you don't need to hide your age."

"I'm not yet twenty-one."

When the gentlemen joined them and tea was over, the card tables were set up. Lady Catherine, Sir William, and Mr. and Mrs. Collins sat down to play quadrille and Miss De Bourgh chose to play cassino, so the two girls joined Mrs. Jenkinson's party. Their conversation was dull, mostly about the game, with Mrs. Jenkinson worrying about Miss De Bourgh being too hot, cold, having too much or too little light. At the other table Lady Catherine was talking a lot, pointing out the mistakes of the other players and telling stories about herself. Mr. Collins was agreeing with everything she said, thanking her for every fish he won and apologizing if he won too many. Sir William was listening and storing everything in his memory.

When Lady Catherine and Miss De Bourgh had finished playing, the tables were cleared, the carriage was offered to Mrs. Collins and she accepted it. Then everyone gathered around the fire to listen to Lady Catherine deciding what the weather would be like the next day. When the coach arrived, Mr. Collins thanked Sir William profusely and they left. As soon as they had gone, Elizabeth was asked by her cousin to give her opinion of what she had seen at Rosings. Elizabeth tried to make her opinion more favorable than it really was, but it was not enough to satisfy Mr. Collins and he had to take Lady Catherine's praise into his own hands.

CHAPTER 30

Sir William only stayed a week at Hunsford, but it was enough for him to see that his daughter was very comfortable with her husband and neighbor. While Sir William was with them, Mr. Collins spent his mornings taking him out in his gig and showing him the countryside. When he left, the whole family returned to their usual activities and Elizabeth was glad that they didn't see more of her cousin because now he spent most of the time between breakfast and dinner either working in the garden, reading and writing, or looking out of his own book room window which faced the road. The room the ladies were sitting in was at the back. Elizabeth initially wondered why Charlotte didn't prefer the dining room for general use as it was a bigger room and had a nicer view. But then she realized Charlotte had a good reason for it as Mr. Collins would have been in his own room less if they had used an equally lively one and she gave Charlotte credit for the arrangement.

From the drawing room they couldn't see anything in the lane, so they were thankful to Mr. Collins for telling them what carriages were passing, especially Miss De Bourgh's phaeton which he mentioned almost every day. She occasionally stopped at the Parsonage to talk to Charlotte, but rarely got out of the carriage.

It was rare for Mr. Collins not to walk to Rosings and for his wife not to go too. Elizabeth didn't understand why they spent so much time there until she remembered there might be other family livings to be given away. Every now and then they were visited by her Ladyship and she noticed everything that was happening in the room during these visits. She looked into what they were doing, observed their work, and suggested that they do it differently; she found fault with the way the furniture was arranged, or noticed that the housemaid had been careless; and if she accepted any food, it seemed to be only to find out that Mrs. Collins was cooking too much food for her family.

Elizabeth soon realized that even though this grand lady was not a magistrate for the county, she was very active in her own parish. Mr. Collins brought her the smallest of matters from the village, and whenever any of the villagers were argumentative, unhappy or too poor, she would go out to the village to sort out their problems, stop their complaints and scold them until they were content and had enough money.

Dining at Rosings was repeated every two weeks, and apart from the absence of Sir William and the lack of a card table in the evening, each occasion was the same as the first. They had few other engagements, as the lifestyle of the neighborhood was beyond the Collinses' means. This however was not a problem for Elizabeth and overall she spent her time quite comfortably; there were moments of pleasant conversation with Charlotte and the weather was so nice for that time of year that she often had great pleasure outdoors. Her favorite walk, and where she usually went when the others were visiting Lady Catherine, was along the open grove that bordered that side of the park, where there was a pleasant sheltered path that no one seemed to appreciate except for her, and where she felt beyond the reach of Lady Catherine's curiosity.

The first two weeks of Elizabeth's visit passed quietly in this manner. Easter was coming up, and the week before it was to bring an addition to the Rosings family, which, in such a small circle, was bound to be important. Elizabeth had heard not long after she arrived that Mr. Darcy was expected to arrive there within a few weeks. Although there were not many people in the circle that she was fond of, his arrival would at least provide someone new to look at during the Rosings parties. Elizabeth might also be amused to see how hopeless Miss Bingley's designs on him were, by his behavior towards his cousin, who he was clearly destined for according to Lady Catherine. Lady

Catherine spoke of Mr. Darcy's arrival with great satisfaction, praised him in the highest terms, and seemed almost angry to learn that he had already been seen frequently by Miss Lucas and Elizabeth.

His arrival was quickly known at the parsonage, as Mr. Collins had spent the entire morning walking within view of the lodges that opened into Hunsford Lane, in order to receive the earliest confirmation of it. After making his bow as the carriage turned into the park, he hurried home with the great news. The following morning, he hastened to Rosings to pay his respects. There were two nephews of Lady Catherine who required them, for Mr. Darcy had brought with him a Colonel Fitzwilliam, the younger son of his uncle, Lord ---- and to the great surprise of all the party, when Mr. Collins returned, the gentlemen accompanied him. Charlotte had seen them from her husband's room, crossing the road, and immediately running into the other room, told the girls what an honor they might expect, adding,

"I may thank you, Eliza, for this piece of civility. Mr. Darcy would never have come so soon to wait upon me."

Elizabeth barely had time to deny any credit for the compliment before they arrived. Colonel Fitzwilliam, who was first to enter, was around thirty years old, not handsome, but had the manners and appearance of a true gentleman. Mr. Darcy looked the same as he had in Hertfordshire, paid his respects to Mrs. Collins with his usual reserve, and met Elizabeth with a composed expression, to which she only curtsied without saying anything.

Colonel Fitzwilliam began talking right away with the ease and readiness of a well-bred man, and had a very pleasant conversation. However, Mr. Darcy, after addressing a slight observation about the house and garden to Mrs. Collins, sat for some time without speaking to anyone. Eventually, his civility was awakened enough to ask Elizabeth about the health of her family. She answered in the usual way and added after a moment's pause, "My eldest sister has been in town these three months. Have you never happened to see her there?" She knew perfectly well that he had never seen Jane, but she wanted to see if he would show any awareness of what had happened between the Bingleys and Jane. He seemed a little confused as he answered that he had not yet met Miss Bennet. The subject was not pursued further, and the gentlemen soon left.

CHAPTER 31

Colonel Fitzwilliam's good manners were greatly admired at the parsonage, and all the ladies felt that he would add considerably to their enjoyment at Rosings. However, they did not receive an invitation to go there for a few days, as visitors were already present in the house. It was not until Easter Sunday, almost a week after the gentlemen had arrived, that they were honored with an invitation. Even then, they were only asked to come to the house in the evening after leaving church. During the last week, they had seen very little of Lady Catherine or her daughter. Colonel Fitzwilliam had visited the parsonage more than once during this time, but Mr. Darcy had only been seen at church.

The invitation was accepted, of course, and they joined the party in Lady Catherine's drawing room at the appropriate time. Her ladyship greeted them politely, but it was clear that their company was not nearly as welcome as it was when she had no one else to entertain. In fact, she was almost entirely focused on her nephews, particularly Darcy, and spoke to them much more than anyone else in the room.

Colonel Fitzwilliam was delighted to see Elizabeth and her party. Anything was a welcome relief to him while staying at Rosings. He was especially taken with Mrs. Collins's charming friend. He sat down next to her and engaged her in a delightful conversation about Kent and Hertfordshire, traveling and staying at home, new books, and music. Elizabeth had never been so entertained in that room before. Their lively discussion drew the attention of Lady Catherine and Mr. Darcy. Mr. Darcy, in particular, showed a keen curiosity about their conversation and frequently glanced their way.

Lady Catherine soon joined in the feeling and called out, "What are you two talking about? Fitzwilliam, what are you telling Miss Bennet? Let me hear it."

"We are discussing music, Madam," he replied, no longer able to avoid answering.

"Music! Then please speak up. It's my favorite subject. I must be included in the conversation if you're talking about music. I don't think there are many people in England who enjoy music more than I do or have a better natural taste for it. If I had ever learned, I would have been very skilled. Anne would have been too, if her health had allowed her to focus. I'm sure she would have done wonderfully. How is Georgiana doing, Darcy?"

Mr. Darcy spoke of his sister's proficiency with fondness.

"I'm very glad to hear such good news of her," said Lady Catherine. "Please tell her from me that she won't be able to do well if she doesn't practice a lot."

"I can assure you, Madam," he replied, "that she doesn't need such advice. She practices very regularly."

"That's even better. It can't be done too much; and when I write to her next, I'll remind her not to neglect it. I often tell young ladies that they won't be able to play music well without constant practice. I've told Miss Bennet multiple times that she won't play well unless she practices more; and even though Mrs. Collins doesn't have an instrument, I've told her many times that she's welcome to come to Rosings every day and play the piano in Mrs. Jenkinson's room. She won't be in anyone's way in that part of the house,"

Mr. Darcy said, looking a bit embarrassed by his aunt's rudeness. He didn't reply.

After they finished their coffee, Colonel Fitzwilliam reminded Elizabeth she had promised to play for him, so she went to the piano. He pulled up a chair near her. Lady Catherine listened to half a song, then started talking to her other nephew again, until he moved slowly towards the piano and positioned himself so he had a good view of Elizabeth. She saw what he was doing and, at the next pause, she looked up at him with a mischievous smile and said,

"You're trying to scare me by coming here like this to listen to me play? But I won't be intimidated, even though your sister is so good. I'm too stubborn to be scared by anyone else. I always get more courageous when someone tries to frighten me."

"I won't say you're wrong," Colonel Fitzwilliam answered, "because I don't think you actually believe I'm trying to scare you. I've known you long enough to know that you enjoy pretending to have opinions that you don't really have."

Elizabeth laughed and said to Colonel Fitzwilliam, "Your cousin will give you a very wrong idea of me and teach you not to believe anything I say. I'm very unlucky to meet someone who knows me so well in a place where I was hoping to present myself in a good light. Mr. Darcy, it was very unfair of you to mention all the bad things you knew about me in Hertfordshire. It was also not very wise of you, because it's making me want to tell things that will shock your family to hear."

"I'm not afraid of you," he said, smiling.

"Let me hear what you have to accuse him of!" exclaimed Colonel Fitzwilliam. "I'd like to know how he behaves around people he doesn't know."

"Well, I'll tell you - but prepare yourself for something terrible. The first time I saw him in Hertfordshire was at a ball. And do you know what he did? He only danced four dances! I'm sorry to tell you this, but it's true, even though there were few gentlemen and I know for a fact that more than one young lady was sitting without a partner. Mr. Darcy, you can't deny it."

"I didn't know any ladies in the room apart from my own party at that time."

"That's true; you can't be introduced in a ballroom. So, Colonel Fitzwilliam, what should I play next? My fingers are waiting for your instructions."

"Perhaps," said Darcy, "I should have made an introduction, but I'm not good at introducing myself to strangers."

"Shall we ask your cousin why this happened?" Elizabeth asked the Colonel.

"No, no!" he exclaimed. "Let's not talk about it any more."

"Should we ask him why a person of intelligence and education, who has experienced life, is not very good at introducing themselves to strangers?"

"I can answer your question without having to ask him," Fitzwilliam said. "It's because he won't put in the effort."

"I don't have the same talent as some people have," Darcy said, "of easily talking to those I've never met before. I can't seem to match their conversation style or act interested in their topics, like I see so many others do."

"My fingers don't move over the piano in the same skillful way that I've seen other women do," Elizabeth said. "They don't have the same strength or speed, and don't create the same sound. But then I always thought it was my own fault, because I didn't bother to practice. It's not that I don't think my fingers are capable of playing better than anyone else's."

Darcy smiled and said, "You're absolutely right. You've used your time much more wisely. Nobody who has heard you play would think anything is missing. We don't perform for strangers."

Lady Catherine heard them and asked what they were talking about. Elizabeth started playing again. Lady Catherine came closer and listened for a few minutes before saying to Darcy,

"Miss Bennet would play much better if she practiced more and had a London teacher. She has a good idea of how to finger the notes, though her taste isn't as good as Anne's. Anne would have been a great performer if she was healthy enough to learn."

Elizabeth glanced at Darcy to see if he agreed with his cousin's compliments, but she couldn't detect any sign of love in him at that moment or at any other time. From observing his behavior towards Miss De Bourgh, Elizabeth took comfort in thinking that Mr. Darcy might have been just as likely to marry Miss Bingley if she were related to him.

Lady Catherine continued to critique Elizabeth's performance, giving her instructions on execution and taste. Elizabeth received the comments with polite patience, and at the gentlemen's request, she continued playing the instrument until Lady Catherine's carriage was ready to take them all home.

CHAPTER 32

The next morning, Elizabeth was alone and writing a letter to Jane while Mrs. Collins and Maria were out on errands in the village. Suddenly, she was startled by the sound of someone ringing the doorbell, which signaled the arrival of a visitor. Since she hadn't heard a carriage, she suspected that it might be Lady Catherine and was preparing to put away her unfinished letter so as to avoid any impertinent questions. However, to her great surprise, it was Mr. Darcy, and he alone, who entered the room.

He appeared to be just as surprised to find her alone and apologized for intruding, explaining that he had assumed all the ladies were present.

They both sat down and when Elizabeth asked about Rosings, they seemed in danger of falling into a total silence. It was necessary, therefore, to think of something to say. Elizabeth recalled the last time she had seen Mr. Darcy in Hertfordshire and, feeling curious about their sudden departure from Netherfield, she commented, "Mr. Darcy, you and your party quitted Netherfield so suddenly last November. It must have been a pleasant surprise for Mr. Bingley to see you all after he had left just the day before. I hope he and his sisters were well when you left London."

"They were all perfectly well, thank you," Mr. Darcy replied.

When Mr. Darcy gave no other answer, Elizabeth added after a short pause, "I understand that Mr. Bingley does not intend to return to Netherfield much?"

"I have never heard him say so, but it's likely that he may not spend much time there in the future. He has many friends, and as he's at an age when friends and engagements are constantly increasing."

"If he doesn't plan to be at Netherfield much, it would be better for the neighborhood if he gave up the place entirely. Then we might possibly have a settled family there. But perhaps Mr. Bingley didn't take the house for the convenience of the neighborhood, but for his own, and we should expect him to keep or quit it on the same principle."

"I wouldn't be surprised," said Darcy, "if Mr. Bingley were to give up Netherfield as soon as a suitable purchase opportunity presents itself."

Elizabeth didn't respond. She was afraid of talking too much about Mr. Bingley, and since she had nothing else to say, she was determined to let him find a new subject to discuss.

Darcy took the hint and began, "This is a very comfortable house. I believe Lady Catherine did a lot of work on it when Mr. Collins first came to Hunsford."

"I believe she did, and I'm sure she couldn't have shown her kindness to a more grateful recipient."

"Mr. Collins seems to be fortunate in his choice of a wife."

"Yes, indeed. His friends can be happy that he has found one of the very few sensible women who would have accepted him, or who could make him happy if they had. My friend has an excellent understanding, although I'm not sure if marrying Mr. Collins was the wisest decision she's ever made. She appears perfectly content, however, and from a practical point of view, it's certainly a good match for her."

"It must be very pleasant for her to be so close to her family and friends," said Elizabeth.

"Do you call it close? It's almost fifty miles away!" her friend exclaimed.

"Fifty miles on a good road is barely more than a half day's journey. I'd say it's a very easy distance," Elizabeth replied.

"I never thought of the distance being an advantage of the match," Elizabeth said with a laugh. "I should never have said Mrs. Collins was settled near her family."

"It is a proof of your own attachment to Hertfordshire. Anything beyond the very neighborhood of Longbourn, I suppose, would seem far away."

As he spoke, there was a sort of smile on his face which Elizabeth thought she understood; he must have been thinking about Jane and Netherfield, and she blushed in response.

"I'm not saying that a woman can't be settled too near her family. The concept of 'far' and 'near' is relative and depends on many factors. If someone has enough money to make travelling inexpensive, then distance isn't a problem. But that's not the case here. Mr. and Mrs. Collins have a comfortable income, but not enough to allow for frequent trips away - and I'm sure my friend wouldn't call herself close to her family if she was any further away than she is now."

Mr. Darcy moved his chair a bit closer to me and said, "You can't have such a strong connection to Longbourn. You can't have always been there."

Elizabeth looked surprised. The gentleman changed his demeanor; he moved his chair back and grabbed a newspaper from the table, looking over it as he said in a colder tone,

"Are you enjoying Kent?"

They then had a short conversation about the countryside, both sides being calm and to the point, before Charlotte and her sister arrived back from their walk. Mr. Darcy explained the mistake that had led him to visit Miss Bennet and, after sitting for a few more minutes without saying much of anything, he left.

"What could this mean?" Charlotte asked as soon as he was gone. "My dear Eliza, he must be in love with you or he wouldn't have come here in such a familiar way," she said.

But when Elizabeth told her of his silence, it didn't seem likely, even to Charlotte's hopes, to be the case. After a lot of guessing, they could only assume that his visit was due to his lack of anything else to do, which was more likely given the time of year since all outdoor activities were over. Inside the house, Lady Catherine had books and a billiard table, but men can't stay inside all the time. The Parsonage was close by, and the walk to it was pleasant, as were the people who lived there. So the two cousins started going there almost every day, either together or separately, sometimes with their aunt. It was obvious to them all that Colonel Fitzwilliam came because he enjoyed their company, which made him even more likable. Elizabeth was reminded of her former favorite, George Wickham, when she was with Colonel Fitzwilliam, although she noticed that he didn't have the same captivating softness in his manner. She thought he might have the most knowledgeable mind.

It was difficult to understand why Mr. Darcy visited the parsonage so often. It couldn't be for the sake of society, since he frequently sat there for ten minutes without saying a word. When he did speak, it seemed like it was out of necessity rather than choice, as if he were sacrificing propriety rather than enjoying himself. He seldom appeared truly animated. Mrs. Collins didn't know what to make of him. Colonel Fitzwilliam occasionally laughed at his stupidity, which showed that he was generally different from what Mrs. Collins knew of him. She would have liked to believe that this change was due to love, and that the object of that love was her friend Eliza, so she seriously set out to discover the truth. She watched him whenever they were at Rosings or whenever he came to Hunsford, but without much success. He certainly looked at her friend a great deal, but the meaning of that look was uncertain. It was an intense, unwavering gaze, but Mrs. Collins often wondered whether there was much admiration in it or whether it was simply absent-mindedness.

Mrs. Collins had suggested to Elizabeth once or twice that Mr. Darcy might have a soft spot for her, but Elizabeth always laughed off the idea. Mrs. Collins didn't think it was right to push the subject any further for fear of raising expectations that could lead to disappointment. She believed that all of Elizabeth's dislike of Mr. Darcy would disappear if Elizabeth thought that she had power over him.

In her kind plans for Elizabeth's future, Mrs. Collins sometimes imagined her marrying Colonel Fitzwilliam. He was by far the most pleasant man, and he certainly admired Elizabeth. His social position was most advantageous. However, Mr. Darcy had significant influence in the church, while his cousin had none at all, which was a disadvantage.

CHAPTER 33

On more than one occasion, Elizabeth encountered Mr. Darcy during her stroll in the Park, which she found to be extremely strange. To prevent it from happening again, she made sure to let him know that it was one of her favorite places to go. It was even stranger that it happened a second and then a third time. It appeared that he was being intentionally mean, or punishing himself, for on these occasions it wasn't just a few formal questions followed by an awkward silence and then he'd leave, but he actually felt the need to turn back and walk with her. He never said much, and she didn't bother to talk or really listen either; but during their third meeting she noticed he was asking some strange, unrelated questions—about how she enjoyed being at Hunsford, her love of taking solitary walks, and her opinion of Mr. and Mrs. Collins' happiness; and when he spoke about Rosings and how she didn't fully understand the house, it seemed like he was expecting her to stay there the next time she came to Kent. His words implied it. Was he thinking about Colonel Fitzwilliam? She figured, if he meant anything, it was a reference to what might happen between them. It made her a bit uncomfortable, and she was relieved when she reached the gate in the fence across from the Parsonage.

She was walking and re-reading Jane's last letter, which made her concerned that Jane wasn't in good spirits, when she saw Colonel Fitzwilliam instead of Mr. Darcy. She put the letter away and forced a smile, saying, "I didn't know you ever walked this way."

"I make this tour of the Park every year," he replied, "and I'm going to finish it with a visit to the Parsonage. Are you going much farther?"

"No, I was just about to turn back." So they walked towards the Parsonage together. She asked,

"Are you definitely leaving Kent on Saturday?"

"Yes, if Darcy doesn't postpone it again. I'm at his disposal. He can arrange things however he wants."

"He certainly seems to enjoy having the freedom to do whatever he wants. I don't know anyone else who does."

"He does like to have his own way very well," replied Colonel Fitzwilliam. "But then again, don't we all? He just has more means of getting it because he's rich and a lot of others aren't. I can relate to that."

"In my opinion, the younger son of an Earl doesn't really know what it's like to have to deny themselves or to depend on someone else. Now, seriously, when have you ever had to deny yourself something or been restricted because of a lack of money?"

"Those are tough questions," replied the Colonel. "I can't really say that I've experienced many hardships because of money. But I do know that when it comes to bigger decisions, I can suffer from not having money. Younger sons can't marry who they want to."

"Unless they want a woman with money, which I think they often do.

"Our spending habits make us too dependent, so there are not many in my social class who can marry without thinking about money."

Elizabeth thought, "Is he talking to me?" and felt embarrassed, but she recovered and said in a cheerful voice, "So, what's the usual price for an Earl's younger son? Unless the elder brother is very ill, I guess you wouldn't ask for more than fifty thousand pounds."

He replied in the same way, and they stopped talking about it. To break the silence and make sure he didn't think she was affected by the conversation, Elizabeth said,

"It seems to me that your cousin brought you here mainly to have someone at his beck and call. It's surprising that he hasn't found a partner to rely on, but perhaps he feels content with his sister's company for now. Since he is responsible for her, he might feel free to do whatever he wants with her."

"No," said Colonel Fitzwilliam, "I share that advantage with him. I am his co-guardian of Miss Darcy."

"Are you really? What kind of guardians are you? Does she give you much trouble? Young ladies of her age can sometimes be hard to handle, and if she has the true Darcy spirit, she may like to have her own way."

As she spoke, she noticed him looking at her intently, and the way he quickly asked her why she thought Miss Darcy was likely to cause them any distress made her think she had stumbled onto the truth. She quickly answered,

"Don't worry. I've never heard anything bad about her; I'm sure she's one of the most obedient people in the world. She's very popular with some of my acquaintances, Mrs. Hurst and Miss Bingley. I think I remember you saying you know them."

"I know them a little. Their brother is a pleasant, gentleman-like man - he's a great friend of Darcy's."

"Oh yes," Elizabeth said drily, "Mr. Darcy is very kind to Mr. Bingley and takes a lot of care of him."

"Care of him? Yes, I really believe Darcy does take care of him in the areas where he needs it most. On our journey here, Darcy told me something that made me think Bingley owes him a lot. But I should apologize, as I have no right to assume it was Bingley he was referring to. It was all just speculation."

"What do you mean?"

"It's something Darcy wouldn't want to be widely known, as it would be embarrassing for the lady's family"

"You can trust me not to mention it."

"And remember, I don't have much reason to think it's Bingley. All he told me was that he was glad he had recently saved a friend from the trouble of an imprudent marriage, but he didn't give any names or details. I only suspected it was Bingley because I think he's the kind of young man to get into such a situation and I know they were together all last summer."

"Did Mr. Darcy tell you his reasons for intervening?"

"I understood that he had very strong objections to the lady."

"And what methods did he use to separate them?"

"He didn't discuss his methods with me," said Fitzwilliam, smiling. "He only told me what I've just told you."

Elizabeth didn't respond and walked on, her heart filled with indignation. After watching her for a moment, Fitzwilliam asked her why she was so thoughtful.

"I'm thinking about what you've just told me," she said. "Your cousin's behavior doesn't sit well with me. Why should he be the judge?"

"It seems like you think his involvement was unnecessary?"

"I don't understand why Mr. Darcy had the right to decide what would make his friend happy, or why he was allowed to determine how his friend should be happy based on his own judgement. But," she continued, "since we don't know the specifics, it's not fair to judge him. I don't think there was much love in the situation."

"That's a reasonable assumption," said Fitzwilliam, "but it really takes away from the honor of my cousin's victory." He said this jokingly, but it seemed like an accurate description of Mr. Darcy to her and she didn't trust herself to answer, so she quickly changed the topic and talked about other things until they got to the parsonage.

Once there, when their guest had left, she was able to think about everything she had heard in the privacy of her own room. It was obvious that the people being talked about were those she was connected to. There couldn't be two people in the world over whom Mr. Darcy had such immense power. She had never doubted that he was involved in the decisions that had been made to separate Mr. Bingley and Jane, but she had always thought Miss Bingley was the one who had come up with the plan and arranged it. If his own vanity wasn't misleading him, he was the cause of all the suffering Jane was going through and had gone through. He had destroyed any chance of happiness for the most loving and generous heart in the world and no one knew how much damage he had caused.

"There were some very strong objections against the lady," Colonel Fitzwilliam had said, and those objections were probably that she had one uncle who was a country lawyer and another who was in business in London.

"Nothing could be said against Jane herself!" she exclaimed. "She is so lovely and kind. Her understanding is excellent, her mind is so advanced, and her manners are so charming. Nothing could be said against my father either, who, despite his quirks, has abilities that Mr. Darcy can't even dream of and respectability that he will probably never have." When she thought of her mother, she was a bit less sure, but she was certain that Mr. Darcy's pride would be more hurt by the lack of importance in her family connections than their lack of intelligence. In the end, she was sure that his pride and his desire to keep Mr. Bingley close to his sister had both played a part in his decision.

Thinking about it made her so upset that she had a headache, and it got worse as the evening went on. Because of that, and her unwillingness to see Mr. Darcy, she decided not to go with her cousins to Rosings. Mrs. Collins, seeing that she was really unwell, didn't try to persuade her to go, and tried to stop her husband from doing the same. However, Mr. Collins couldn't hide his worry that Lady Catherine would be displeased with her for staying at home."

CHAPTER 34

After they had left, Elizabeth, as if intending to aggravate her anger against Mr. Darcy as much as possible, chose to spend her time examining all the letters that Jane had written to her since her arrival in Kent. The letters contained no direct complaints, nor were there any reminders of past events or any updates on present sufferings. However, in almost every line of each letter, there was a lack of the cheerfulness that had characterized Jane's previous letters. This cheerfulness, which had stemmed from the serenity of a mind at ease with itself and kindly disposed towards everyone, had been scarcely ever dimmed. Elizabeth noticed every sentence conveying an idea of unease with an attention that she had not given during her initial reading. Mr. Darcy's shameful boasting about the misery he had been able to inflict gave her a sharper sense of her sister's sufferings. She found some consolation in the thought that his visit to Rosings was to end on the day after the next, and even greater consolation in the fact that in less than a tow weeks, she would be with Jane again, able to contribute to her sister's recovery by everything that affection could offer.

She couldn't think of Darcy's departure from Kent without remembering that his cousin was going with him. However, Colonel Fitzwilliam had made it clear that he had no intentions, and while he was a pleasant company, Elizabeth didn't mean to worry about him.

As she was settling this thought, she was suddenly startled by the sound of the doorbell. Her spirits were slightly fluttered by the idea of it being Colonel Fitzwilliam himself, who had called late in the evening before and might now come to inquire specifically about her. However, this idea was quickly dismissed, and her spirits were very differently affected when, to her complete amazement, she saw Mr. Darcy walk into the room. In a hurried manner, he immediately began to inquire about her health, attributing his visit to a desire to hear that she was doing better. She responded to him politely but coldly. He sat for a few moments, then got up and paced around the room. Elizabeth was surprised, but said nothing. After a few minutes of silence, he approached her in a state of agitation and said,

"I've been trying to fight it, but I can't. I have to tell you how much I admire and love you."

Elizabeth was speechless. She was shocked, blushed, and was silent. He took her silence as encouragement and proceeded to tell her all the feelings he had for her. He spoke well, but also discussed the family obstacles that had always stood in the way of his love for her. He spoke with a passion that was meant to show how much he cared, but it was unlikely to help his case.

In spite of her strong dislike, she couldn't help but feel flattered by the affections of such a man, but her intentions didn't change. She felt sorry for the pain he would suffer, but her compassion turned to anger when he spoke. She tried to remain calm and answer him patiently. He expressed his attachment which he had been unable to conquer and asked for her hand in marriage. She could see he was sure of her answer, and her cheeks blushed with anger. She said,

"In such cases it is customary to express gratitude for the sentiments, even if they are not returned. I wish I could feel grateful, but I never wanted your approval and you clearly gave it reluctantly. I'm sorry to have caused anyone pain, though it was unintentional and I hope it will be short-lived. The feelings that have stopped you from acknowledging your affections before should have no trouble overcoming them after this explanation."

Mr. Darcy, who was standing by the mantel-piece with his eyes fixed on her face, seemed to take in her words with as much anger as surprise. His face went pale with rage and his emotions were visible in every feature. He was trying to keep his composure, and he wouldn't speak until he thought he had achieved it. The silence was excruciating for Elizabeth. Finally, in a voice that was obviously forced to stay calm, he said,

"And this is all the response I'm going to get? I might have expected a bit more politeness. But it doesn't matter."

"I might as well ask why, if you had the intention of offending and insulting me, you told me that you liked me even though it was against your will, reason and character? Was that not a way of excusing your rudeness if I was rude? But I have other reasons to be angry with you. You know I do. Even if I hadn't had my own feelings to consider, do you think I would have accepted someone who had ruined the happiness of my beloved sister, possibly forever?"

As Elizabeth spoke these words, Mr. Darcy's face changed color, but he quickly regained his composure and listened to her without interrupting.

"I have every reason to think poorly of you. No justification can excuse the unjust and ungenerous role you played in separating them. You cannot deny that you were the primary, if not the sole, means of driving them apart, of exposing one to the censure of the world for fickleness and instability, and the other to ridicule for dashed hopes, and bringing them both to acute misery."

She paused and saw with indignation that he listened with an air that showed he was completely unaffected by any sense of remorse. He even looked at her with a smile of feigned incredulity.

"Can you deny that you did it?" she asked again.

With feigned calmness, he replied, "I have no wish to deny that I did everything in my power to separate my friend from your sister, or that I am pleased with my success. I have been kinder to him than I have been to myself."

Elizabeth disdained to acknowledge the civility of his comment, but she understood its meaning and was not likely to be won over by it.

"But it is not only this incident on which my dislike for you is based. Long before this, my opinion of you was formed. Your character was revealed to me months ago in the account given to me by Mr. Wickham. What can you say on this subject? In what imaginary act of friendship can you defend yourself, or how can you deceive others?"

"You are very interested in that gentleman's affairs," said Darcy, his tone less calm and his face reddening.

"I cannot imagine anyone who knows what he has gone through not feeling an interest in him," Elizabeth said.

"His misfortunes!" Darcy repeated with disdain. "Yes, his misfortunes have indeed been great."

"And it's because of your doing," she continued, her voice full of emotion. "You have left him in his current state of poverty. You have denied him the opportunities that should have been his right. You have taken away the best years of his life and his chance at independence. You have done all of this, yet you have the audacity to mock his misfortune!"

"And this is how you see me? This is your opinion of me? I'm thankful you made it so clear. My mistakes, as you see it, must be really bad! But maybe," he said, stopping and turning to her, "these mistakes could have been overlooked if I had been more careful in how I presented the reservations that had kept me from any serious plans. These harsh accusations could have been avoided if I had been more strategic in hiding my struggles and made you think I was only motivated by pure and genuine interest. But I hate all forms of deception. And I'm not ashamed of the feelings I expressed. They were natural and appropriate. Did you expect me to be happy about your lower social standing? Can you really congratulate yourself for hoping to have a relationship with someone whose social status is so much lower than your own?"

Elizabeth felt her anger rising, but she tried to remain composed as she said,

"You're wrong, Mr. Darcy. The way you declared your feelings didn't affect me in any other way than to spare me the discomfort of having to reject you if you had acted like a gentleman."

She saw him flinch at her words, but he said nothing. Elizabeth continued, "No matter how you had asked, you couldn't have convinced me to accept your proposal."

Again, he looked at her in disbelief and embarrassment. She continued.

"From the very start, almost from the first moment I met you, your manners made me believe completely in your arrogance, conceit, and your disregard for the feelings of others, and it wasn't long before I realized that you were the last person I would ever want to marry."

"That's enough, ma'am. I understand your sentiments perfectly and I'm ashamed of my own. Please forgive me for taking up so much of your time and accept my best wishes for your health and happiness."

With that, he quickly left the room and Elizabeth heard him open the front door and leave the house.

She was overwhelmed with emotion. She didn't know how to cope and, from sheer exhaustion, she sat down and cried for half an hour. Every time she thought about what had happened, her astonishment grew. That she could not believe it when she heard that Mr. Darcy had offered her marriage, despite all the reasons he had given for not wanting his friend to marry her sister and the same reasons must have applied to him! She was pleased to think that she had unknowingly inspired such strong feelings in him. But then she remembered his pride, his awful pride, and his shameless admission of what he had done to Jane, and his refusal to excuse his cruel treatment of Mr. Wickham. This soon replaced the pity she had felt for him.

Elizabeth remained lost in deep and troubling thoughts until she heard the sound of Lady Catherine's carriage. It reminded her of Charlotte's presence and how unprepared she was to face any scrutiny. She quickly left for her room.

CHAPTER 35

Elizabeth woke up the next morning still thinking about it all. She was unable to get over her surprise at what had happened; she couldn't concentrate on anything else and feeling too unwell to work, she decided to go out for some fresh air and exercise after breakfast. She was heading directly to her favorite walk when she remembered that Mr. Darcy sometimes went there, so instead of entering the park, she turned up the lane which took her further away from the main road. The park fence was still on one side and she soon reached one of the gates.

After walking up and down the lane a few times, she was drawn in by the beauty of the morning and stopped at the gates to look into the park. The five weeks she had spent in Kent had changed the countryside considerably and every day the early trees were becoming greener. She was about to continue her walk when she caught a glimpse of a man in the grove which bordered the park; he was walking in her direction and, fearing it might be Mr. Darcy, she quickly turned back. He stepped forward eagerly and called her name. She had turned away, but when she heard it was Mr. Darcy, she turned back towards the gate. He had reached it by then and was holding out a letter. She took it without thinking and he said, in a haughty voice, "I have been walking in the grove hoping to meet you. Will you do me the honor of reading this letter?" He gave a slight bow and then walked back into the plantation and out of sight.

Elizabeth opened the letter with no anticipation of pleasure but with great curiosity. Inside was an envelope containing two sheets of letter paper, written in a very neat hand, and the envelope was also full. She started reading as she continued walking along the lane.

"It was eight o'clock in the morning when I received a letter from Rosings. I was worried that it might contain sentiments or offers that disgusted me last night. I am writing this letter without any intention of hurting you or making myself look bad. I simply ask for your attention, although I know you don't want to give it to me. Last night you accused me of two things. The first was that I had taken Mr. Bingley away from your sister, and the other was that I had ruined Mr. Wickham's immediate prosperity and destroyed his future prospects, despite his valid claims and despite my honor and humanity. To have deliberately thrown away the companion of my youth, the acknowledged favorite of my father, a young man with no other support than our patronage, and who had been raised to expect our help, would be a terrible thing, incomparable to the separation of two people who had only been in love for a few weeks. But I hope to be spared from such harsh judgement in the future after my actions and their motives have been explained. If I have to relate feelings which may be hurtful to you, I can only say that I am sorry. I must obey the necessity and any further apology would be pointless. I did not stay in Hertfordshire for long before I saw, like everyone else, that Bingley was more interested in your eldest sister than any other woman in the area. But it was not until the evening of the dance at Netherfield that I suspected he had a serious attachment. I had seen him in love many times before. At that ball, while I was dancing with you, I was informed by Sir William Lucas that Bingley's attentions to your sister had led to the general assumption that they would get married. He spoke of it as if it were an event that was certain to happen, but the only thing that was uncertain was when it would happen. From that moment on, I paid close attention to my friend's behavior and I could tell that his affection for Miss Bennet was more than I had ever seen before. I also watched your sister — her look and behavior were as open, cheerful, and inviting as ever, but there was no sign that she felt any special attachment to him. If I am wrong about this and I have caused her pain, then your anger is justified. But I won't hesitate to say that the calmness of your sister's face and demeanor was such that even the most observant person would have been convinced that, as pleasant as her disposition was, her heart was not likely to be easily moved. It's certain that I wanted to believe she was not interested, but I can confidently say that my judgment is *not usually swayed by my hopes or fears. I didn't think she was uninterested because I wanted it to be true; I believed it based on an unbiased assessment, as much as I wanted it to be the case. My objections to the marriage were not just the ones I admitted last night required a powerful emotion to ignore in my own case; the lack of connection wouldn't be as bad for my friend as it would be for me. But there were other reasons I didn't want it to happen; reasons that were still there and equally applicable in both cases, but that I had tried to forget because they weren't right in front of me. I must mention them, though briefly. Your mother's family's situation, though not ideal, was nothing compared to the complete lack of propriety often shown by your mother, your three younger sisters, and sometimes even your father. Please forgive me; it pains me to upset you. Amidst your worry about the faults of your closest family members and your displeasure at this portrayal of them, take comfort in knowing that you and your eldest sister have conducted yourselves in such a way that you have avoided any similar criticism - a praise which is both honorable to both of your senses and dispositions. I can only add that my opinion of all parties was confirmed and every incentive increased after what happened that evening, which had already led me to try and prevent my friend from what I thought was an unfortunate union. He left Netherfield for London the next day, as you surely remember, with the intention of returning soon. I will now explain my part in this. His sisters were as troubled as I was and it was soon clear that we both felt the same way; understanding that no time was to be wasted in separating their brother, we decided to go to London to join him. I was quick to take on the role of pointing out to my friend the certain dangers of such a choice. I described and emphasized them strongly. Even if my remonstration had made him hesitate or delay his decision, I do not think it would have stopped the marriage in the end, had it not been backed up by my assurance of your sister's lack of interest. He had previously thought she felt the same affection for him, even if it wasn't as strong. But Bingley was very modest and relied more on my opinion than his own. So it wasn't too hard to make him realize he was wrong. It was a lot harder to convince him not to go back to Hertfordshire. I can't be too mad at myself for doing this much. The only part of my conduct that I'm not proud of is that I didn't tell him that your sister was in town. I knew it, as did Miss Bingley, but he still doesn't know. It's possible they could have met without any harm, but* his feelings for her didn't seem to have faded enough for that. I guess this deception was beneath me, but it was done for the best. I have nothing more to say about it, no other way to apologize. If I have hurt your sister's feelings, it was done without knowing it; and even though the reasons that drove me may seem inadequate to you, I have not yet learned to condemn them. As for the more serious accusation of having wronged Mr. Wickham, I can only refute it by telling you the whole story of his relationship with my family. I do not know what he has accused me of specifically, but I can call on more than one reliable witness to confirm what I am about to say. Mr. Wickham is the son of a very respectable man who was in charge of all the Pemberley estates for many years and his good service made my father want to be helpful to him. My father paid for George Wickham's schooling and later at Cambridge – a very important help as his own father, who was always poor due to his wife's extravagance, could not have given him a gentleman's education. My father was very fond of this young man and found his manners to be very charming. He also had a high opinion of him and was hoping he would choose to become a clergyman, so he was intending to provide for him in the church. As for me, it has been many years since I began to think of him in a completely different way. He was careful to hide his bad behavior and lack of principles from his best friend, but I, being only slightly younger than him, had the opportunity to see him in moments when he was not so guarded. I know this will cause you pain, but no matter what feelings Mr. Wickham has made you feel, I must still tell you the truth about his character. This only gives me more reason to do so. My father passed away about five years ago and he was very fond of Mr. Wickham. In his will, he asked me to do all I could to help Mr. Wickham advance in his profession. He also left him a legacy of one thousand pounds. Not long after, Mr. Wickham wrote to me to say that he had decided against taking orders and asked for some more immediate financial help instead. He said he was thinking of studying law and that one thousand pounds wouldn't be enough to support him. I wasn't sure if he was being sincere, but I agreed to his proposal. I knew Mr. Wickham wasn't meant to be a clergyman, so we soon settled the matter. He gave up any claim to help in the church and I gave him three thousand pounds in return. It seemed like all ties between us were now severed. I thought too poorly of him to invite him to Pemberley or to welcome him in town. I believe he mostly *stayed in town, but his studying the law was just a sham, and now being free from all obligations, he lived a life of idleness and debauchery. For around three years I heard little of him; however, when the incumbent of the living he was meant to have passed away, he wrote to me again asking for the position. He assured me his circumstances were very dire, and I had no trouble believing him, since he had no other person to provide for and I could not have forgotten my late father's wishes. You won't blame me for not agreeing to this request or for not wanting to hear it again. His anger matched how desperate his situation was, and he probably said bad things about me to other people as much as he did to me. After that, we didn't act like we knew each other at all. I don't know how he lived, but last summer he was forced back into my life. I don't want to tell you this, but since I have to, I know you'll keep it a secret. My sister, who is more than 10 years younger than me, was taken care of by my mom's nephew, Colonel Fitzwilliam, and me. About a year ago, she was taken out of school and set up in London and last summer she went to Ramsgate with the woman who was in charge of her. Mr. Wickham was there too, on purpose because he had known Mrs. Younge before and she helped him make Georgiana, who had a good memory of how nice he was to her when she was a child, think she was in love with him and agree to elope. She was only fifteen, so that must be taken into account; and I am glad to say I only found out about it because she told me herself. I arrived unexpectedly a few days before they were due to elope, and Georgiana, not being able to bear the thought of upsetting and angering a brother she almost thought of as a father, confessed everything to me. You can imagine how I felt and what I did. I wanted to protect my sister's reputation and feelings, so I didn't make it public, but I wrote to Mr. Wickham and he left straight away, and Mrs. Young was removed from her position. Mr. Wickham's main aim was obviously my sister's thirty thousand pounds in inheritance, but I can't help thinking that he also wanted to take revenge on me. His revenge would have been complete indeed. This, ma'am, is a true account of every event in which we were involved together; and if you don't completely reject it as false, I hope you will accept that I have not been cruel to Mr. Wickham. I do not know how, under what false pretense he has deceived you; but his success is not surprising. As you were previously unaware of anything concerning either of them, you could not have detected it and you had no reason to be suspicious.*

You may wonder why I didn't tell you all this last night. But I was not in control of myself enough to know what should be revealed. I can particularly call upon Colonel Fitzwilliam to testify to the truth of everything I have related here. He, due to our close relationship and constant friendship, and even more so as one of the executors of my father's will, has unavoidably been made aware of every detail of these events. If you are so disgusted with me that you don't trust my words, you can still talk to my cousin. I will try to find a way to give you this letter today. May God bless you.

"*Fitzwilliam Darcy.*"

CHAPTER 36

Elizabeth, upon receiving Mr. Darcy's letter, did not expect it to include a renewal of his proposal. However, she had no idea what to anticipate. As she read through the letter, her emotions were difficult to define. She was amazed that he believed he could apologize, and she was convinced that he would have nothing to say that shame would not prevent him from revealing. She began reading about what had happened at Netherfield with a strong prejudice against anything he might say. She read with such eagerness that she barely comprehended the text and could not focus on the current sentence. She immediately decided that he was wrong about her sister's indifference, and she was too furious to give him a fair hearing when he detailed the actual objections to the match. She was unsatisfied with his lack of regret, and his tone was proud and insolent.

But when the subject changed to Mr. Wickham and she read the events more carefully, which if true would prove his worthlessness and which were similar to his own story, her feelings were even harder to describe. She felt astonishment, fear, and even terror. She wished to completely discredit it, repeatedly exclaiming, "This must be false! This cannot be! This must be the biggest lie!", and after she had read the whole letter, not understanding much of the last page or two, she quickly put it away, insisting that she would not look at it again.

In her disturbed state of mind, unable to focus on anything, she walked on; but it didn't work, within half a minute she had unfolded the letter again, and trying to compose herself as best she could, she started to read through it all again, paying close attention to every sentence. The account of his connection with the Pemberley family was exactly what he had told her himself;

and the kindness of the late Mr. Darcy, though she hadn't known before how much he had done, matched up with what he had said. So far each story matched the other; but when she got to the will, there was a big difference. What Wickham had said about the living was still fresh in her mind, and as she recalled his exact words, it was impossible not to think that someone was being dishonest. For a few moments she hoped that her wishes weren't wrong. But when she read and re-read the details of Wickham giving up any claim to the living and receiving three thousand pounds in return, she was unsure again. She put down the letter, tried to be fair and consider every point of view, but with little success. Both sides were simply making assertions. She read on, and every line showed her that the situation, which she had thought could not be presented in a way that would make Mr. Darcy's actions less than disgraceful, could be interpreted so that he would be completely innocent.

She was exceedingly shocked by the extravagance and general recklessness which Mr. Darcy accused Mr. Wickham of, and she had no proof to refute it. She had never heard of him before he joined the Militia, which he did at the suggestion of the young man whom he had met in town and had a slight acquaintance with. No one in Hertfordshire knew anything of his past life, except what he told himself. His appearance, his voice and his manner had made her think he was a good person, and she tried to remember any good deeds or any signs of integrity or kindness he had done to prove Mr. Darcy wrong. But she couldn't recall any. She could easily picture him in her mind, with his charming looks and manners, but she could not think of any substantial good he had done, except being well-liked in the neighborhood and his popularity in the mess. After thinking about this for a while, she went back to reading. But, unfortunately, what she read next confirmed what Colonel Fitzwilliam had told her the day before about Mr. Darcy's plans for Miss Darcy. She was told to ask Colonel Fitzwilliam for more details, since she already knew he was involved in his cousin's affairs and she trusted his character. At one point, she considered asking him directly, but she was worried about how awkward it would be and eventually she decided that Mr. Darcy would never have made the proposal if he hadn't been sure of his cousin's support.

She remembered exactly what had been said between Wickham and her the first night at Mr. Philips's. She recalled many of his expressions and was now appalled by how inappropriate it was for him to have said such things to a stranger. She was embarrassed that she had not noticed this before. She was aware of how forward he had been and how his words did not match his actions. She remembered that he had boasted of not being afraid to see Mr. Darcy, saying that even if Mr. Darcy left the country, he would stay put. But then he had avoided the Netherfield ball the following week. Up until the Netherfield family had left the area, he had only told his story to her. But then afterwards, it had been discussed everywhere. He had then had no qualms about tarnishing Mr. Darcy's reputation, even though he had previously told her that his respect for the father would stop him from exposing the son.

How different everything now looked concerning him! His attentions to Miss King were now motivated solely by money; and her lack of money showed that he was not content with what he had, but was eager to get more. His behavior towards her could no longer be justified; he had either been misled about her wealth, or was trying to boost his own ego by encouraging her feelings for him. Every lingering thought that he was in the right was fading away; and in defense of Mr. Darcy, she had to admit that Mr. Bingley had long ago declared his innocence in the matter; and that although his manners were proud and unapproachable, she had never seen anything in their acquaintance that indicated he was unprincipled or unjust, or had immoral or irreligious habits. She acknowledged that she had heard him speak affectionately of his sister and that even Wickham had allowed him merit as a brother, which showed he was capable of some amiable feeling. It would have been impossible for him to have done such a gross violation of everything right and still be able to keep it hidden from the world and that she couldn't understand how a person capable of such a thing could be friends with such an amiable man as Mr. Bingley.

She felt ashamed of herself and realized that she had been blind, partial, prejudiced and absurd. She exclaimed,

"How despicably have I acted! I, who have prided myself on my discernment! I, who have valued myself on my abilities! Who have often disdained the generous candor of my sister, and gratified my vanity in useless or blamable distrust. How humiliating is this discovery! Yet, how just a humiliation! Had I been in love, I could not have been more wretchedly blind. But vanity, not love, has been my folly. Pleased with the preference of one, and offended by the neglect of the other, on the very beginning of our acquaintance, I have courted prepossession and ignorance, and driven reason away, where either were concerned. Till this moment I never knew myself."

Elizabeth's thoughts were consumed with Mr. Darcy's letter, leading her from herself to Jane, and then to Bingley. She recalled how insufficient his explanation had seemed and decided to read it again. However, the effect was quite different the second time. She couldn't deny that his assertions in one instance were just as valid as the other. He declared he had no idea of Jane's attachment to Bingley, and Elizabeth couldn't help remembering Charlotte's similar opinion. She also couldn't deny the truth in his description of Jane. While her feelings were strong, they were not often displayed, and her air and manner were consistently pleasant but lacking in great sensibility.

As Elizabeth read the part of the letter where her family was mentioned with mortifying reproach, she felt severe shame. The charge was too just to be denied, and the circumstances referred to, particularly those that occurred at the Netherfield ball and which confirmed his initial disapproval, made as strong an impression on her mind as they did on his.

The compliment to herself and Jane was not ignored, but it couldn't make up for the contempt shown towards the rest of her family. As she realized that Jane's disappointment was due to the actions of their closest relatives and thought about how much damage their conduct would do to their reputations, she felt more depressed than she had ever felt before.

After wandering along the lane for two hours, giving way to every variety of thought; re-considering events, determining probabilities, and reconciling herself as well as she could, to a change so sudden and so important, fatigue, and a recollection of her long absence, made her at length return home; and she entered the house with the wish of appearing cheerful as usual, and the resolution of repressing such reflections as must make her unfit for conversation. She was immediately told, that the two gentlemen from Rosings had each called during her absence; Mr. Darcy, only for a few minutes to take leave, but that Colonel Fitzwilliam had been sitting with them at least an hour, hoping for her return, and almost resolving to walk after her till she could be found.—Elizabeth could but just *affect* concern in missing him; she really rejoiced at it. Colonel Fitzwilliam was no longer an object. She could think only of her letter.

Elizabeth spent two hours walking and thinking about recent events, considering different possibilities and trying to come to terms with the sudden and significant change. She returned home feeling tired and aware of her long absence. She wished to appear as usual and avoid thinking about anything that would make her unsuitable for conversation. She was informed that both Mr. Darcy and Colonel Fitzwilliam had visited during her absence. Mr. Darcy only came to say goodbye, but Colonel Fitzwilliam had been waiting for her for an hour, considering following her until she returned. Elizabeth only pretended to be concerned about missing him; she was actually glad to hear it. Her focus was solely on the letter she had received from Mr. Darcy.

CHAPTER 37

The two gentlemen left Rosings the next morning and Mr. Collins having been in waiting near the lodges to bid them farewell was able to bring home the good news that they seemed to be in good health, and in as tolerable spirits as could be expected, considering the melancholy scene so lately had just gone through at Rosings. To Rosings he then hastened, to console Lady Catherine and her daughter; and on his return, brought back with great satisfaction, a message from her Ladyship saying that she was so dull as to make her very desirous of have them all over for dinner.

Elizabeth could not see Lady Catherine without, had she chosen to, she could hardly help thinking of Miss de Bourgh as Catherine as her future niece, nor without a smile coming to her face, as she wondered what Lady Catherine's response would have been.

Their initial topic of conversation was the decrease in the number of guests at Rosings. "I can assure you that I feel it very much," said Lady Catherine. "I believe no one feels the loss of friends as much as I do. But I am particularly fond of these young men and I know that they are equally fond of me. They were extremely sorry to leave! But they always are. The dear Colonel managed to keep his spirits up reasonably well until the very end, but Darcy seemed to feel it most keenly, more so than last year. His attachment to Rosings is certainly growing stronger."

Mr. Collins had something to say that was complimentary and hinted at something else, and both remarks were received warmly by the mother and daughter.

After dinner, Lady Catherine noticed that Miss Bennet appeared downcast. She quickly assumed that it was because Miss Bennet did not want to leave so soon and said, "But if that is the case, you must write to your mother and request to stay a little longer. I am sure Mrs. Collins would be delighted to have your company."

Elizabeth replied, "I am very grateful for your invitation, your ladyship, but I cannot accept it. I must be in town next Saturday."

Lady Catherine responded, "At that rate, you will have only been here for six weeks. I expected you to stay for two months. I had told Mrs. Collins so before you arrived. There is no need for you to leave so soon. Mrs. Bennet could certainly spare you for another two weeks."

"But my father cannot," Elizabeth said. "He wrote to me last week, urging me to return home."

Lady Catherine replied, "Your father can spare you if your mother can. Daughters are never as important to a father. If you stay another month, I can take one of you to London. I'm going there early in June for a week and there will be plenty of room in the carriage. If it's cool, I wouldn't mind taking both of you, since you're not very big."

"You're so kind, Lady Catherine, but we must stick to our plan."

Lady Catherine seemed resigned. "Mrs. Collins, you must send a servant with them. I can't stand the idea of two young women travelling alone by post. It's not right. You must arrange for someone to accompany them. I hate that sort of thing. Young women should always be properly looked after and accompanied, depending on their station in life. When my niece Georgiana went to Ramsgate last summer, I made sure she had two male servants accompanying her. It would not have been appropriate for Miss Darcy, the daughter of Mr. Darcy of Pemberley, and Lady Anne, to go any other way. I'm very particular about these kinds of things. You should send John with the young ladies, Mrs. Collins. I'm glad I thought of it, it would have been embarrassing for you to let them go alone."

"My uncle is going to send a servant for us."

"Oh! Your uncle has a man-servant? I'm glad someone is looking out for those details. Where are you changing horses? Oh, of course, Bromley. If you mention my name at the Bell, they'll take care of you."

Lady Catherine had many more questions about their journey, and since she didn't answer them all herself, Elizabeth had to pay attention. She was grateful for this, as otherwise, with her mind so preoccupied, she might have forgotten where she was. Reflection had to be kept for when she was alone; whenever she was by herself, she welcomed it as a great relief; and not a single day passed by without her taking a solitary walk, where she could indulge in all the pleasure of unpleasant memories.

She was well on her way to being able to recite Mr. Darcy's letter from memory. She analyzed every sentence: and her feelings towards its writer fluctuated greatly. When she recalled the way he had addressed her, she was still filled with indignation; but when she thought about how unfairly she had judged and scolded him, her anger turned to herself; and his thwarted emotions became an object of pity. His affection gave her a sense of gratitude, and his overall character was respected; but she could not approve of him; nor could she for a single moment regret her refusal, or feel the slightest desire to ever see him again. In her own past behavior, there was a constant source of frustration and remorse; and in the unfortunate flaws of her family, a source of even greater distress. There was no way to fix them. Her father, contented with just laughing at them, would never put in any effort to stop the wild behavior of his youngest daughters; and her mother, with her own manners being far from proper, was completely oblivious to the wrongness of it. Elizabeth and Jane had often tried to stop the foolishness of Catherine and Lydia, but as long as their mother let them get away with it, what chance was there of them changing? Catherine, having no strength of character, being easily irritated and completely under Lydia's control, would always take offence when they tried to give her advice; and

Lydia, being stubborn and careless, would not even listen to them. They were ignorant, lazy, and vain. Whenever there was an officer in Meryton, they would flirt with him; and as long as Meryton was within walking distance of Longbourn, they would be going there all the time.

The prevailing concern was anxiety for Jane, and Mr. Darcy's explanation had only made matters worse by reminding them of all that Jane had lost. However, it also restored Bingley to the good graces of the group, as it proved that his affection for Jane had been genuine, and his behavior was no longer in question, except for perhaps his unwavering trust in his friend.

It was a sorrowful thought that Jane had been denied a situation that was so desirable in every way, filled with advantages, and promising happiness, all due to the foolishness and impropriety of her own family.

When these memories were combined with the revelation of Wickham's true character, it was no surprise that Jane's usually cheerful disposition was so adversely affected that it was almost impossible for her to appear happy.

They kept their engagements at Rosings during the last week of Jane's stay, and on the very last evening, Lady Catherine again asked for details about their journey, gave them instructions about the best way to pack, and was so insistent that the gowns should be packed in a certain way that Maria had to unpack her trunk and repack it when she returned.

When they parted, Lady Catherine, with great politeness, wished them a safe journey and invited them to come to Hunsford again next year; and Miss De Bourgh made an effort to curtsey and hold out her hand to both of them.

CHAPTER 38

On Saturday morning Elizabeth and Mr. Collins met for breakfast a few minutes before the others arrived; and he took the opportunity to express his appreciation for her visit.

"I do not know, Miss Elizabeth," said he, "whether Mrs. Collins has expressed her gratitude for your kind visit, but I am certain that you will not leave our house without her thanks. We are very aware of how little there is to encourage anyone to come to our humble home. Our plain lifestyle, small rooms, few servants, and lack of contact with the outside world must make Hunsford seem very dull to a young lady like yourself; but I hope you will believe us to be grateful for your presence, and that we have done our best to make your stay enjoyable."

Elizabeth was grateful and expressed her happiness. She had enjoyed her six weeks at Hunsford tremendously, and felt indebted to Charlotte for her kind attentions. Mr. Collins was pleased and replied with a more cheerful tone,

"I am delighted to hear that you had a pleasant time. We did our best to ensure it, and fortunately, we were able to introduce you to high society. Thanks to our connection to Rosings, we had many opportunities to provide some variety to your stay in this humble home. I hope you didn't find your visit to Hunsford too dull. Our relationship with Lady Catherine's family is indeed an extraordinary advantage and a blessing that few can boast of. You can see how close we are with them and how frequently we engage with them. Despite the disadvantages of living in this small parsonage, I do not believe anyone living here should be pitied as long as they share our intimacy with Rosings."

Words were not enough to express his feelings, so he paced around the room while Elizabeth attempted to combine politeness and honesty in a few short sentences.

"My dear cousin, you can give a very positive report of us in Hertfordshire. At least, I hope you can. You have seen Lady Catherine's great attentions to Mrs. Collins every day. I trust that it does not seem as though your friend has had an unfortunate experience, but it's best not to say any more on this subject. I only want to assure you, Miss Elizabeth, that I wholeheartedly wish you the same happiness in marriage that I have found with my dear Charlotte. We share one mind and one way of thinking. There is an extraordinary resemblance between us in character and ideas. It's as if we were made for each other."

Elizabeth happily agreed that it was a great happiness to have such a strong connection and believed, with equal sincerity, that he had found comfort in his domestic life. She was, however, relieved when their conversation was interrupted by the arrival of the lady who was the subject of their discussion.

Elizabeth felt sorry for poor Charlotte, who had to endure such company, but she had chosen to marry Mr. Collins with her eyes wide open. Even though she clearly regretted their departure, Charlotte did not seem to be asking for pity. Her home, her household management, her parish, her chickens, and all of their related concerns had not lost their appeal.

Finally, the chaise arrived, the trunks were secured, and the parcels were placed inside. After an affectionate farewell between the friends, Mr. Collins accompanied Elizabeth to the carriage. As they walked down the garden, he asked her to convey his best regards to her entire family, thanking them for their kindness during his winter stay at Longbourn. He also extended his compliments to Mr. and Mrs. Gardiner, despite not knowing them. After helping Elizabeth into the carriage, Maria followed, and as the door was about to close, Mr. Collins suddenly remembered, with some panic, that they had forgotten to leave a message for the ladies of Rosings.

"But," he quickly added, "you will surely want to send your humble regards and grateful thanks to them for their kindness during your stay here."

Elizabeth had no objections, and the door was closed before the carriage drove away.

After a few minutes of silence, Maria exclaimed, "Goodness gracious! It feels like we've only just arrived, and yet so much has happened!"

"Yes, indeed," replied her companion with a sigh.

"We've dined nine times at Rosings, and had tea there twice as well! I've got so much to tell you!"

Elizabeth thought to herself, "But I've also got so much to keep to myself."

They didn't talk much during their journey, and after four hours they arrived at Mr. Gardiner's house, where they were going to stay for a few days.

Jane seemed to be doing well, and Elizabeth didn't get a chance to really observe her spirits, because of all the activities her aunt had planned for them. But Jane was going back home with Elizabeth, and at Longbourn they would have plenty of time for observation.

Elizabeth was finding it hard to wait until they got to Longbourn before she told Jane about Mr. Darcy's proposal. She knew that she had the power to tell Jane something that would shock her greatly, but also something that would make her feel very pleased with herself. She couldn't decide how much to tell her, and was scared that if she started talking about it, she would end up saying something about Bingley that would make her sister even more upset.

CHAPTER 39

It was the second week of May when the three young ladies departed together from Gracechurch Street to travel to the town in Hertfordshire. As they approached the designated inn where Mr. Bennet's carriage was to meet them, they saw Kitty and Lydia eagerly peering out of an upstairs dining room, a clear indication of the coachman's punctuality. The two girls had been at the inn for over an hour, happily occupied with a visit to a nearby milliner, watching the guard on duty, and preparing a salad and cucumber.

After welcoming their sisters, they proudly showed them a table filled with cold meat, like what you'd usually find in an inn, and exclaimed, "Isn't this nice? Isn't this a pleasant surprise?"

"And we plan to treat you all," Lydia added, "but you'll have to lend us the money, because we just spent ours at the shop out there." Then she showed them her purchases: "Look at this bonnet. I don't think it's very attractive, but I figured I might as well buy it. As soon as I get home, I'll take it apart and see if I can make it look better."

When her sisters said it was ugly, she replied, completely unconcerned, "Oh, there were two or three even uglier ones in the shop. Once I buy some prettier-colored satin to trim it with, I think it'll be alright. Besides, it won't really matter what we wear this summer, once the regiments have left Meryton, and that's in two weeks."

"Really?" Elizabeth said, delighted.

"They are going to camp near Brighton, and I really want Father to take us all there for the summer! It would be such a fantastic plan and I don't think it would cost much at all. Mother would love to go too! Just imagine what an awful summer we'll have otherwise!"

Elizabeth thought to herself, "Yes, that would be a truly wonderful plan and it would solve everything for us. Goodness me! Brighton and an entire camp of soldiers, for us, who were already overwhelmed by just one poor regiment of militia and the monthly balls in Meryton."

"I've got some news for you," said Lydia as they sat down to eat. "Guess what? It's really good news and it's about someone we all like."

Jane and Elizabeth looked at each other and told the waiter he could go. Lydia laughed and said,

"Ha, that's just like you two being so formal. You thought the waiter couldn't hear us, like he would care! I'm sure he's heard much worse. But he's ugly! I'm glad he's gone. I've never seen such a long chin in my life. Anyway, my news is about Wickham. Isn't it too good for the waiter? Mary King isn't going to marry him. There you go! She's gone to stay with her uncle in Liverpool so Wickham is safe."

"And Mary King is safe!" Elizabeth added. "Safe from a connection that would have been bad for her finances."

"She's a real idiot for leaving if she liked him," said Jane.

"But I hope there's no strong feelings from either side," Jane said.

"I'm sure he wasn't interested in her at all. I guarantee he never cared about her, not even a little bit. Who could be interested in such a disgusting little freckled thing?"

Elizabeth was taken aback to realize that, although she herself was not capable of expressing such coarseness, the sentiment was not much different from what she had harbored in her own mind and had once considered to be liberal.

After the meal was finished and the elder members of the party had settled the bill, they ordered the carriage. With some maneuvering, they managed to fit the entire group, along with all of their luggage, workbags, and parcels, as well as Kitty's and Lydia's shopping, into the carriage.

"How tightly we are all packed in here!" shouted Lydia. "I'm glad I bought my bonnet, if only for the fun of having another box! Now let's be comfortable and cozy and have a good time talking and laughing on our way home. First, tell us what happened to all of you since you left. Did you see any interesting men? Did you do any flirting? I was really hoping one of you would have gotten married before you came back. Jane is going to be an old maid soon, I'm telling you. She's almost twenty-three! Lord, I'd be so embarrassed if I wasn't married by twenty-three! My aunt Philips really wants you to find husbands, you can't imagine. She says Lizzy should have taken Mr. Collins, but I don't think it would have been any fun. Wow, I'd love to be married before any of you; then I could chaperone you to all the balls. We had so much fun the other day at Colonel Forster's. Kitty and I were spending the day there and Mrs. Forster said she'd have a dance in the evening (we're such good friends!). So she asked the two Harringtons to come, but Harriet was sick so Pen had to come alone. And then, guess what we did? We dressed up Chamberlayne in women's clothes so he could pass as a lady - can you imagine how funny that was! No one knew about it except Colonel and Mrs. Forster, Kitty and me, and my aunt - we had to borrow one of her gowns. You can't believe how good he looked! Forster, Kitty and I, apart from my aunt, went in borrowed gowns; and you cannot imagine how handsome he looked! When Denny, Wickham, Pratt and a few other guys came in, they didn't recognize him at all. I couldn't help laughing, and neither could Mrs. Forster. I thought I was going to die! The men got suspicious, and soon realized what was going on".

With stories like these and funny jokes, Lydia, with help from Kitty's hints and additions, tried to entertain everyone on the way to Longbourn. Elizabeth tried to listen as little as possible, but she couldn't avoid hearing Wickham's name mentioned frequently.

When they arrived home, they were welcomed warmly. Mrs. Bennet was delighted to see Jane looking as beautiful as ever, and during dinner, Mr. Bennet said to Elizabeth more than once,

"I'm glad you're back, Lizzy."

They had a large group in the dining room, since almost all the Lucases had come to meet Maria and hear the news. Lady Lucas was asking Maria, on the other side of the table, how her eldest daughter was doing and how her poultry were. Mrs. Bennet was doing two things at once: getting the latest fashion news from Jane, who was sitting a bit further away, and then telling it all to the younger Miss Lucases. And Lydia was loudly telling everyone at the table about all the fun she had that morning.

"Oh, Mary," she said. "I wish you had come with us. We had so much fun! As we were going, Kitty and I pulled all the blinds down and pretended there was nobody in the coach. I would have kept doing that the whole way if Kitty hadn't been feeling sick. When we got to the George, I think we were really generous. We treated the other three to the nicest cold lunch you could imagine. If you had been there, we would have treated you too. On the way home, it was so funny! I thought I was going to die laughing. We talked and laughed so loud that you could have heard us from ten miles away!"

Mary replied very seriously, "I wouldn't want to put down such fun. I'm sure it would be enjoyable for most people. But it's not something I would enjoy. I would much rather have a book."

But Lydia didn't hear a word of this. She rarely paid attention to anyone for more than half a minute and never paid any attention to Mary at all.

In the afternoon Lydia was very keen for the other girls to go to Meryton and see what was happening, but Elizabeth was firmly against it. She didn't want it to be said that the Miss Bennets couldn't stay at home for half a day before they were off chasing the officers. She also had another reason for not wanting to go - she was dreading seeing Wickham again and was determined to avoid it for as long as possible. The thought of the regiment leaving in two weeks was a huge comfort to her, and she was sure that once they were gone, she would be free from worrying about him.

After arriving home, it didn't take long for Elizabeth to realize that the Brighton plan, which Lydia had mentioned at the inn, was being frequently discussed by her parents. Elizabeth could tell that her father had no intention of giving in, but his responses were so ambiguous and noncommittal that her mother, despite becoming disheartened at times, had not yet given up hope of convincing him.

CHAPTER 40

Elizabeth couldn't contain her urge to tell Jane what had happened any longer, and so, deciding to leave out any details that involved her sister, she told Jane the main points of the conversation between Mr. Darcy and herself the next morning.

Miss Bennet's astonishment quickly diminished when she realized that Elizabeth's admiration of Mr. Darcy was only natural due to her strong sisterly love, and any surprise was soon replaced by other emotions. She was sorry that Mr. Darcy had expressed his feelings in a way that didn't make them sound very appealing, but she was even more upset by the unhappiness that her sister's rejection must have caused him.

"His assurance of succeeding was wrong," she said. "And he should not have acted in such a way. But imagine how much more disappointed he will be now."

"I really feel sorry for him," Elizabeth said. "But he will soon have other feelings that will make him forget me. Do you think I was wrong to refuse him?"

"No, of course not."

"Do you think I was wrong to speak so highly of Wickham?"

"No, I don't think you were wrong."

"Let me tell you what happened the very next day."

She then talked about the letter, reciting the entire content that pertained to George Wickham. This was a heavy blow for poor Jane, who would have preferred to go through life without believing that so much evil existed in all of humanity, as was found in this one individual. Although Darcy's defense was appreciated by her, it was not enough to console her for such a revelation. She worked fervently to prove that there was a possibility of a mistake, and tried to clear one person's name without implicating the other.

"This won't do," said Elizabeth. "You will never be able to make both of them good for anything. Choose one, but you must be satisfied with just one. There is only enough merit between them to make one good man, and lately it has been shifting back and forth quite a bit. For my part, I am inclined to believe it is all Mr. Darcy's doing, but you can do as you please."

It took some time, however, before Jane could be coaxed into a smile.

"I don't know when I've been more shocked," she said. "Wickham is so very bad! It's almost unbelievable. And poor Mr. Darcy! Dear Lizzy, think about what he must have suffered. Such a disappointment, and with the knowledge of your poor opinion too! And having to reveal such a thing about his sister! It's truly too distressing. I'm sure you must feel it too."

"Oh no, my regret and sympathy are gone now that I see you feeling them so strongly. Your generosity makes me more frugal; and if you keep lamenting over him, my heart will be as light as a feather."

"Poor Wickham; there is such kindness in his face! Such openness and gentleness in his manner."

"Clearly there was something wrong with the way those two young men were raised. One has all the goodness and the other all the appearance of it."

"I never thought Mr. Darcy was so lacking in the appearance of it like you used to."

"And yet I was trying to be really clever in having such a strong dislike for him without any reason. It's such an encouragement to one's intelligence, such an opportunity for wit to have that kind of dislike. You can be constantly critical without saying anything right; but you can't keep making fun of a man without occasionally coming up with something funny."

"Lizzy, when you first read that letter, I'm sure you didn't look at it the same way you do now."

"No, I couldn't. I was really uneasy. I was very uncomfortable, I can say, I was unhappy. And with no one to talk to about how I felt, no Jane to comfort me and tell me I hadn't been so weak and vain and silly as I knew I had been! Oh, how I wished you were here!"

"It's too bad you said such harsh things about Wickham to Mr. Darcy, since it seems now that they weren't deserved."

"Yes, that was unfortunate. But it's a natural consequence of the bad opinion I had of him. I wanted to ask your advice about something. Should I tell everyone else what Wickham's really like?"

Miss Bennet paused for a moment and then said, "I don't think you should expose him like that. What do you think?"

"I think it shouldn't be done. Mr. Darcy didn't authorize me to tell anyone else about his sister. He wanted me to keep it to myself. Besides, the general opinion of Mr. Darcy is so negative that if I tried to show him in a better light, it would ruin the reputations of a lot of people in Meryton. I'm not brave enough to do that. Wickham will be gone soon, so it won't matter to anyone here what he's really like. Eventually, everyone will find out and we'll laugh at how ignorant they were. I won't say anything about it now."

"You're right, if his mistakes were made public, it could ruin him. He may be regretful now and trying to restore his reputation."

This conversation helped Elizabeth to calm down. She had shared two of the secrets that had been on her mind for two weeks, and knew she could talk to Jane about them whenever she wanted. But there was still something else she couldn't tell anyone. She was too afraid to tell Jane the rest of Mr. Darcy's letter, or how much he valued her. She knew that only if there was a perfect understanding between them could she let go of this secret. "And even then," she thought, "if that highly unlikely event ever happens, I'll just be able to tell what Bingley can say in a much more pleasant way himself. I won't be able to share this news until it's lost all its value!"

Now that she was home, she had time to see how Jane really felt. Jane was not happy. She still had strong feelings for Bingley. Having never been in love before, she had a strong fondness for him and was more stable than usual for someone in her situation; she treasured his memory so much and preferred him to any other man that she had to use all her common sense and be mindful of her friends' feelings to stop herself from getting too sad, which would have been detrimental to her health and their peace.

Mrs. Bennet asked her one day, "Lizzy, what do you think of this sad affair with Jane now? I told my sister Philips the other day that I'm never going to talk about it with anyone ever again. I haven't heard that Jane saw him in London either. He's an undeserving young man and I don't think there's any chance of her getting him back now. There's no talk of him coming back to Netherfield in the summer and I've asked around to see if anyone knows."

"It's his choice. Nobody's forcing him to come back. But I'll always say he treated my daughter terribly and if I was her, I wouldn't have put up with it. The only thing that comforts me is that I'm sure Jane will die of a broken heart and then he'll be sorry for what he's done."

Elizabeth didn't respond to that.

"Well, Lizzy," her mother continued soon after, "so the Collinses are living comfortably, are they? Well, well, I hope it will continue. And what kind of meals do they have? Charlotte is an excellent manager, I'm sure. If she's half as clever as her mother, she's saving plenty. I don't think there's anything extravagant in their household."

"No, nothing at all."

"It's all about good management, mark my words. Yes, yes. They'll make sure not to overspend. They'll never be short of money. Well, I hope it serves them well! And so I suppose they often discuss inheriting Longbourn when your father dies. I'm sure they see it as their own whenever that happens."

"It was a topic they couldn't discuss in my presence."

"Of course not. It would have been odd if they had. But I have no doubt they often talk about it in private. Well, if they can be content with an estate that doesn't rightfully belong to them, all the better for them. I'd be ashamed to have an inheritance that was only legally mine."

CHAPTER 41

The first week back had gone by quickly. The second was beginning. It was the last week the regiment was in Meryton and all the young ladies in the area were feeling down. The sadness was almost universal. The elder Miss Bennets were still able to eat, drink, sleep and do their usual activities. Kitty and Lydia often criticized them for being unfeeling, since their own misery was so great and they couldn't understand such lack of compassion from anyone in the family.

"Oh, what will become of us! What should we do!" they often exclaimed in despair. "How can you smile, Lizzy?"

Their loving mother shared their sorrow and remembered the pain she had endured twenty-five years ago on a similar occasion.

"I cried for two whole days when Colonel Millar's regiment left," she said. "I thought my heart would break."

"I'm sure mine will break," said Lydia.

"If only we could go to Brighton!" Mrs. Bennet exclaimed.

"Yes, if only we could go to Brighton! But Papa is so disagreeable."

"A little sea-bathing would rejuvenate me," said Mrs. Bennet.

"And my aunt Phillips is certain it would do me a world of good," added Kitty.

There were constant laments of this kind echoing perpetually through Longbourn house. Elizabeth tried to be entertained by them, but she felt no pleasure and was only embarrassed. She felt anew the fairness of Mr. Darcy's objections; and never before had she been so willing to forgive his interference in his friend's plans.

But Lydia's dismal outlook was soon brightened; for she received an invitation from Mrs. Forster, the wife of the Colonel of the regiment, to go to Brighton with her. This invaluable friend was a very young woman, and had recently been married. They had become close friends in the three months they had known each other.

Lydia was ecstatic on this occasion, adoring Mrs. Forster, while Mrs. Bennet was overjoyed and Kitty was mortified. Completely disregarding her sister's feelings, Lydia roamed around the house in a restless frenzy, seeking everyone's congratulations and laughing and talking more forcefully than ever. Meanwhile, the unfortunate Kitty remained in the parlor, complaining about her fate in terms that were as unreasonable as her tone was irritable.

"I don't see why Mrs. Forster can't invite me too," she said, "even though we're not that close. I have just as much right to be asked as she does, and more too, since I'm two years older."

But Elizabeth's attempts to make her mother and Lydia be reasonable and resigned were in vain. Elizabeth herself didn't feel the same excitement as her mother and Lydia about the invitation and thought it would be the death of Lydia's common sense. Even though she knew it would be seen as detestable, she couldn't help secretly advising her father not to let Lydia go. She told him about Lydia's general behavior and the little advantage she would get from the friendship of Mrs. Forster, and the likelihood of her being even more imprudent if she went to Brighton, where the temptations would be greater than at home. He listened to her carefully and then said,

"Lydia will never be content until she has done something outrageous in public, and it would be too much to expect her to do it without putting her family out of pocket."

Elizabeth replied, "If you knew the harm that has already come from Lydia's reckless and thoughtless behavior, you would think differently about the situation." Mr. Bennet said,

"Already done harm? What, has she scared away some of your admirers? Poor Lizzy! Don't be too upset. Anyone who can't put up with a bit of foolishness isn't worth worrying about. Come on, let me see the list of these poor fellows who have been scared off by Lydia's foolishness."

"You're mistaken. I'm not angry about any particular person, I'm talking about the general damage that has been done. Our standing in society is affected by Lydia's wild behavior and her disregard for any kind of restraint. Excuse me, I must be blunt. If you, my dear father, don't take the time to reign in her reckless behavior and remind her that her current activities are not to be her life's work, she will soon be too far gone to be corrected. Her character will be set and at sixteen she will be the most determined flirt that ever brought shame to her family. A flirt in the worst and most despicable way, with nothing to recommend her beyond her youth and looks, and with her mind being too empty to protect herself from the scorn that her need for attention will bring. Kitty is also in danger of this. She will follow Lydia wherever she goes. Vain, ignorant, idle, and completely out of control. Oh my dear father, can you really believe that they won't be looked down upon and despised wherever they go and that their sisters won't be dragged into the shame?"

Mr. Bennet, seeing that she was truly passionate about the matter, affectionately took her hand and said,

"Don't worry my love. Wherever you and Jane are known you will be respected and valued, and you won't appear any less favorable for having a couple of—or I should say, three, very silly sisters. We won't have any peace at Longbourn if Lydia doesn't go to Brighton. Let her go then. Colonel Forster is a sensible man, and he will keep her out of any real trouble; and luckily she is too poor to be a target for anyone. At Brighton she will be less noteworthy even as a common flirt than she was here. The officers will find women who are more worthy of their attention. Let us hope, then, that her being there may teach her her own worthlessness. At any rate, she can't become much worse, without us having to lock her up for the rest of her life."

With this response Elizabeth had to be content; but her own opinion stayed the same, and she left him disappointed and sorry. However, it was not in her character to worsen her frustrations by thinking about them. She was sure she had done her duty, and she didn't want to make her troubles worse by worrying about them.

If Lydia and her mother had known what she had talked about with her father, they would have been very angry. Lydia thought that going to Brighton would be the best thing ever. She imagined the streets full of officers and herself as the center of attention, surrounded by them. She imagined the camps, with their tents in neat lines and everyone dressed in bright colors. She imagined herself sitting under a tent, flirting with six officers at once.

If she had known that her sister was trying to stop her from having these experiences, she would have been very upset. Her mother would have understood how she felt. Lydia's trip to Brighton was the only thing that cheered her up, despite her husband's refusal to go with her.

They were completely unaware of what had happened, and they stayed excited until the day Lydia left.

Elizabeth was now going to see Mr. Wickham for the last time. She had been around him often since her return, so her initial excitement had worn off. She had even started to notice the artificiality and monotony of his behavior which had once charmed her. Additionally, his attempts to rekindle their old relationship only served to anger her, given the circumstances. She completely lost interest in him when she realized he was flirting with her out of boredom and vanity; and while she tried to hide her feelings, she couldn't help but be offended that he thought she would be so easily swayed by his attention.

On the last day of the regiment's stay in Meryton, he ate dinner with the other officers at Longbourn. Elizabeth was not in a good mood when it came time to part ways, so when he asked her how her time at Hunsford had been, she mentioned that Colonel Fitzwilliam and Mr. Darcy had both spent three weeks at Rosings.

He looked surprised, displeased, and alarmed, but then recovered and said he had seen him often before and that he was a very polite man. He then asked her what she thought of him, and she gave a positive response. With a nonchalant expression, he then asked, "How long did you say he stayed at Rosings?"

"Almost three weeks," she replied.

"And you saw him often?"

"Yes, almost every day."

"His manners are so different from his cousin's."

"Yes, very different. But I think Mr. Darcy gets better the more you get to know him."

"Really?" exclaimed Wickham with a look that Elizabeth noticed. "May I ask how?" he asked, but then quickly changed the subject, "Has he at least been more polite in his manner?" He continued in a more serious tone, "I can't hope that he's changed in any other way."

"Oh, no!" exclaimed Elizabeth. "I believe that, in the most important aspects, he is still very much the same person he has always been."

As Elizabeth spoke, Wickham appeared unsure whether to be pleased or suspicious of her words. There was something in her expression that made him listen with apprehension and anxiety as she continued,

"When I remarked that he improved on acquaintance, I did not intend to suggest that his mind or manners were undergoing any sort of improvement. Rather, I meant that as I got to know him better, I began to understand his true disposition more clearly."

Wickham's face flushed and he looked anxious. He was quiet for a few moments, then he spoke again in a gentle voice,

"As you are well aware of my feelings towards Mr. Darcy, you will understand how genuinely I must rejoice that he is wise enough to at least appear to do what is right. His pride, in this regard, may serve a useful purpose, if not for himself, then for many others, as it may deter him from engaging in the kind of despicable behavior I have personally suffered from. However, I fear that the caution to which you referred earlier is only put on when he visits his aunt, as he greatly values her good opinion and judgment. I know that he has always been afraid of her when they are together, and much of his behavior can be attributed to his desire to promote a match with Miss De Bourgh, which I am certain is of great importance to him."

Elizabeth couldn't help but smile at this, but she only nodded slightly in response. She could tell that he wanted to bring up the old topic of his grievances, but she wasn't in the mood to entertain him. The rest of the evening passed with him putting on a façade of his usual cheerfulness, but without any further attempt to engage with Elizabeth. Finally, they parted ways with mutual civility, and perhaps with a mutual desire to never see each other again.

When the party dispersed, Lydia returned with Mrs. Forster to Meryton, from where they were to set out early the next morning. The separation between her and her family was more noisy than emotional. Kitty was the only one who shed tears, but they were tears of vexation and envy. Mrs. Bennet expressed her good wishes for her daughter's happiness and strongly advised her not to miss any opportunities to enjoy herself, advice which there was every reason to believe Lydia would follow. Amidst Lydia's noisy joy in saying goodbye, her sisters' more subdued farewells went unheard.

CHAPTER 42

If Elizabeth had only taken her cues from her own family, she wouldn't have had a very positive view of marriage and domestic life. Her father, captivated by youth and beauty, had married a woman whose weak understanding and illiberal mind had extinguished any real affection between them. Respect, esteem, and confidence had been lost forever and all his hopes of a happy home life were destroyed. Mr. Bennet, however, was not one to seek consolation in the usual vices and pleasures of the unfortunate. He was fond of the countryside and reading; these were his main sources of pleasure. He was only really indebted to his wife in that her ignorance and foolishness provided him with some amusement. This is not the kind of happiness that a man would usually want to owe to his wife, but when there are no other sources of entertainment, a true philosopher will take what they can get.

Elizabeth had always been aware of her father's inappropriate behavior as a husband, and it caused her pain. However, she respected his abilities and was grateful for his affectionate treatment of her, so she tried to ignore what she couldn't overlook and to put out of her mind the continual breach of marital duty and propriety which was so wrong, as it made his wife the object of her children's contempt. But she had never felt so strongly as now, the disadvantages which must come with the children of such an unsuitable marriage, nor ever been so aware of the problems that come with such poor decisions about using talents; talents that if used properly could have at least kept the respectability of his daughters, even if they could not have improved his wife's mind.

When Elizabeth was glad that Wickham had gone, she found little else to be happy about with the regiment leaving. Their activities outside the home were not as varied as before; and at home she had a mother and sister who constantly complained about the dullness of everything around them, casting a real gloom over their family life; and, though Kitty might eventually recover her sense of reason now that the things that confused her mind were gone, her other sister, from whom even greater trouble could be expected, was likely to become even more confident and foolish in a place like a beach resort and a military camp. Altogether, she found what has been found before; that an event she had been eagerly looking forward to did not bring the satisfaction she had expected. So she had to set a different time for when she would start to be truly happy, and have something new to look forward to, to make up for her current unhappiness caused by her mother and Kitty. Her tour to the Lakes was now the source of her happiest thoughts, and was the best way to make up for the uncomfortable hours. If Jane could have come along, everything would have been perfect. But, she thought, it was a good thing that she had something to hope for; if everything had worked out, she would have been certain to be disappointed. By having the constant reminder of Jane not being there, she could reasonably hope that all her expectations of pleasure would be fulfilled.

"But it's fortunate," she thought to herself, "that I have something to look forward to. If the entire plan were complete, my disappointment would be inevitable. However, by bringing with me the constant source of regret that comes with my sister's absence, I can reasonably expect to have all my hopes of enjoyment fulfilled. A plan in which every part promises delight can never truly succeed, and general disappointment can only be avoided by the presence of some small, specific annoyance."

Lydia went away, promising to write often and in detail to her mother and Kitty. But her letters were always long awaited and always very short. Those to her mother contained little else than that they had just returned from the library with some officers in attendance and that she had seen some beautiful ornaments that made her go wild; that she had a new gown or parasol which she would have described more but had to stop in a hurry as Mrs. Forster called her and they were off to the camp. Her letters to Kitty were slightly longer but still full of lines under the words.

After her absence of a two or three weeks, health, good spirits, and cheerfulness began to return to Longbourn. Everything seemed happier. The families who had spent the winter in town returned, and summer finery and engagements emerged. Mrs. Bennet regained her usual querulous serenity, and by mid-June, Kitty had recovered enough to be able to go to Meryton without tears. This was such a happy development that Elizabeth hoped that by the following Christmas, Kitty would be reasonably well-behaved and not mention an officer more than once a day, unless some cruel and malicious arrangement at the War Office resulted in another regiment being quartered in Meryton.

The time for the start of their Northern tour was fast approaching, and only a two weeks remained when a letter arrived from Mrs. Gardiner that both delayed and reduced the tour's duration. Mr. Gardiner's business commitments would prevent him from leaving for another two weeks in July, and he needed to be back in London within a month. Given the short amount of time left, they could not go as far or see as much as they had planned, nor do it with the leisure and comfort they had hoped for. Therefore, they were obliged to give up the Lakes and instead settle for a more restricted tour that would take them no farther north than Derbyshire. There was enough to see in that county to occupy the majority of their three weeks, and it held a particularly strong attraction for Mrs. Gardiner. The town where she had previously spent several years of her life and where they would now stay for a few days was probably as fascinating to her as all the renowned beauties of Matlock, Chatsworth, Dovedale, or the Peak.

Elizabeth was extremely disappointed as she had set her heart on seeing the Lakes and still believed there was enough time. However, it was her responsibility to be content, and she certainly had the temperament to be happy, so everything was soon right again.

The mention of Derbyshire triggered many thoughts for her. She couldn't see the word without thinking of Pemberley and its owner. "But surely," she thought to herself, "I can enter his county without consequence and take a few petrified spars without him noticing."

The waiting period was now doubled. Four weeks had to pass before her uncle and aunt's arrival. But they did pass, and Mr. and Mrs. Gardiner, with their four children, eventually arrived at Longbourn. The two girls, aged six and eight, and the two younger boys were to be under the particular care of their cousin Jane, who was the general favorite. Her steady sense and sweet temperament made her perfectly suited to attend to them in every way, teaching them, playing with them, and loving them.

The purpose of this work is not to provide a description of Derbyshire or any of the remarkable places on the way there, such as Oxford, Blenheim, Warwick, Kenilworth, Birmingham, and so on, as these are well-known enough. Only a small part of Derbyshire is currently relevant. After seeing all the principal wonders of the country, they headed towards the little town of Lambton, where Mrs. Gardiner used to live and where she had recently discovered that she still had some acquaintances. Elizabeth learned from her aunt that Pemberley was situated within five miles of Lambton, although it was not directly on their route and only a mile or two out of it. When they discussed their itinerary the evening before, Mrs. Gardiner expressed a desire to see Pemberley again. Mr. Gardiner declared his willingness to do so, and Elizabeth was asked for her approval.

"My love, wouldn't you like to see a place that you have heard so much about?" her aunt asked. "And a place where so many of your acquaintances have connections to. You know Wickham spent his youth there."

Elizabeth was distressed. She felt she had no right to be at Pemberley and had to pretend she wasn't interested in seeing it.

She admitted she was bored of visiting grand houses; after seeing so many, she didn't get any pleasure from looking at fancy carpets and silk curtains.

Mrs. Gardiner scolded her for being so silly. "If it was just a beautiful house with nice furniture, I wouldn't be interested," she said. "But the grounds are gorgeous. It has some of the best woods in the country."

Elizabeth didn't say anymore but she couldn't agree. The thought of possibly running into Mr. Darcy while exploring the place made her blush. She thought it would be better to be honest with her aunt than to take such a risk. But despite this, there were objections; and she eventually decided it could be a last resort, if her private investigations into the family's absence gave her an unfavorable response.

So, when she went to bed, she asked the chambermaid if Pemberley was a nice place, what the owner's name was, and - with some alarm - if the family were there for the summer. Much to her relief, the last question was answered in the negative - and with her worries gone, she was eager to see the house for herself; and when the subject was brought up the next morning, and she was asked again, she could quickly answer, and with a suitable air of indifference, that she didn't really have any problem with the plan.

So, off to Pemberley they went.

CHAPTER 43

Elizabeth, as they drove along, was anxiously looking out for the first sight of Pemberley Woods and when they finally arrived at the entrance, she was extremely excited.

The park was very large and had a lot of different areas. They drove in at one of the lowest points and drove through a beautiful wood for a while.

Elizabeth's mind was too preoccupied for conversation, but she observed and admired every remarkable spot and viewpoint. They gradually ascended for half a mile and then found themselves at the top of a considerable hill where the forest ended, and Pemberley House instantly caught their eye on the opposite side of a valley, into which the road wound abruptly. It was a large, attractive, stone building situated on rising ground, backed by a ridge of tall, woody hills. In front of the house, a stream of some natural importance was swollen but without any artificial features. The banks were neither formal nor artificially adorned. Elizabeth was overjoyed. She had never seen a place where nature had done more or where natural beauty had been so little disrupted by awkward taste. They were all warmly admiring the scene, and at that moment Elizabeth felt that being the mistress of Pemberley would be quite something!

They descended the hill, crossed the bridge, and drove up to the door. As they examined the house's nearer aspect, all of Elizabeth's fears of meeting its owner returned. She feared that the chambermaid had been mistaken. When they asked to see the place, they were allowed into the hall, and Elizabeth had time to ponder how she found herself there as they waited for the housekeeper.

The housekeeper arrived, an older, respectable-looking woman who was much less fancy and more polite than

Elizabeth had expected. They followed her into the dining room. It was a large, well-proportioned room that was nicely decorated. Elizabeth glanced around before going to the window to admire the view. The hill, covered in trees, which they had just come down, looked even more impressive from a distance. Every aspect of the landscape was pleasing and she looked at the entire scene, the river, the trees scattered along its banks, and the winding of the valley as far as she could see it, with joy. As they moved into other rooms, the views outside changed, but from every window there were beautiful things to be seen. The rooms were high and attractive, and their furniture was appropriate to the wealth of their owner; but Elizabeth noticed, with admiration of his taste, that it was neither overly ornate nor excessively luxurious; with less showiness and more true elegance than the furniture of Rosings.

Her thoughts turned to what could have been, "I could have been the mistress of this place," she mused, "familiar with every room and taking pleasure in them as my own. I would have been able to welcome my uncle and aunt here as guests instead of feeling like a stranger. But alas," she recalled, "that was never a possibility. If I had become mistress of the place, my uncle and aunt would have been taken away from me. I would never have been allowed to invite them over."

This was a fortunate remembrance—it prevented her from feeling any regret.

She wanted to ask the housekeeper if her master was really away, but she was too scared. Eventually, her uncle asked the question, and Elizabeth was filled with dread as Mrs. Reynolds replied that he was, but that he was expected back the next day with a lot of friends. Elizabeth was so relieved that their journey hadn't been delayed a day.

Her aunt asked her to look at a picture, and when she did, she saw a likeness of Mr. Wickham hanging among several other miniatures over the mantle-piece. Her aunt asked her, smilingly, how she liked it. The housekeeper came forward and told them it was a picture of a young man who was the son of her late master's steward, and had been taken care of by him. She added that he had gone into the army, but was afraid he had turned out wild.

Mrs. Gardiner looked at her niece with a smile, but Elizabeth couldn't return it.

"And that," Mrs. Reynolds said, pointing to another miniature, "is my master, and it resembles him very closely. It was drawn about eight years ago, at the same time as the other."

"I've heard a lot about your master's good looks," Mrs. Gardiner remarked, looking at the picture. "It's a handsome face. But, Lizzy, you can tell us whether it resembles him or not."

Mrs. Reynolds appeared to have a higher regard for Elizabeth upon hearing that she knew her master.

"Does that young lady know Mr. Darcy?"

Elizabeth blushed and replied, "A little."

"Do you not think he is a very handsome gentleman, ma'am?" asked Mr. Gardiner.

"Yes, very handsome," Elizabeth replied.

"I am sure I know none so handsome. Upstairs in the gallery you will see a larger, finer picture of him. This room was my late master's favorite and these miniatures are just as they were when he was alive. He was very fond of them."

Elizabeth understood why Mr. Wickham was in the room.

Mrs. Reynolds then showed them a picture of Miss Darcy when she was eight years old.

"Is Miss Darcy as handsome as her brother?" asked Mr. Gardiner.

"Oh yes, she is the most beautiful young lady ever seen, and so accomplished! She plays and sings all day long. In the next room is a new instrument that my master got for her as a present; she's coming here tomorrow with him."

Mr. Gardiner, who had a friendly and agreeable demeanor, prompted her to speak more by asking questions and making comments. Mrs. Reynolds, either out of pride or attachment, clearly took great pleasure in discussing her master and his sister.

"Does your master spend much time at Pemberley during the year?" asked Mr. Gardiner.

"Not as much as I'd like, sir, but I'm sure he spends half his time here, and Miss Darcy always comes down for the summer months," said Mrs. Reynolds.

"Except when she goes to Ramsgate," thought Elizabeth.

"If your master were to get married, you'd see more of him," said Mr. Gardiner.

"Yes, sir, but I don't know when that will be. I don't know who would be good enough for him," said Mrs. Reynolds.

Mr. and Mrs. Gardiner smiled. Elizabeth couldn't help but say, "It's really to his credit that you think that way."

"I'm just speaking the truth, and what everyone who knows him would say," said Mrs. Reynolds.

Elizabeth thought this was going too far; and she listened with increasing shock as the housekeeper added, "I have never had an argument with him in my life, and I have known him since he was four years old."

This was praise, unlike anything she had heard before, completely opposite to her beliefs. That he was not a good-tempered man, had been her strongest opinion. Her curiosity was piqued; she wanted to hear more, and was thankful to her uncle for saying,

"There are very few people of whom so much can be said. You are fortunate to have such a master."

"Yes, Sir, I know I am. If I were to go through the world, I could not find a better. But I have always noticed, that those who are good-natured when they are young, are good-natured when they grow up; and he was always the most even-tempered, kindest-hearted, boy in the world."

Elizabeth was almost speechless. "Can this be Mr. Darcy!" she thought.

"His father was an excellent man," said Mrs. Gardiner.

"Yes, ma'am, he certainly was, and his son will be just like him, just as kind to the poor."

Elizabeth listened, but she was curious for more information. Mrs. Reynolds spoke about the pictures, the sizes of the rooms, and the cost of the furniture, but Elizabeth was not satisfied. Mr. Gardiner, amused by the family loyalty that Mrs. Reynolds had for her master, asked her more questions and she spoke with enthusiasm about his many merits as they walked up the staircase.

"He is the best landlord and the best master that ever lived," she said. "Not like the wild young men these days who only think of themselves. None of his tenants or servants will ever speak ill of him. Some people say he's proud, but I've never seen it. I think it's just because he doesn't talk as much as other young men."

Elizabeth thought to herself, "What a wonderful light this paints him in!"

"This favorable description of him," whispered her aunt as they walked, "doesn't quite match up with how he treated our poor friend."

"Maybe we got it wrong."

"That's unlikely; our source was reliable."

When they arrived in the large entryway upstairs, they were taken to a very pretty sitting room that had been recently decorated with more sophistication and brightness than the rooms below. They were told it had been done to please Miss Darcy, who had taken a liking to it when she had last visited Pemberley.

"He's certainly a good brother," said Elizabeth as she walked towards one of the windows.

Mrs. Reynolds knew Miss Darcy would be delighted when she saw the room. "And this is always how he is," she added. "Whatever will make his sister happy, he'll do it in a second. He wouldn't refuse her anything."

The picture gallery and two or three of the main bedrooms were the only remaining areas to be shown. The gallery contained many good paintings, but Elizabeth was ignorant of the art. From what she had already seen on the lower level, she was happy to look at some of Miss Darcy's crayon drawings, which were usually more interesting and understandable.

There were many family portraits in the gallery, but they would have held little interest for a stranger. Elizabeth continued to walk, searching for the only face whose features she knew. Finally, she found it - a striking resemblance of Mr. Darcy, with a smile on his face that she remembered seeing before when he looked at her. She stood in front of the picture for several minutes, lost in thought, and returned to it again before leaving the gallery. Mrs. Reynolds informed them that it had been painted during his father's lifetime.

At this moment, Elizabeth felt a kinder feeling towards Mr. Darcy than she ever had before, even during their previous acquaintance. Mrs. Reynolds' high praise of him was not insignificant, for what praise is more valuable than that of an intelligent servant? Elizabeth considered how many people's happiness depended on Mr. Darcy as a brother, landlord, and master. She also considered how much pleasure or pain he could bestow, and how much good or evil he had the power to do. Every idea that the housekeeper had presented about Mr. Darcy's character was favorable, and as Elizabeth looked at his portrait and caught his gaze upon her, she felt a deeper sense of gratitude for his regard and remembered its warmth and forgave any impropriety in its expression.

After seeing all of the parts of the house that were open for general inspection, they went back downstairs and said goodbye to the housekeeper. Then they were handed over to the gardener, who met them at the hall door.

As they walked across the lawn towards the river, Elizabeth looked back at the house. Her uncle and aunt also stopped and her uncle wondered about the date of the building. Suddenly, the owner of the house himself appeared from the road that led behind the house to the stables.

They were within twenty yards of each other, and his sudden appearance was unavoidable. When their eyes met, they both blushed deeply. He was shocked and stood still for a moment, but then he walked towards the group and spoke to Elizabeth with a polite and courteous tone, albeit not with complete composure.

Although she had turned away on instinct, she stopped when he approached and received his compliments with an impossible-to-overcome sense of embarrassment. If his first appearance or resemblance to the painting they had just examined was not enough to confirm to the others that they were looking at Mr. Darcy, then the gardener's expression of surprise at seeing his master would have confirmed it. They stood a little apart while he spoke to their niece, who was astonished and confused and hardly dared to look at his face, let alone answer his civil inquiries about her family. Every sentence he spoke increased her embarrassment, and the thought of the impropriety of being found there kept recurring in her mind. The few minutes they spent together were some of the most uncomfortable of her life. He didn't seem much more at ease either; his usual calm tone was absent, and he repeatedly asked her about the time she had left Longbourn and her stay in Derbyshire in a hurried and repetitive manner that clearly showed his distracted state of mind.

Eventually, he seemed to run out of things to say and, after standing in silence for a few moments, he suddenly remembered himself and said goodbye.

The others then joined her and expressed their admiration of his appearance, but Elizabeth did not hear a word. She was completely absorbed in her own thoughts and followed them in silence. She was overwhelmed with shame and vexation. Her decision to come here was the most unfortunate and ill-advised thing in the world! How strange it must appear to him! In what a disgraceful light might he see her, given his vanity! It might seem as if she had purposely thrown herself in his way again! Oh, why did she come, or why did he arrive a day earlier than expected? If they had been only ten minutes earlier, they would have been out of his reach, for it was clear that he had just arrived and gotten off his horse or carriage. She blushed again and again at the perverseness of the encounter. And his behavior, so strikingly different - what could it mean? It was amazing that he even spoke to her, but to speak with such civility, to inquire after her family! Never in her life had she seen him act with such little dignity, nor had he spoken with such gentleness as he did during this unexpected meeting. What a contrast to his last conversation in Rosing's Park, when he handed her his letter! She didn't know what to think or how to explain it.

They had now entered a beautiful walk by the side of the water, and with every step, the landscape became more impressive, or the woods they were approaching became more beautiful; but it was some time before Elizabeth noticed any of it; and although she responded to the repeated questions of her uncle and aunt and seemed to be looking at the things they pointed out, she didn't really take in any of the scenery. Her thoughts were all on Pemberley House, wherever it might be, and what Mr. Darcy was thinking at that moment. She longed to know what was going through his mind, how he thought of her, and whether, despite everything, she was still dear to him. Maybe he had been polite just because he felt comfortable; yet there had been something in his voice that didn't sound like comfort. She couldn't tell if he had felt more pain or pleasure at seeing her, but he certainly hadn't seen her calmly.

Finally, the remarks of her companions on her absent-mindedness roused Elizabeth, and she felt the need to appear more like herself. They entered the woods and, bidding farewell to the river for a while, climbed to some of the higher grounds. From there, in spots where the trees opened up the view, they could see many lovely sights of the valley, the opposite hills, the long range of woods covering many of them, and occasionally part of the stream. Mr. Gardiner expressed a desire to walk around the entire park, but feared it might be too far. They were triumphantly told that it was ten miles around, settling the matter, and they proceeded on the usual circuit. After some time, they descended among hanging woods to the edge of the water in one of its narrowest parts, crossing it by a simple bridge that fit the general air of the scene. It was a less adorned spot than any they had visited, and the valley, here narrowed into a glen, allowed only enough room for the stream and a narrow walk amidst the rough coppice wood that bordered it. Elizabeth longed to explore its windings, but when they had crossed the bridge and perceived how far they were from the house, Mrs. Gardiner, who was not a great walker, could go no further and thought only of returning to the carriage as quickly as possible. Her niece was, therefore, obliged to submit, and they made their way towards the house on the opposite side of the river in the nearest direction. However, their progress was slow, as Mr. Gardiner, though seldom able to indulge his taste, was very fond of fishing and was so engrossed in watching the occasional appearance of some trout in the water and talking to the man about them that he made little headway. While wandering slowly, they were surprised again, and Elizabeth's astonishment was quite equal to what it had been at first, by the sight of Mr. Darcy approaching them and not far away. The walk was less sheltered here than on the other side, allowing them to see him before they met. Elizabeth, although astonished, was at least more prepared for an interview than before and resolved to appear and speak calmly if he truly intended to meet them. For a few moments, she felt that he would probably take another path. This idea lasted until a turn in the walk concealed him from their view; once past the turn, he was immediately before them. With a glance, she saw that he had lost none of his recent civility, and to imitate his politeness, she began, as they met, to admire the beauty of the place. But she had not gone beyond the words "delightful" and "charming" when some unlucky recollections came to mind, and she fancied that praise of Pemberley from her might be mischievously construed. Her color changed, and she said no more.

Mrs. Gardiner was standing a little behind and, when she paused, he asked her if she would do him the honor of introducing him to her friends. She was taken aback by his politeness, and she couldn't help but smile at the fact that he was now trying to make the acquaintance of people he had previously looked down on when he proposed to her. "What will he think when he finds out who they really are?" she thought. "He must think they're fashionable."

The introductions were made and, as she said how they were related to her, she glanced at him to see how he was taking it. She was expecting him to run away, embarrassed by such undignified companions. He was clearly surprised, but he stayed and started talking to Mr. Gardiner. Elizabeth was pleased and triumphant. It was a relief to know that she had family she didn't have to be ashamed of. She listened intently to the conversation between them and was proud of every word her uncle said that showed his intelligence, taste, and good manners.

The conversation then turned to fishing and she heard Mr. Darcy politely invite her uncle to fish there as often as he wanted while he was in the area, offering to provide him with the necessary equipment and pointing out the best spots to catch fish. Mrs. Gardiner, who was walking with Elizabeth, gave her a look of surprise. Elizabeth said nothing but was very pleased. She was amazed and kept saying to herself, "Why has he changed so much? What could have caused it? It can't be because of me. My reproaches at Hunsford couldn't have caused this kind of change."

After walking for some time in this way, the two ladies in front and the two gentlemen behind, they happened to make a small change when they resumed their places, having descended to the brink of the river to inspect a curious water plant. Mrs. Gardiner, fatigued by the morning's exercise, found Elizabeth's arm insufficient for support and thus preferred her husband's. Mr. Darcy took her place beside her niece, and they walked on together. After a short silence, Elizabeth spoke first. She wanted him to know that she had been assured of his absence before coming to the place and therefore began by saying that his arrival had been very unexpected. "Your housekeeper," she added, "informed us that you would certainly not be here until tomorrow, and before we left Bakewell, we understood that you were not immediately expected in the country." He acknowledged that it was all true and explained that business with his steward had caused him to arrive a few hours before the rest of the party with whom he had been traveling. "They will join me early tomorrow," he continued, "and among them are some who will claim an acquaintance with you—Mr. Bingley and his sisters."

Elizabeth gave only a slight bow in response. She was immediately taken back to the last time Mr. Bingley's name had been mentioned between them; and judging by his expression, his mind was occupied with similar thoughts.

"There is also one other person in the party," he said after a moment of silence, "who is particularly eager to make your acquaintance. Would you allow me, or am I asking too much, to introduce my sister to you while you are staying in Lambton?"

She was greatly surprised by his request; it was so unexpected that she did not know how to respond. She quickly realized that Miss Darcy's desire to meet her must have been her brother's doing, and this was satisfying; it showed that his anger had not caused him to think badly of her.

They continued walking in silence, each of them lost in their own thoughts. Elizabeth was not comfortable; that was impossible; but she was flattered and pleased. His wish to introduce his sister to her was a compliment of the highest order. They soon outpaced the others and when they reached the carriage, Mr. and Mrs. Gardiner were a quarter of a mile behind.

He then asked her to walk into the house, but she said she wasn't tired and they stood together on the lawn. There was much to be said, but the silence was awkward. She wanted to talk, but it seemed like every topic was off limits. Finally, she remembered she had been travelling and they talked about Matlock and Dove Dale with great determination. Yet time and her aunt moved slowly and her patience and ideas were nearly gone before the conversation was over. When Mr. and Mrs.

Gardiner arrived, they were all asked to go into the house and have some refreshment; but this was declined and they parted on each side with politeness. Mr. Darcy helped the ladies into the carriage and when it drove off, Elizabeth saw him walking slowly towards the house.

Her uncle and aunt began to observe him closely; and each of them declared him to be much better than they had expected. "He's very well-mannered, polite, and humble," said her uncle.

"He does have a bit of a stately air," her aunt replied, "but it's not unbecoming. I can now agree with the housekeeper that though some may call him proud, I haven't seen any of that."

"I was so surprised by his behavior towards us. It was more than civil; it was really attentive; and there was no need for it. He didn't even know Elizabeth very well."

"Yes, Lizzy," her aunt said, "he's not as good-looking as Wickham, or rather he doesn't have Wickham's face, because his features are quite good. But why did you tell us he was so unpleasant?"

Elizabeth tried to excuse herself as best she could; she said she had liked him more when they met in Kent than before, and that she had never seen him so pleasant as that morning.

"But maybe he can be a bit capricious with his politeness," replied her uncle. "Your great men often are; so I won't take him at his word about fishing, as he might change his mind another day and tell me to stay off his land."

Elizabeth thought they had completely misunderstood his character, but she said nothing.

"From what we've seen of him," continued Mrs. Gardiner, "I really wouldn't have thought he could be so cruel to anyone like he was to poor Wickham. He doesn't have an unkind look. On the contrary, his mouth looks quite pleasant when he talks. And there's a certain dignity in his face that doesn't make you think badly of his heart. But of course, the nice lady who showed us the house did give him a very glowing description! I could barely keep from laughing out loud at times. But he's a nice guy, good company, and I'm sure he has some good qualities."

Elizabeth felt obliged to defend his treatment of Wickham and so she told them, in a very careful way, that from what she had heard from his family in Kent, his behavior could be seen in a different light and that neither his character nor Wickham's was as bad as people in Hertfordshire thought. To prove this, she described all the financial dealings they had been involved in, without saying who had told her, but making it clear that the information was reliable.

Mrs. Gardiner was shocked and upset, but as they were now approaching the place where she had spent so many happy times, all other thoughts were forgotten and she was too busy pointing out to her husband all the interesting places nearby to think of anything else. Exhausted from her morning walk, they had no sooner finished their meal than she set off again to look for her old acquaintance and the evening was spent in the joys of being reunited after many years apart.

The events of the day left Elizabeth with little time to think of her new friends; all she could do was marvel at Mr. Darcy's politeness and, most of all, his desire for her to meet his sister.

CHAPTER 44

Elizabeth had decided that Mr. Darcy would bring his sister to visit her the very day after she arrived at Pemberley and was therefore determined not to be out of sight of the inn for the entire morning. However, her assumption was wrong, for on the very next morning after their arrival in Lambton, these visitors came. They had been walking around the area with some of their new friends and had just returned to the inn to get ready for dinner with the same family when they heard the sound of a carriage and saw a gentleman and lady in a curricle driving up the street. Elizabeth immediately recognized the livery and guessed what it meant, causing great surprise to her family when she informed them of the expected visit. Her uncle and aunt were amazed, and her embarrassed manner, combined with the circumstance itself and many of the events of the previous day, gave them a new idea of the situation. Nothing had ever suggested it before, but they now felt that there was no other way to account for such attention from such a quarter than by supposing a partiality for their niece. While these newly formed thoughts were swirling in their minds, Elizabeth's emotions were becoming more and more tumultuous. She was amazed at her own lack of composure, but among other causes of anxiety, she feared that Mr. Darcy's fondness for her had been too openly expressed to his sister. More than ever, she was anxious to please, but she naturally suspected that every effort to please would fail her.

She moved away from the window, afraid of being seen, and as she paced the room trying to calm herself, she noticed her uncle and aunt looking at her with enquiring surprise, making the situation even worse.

Miss Darcy and her brother then arrived and the awkward introduction began. Elizabeth was astonished to see that her new acquaintance was just as embarrassed as she was. She had heard that Miss Darcy was very proud, but after a few minutes she realized that she was just very shy. Elizabeth found it hard to get more than a one-word answer from her.

Miss Darcy was tall and bigger than Elizabeth, and although she was only sixteen, her figure was elegant and her appearance womanly and graceful. She was not as attractive as her brother, but her face showed intelligence and humor, and her manner was humble and gentle. Elizabeth had expected her to be as sharp and unembarrassed as Mr. Darcy, so she was relieved to find her so different.

They had not been together for long before Darcy told her that Bingley was coming to visit her. She had just enough time to express her pleasure and prepare for him when his quick footsteps were heard on the stairs and he entered the room. All Elizabeth's anger towards him had long gone, and even if she had still felt it, it could not have withstood the warm welcome he gave her. He asked in a friendly way after her family and spoke with the same good humor he had always done.

Mr. and Mrs. Gardiner were almost as interested in him as she was. The whole group excited lively attention. The suspicions that had just arisen about Mr. Darcy and their niece caused them to observe both of them closely, though cautiously, and they soon realized that at least one of them was in love. They weren't sure about the lady's feelings, but it was obvious that the gentleman was overflowing with admiration.

Elizabeth had a lot to do. She wanted to figure out the feelings of each of her visitors, she wanted to control her own, and to make everyone happy; and in this last endeavor, which she was most afraid of failing in, she was most successful, because those she tried to please were already predisposed to liking her. Bingley was ready, Georgiana was eager, and Darcy determined to be pleased.

When Elizabeth saw Bingley, her thoughts immediately went to her sister; and oh, how desperately she wanted to know if any of his thoughts were directed in a similar way. Sometimes she could imagine that he talked less than on previous occasions, and she even allowed herself to think that when he looked at her, he was trying to see if she looked like someone else. But, although this was only her imagination, she was certain that he and Miss Darcy were not showing any signs of special fondness for each other. Nothing happened between them that could give his sister any hope. She soon became certain of this and a few other little things happened before they parted that, in her anxious interpretation, seemed to show he remembered Jane fondly and wanted to mention her, if only he had been brave enough. He said to her, while the others were talking, in a tone that seemed to show real regret, "It's been a long time since I've seen you; it's more than eight months. We haven't met since the twenty-sixth of November when we were all dancing at Netherfield."

She was pleased that he remembered so precisely. Later, when no one else was around, he asked her if all her sisters were at Longbourn. His words and expression made the question meaningful.

She rarely had the chance to look directly at Mr. Darcy, but when she did, she saw a look of politeness. In everything he said, his tone was so far from being arrogant or disdainful of the others that she was convinced that the improvement in his manners, however temporary it might be, had lasted at least one day. As she observed him making an effort to befriend and gain the approval of individuals whom he would have been embarrassed to associate with merely months prior, her amazement was palpable. Not only was he courteous to her, but he was also polite to the family that he had previously disregarded. As she reminisced about their last conversation at Hunsford Parsonage, the stark contrast in his behavior left her nearly speechless. Never before had she seen him so eager to please, so humble, and so relaxed, even more so than when he was with his dear friends at Netherfield or esteemed relatives at Rosings. Despite the fact that being acquainted with the individuals he was trying to impress would draw ridicule and criticism from the ladies of Netherfield and Rosings, he made no attempt to gain any benefits from his efforts.

Their visitors stayed with them for over half an hour, and when they got up to leave, Mr. Darcy asked his sister to join him in expressing their desire to have Mr. and Mrs. Gardiner, and Miss Bennet, to dinner at Pemberley before they left the country. Miss Darcy, though somewhat hesitant as she was not used to giving invitations, readily agreed. Mrs. Gardiner looked at her niece, wanting to know how Elizabeth, whom the invitation most concerned, felt about accepting it, but Elizabeth had turned her head away. Presuming, however, that this deliberate avoidance indicated only momentary embarrassment rather than any dislike of the proposal, and seeing in her husband, who enjoyed company, a willingness to accept it, she dared to commit to attending, and the day after the next was chosen.

Bingley expressed great delight at the prospect of seeing Elizabeth again, as he still had much to say to her and many questions to ask about all their friends in Hertfordshire. Elizabeth, interpreting all of this as a desire to hear her speak about her sister, was pleased. For this reason, as well as others, she found herself capable of looking back on the last half-hour with some satisfaction after their visitors had departed, even though she had not enjoyed it much while it was happening. Eager to be alone and afraid of any inquiries or hints from her uncle and aunt, she stayed with them only long enough to hear their favorable opinion of Bingley before hurrying off to get dressed.

But she had no reason to be concerned about Mr. and Mrs. Gardiner's curiosity; they did not intend to pressure her into talking. It was clear that she was much more familiar with Mr. Darcy than they had previously thought and it was clear that he was very much in love with her. They noticed lots of things that were interesting, but nothing that would cause them to ask questions.

It was now important to them to think of Mr. Darcy in a good light and, as far as they knew him, there was nothing wrong with him. If they had based their opinion of him on their own feelings and the reports of his servant, without referring to any other accounts, the people in Hertfordshire who knew him wouldn't have recognized him as Mr. Darcy. There was now an interest in believing the housekeeper, and they soon realized that the opinion of a servant who had known him since he was four years old, and who seemed respectable, should not be quickly dismissed. Nothing they had heard from their friends in Lambton had weakened the weight of her statement. All they could accuse him of was pride; he probably had pride, and if not, it would certainly be assumed by the people of a small town where the family did not visit. It was acknowledged, however, that he was generous and did a lot of good for the poor.

Regarding Wickham, the travelers soon found out he was not highly regarded there; although the details of his dealings with the son of his patron were not completely understood, it was a well-known fact that when he left Derbyshire he had left behind many debts which Mr. Darcy later paid off.

Elizabeth's thoughts were with Pemberley this evening more than the night before. The night seemed to pass slowly, but it wasn't long enough for her to figure out her feelings for the person living there. She realized she didn't hate him anymore. In fact, she was embarrassed that she ever felt anything close to dislike for him. She had come to respect him for his good qualities and this had grown into something more like friendship. Most of all, she was grateful for his willingness to forgive her for her rude rejection of him and the false accusations she had made. He, whom she had been convinced would avoid her as if she were his greatest enemy, seemed, on this unexpected meeting, to be very keen to keep in touch, and without any inappropriate display of affection, or any strange behavior, just between the two of them, was trying to make a good impression on her friends, and was determined to introduce her to his sister. Such a change in a man who was so proud surprised and pleased her; it could only be attributed to his passionate love for her, and it made her feel a mixture of emotions that were not unpleasant, though she couldn't quite put her finger on them. She respected him, she admired him, she was thankful to him, she genuinely cared about his well-being; and she just had to figure out how much of that well-being she wanted to be responsible for, and how much it would benefit them both if she used the power, which her imagination told her she still had, to encourage him to start courting her again.

It was agreed between the aunt and niece that they should show Miss Darcy a great deal of politeness by visiting her at Pemberley the next morning.

CHAPTER 45

Elizabeth was pleased with the plan, but she couldn't explain why. Mr. Gardiner left them after breakfast to go fishing with some of the gentlemen at Pemberley. Elizabeth was sure that Miss Bingley disliked her out of jealousy and she was curious to see how civil Miss Bingley would be when they met again.

When they reached the house, they were taken through the hall into the living room, which was lovely in the summertime because its northern windows gave a pleasant view of the high, wooded hills behind the house and the beautiful oaks and Spanish chestnut trees on the lawn in between.

Miss Darcy was in the room with Mrs. Hurst and Miss Bingley, and the woman she lived with in London. Georgiana was polite to them, but obviously very shy and afraid of making a mistake, which made them think she was proud and aloof. Mrs. Gardiner and her niece were sympathetic towards her.

Mrs. Hurst and Miss Bingley only acknowledged them with a curtsey and then an awkward pause, as such pauses always are, followed for a few moments after they were seated. The silence was first broken by Mrs. Annesley, a genteel and pleasant-looking woman, whose attempt to introduce some form of conversation demonstrated that she was more truly well-mannered than either of the others. The conversation was carried on between her and Mrs. Gardiner, with occasional input from Elizabeth. Miss Darcy appeared as if she wished for enough courage to join in but sometimes dared to speak a short sentence when there was little danger of it being heard.

Elizabeth soon noticed that Miss Bingley was watching her carefully, and that she couldn't say anything, especially to Miss Darcy, without drawing her attention. This meant she didn't have to say much, as she was busy thinking. She was expecting some of the men to come into the room at any moment and wasn't sure if she wanted or feared the owner of the house to be amongst them. After sitting in this manner for a quarter of an hour without hearing Miss Bingley's voice, Elizabeth was startled when she received a cold inquiry about the health of her family. She answered with equal indifference and brevity and the other said nothing else.

The next thing that happened was that servants entered with cold meat, cake, and a variety of fruits in season; but this did not occur until Mrs. Annesley had given Miss Darcy many meaningful looks and smiles to remind her of her duties. Now everyone had something to do; even though they couldn't all talk, they could all eat, and the beautiful pyramids of grapes, nectarines, and peaches soon gathered them around the table.

While they were occupied, Elizabeth had a chance to decide whether she most feared or wished for the appearance of Mr. Darcy, based on her feelings when he entered the room. Before she had thought her wishes would take precedence, but now she began to regret that he had come.

He had been spending some time with Mr. Gardiner and some other gentlemen from the house who were fishing by the river. When he arrived, Elizabeth decided to be calm and composed, as she could tell that everyone was suspicious of them and all eyes were on him when he entered the room. Miss Bingley was especially curious, despite the smiles she gave when she spoke to either of them; as she was still jealous, her attentions to Mr. Darcy were still obvious. When her brother came in, Miss Darcy tried harder to talk and Elizabeth could tell that he wanted her and his sister to get to know each other, so she encouraged any conversation. Miss Bingley also noticed this and, in her anger, took the opportunity to say with a sneering politeness,

"Tell me, Miss Eliza, have the militia left Meryton? They must have been a great loss to your family."

Although she was unable to mention Wickham's name in Darcy's presence, Elizabeth understood immediately that he was the one on her mind. This caused her some distress, but she quickly recovered and answered the question in an unaffected manner. As she spoke, she noticed Darcy had flushed cheeks and was intently watching her, while his sister was too embarrassed to look up. Had Miss Bingley been aware of the pain she was causing her beloved friend, she would have avoided the suggestion; however, she only wanted to embarrass Elizabeth by bringing up the idea of a man she thought she was partial towards, so that she would reveal her emotions and potentially damage her standing in Darcy's eyes. Furthermore, Bingley wanted to remind Darcy of all the foolishness and absurdity his family had with the regiment. To no one had it been revealed, when secrecy was possible, except to Elizabeth. Bingley's brother was particularly anxious to conceal it from all of Bingley's connections, including his own wish for them to become Elizabeth's connections in the future, which Elizabeth had long ago suspected. He had undoubtedly made such a plan, and while he did not intend for it to affect his efforts to separate Bingley from Miss Bennet, it is possible that it might have added to his deep concern for his friend's welfare.

Elizabeth's behavior, however, soon calmed his emotions; and as Miss Bingley, frustrated and disappointed, did not dare to approach Wickham, Georgiana also eventually recovered, though not enough to be able to speak. Her brother, who she was afraid to meet his gaze, hardly remembered her involvement in the matter, and the very thing that was meant to take his thoughts away from Elizabeth seemed to have made him think of her more cheerfully.

They did not stay for much longer after the question and answer mentioned before; and as Mr. Darcy was seeing them to their carriage, Miss Bingley was expressing her feelings about Elizabeth's appearance, behavior, and clothing. But Georgiana didn't join her. Her brother's opinion was enough to win her over: his judgement could not be wrong, and he had spoken so highly of Elizabeth that Georgiana could not see her any differently than lovely and amiable. When Darcy returned to the room, Miss Bingley couldn't help but tell him some of what she had said to his sister.

"How terrible Eliza Bennet looks this morning, Mr. Darcy," she exclaimed. "I've never seen anyone change so much since last winter. She's become so dark and coarse-looking! Louisa and I were just saying that we wouldn't have recognized her."

However much Mr. Darcy might not have liked this comment, he simply responded that he only noticed she was a bit tanned, nothing too out of the ordinary.

"Personally," she continued, "I never thought she was attractive. Her face is too thin, her complexion lacks luster, and her features are not at all pretty. Her nose lacks character and her eyes, which some have said are lovely, don't seem extraordinary to me. They have a harsh, unpleasant look that I don't like. Her overall demeanor is arrogant and unfashionable, which is unbearable."

Although Miss Bingley was convinced that Darcy admired Elizabeth, insulting her was not the best way to make herself more attractive to him. However, angry people do not always act wisely, and Miss Bingley had the satisfaction of seeing Darcy become somewhat annoyed by her behavior. Despite this, he remained resolutely silent, and in an attempt to make him speak, she persisted.

"I remember when we first met her in Hertfordshire, we were all so surprised to hear she was considered beautiful. I remember you said one night after they had dinner at Netherfield, 'She a beauty? I'd sooner call her mother a wit.' But then you seemed to think she was attractive at some point."

"Yes," Darcy replied, no longer able to keep quiet. "But that was only when I first met her. It's been months since I thought of her as one of the prettiest women I know."

He then left, leaving Miss Bingley feeling pleased that she had made him say something that didn't bother anyone but her.

On the way back, Mrs. Gardiner and Elizabeth talked about everything that had happened during their visit, except for the things that had really interested them. They discussed the looks and behavior of everyone they had seen, except for the person who had taken up most of their attention. They talked about his sister, his friends, his house, his fruit, everything but himself; and Elizabeth was eager to know what Mrs. Gardiner thought of him. Mrs. Gardiner would have been delighted if Elizabeth had started the conversation about him.

CHAPTER 46

Elizabeth had been quite disappointed to not find a letter from Jane upon their arrival at Lambton, and this disappointment had continued each morning they spent there. However, on the third morning, her disappointment faded away as she received two letters from Jane at once, one of which was marked as having been sent to the wrong address. Elizabeth was not surprised, as Jane had written the address quite poorly.

Just as the letters arrived, they were preparing to go for a walk, and her uncle and aunt left her to read the letters in peace while they set off on their own. The missent letter had to be read first; it had been written five days prior. The beginning of the letter contained accounts of their various social events and engagements, along with any news from the countryside. However, the latter half of the letter, dated a day later and written with obvious agitation, contained more important information. It read as follows:

"After writing the above, my dearest Lizzy, something unexpected and serious has occurred, but I am afraid of alarming you—rest assured that we are all well. What I have to say concerns poor Lydia. An express arrived at twelve last night, just as we were all going to bed, from Colonel Forster, informing us that she had eloped to Scotland with one of his officers, to be frank, with Wickham! Imagine our surprise. However, Kitty does not seem so shocked. I am very, very sorry. Such an imprudent match on both sides! But I am willing to hope the best and that his character has been misunderstood. I can easily believe him thoughtless and indiscreet, but this step (and let us rejoice over it) shows that he has no bad intentions. His choice is disinterested at least, for he must know that my father can give her nothing. Our poor mother is sadly grieved, but my father bears it better. I

am so thankful that we never let them know what has been said against him; we must forget it ourselves. They left on Saturday night around twelve, as is assumed, but were not missed until yesterday morning at eight. The express was sent off immediately. My dear Lizzy, they must have passed within ten miles of us. Colonel Forster gives us reason to expect him here soon. Lydia left a few lines for his wife, informing her of their intentions. I must conclude, for I cannot be away from my poor mother for long. I am afraid you may not be able to read this, but I hardly know what I have written."

Without giving herself time to think and not really knowing how she felt, Elizabeth finished the letter and immediately grabbed the other one and, with the greatest impatience, read the following: it had been written a day after the end of the first.

"My dearest sister, I hope this letter finds you well. I apologize for my previous hurried letter as my head is still in a state of confusion. I have bad news for you that cannot be delayed any longer. We are anxious to confirm whether Mr. Wickham has married our poor Lydia, despite the imprudence of such a match. There is reason to fear that they did not go to Scotland as they had planned. Colonel Forster arrived yesterday from Brighton, having left the day before, shortly after receiving an express. Lydia's letter to Mrs. F. had mentioned that they were going to Gretna Green, but something was said by Denny to suggest that Mr. Wickham had no intention of marrying her and was not going to Gretna Green. This information alarmed Colonel Forster, and he immediately set off to trace their route. He found them in Clapham but lost sight of them when they got into a hackney-coach and dismissed the chaise that brought them from Epsom. All that is known after this is that they were seen continuing on the London road. We are distressed and worried, but my father and mother believe the worst, whereas I cannot think so poorly of Mr. Wickham. Even if he did intend to deceive a young woman of Lydia's standing, I cannot believe that she would be so naive as to fall for it. I am saddened to hear that Colonel Forster does not trust that they are married, but I still have hope. My mother is unwell and my father is deeply affected by this news. Kitty is angry for being kept in the dark about their attachment, but I cannot blame Lydia for confiding in

someone. *I long for your return now that the initial shock has passed. I am not being selfish, but I must admit that your presence would be a comfort. Please come as soon as possible, and if it's not too much to ask, please bring our dear uncle and aunt with you. My father and Colonel Forster are going to London to try to find Lydia, and we could use all the advice and assistance we can get. I know I can rely on our uncle's kindness and understanding in this matter."*

"Oh, where's my uncle?" Elizabeth exclaimed, jumping up from her seat as she finished the letter, desperate to follow him and not waste a second. But as she reached the door, it opened and Mr. Darcy appeared. Her pale face and impulsive manner made him jump, and before he could compose himself enough to speak, she, who's every thought was preoccupied by Lydia's situation, hastily exclaimed, "I apologize, but I must go. I must find Mr. Gardiner right away, on a matter that can't wait; I don't have a second to spare."

"Good God! What's wrong?" he exclaimed, with more emotion than politeness; then recollecting himself, "I won't keep you a minute, but let me, or let the servant, go after Mr. and Mrs. Gardiner. You're not well enough;--you can't go yourself."

Elizabeth hesitated, but her knees were shaking so much she realized how little she would accomplish by trying to follow them. So, calling the servant back, she told him, in a voice so rushed it was almost incomprehensible, to bring his master and mistress home immediately.

After he left the room, she sat down, too weak to stand, and looking so wretchedly ill, that it was impossible for Darcy to leave her, or to resist saying, in a tone of kindness and sympathy, "Let me call your maid. Is there anything I can get for you to make you feel better?--Can I get you a glass of wine?--You look really unwell."

"No, thank you," she responded, trying to compose herself. "There's nothing wrong with me. I'm perfectly fine. I'm just really upset about some terrible news I just received from Longbourn."

She burst into tears as she mentioned it and couldn't say anything else for several minutes. Darcy, filled with dread, could only mumble something about being sorry and watched her in sympathy. Eventually, she spoke again.

"I just received a letter from Jane with some awful news. It can't be kept a secret. My youngest sister has abandoned everyone she knows—she's eloped—she's gone off with Mr. Wickham. They left Brighton together. You know him too well to doubt the rest. She doesn't have any money, any family, nothing that would make him stay with her—she's gone forever."

Darcy was stunned. "When I think," she said, her voice trembling, "that I could have stopped this!--I, who knew what he was like. If I had only shared some of what I knew with my family! If his character had been known, this wouldn't have happened."

"I am really sorry," said Darcy, "saddened and shocked. But is it absolutely certain?"

"Oh yes! They left Brighton together on Sunday night and were followed almost to London, but not beyond; they definitely haven't gone to Scotland."

"And what has been done, what attempts have been made, to get her back?"

"My father has gone to London and Jane has written to ask my uncle for his urgent help and I hope we will be leaving in half an hour. But nothing can be done; How can you make a man like that do anything? How can you even find them? I have no hope at all. It is awful in every way!"

Darcy nodded his head in agreement.

"When I realized his true character. Oh! If I had only known what I should have done, what I was brave enough to do! But I didn't know, I was scared of doing too much. What a terrible mistake!"

Darcy said nothing. He seemed to barely listen to her, and was pacing the room in deep thought; his forehead furrowed, his expression grim. Elizabeth quickly noticed, and immediately understood the situation. Her power was fading; everything must be lost due to such a display of family weakness, such a confirmation of the utmost shame. She could neither be surprised nor blame him, but the idea that he had conquered himself brought her no comfort, gave her no relief from her suffering. On the contrary, it made her acutely aware of her own desires; never before had she so honestly admitted to herself that she could have loved him, even though it was now impossible.

But she could not focus solely on herself; there was too much else to consider. Lydia—the shame and misery she was causing them all, soon overshadowed any personal worries Elizabeth had; and, covering her face with her handkerchief, Elizabeth was soon oblivious to her surroundings; and, after a few moments of silence, she was only brought back to reality by the voice of her companion, who, in a way that showed compassion but also restraint, said, "I'm afraid you have been waiting for me to leave for some time, and I have no excuse for staying other than genuine, though unhelpful, sympathy. I wish there was something I could say or do to offer you comfort—but I won't torture you with empty wishes that would just require your thanks. I'm afraid this unfortunate event will prevent my sister from having the pleasure of seeing you at Pemberley today."

"Yes, please. Be so kind as to apologize to Miss Darcy on our behalf. Say that urgent business requires us to go home immediately. Hide the unfortunate truth for as long as possible."

He assured her of his discretion—expressed his sympathy for her distress, wished her a better outcome than what seemed likely at the moment, and after leaving his best regards for her family and giving her one serious, parting look, he left.

As he left the room, Elizabeth realized how unlikely it was that they would ever see each other again on friendly terms like they had in Derbyshire; and as she looked back on their entire relationship, so full of ups and downs, she sighed at how her feelings had changed—where once she would have been glad for it to end, now she wished it could continue.

If gratitude and respect can form the basis of affection, then Elizabeth's change of heart is neither unlikely nor wrong. But if, on the other hand, the admiration she felt was not genuine, and was instead based on something unreasonable or unnatural, then there was nothing to be said in her defense, apart from the fact that she had tried to form an attachment with Wickham, and that it had been unsuccessful. Regardless, she watched him leave with sadness, and this early example of what Lydia's scandalous behavior had caused made her feel even worse. She had never expected Wickham to marry her, she thought that only Jane could think that. She had been surprised by the contents of the first letter, wondering how Lydia could have been so taken with him, but now it all made sense. Lydia could have been attractive enough for him, and although she didn't think that Lydia had planned to elope without the intention of marriage, she had no doubt that her virtue and understanding would not protect her from the advances of men like Wickham.

She had never noticed while the regiment was in Hertfordshire that Lydia had any special fondness for him, but she was certain that Lydia would have attached herself to whoever had paid her attention. Her affections had been constantly changing, but never without a focus. The harm that came from neglecting and wrongly spoiling such a girl—Oh! How painfully she felt it now.

She was desperate to be at home - to hear, to see, to be on the scene, to help Jane with the responsibilities that had now fallen completely on her, in a family so disrupted; a father away, a mother incapable of doing anything and requiring constant care; and although she was almost convinced that nothing could be done for Lydia, her uncle's involvement seemed of the utmost importance, and until he entered the room, the distress of her impatience was intense. Mr. and Mrs. Gardiner had hurried back in panic, assuming, from the servant's report, that their niece had suddenly fallen ill; but reassuring them immediately on that point, she eagerly shared the reason for their summons, reading the two letters out loud and dwelling on the postscript of the last with trembling intensity. Even though Lydia had never been a favorite of theirs, Mr. and Mrs. Gardiner could not help but be deeply affected. Not just Lydia, but everyone was involved in it; and after the initial shock and surprise, Mr. Gardiner readily offered any help he could. Elizabeth, although expecting no less, thanked him with tears of gratitude; and since they all had the same goal, everything related to their journey was quickly sorted out. They were to leave as soon as possible. "But what are we going to do about Pemberley?" Mrs. Gardiner asked. "John told us Mr. Darcy was here when you sent for us; was that true?"

"Yes; and I told him we would not be able to keep our appointment. That's all sorted."

"That's all sorted," she repeated as she ran into her room to get ready. "Are they on such terms that she can tell the truth? Oh, if only I knew how it was!"

But wishes were futile; or at best, they could only provide her with a distraction in the rush and confusion of the following hour.

If Elizabeth had the luxury of being idle, she would have believed that no task could be accomplished by someone as miserable as herself. However, she had her fair share of responsibilities to attend to, just like her aunt. One of these tasks was to write notes to all their friends in Lambton, fabricating false reasons for their abrupt departure. Within an hour, all the notes were written and Mr. Gardiner had settled his account at the inn. There was nothing left to do but to leave. Despite the anguish she had felt earlier that morning, Elizabeth found herself seated in the carriage and on the way to Longbourn in a shorter amount of time than she had expected.

CHAPTER 47

"I've been reconsidering, Elizabeth," said her uncle as they left town. "And upon serious reflection, I find myself more inclined to agree with your eldest sister's assessment of the situation. It seems very unlikely that a young man would attempt to deceive a girl who is not without protection or friends, and who was actually staying with his colonel's family. I am strongly inclined to hope for the best. Could he have expected that her friends would not come forward? Could he have expected to be accepted by the regiment after disrespecting Colonel Forster in such a way? The potential reward does not justify the risk."

Mrs. Gardiner replied, "Do you really think so? I'm starting to agree with your uncle. It's a huge breach of decency, honor, and self-interest for him to do this. Lizzy, can you really give up on him so completely to believe he's capable of this?"

"I don't think he'd neglect his own interests. But I can believe he's capable of anything else. What if it's true? But I don't want to hope for it. Why wouldn't they just go to Scotland if that was the case?"

"Well, firstly," he replied, "there's no definite proof that they haven't gone to Scotland."

"But changing from a chaise to a hackney coach is quite suspicious and there were no signs of them on the Barnet road."

"Okay, so let's say they are in London. It's possible they're there to hide, since neither of them have much money. It may be cheaper to get married in London than in Scotland"

"But why all the secrecy? Why the fear of being discovered? Why must their marriage be private? Oh no, this is unlikely. You can see from Jane's account that even Wickham's closest friend was convinced that he had no intention of marrying Lydia.

Wickham will never marry a woman without some money. He cannot afford it. And what does Lydia have to offer? What qualities does she possess beyond youth, health, and good humor that would cause him to give up the chance of marrying well for her sake? As for the fear of disgrace in the regiment restraining him from eloping dishonorably with her, I cannot say. I don't know what effects such an action might have. But I don't think your other objection is valid. Lydia has no brothers to defend her honor, and Wickham might have thought that my father, with his indolence and lack of attention to family matters, would do as little as any father could in such a situation."

"Do you think that Lydia is so in love with him that she would agree to live with him without getting married?"

"It does seem that way, and it's really upsetting," Elizabeth replied, with tears in her eyes. "I'm not sure what to say. Maybe I'm not being fair to her. But she's very young; she's never been taught to think about important things. For the last six months, or even a year, she's been doing nothing but having fun and being vain. She's been allowed to do whatever she wants and to accept any ideas that come her way. Since the militia first arrived in Meryton, all Elizabeth could think and talk about was love, flirting, and the officers. She was doing her best to make her feelings, which were already quite strong, even stronger. We all know that Wickham has every charm that could make a woman fall for him."

"But you see, Jane," said her aunt, "does not think so poorly of Wickham to believe that he is capable of such an attempt."

"Who does Jane ever think poorly of? And who is there, no matter how they have behaved in the past, that she would believe capable of such an action until it is proven against them? But Jane knows, just as I do, what Wickham truly is. We both know that he has been immoral in every sense of the word. That he has neither honesty nor honor. That he is as dishonest and deceitful as he is charming."

"And do you truly know all of this?" cried Mrs. Gardiner, whose curiosity about the source of Elizabeth's information was piqued.

"I do, indeed," replied Elizabeth, blushing. "I told you the other day about his dishonorable behavior towards Mr. Darcy. And you, yourself, when you were last at Longbourn, heard how he spoke about the man who had treated him with such patience and generosity. There are other circumstances that I am not at liberty to disclose, and they are not worth mentioning. But his lies about the entire Pemberley family are endless. From what he said about Miss Darcy, I was expecting to meet a proud, reserved, disagreeable girl. Yet he knew otherwise. He must have known that she was just as kind and unassuming as we have found her to be."

"Does Lydia know nothing about this? Is she unaware of what you and Jane seem to know so well?"

"Oh yes, that's the worst of it. I didn't know the truth myself until I was in Kent and saw Mr. Darcy and his cousin Colonel Fitzwilliam. When I got home, the regimen was due to leave Meryton in a week or two. So neither Jane, who I told the whole story to, nor I, thought it necessary to make our knowledge public, since it wouldn't be of any use to anyone to ruin the good opinion that everyone in the neighborhood had of him. I never even thought of the possibility that Lydia could be deceived. The idea of such a consequence never crossed my mind. When they all moved to Brighton, I didn't think that they were fond of each other. I didn't see any signs of affection from either of them. When he first joined the corps, Lydia was ready to admire him, but so were all the other girls. Every girl in or near Meryton was completely obsessed with him for the first two months; however, he never paid her any special attention and so, after a while, her infatuation with him faded and she started to pay attention to other members of the regiment who paid her more attention."

It can be easily imagined that, as they had discussed the topic so much, they had nothing new to say about it, but they could not stay away from it for long during the journey. Elizabeth could not escape her anguish and regret; it was constantly on her mind.

They travelled as quickly as possible and, after sleeping one night on the road, they arrived at Longbourn by dinner time the next day. Elizabeth was relieved that Jane had not had to wait for them for a long time.

The little Gardiners were standing on the steps of the house as they drove up and when the carriage stopped, their faces lit up with joy and they began to dance around in excitement.

Elizabeth jumped out and after giving each of them a quick kiss, she rushed into the vestibule where Jane was waiting for her. Elizabeth hugged her and tears filled their eyes as she asked if there had been any news from the fugitives.

"Not yet," Jane replied, "but now that my uncle is here, I hope everything will be okay."

Elizabeth asked if her father was in town and Jane said,

"Yes, he went on Tuesday like I told you in my letter. Have you heard from him?"

"We've only heard from him once. He wrote me a few lines on Wednesday to say he had arrived safely and to give me his instructions, which I asked him to do. He added that he wouldn't write again until he had something important to tell us."

"How is mother? How are all of you?"

"Mother is doing alright, I think, but she's very shaken up. She's upstairs and will be very happy to see you all. Mary and Kitty, thank goodness, are both fine."

Elizabeth exclaimed, "But how are you? You look pale. You must have gone through so much!"

However, her sister reassured her that she was perfectly fine. Their conversation was interrupted by the arrival of Mr. and Mrs. Gardiner and their children. Jane greeted her uncle and aunt with smiles and tears, thanking them both.

In the drawing-room, Elizabeth's previous questions were repeated by the others, but Jane had no news to give. Despite this, Jane's kind heart remained hopeful and she believed that everything would turn out well. She hoped to receive a letter every morning from either Lydia or their father to explain their situation and possibly announce the marriage.

Mrs. Bennet, with tears and lamentations of regret, received them as expected; blaming everyone but the person whose poor judgement had allowed her daughter to make such a mistake. She said,

"If only I had been able to convince my entire family to go with me to Brighton, this would not have happened," she said. "But poor dear Lydia had no one to take care of her. Why did the Forsters ever let her out of their sight? I am certain that they were neglectful in some way or another, for Lydia is not the type of girl to do such a thing if she had been properly looked after. I always believed that they were unsuitable to be in charge of her, but my opinion was overruled, as it always is. Poor dear child! And now Mr. Bennet has left, and I know he will fight Wickham wherever he finds him, and then he will be killed. What will become of us all? The Collinses will throw us out before Mr. Bennet's body is even cold, and if you are not kind to us, brother, I do not know what we shall do."

They all objected to such dreadful thoughts, and Mr. Gardiner, after expressing his affection for her and her family, informed her that he intended to be in London the next day and would help Mr. Bennet in all efforts to find Lydia.

"Try not to worry unnecessarily," he added. "Although it is wise to prepare for the worst, there is no need to assume the worst outcome. It hasn't even been a week since they left Brighton. In a few more days, we may receive some news about them, and until we know for certain that they have married or intend to marry, let's not give up hope. As soon as I reach London, I will go to my brother and persuade him to come with me to Gracechurch Street so that we can discuss what to do together."

"Oh, my dear brother," Mrs. Bennet replied, "that's exactly what I wish for. When you get to town, find them wherever they are and if they are not married yet, make them get married. And don't let them wait for wedding clothes, tell Lydia she can have as much money as she wants to buy them once they are married. And, most importantly, keep Mr. Bennet from getting into a fight. Tell him how terrified I am—I'm shaking, I'm trembling, I'm having spasms in my side, pains in my head, and my heart is pounding so hard I can't get any rest. Tell my dear Lydia not to buy any clothes until she sees me, because she doesn't know which stores are the best. Oh, brother, how kind you are! I know you'll figure it out."

But Mr. Gardiner, although he promised to do his best, urged me to be realistic in my expectations and fears. After talking with me like this until dinner was ready, he and I left the room so I could express my feelings to the housekeeper who was there in the absence of my daughters.

Though her brother and sister were convinced that there was no need for her to be so distant from the family, they didn't try to stop her as they knew she wasn't careful enough to keep quiet while the servants were in the room. So they thought it would be better if only one of them, the one they trusted the most, knew of her worries.

In the dining room, Mary and Kitty joined them soon after. They had been too occupied in their separate rooms to come earlier. One had been studying, and the other had been preparing herself. However, both of their faces were relatively calm, and no significant change could be seen in either of them, except that Kitty's voice was a bit more irritable than usual due to the loss of her favorite sister or the anger she had caused in the matter. As for Mary, she was composed enough to whisper to Elizabeth with a serious expression on her face shortly after they had all taken their seats at the table,

"This is a very unfortunate event that will likely be widely discussed. But we must counteract the tide of malice and soothe each other's wounded hearts with sisterly comfort."

Noticing that Elizabeth did not seem inclined to respond, Mary added, "As unfortunate as this event is for Lydia, we can learn a useful lesson from it: the loss of virtue in a woman is irreversible - one mistake can lead to endless ruin - her reputation is as fragile as it is beautiful, and she cannot be too cautious in her interactions with undeserving men."

Elizabeth looked at Mary in astonishment but was too overwhelmed to say anything. Nevertheless, Mary continued to console herself by extracting such moral lessons from the unfortunate situation they were in.

In the afternoon, the two older Miss Bennets were able to spend half an hour alone. Elizabeth immediately took advantage of the opportunity to ask many questions, which Jane was equally eager to answer. After expressing their grief over the terrible outcome of this event, which Elizabeth considered almost certain, and Miss Bennet could not deny was at least possible, the former continued by saying, "But tell me everything about it that I have not already heard. Give me more details. What did Colonel Forster say? Did they have no suspicion of anything before the elopement? They must have seen them together all the time."

Miss Bennet replied, "Colonel Forster admitted that he had sometimes suspected there was something going on, especially on Lydia's side, but nothing that gave him cause for alarm. I'm so sorry for him. He was very kind and attentive. He was coming to us to reassure us before he had any idea they weren't going to Scotland. When the idea of them not going there started to spread, it made him hurry his journey."

Elizabeth asked, "Was Denny sure that Wickham wouldn't marry? Did he know about their plan to elope? Had Colonel Forster seen Denny himself?"

"Yes, but when questioned by him, Denny denied knowing anything about their plan and wouldn't give his true opinion on it. He didn't repeat his belief that they wouldn't get married, so I'm hopeful that he was misunderstood before."

"And since this sad affair has taken place, it is said that he left Meryton greatly in debt; but I hope this may be false."

"Before Colonel Forster arrived, none of you had any doubts that they were really married, right?"

"How could we possibly think otherwise? I was a bit worried about my sister's happiness with him in marriage because I knew his behavior hadn't always been good. My parents didn't know that, they just thought it was a foolish match. Kitty then proudly informed us that in Lydia's last letter she had already mentioned that they were in love. She had known for weeks."

"But not before they went to Brighton?"

"No, I don't think so."

"Did Colonel Forster seem to think badly of Wickham? Does he know his true character?"

"I have to admit he didn't speak of Wickham as highly as he used to. He thought he was irresponsible and wasteful. After this happened, I heard he left Meryton with a lot of debt, but I hope that's not true."

"Oh Jane, if we had not been so secretive, if we had told what we knew about him, this would not have happened!"

"Maybe it would have been better," Jane said. "But to reveal someone's past mistakes without knowing what their current feelings are, seemed wrong. We acted with the best of intentions."

"Could Colonel Forster tell his wife the details of Lydia's letter?" Elizabeth asked.

"He brought it with him for us to see."

Jane took the letter from her pocketbook and gave it to Elizabeth. The letter said:

"My dear Harriet,

"You will laugh when you find out where I have gone and I can't help but laugh at your surprise tomorrow morning when I am gone. I am going to Gretna Green and if you can't guess who I'm with, you must be a fool, because there is only one man in the world that I love and he is an angel. I could never be happy without him, so don't think it's wrong that I'm leaving. You don't have to tell the people at Longbourn that I'm gone if you don't want to, because it will make the surprise even greater when I write to

them and sign my name 'Lydia Wickham.' It will be so funny! I'm laughing so hard I can hardly write. Please make my apologies to Pratt for not keeping my promise to dance with him tonight. Tell him I hope he will forgive me when he finds out why and tell him I'll happily dance with him at the next ball we meet. I'll send for my clothes when I get to Longbourn, but could you ask Sally to mend a large tear in my embroidered muslin dress before they're packed away? Goodbye. Give my love to Colonel Forster, I hope you'll drink to our successful journey.

Your affectionate friend,
Lydia Bennet."

"Oh, thoughtless, thoughtless Lydia!" cried Elizabeth. "What kind of letter is this to be written at such a moment? But at least it shows that she was serious about the purpose of her journey. Whatever he might have convinced her to do later, it was not her intention to do anything dishonorable. Poor father, how he must have felt it!"

"I have never seen anyone so shocked. He couldn't say a word for ten minutes. My mother fell ill right away, and the whole house was in such chaos!"

"Oh Jane," Elizabeth exclaimed, "was there any servant in the house who didn't know the whole story by the end of the day?"

"I don't know. I hope so. But it is hard to stay discreet in such a situation. My mother was in hysterics, and although I tried to help her as much as I could, I'm afraid I didn't do enough. But the fear of what could happen almost took away my ability to think."

"Your care of her has been too much for you. You don't look well. Oh, if only I had been with you!"

"Mary and Kitty have been so kind, and they would have helped with anything, I'm sure, but I didn't think it was right for either of them. Kitty is small and fragile, and Mary studies so much that her rest times shouldn't be interrupted. My aunt Philips came to Longbourn on Tuesday after my father left; and was so kind as to stay until Thursday with me. She was really helpful and comforting to us all, and Lady Lucas was really kind; she walked here on Wednesday morning to offer her sympathies and offered her services, or any of her daughters, if they could be of use to us."

"She would have been better staying at home," said Elizabeth; "maybe she meant well, but in a situation like this, you can't be around your neighbors too much. Helping is impossible; sympathy is unbearable. Let them be happy for us from afar and be content."

She then asked what plans her father had made to try and get her back.

"He intended, I believe," replied Jane, "to go to Epsom, the place where they last changed horses, see the postilions, and try to gather any information from them. His main goal must be to find out the number of the hackney coach that took them from Clapham. It had come with a fare from London, and as he thought that the circumstance of a gentleman and lady changing from one carriage to another might be noteworthy, he intended to inquire at Clapham. If he could discover where the coachman had previously dropped off his fare, he planned to investigate there and hoped it might not be impossible to find out the stand and number of the coach. I don't know of any other plans he had made, but he was so anxious to leave and so upset that I had difficulty in extracting even this much information from him."

CHAPTER 48

The entire group hoped to receive a letter from Mr. Bennet the following morning, but to their disappointment, the post arrived without a single line from him. Although they knew Mr. Bennet to be a negligent correspondent, they had hoped for more effort during such trying circumstances. They were forced to assume that he had no positive news to share, but even that would have been preferable to not knowing. Mr. Gardiner had been waiting for the letters before leaving and once he departed, the family could only rely on him for updates.

With Mr. Gardiner gone, the family hoped to receive constant updates and at parting, their uncle promised to persuade Mr. Bennet to return to Longbourn as soon as possible. This was a great consolation to Mr. Bennet's sister who believed that his return was the only way to prevent her husband from being killed in a duel. The family anxiously awaited any news that might alleviate their worries.

Mrs. Gardiner and the children decided to stay in Hertfordshire for a few more days, as Mrs. Gardiner believed her presence would be useful to her nieces. She joined them in caring for Mrs. Bennet and was a great source of comfort to them during their free hours. Their other aunt also visited them frequently, claiming to have the intention of cheering and encouraging them. However, she never came without reporting a new instance of Wickham's reckless behavior or irregularity. As a result, she often left them feeling more dejected than when she arrived.

Everyone in Meryton seemed to be trying to make Wickham look bad, even though a few months ago he had seemed like an angel. He was said to owe money to every shop in town and his affairs, which were all called seductions, had spread to every shopkeeper's family. Everyone said he was the worst young man in the world and people started to realize they had never really trusted his goodness. Elizabeth, though she didn't believe much of what was said, still thought it was likely enough that her sister was in trouble; Jane, who believed even less, had almost given up hope, especially since the time had come when if they had gone to Scotland, they probably would have heard something about them.

Mr. Gardiner departed Longbourn on Sunday, and by Tuesday, his wife received a letter from him. The letter stated that upon his arrival, he had immediately sought out his brother and convinced him to come to Gracechurch Street. Before Mr. Gardiner's arrival, Mr. Bennet had visited Epsom and Clapham, but had not obtained any useful information. He was now determined to investigate all the major hotels in town, as he believed it was possible that his daughters had stayed in one of them before finding lodging. Although Mr. Gardiner did not expect much success from this, he intended to support his brother in this endeavor. He also mentioned that Mr. Bennet had no plans to leave London at present and promised to write again soon. The letter contained a postscript to this effect:

"I have written to Colonel Forster, asking him to try and find out from some of the young man's close associates in the regiment whether Wickham has any family or acquaintances who might have an idea of his current whereabouts in town. If we could find someone who has that kind of information, it would be of immense importance. Right now, we don't have any leads to follow. I am confident that Colonel Forster will do everything in his power to help us in this matter. However, upon further consideration, perhaps Lizzy could provide us with better information regarding his living family members than anyone else."

Elizabeth had no difficulty in understanding why this respect for her authority had developed. However, she was unable to provide any information that was as satisfactory as the compliment deserved.

Each day at Longbourn was filled with anxiety, but the most tense moments were those when they anticipated the post. The arrival of letters was the first significant event of each morning. Letters would contain any good or bad news, and every day was expected to bring news of some importance.

However, before they received any further communication from Mr. Gardiner, a letter arrived for their father from Mr. Collins, from a different source. Jane had been instructed to open all letters that came for him during his absence, so she read it. Elizabeth, who knew how curious Mr. Collins's letters tended to be, also looked over her sister's shoulder and read it. The letter read as follows:

"*Dear Sir,*

I feel it is my duty, as a relative and due to my position in society, to offer my condolences for the grievous affliction that has befallen you. We were informed yesterday by a letter from Hertfordshire about your present distress, which must be the bitterest kind, because it stems from a cause which no time can heal. Please be assured, my dear Sir, that Mrs. Collins and I sincerely sympathize with you and your respectable family. No arguments shall be spared from my side to alleviate such a severe misfortune or comfort you under circumstances that must be the most afflicting to a parent's mind. It is to be lamented that the death of your daughter would have been a blessing in comparison to this. Moreover, it is to be supposed, as my dear Charlotte has informed me, that your daughter's licentious behavior has proceeded from a faulty degree of indulgence. Though, for the consolation of yourself and Mrs. Bennet, I am inclined to think that her own disposition must be naturally bad or she could not have been guilty of such an enormity at such an early age. However, you are grievously to be pitied, and Mrs. Collins and Lady Catherine and her daughter join me in apprehending that this false step by one daughter will be injurious to the fortunes of all the others. Lady Catherine herself has condescended to say who will connect themselves with such a family. This consideration leads me to reflect with augmented satisfaction on a certain event of last November, for had it been otherwise, I must have been involved in all your sorrow and disgrace. Let me advise you then, my dear Sir, to console yourself as much as possible, to disown your unworthy child forever, and leave her to reap the consequences of her own heinous offense.

I am, dear Sir, etc., etc."

Mr. Gardiner did not write again until he had received a reply from Colonel Forster, and it was not good news. It was not known that Wickham had any relatives with whom he kept in contact, and it was certain that he had no close family members living. He had many acquaintances in the past, but since he had been in the militia, it did not seem that he was especially close with any of them. So there was no one who could be identified as likely to have any information about him. Furthermore, due to his financial difficulties, there was a strong incentive for him to stay hidden, as it had recently been revealed that he had left behind gambling debts amounting to a large sum. Colonel Forster thought it would take more than a thousand pounds to pay off his debts in Brighton. He owed money to people in the town, but his debts of honor were even more significant. Mr. Gardiner did not attempt to hide these facts from the Longbourn family; Jane was shocked upon hearing them. "A gambler!" she exclaimed. "I had no idea of it."

Mr. Gardiner wrote in his letter that they could expect their father to come home the next day, which was Saturday. Defeated and broken by the failure of their efforts, he had agreed to his brother-in-law's request that he return to his family and leave it to him to decide what should be done to continue their search. When Mrs. Bennet was told this, she was not as pleased as her children had expected, considering her worry for his life previously.

"What, he's coming home without poor Lydia?" she cried. "Surely he won't leave London before finding them. Who will make Wickham marry her if he leaves?"

As Mrs. Gardiner wanted to be back home, it was decided that she and her children would go to London at the same time Mr. Bennet was coming from it. So, the coach took them on the first part of their journey and brought its master back to Longbourn."

Mrs. Gardiner left Longbourn with the same confusion about Elizabeth and her friend from Derbyshire that had accompanied her from that area. Elizabeth had never mentioned his name in front of them on her own, and the vague hope Mrs. Gardiner had held that they might receive a letter from him had come to nothing. Elizabeth had not received any letter from Pemberley since her return home.

Elizabeth's low spirits were understandable, given the current unhappy state of the family. She was aware that if she hadn't known about Darcy, she would have been able to cope with the worry about Lydia's reputation better, as it would have saved her a sleepless night or two.

When Mr. Bennet arrived, he looked as composed as usual. He said as little as he usually did, not mentioning the reason for his absence, and it took some time for his daughters to have the courage to bring it up.

It was not until the afternoon, when he joined them for tea, that Elizabeth had the nerve to bring it up. After she briefly expressed her sorrow for what he must have gone through, he replied, "Don't say that. Who should suffer but me? I brought this on myself and I should feel it."

"You shouldn't be too hard on yourself," Elizabeth said.

"You can warn me against the same mistake. People are so prone to it! No, Lizzy, let me experience this once in my life and understand how wrong I was. I'm not afraid of being overwhelmed by it. It will pass soon enough."

"Do you think they're in London?"

"Yes, where else could they be so well hidden?"

"Lydia used to want to go to London," Kitty added.

"She's happy then," her father said drily. "And it looks like she'll be staying there for a while."

After a brief pause, he went on, "Lizzy, I don't hold it against you for giving me advice last May. It shows you have a strong character, considering what happened."

Miss Bennet arrived to bring her mother's tea.

"What a show!" he exclaimed. "It's so uplifting to see someone make the best of a bad situation! One of these days I'll do the same. I'll sit in the library in my night cap and robe, and cause as much trouble as I can - or maybe I'll wait until Kitty runs away."

"I am not running away, Father," Kitty said in a peevish tone. "If I ever go to Brighton, I will behave better than Lydia."

"You go to Brighton! I wouldn't trust you to be that close, not even to Eastbourne for fifty pounds! No, Kitty, I have learned to be cautious at last, and you will feel the effects of it. No officer will ever enter my house again, nor will they even be allowed to pass through the village. Balls will be strictly prohibited, unless you dance with one of your sisters. And you will not be allowed to go outside until you can prove that you have spent at least ten minutes of each day in a rational manner."

Kitty, feeling overwhelmed by the rules, started to cry.

"Well, well," he said, "don't make yourself unhappy. If you're a good girl for the next ten years, I'll take you to a military parade at the end of them."

CHAPTER 49

Two days after Mr. Bennet's return, Jane and Elizabeth were walking together in the shrubbery behind the house when they saw the housekeeper approaching. Assuming she was coming to summon them to their mother, the sisters walked forward to meet her. However, instead of calling them, the housekeeper said to Miss Bennet, "I beg your pardon, madam, for interrupting you, but I was hoping you might have received some good news from town, so I took the liberty of coming to ask."

Confused, Elizabeth asked, "What do you mean, Hill? We have heard nothing from town."

Mrs. Hill replied with great surprise, "Dear madam, don't you know that there is an express that has come for master from Mr. Gardiner? He has been here for half an hour, and master has received a letter."

The girls were too eager to wait for any more information and ran to find their father. They searched through the vestibule and breakfast room, but he was in neither. They were about to go upstairs with their mother to find him when the butler intercepted them and said, "If you are looking for my master, ma'am, he is walking towards the little grove."

On hearing this, they hurried through the hall again and ran across the lawn after their father, who was strolling towards a small wood on one side of the paddock.

Jane, who wasn't as fast or used to running as Elizabeth, soon lagged behind, while her sister, out of breath, caught up with him and eagerly asked,

"Oh, Papa, what news? What news? Have you heard from my uncle?"

"Yes, I have had a letter from him by express."

"Well, and what news does it bring? Good or bad?"

"What can we expect that's good?" He took the letter out of his pocket and said, "Maybe you'd like to read it."

Elizabeth snatched it from his hand. Jane came over and said,

"Read it aloud," said her father, I'm not even sure what it's about."

So Elizabeth read,

"Gracechurch-street, Monday, August 2.
"My dear brother,
Finally, I can give you an update on my niece that I hope will satisfy you. Not long after you left me on Saturday, I was lucky enough to discover where in London they were. I'll give you the details when we meet, but for now, it's enough to know that they've been found. I've seen them both."

Jane exclaimed, "So it's true, they are married!"

Elizabeth continued reading,

"They are not married, nor do I believe there was ever any intention of them being so. However, if you agree to the terms I have negotiated on your behalf, I hope they will soon be engaged. All that is required of you is to ensure that your daughter is guaranteed an equal share of the five thousand pounds that is to be divided among your children after you and my sister have passed away. Additionally, you must commit to providing her with one hundred pounds per annum during your lifetime. Given the circumstances, I had no hesitation in agreeing to these conditions on your behalf. I am sending this message by express so that there is no delay in receiving your response. From these details, you can see that Mr. Wickham's financial situation is not as dire as many believe it to be. Contrary to popular belief, he will have some money left over after his debts are paid off, which will be added to my niece's fortune. If you give me full authority to act on your behalf in this matter, I will instruct Haggerston to prepare the necessary settlement documents. There will be no need for you to return to London; simply remain at Longbourn and trust in my abilities. Please respond as soon as possible and provide detailed instructions. We have decided that it

would be best for my niece to be married from this house, and I hope you agree. She will be arriving today. I will write again as soon as further arrangements have been made.

Yours truly, Edward Gardiner."

"Can it be possible that he will marry her?" cried Elizabeth when she had finished reading.

"Wickham isn't as bad as we thought," her sister said. "Congratulations, my dear father."

"Have you answered the letter?" Elizabeth asked.

"No, but it must be done soon."

Elizabeth begged him to write back quickly.

"Oh my dear father, come back and write right away. You know how important every moment is in this case."

"Let me write for you if you don't want to do it yourself," Jane offered.

"I really don't want to," he replied, "but it has to be done."

With that, he turned and walked back to the house with them.

"May I ask what the terms are? I suppose they must be complied with" said Elizabeth.

"Complied with! I'm ashamed that he's asking for so little."

"And they must get married! But he's such a scoundrel!"

"Yes, they must get married. There's no other option. But there are two things I really want to know: first, how much money has your uncle put down to make it happen, and second, how will I ever repay him?"

"Money! My uncle!" exclaimed Jane. "What do you mean, sir?"

"I mean that no man in his right mind would marry Lydia for such a small sum as one hundred pounds a year during my lifetime and fifty pounds after I'm gone."

"That's very true," said Elizabeth. "Although I hadn't thought of it before. His debts to be paid off and still something left over! Oh, it must be my uncle's doing! He's a generous, good man, but I'm afraid he's caused himself some trouble. A small sum of money couldn't have done all this."

"No," said her father. "Wickham would be a fool to take her for anything less than ten thousand pounds. I would hate to think so poorly of him, especially at the start of our relationship."

"Ten thousand pounds! Heaven forbid! How can half of that be paid back?"

Mr. Bennet didn't answer, and each of them thought about it in silence until they got home. Then their father went to the library to write, and the girls went to the breakfast room.

"They're really going to get married!" exclaimed Elizabeth as soon as they were alone. "How strange this is! We're supposed to be thankful for this even though their chances of being happy are so small and his character is so bad. Oh, Lydia!"

"I'm trying to think positively," replied Jane. "He must have some real feelings for her if he's willing to marry her. Though our kind uncle has done something to help him out, I cannot believe that he has advanced ten thousand pounds, or anything close to that."

Elizabeth said, "If we ever manage to find out what Wickham's debts were and how much money was set aside for our sister, we will know exactly what Mr. Gardiner did for them since Wickham doesn't have a penny to his name. Our uncle and aunt's kindness can never be repaid. Taking her into their home and providing her with their personal protection and support is such a great benefit to her that years of gratitude won't be enough to acknowledge it. By now she must be with them! If such goodness doesn't make her unhappy now, she will never deserve to be happy! How overwhelming it must be when she first meets my aunt!"

"We must try to forget everything that has happened on both sides," said Jane. "I hope and trust that they will still be happy. His agreement to marry her is proof, I believe, that he has come to his senses. Their mutual affection will guide them, and I hope that they will settle down quietly and live rationally, which will eventually make people forget their past foolishness."

"Their behavior has been such," replied Elizabeth, "that neither you nor I nor anyone else can ever forget it. Talking about it is pointless."

The girls then realized that their mother probably did not know what had happened. They went to the library and asked their father if they should tell her. He was writing and without looking up he said,

"Do whatever you want."

"Can we take my uncle's letter to read to her?"

"Take whatever you want and go."

Elizabeth grabbed the letter from her father's writing table, and they went upstairs together. Mary and Kitty were both with Mrs. Bennet, so one announcement would suffice for all. After a brief introduction of good news, the letter was read aloud. Mrs. Bennet could barely contain herself. When Jane read aloud Mr. Gardiner's hope that Lydia would soon be married, her joy erupted and every subsequent sentence only added to her excitement. She was now as agitated by her delight as she had been fidgety from worry and annoyance before. Simply knowing that her daughter was going to be married was enough. She was not worried about her daughter's happiness or ashamed of her misconduct in any way.

"My dear, dear Lydia!" she exclaimed. "This is wonderful! She will be married! I'll get to see her again! She'll be married at sixteen! My kind brother! I knew he'd make it work out. I can't wait to see her! And Wickham too! But the clothes! The wedding clothes! I'll write to my sister Gardiner about them right away. Lizzy, darling, go downstairs to your father and ask him how much he'll give her. Wait, I'll go myself. Ring the bell, Kitty, for Hill. I'll get dressed in a moment. My dear, dear Lydia!" cried out Mrs. Bennet. "How happy we will be when we are together again!"

Her eldest daughter tried to ease her mother's excitement by reminding her of the debt of gratitude they owed to Mr. Gardiner.

"After all," she said, "we must thank him for making this happy ending possible. We are sure he has promised to help Mr. Wickham financially."

"Well," said Mrs. Bennet, "it's all very right that he should do it. If he didn't have his own family, all his money would have gone to me and my children. This is the first time he has done anything for us, apart from a few gifts. I'm so happy. In a little while I will have a daughter married! Mrs. Wickham! How nice it sounds. She was only sixteen last June. My dear Jane," Mrs. Bennet said, getting so excited she couldn't write. "I will dictate and you can write for me. We will discuss the money with your father later, but the things should be ordered right away."

She was about to go into great detail about calico, muslin, and cambric, and would have soon dictated a very large order if Jane, though with some difficulty, had not persuaded her to wait until her father was available to be consulted. She noted that one day's delay would not make much of a difference, and her mother was too happy to be as stubborn as she normally was. Other plans also came to her mind.

"I'll go to Meryton as soon as I'm dressed and tell my sister Philips the good news," she said. "And on the way back, I can drop in to visit Lady Lucas and Mrs. Long. Kitty, go and order the carriage. A drive would do me a lot of good. Girls, is there anything I can get for you in Meryton? Oh, here comes Hill. My dear Hill, have you heard the good news? Miss Lydia is getting married and you'll all get a bowl of punch to celebrate at her wedding."

Mrs. Hill immediately started expressing her joy. Elizabeth received her congratulations among the others, and then, feeling embarrassed by the foolishness of the situation, she retreated to her own room so that she could think freely.

Poor Lydia's situation was certainly not ideal, but Elizabeth was thankful that it could have been worse. Looking back to the fear they had felt only two hours ago, she was relieved by the advantages they had gained.

CHAPTER 50

Mr. Bennet had often wished before this period of his life that, instead of spending all his income, he had saved some of it each year to provide better for his children and his wife if she outlived him. Now he wished it more than ever. If he had done his duty in that respect, Lydia would not have had to rely on her uncle to buy her any honor or credit. The satisfaction of convincing one of the most worthless young men in Britain to marry her would have been enough.

He was very worried that something of such little benefit to anyone should be done at the expense of his brother-in-law, and he was determined to figure out how much help he had given and to repay him as soon as he could.

When Mr. Bennet had first gotten married, being thrifty was seen as unnecessary; after all, they were expecting to have a son. This son would cut off the entail as soon as he was of age, and the widow and younger children would be taken care of. Five daughters were born instead, but Mrs. Bennet was still convinced that the son was coming. By the time they had given up hope, it was too late to start saving. Mrs. Bennet had no interest in being thrifty and her husband's love of independence was the only thing that had kept them from spending more than their income.

Five thousand pounds had been settled on Mrs. Bennet and the children through marriage articles. However, the proportions in which it would be divided among the children depended on the will of the parents. At least with regards to Lydia, this issue had now been settled, and Mr. Bennet had no qualms about agreeing to the proposal before him. He expressed his complete approval of everything that had been done and his willingness to fulfill the obligations that had been made for him, thanking his brother for his kindness in the most concise terms possible. He had never thought that if Wickham could be convinced to marry his daughter, it could be done with so little inconvenience to himself, as with the present arrangement. He would hardly lose ten pounds a year from the hundred that was to be paid to them, as Lydia's expenses had been very little within that amount, what with her board and pocket allowance and the continuous cash gifts that were passed on to her through her mother's hands.

It was a pleasant surprise that he didn't have to put in much effort to accomplish it. He was hoping to avoid any unnecessary trouble in this matter. After his initial burst of anger that led him to search for her, he went back to his usual laziness. He wrote a letter quickly because although he was slow to start work, he was efficient once he began. He asked for more information about his debts to his brother but was too angry with Lydia to send her a message.

The good news quickly spread throughout the house, and then throughout the neighborhood at a similar pace. People in the neighborhood took the news in stride. It would have been better for gossip if Miss Lydia Bennet had come to town or been secluded in a distant farmhouse. However, there was much to talk about regarding her marriage. The kind-hearted wishes for her well-being that had come from all the spiteful old ladies in Meryton before the news did not lose much of their spirit in light of the new circumstances because everyone thought that with such a husband, her misery was certain.

It had been two weeks since Mrs. Bennet had been down stairs, but on this joyous day, she had taken her seat at the head of the table once again, and was in a state of overwhelming elation. No feelings of embarrassment put a damper on her joy. She had been wishing for her daughter to get married since Jane was sixteen, and now it was about to happen, and all her thoughts and words were on the accompanying luxuries of an elegant wedding, such as fine muslin, new carriages and servants. She was searching the neighborhood for a suitable home for her daughter, and without considering their income, she rejected many as not grand enough.

"Haye-Park could do," she said, "if the Gouldings would move out, or the big house at Stoke if the drawing-room was bigger; but Ashworth is too far away! I couldn't bear for her to be ten miles from me; and as for Purvis Lodge, the attics are awful."

Her husband let her talk without stopping while the servants were still there. But when the servants had left, he said to her, "Mrs. Bennet, before you take any or all of these houses for your son and daughter, let's come to a clear understanding. They will never be allowed into one particular house in this neighborhood. I won't encourage the boldness of either of them by letting them come to Longbourn."

A long argument followed this statement, but Mr. Bennet was determined. It quickly led to another argument and Mrs. Bennet was astonished and horrified to find that her husband would not even give a guinea to buy clothes for his daughter. He insisted that he should not show her any form of affection on this occasion. Mrs. Bennet could hardly believe it. She was shocked that his anger could be so strong that he would deny his daughter something which was essential for her marriage to be considered valid. She was more concerned about the disgrace that not having new clothes would bring to her daughter's wedding than the fact that she had eloped and been living with Wickham two weeks before the ceremony.

Elizabeth was now deeply regretful that, in her distress, she had informed Mr. Darcy about their worries concerning Lydia. As her marriage would soon put an end to the elopement, they could hope to keep its unfortunate start a secret from everyone who wasn't there at the time.

She had no fear of it spreading further through his means. There were few people whose secrecy she would have trusted more, but at the same time, there was no one whose knowledge of her sister's recklessness would have embarrassed her so much. Not that she was worried about any consequences for herself; it was clear that there was an impassable gap between them. Even if Lydia's marriage had been arranged in the most honorable way, she could not expect Mr. Darcy to connect himself to a family that, in addition to all its other problems, now had the closest ties to the man he so rightly despised.

She could not be surprised that he wanted to distance himself from such a connection. The thought of gaining her affection, which she had been certain he felt for her in Derbyshire, was now impossible to even consider. She was embarrassed, she was sad; she felt regret, even though she didn't know what for. She was jealous of his admiration, when she no longer had any chance of benefiting from it. She wanted to hear news of him, when there seemed to be a small chance of getting it. She was sure she would have been happy with him; even though it was unlikely they would meet again.

How triumphant he would feel, she often thought, if he knew that the proposals she had haughtily rejected four months ago, would now have been gladly and thankfully accepted! She was sure he was as generous as any man could be. But while he was alive, there would be a sense of victory.

She now began to understand that he was the perfect man for her, in terms of character and talents. His mind and temper, though different to her own, would have fulfilled all her desires. It was a union that would have been beneficial for both of them; her cheerfulness and liveliness could have softened his mind and improved his manners, and he could have provided her with great benefits from his wisdom, knowledge, and experience of the world.

But such a happy marriage could no longer show the admiring public what a truly blissful connection looked like. A union of a different kind, one that prevented the possibility of the other, was soon to be formed in their family.

She could not imagine how Wickham and Lydia were going to be supported in tolerable independence. But she could easily guess how little permanent happiness could belong to a couple who were only brought together because their passions were stronger than their virtue.

* * * * *

Mr. Gardiner soon wrote back to his brother. He replied briefly to Mr. Bennet's gratitude, promising to do all he could to help any of his family, and concluded by begging that the topic never be brought up again. The main purpose of his letter was to inform them that Mr. Wickham had decided to leave the Militia.

"It was greatly my wish that he should do so as soon as his marriage was fixed on. And I think you will agree with me in considering a removal from that corps as highly advisable, both on his account and my niece's. It is Mr. Wickham's intention to go into the regulars, and among his former friends there are still some who are able and willing to assist him in the army. He has the promise of an ensigncy in the General's regiment, now quartered in the North. It is an advantage to have it so far from this part of the kingdom. He promises fairly, and I hope among different people, where they may each have a character to preserve, they will both be more prudent. I have written to Colonel Forster to inform him of our present arrangements and to request that he will satisfy the various creditors of Mr. Wickham in and near Brighton, with assurances of speedy payment, for which I have pledged myself. And will you give yourself the trouble of carrying similar assurances to his creditors in Meryton, of whom I shall subjoin a list according to his information? He has given in all his debts; I hope at least he has not deceived us. Haggerston has our directions, and all will be completed in a week. They will then join his regiment unless they are first invited to Longbourn. And I understand from Mrs. Gardiner that my niece is very desirous of seeing you all before she leaves the South. She is well and begs to be dutifully remembered to you and her mother.
Yours, etc. E. Gardiner."

Mr. Bennet and his daughters saw all the advantages of Wickham moving away from the regiment, just as Mr. Gardiner did. But Mrs. Bennet was not so happy about it. Lydia being sent to the North when she was expecting to have the most fun and be proud of her company, for she had not given up her plan of them living in Hertfordshire, was a big disappointment; and it was such a shame that Lydia had to leave a regiment where she knew everyone and had so many friends.

"She is so fond of Mrs. Forster," she said, "it would be terrible to make her go!—and there are several of the young men she likes a lot too. The officers in the General's regiment might not be as pleasant."

At first, Mr. Bennet completely refused his daughter's request to be welcomed back into the family before she left for the North. However, Jane and Elizabeth wanted their sister to have the respect and honor of being welcomed back by their parents after she was married, so they pleaded with him rationally and kindly to allow her and her husband to come to Longbourn when they were married. Their mother was pleased that she would be able to show her married daughter to the neighborhood. Thus, Mr. Bennet wrote to his brother and gave them permission to come, and it was settled that they would go to Longbourn as soon as the ceremony was over.

Elizabeth was surprised, however, that Wickham would agree to such a plan, and, if she had only followed her own desires, she would have wanted nothing more than to avoid any meeting with him.

CHAPTER 51

The day of their sister's wedding had arrived; and Jane and Elizabeth likely felt more for her than she felt for herself. The carriage was sent to pick them up and they were due back in time for dinner. The older Miss Bennets dreaded their arrival; and Jane, in particular, who felt for Lydia the same as she would have felt had she been the one in trouble, was distressed at the thought of what her sister would have to go through.

They arrived. The family was gathered in the breakfast room to welcome them. Mrs. Bennet had a smile on her face as the carriage pulled up to the door; her husband had an unreadable expression; and her daughters were anxious and uneasy.

Lydia's voice was heard in the vestibule; the door was opened, and she ran into the room. Her mother stepped forward, embraced her, and welcomed her with great joy; she then gave her hand with an affectionate smile to Wickham, who followed his partner, and wished them both joy with enthusiasm, which showed no doubt of their happiness.

Mr. Bennet's reception of them was not as warm. His expression became more serious and he hardly said a word. The confident attitude of the young couple was enough to annoy him. Elizabeth was disgusted and even Miss Bennet was shocked. Lydia was still the same; untamed, unashamed, wild, noisy, and fearless. She went from one sister to the other, asking them to congratulate her, and when they all sat down, she looked around the room, noticed some changes and laughed, saying it had been a long time since she had been there.

Wickham was no more upset than Elizabeth herself, but he had such pleasant manners that if his character and marriage had been what they should have been, his smiles and easy manner while claiming their relationship would have delighted them all.

Elizabeth had not previously believed him capable of such confidence, but she sat down, deciding not to set any limits in the future to the impudence of an impudent man. Elizabeth and Jane blushed, but the two who caused their confusion showed no change in color in their cheeks.

There was no lack of conversation. The bride and her mother could not talk fast enough; and Wickham, who happened to be sitting near Elizabeth, began asking about his acquaintances in the area with a good-natured ease that she felt unable to match in her replies. They both seemed to have the happiest memories. Nothing of the past was remembered with pain; and Lydia willingly brought up topics which her sisters would never have mentioned in a million years.

"Just think, it's been three months since I left!" she exclaimed. "It only feels like a couple of weeks, I declare; and yet so much has happened in that time. Goodness me! When I left, I definitely didn't think I'd be married when I got back, although I thought it would be really fun if I was."

Her father raised his eyes in surprise. Jane was distressed. Elizabeth shot a look of dismay at Lydia, who, oblivious to all else, cheerfully continued, "Oh, Mama, do the people around here know I'm married today? I was worried they wouldn't, so when we passed William Goulding in his carriage, I made sure he knew. I lowered the window next to him, took off my glove and let him see my ring, then I bowed and smiled."

Elizabeth could take it no more. She got up and ran out of the room and didn't come back until she heard them heading to the dining room. Lydia then quickly joined them and, with a show of eagerness, walked up to her mother's right side and said, "Ah! Jane, I'm taking your place now because I'm a married woman so you have to move down."

It was obvious that time hadn't made Lydia become embarrassed, something she had been completely free of when she first arrived. Her ease and cheerfulness only increased. She wanted to see Mrs. Philips, the Lucases, and all the other neighbors and to hear them call her "Mrs. Wickham". After dinner, she went to show off her ring and brag about being married to Mrs. Hill and the two housemaids.

When they were all back in the breakfast room, she said to her mother, "Well, mamma, what do you think of my husband? Isn't he a great guy? I'm sure my sisters must all be jealous of me. I only hope they can have half my luck. They should all go to Brighton. That's the place to get husbands. It's such a shame we didn't all go there, mamma."

"I agree, if I had my way we would. But Lydia, I don't like the idea of you going so far away. Is it really necessary?"

"Oh, yes, there's nothing to worry about. You, Papa, and my sisters should come visit us. We'll be in Newcastle all winter, and I'm sure there will be some balls. I'll make sure to get good partners for all of you."

"I would love that!" said her mother.

"And then when you leave, you can leave one or two of my sisters behind and I'm sure I'll get them husbands before the winter is over."

"Thanks for the offer," said Elizabeth, "but I'm not too fond of your way of finding husbands."

Their visitors weren't staying more than ten days. Mr. Wickham had received his commission before leaving London and was to join his regiment in two weeks.

Everyone except Mrs. Bennet was sad that the stay was so short and she made the most of the time by taking Lydia around and having frequent parties at home. Everyone enjoyed these parties, as it was preferable to staying in a family circle.

Elizabeth could easily tell that Wickham's feelings for Lydia weren't as strong as hers for him. She didn't need any more evidence to prove that Lydia had eloped with him out of love, rather than the other way around. Elizabeth would have been surprised if Wickham had eloped with her, had she not been certain that he had been forced to do it due to his financial situation.

Lydia was extremely fond of him. He called him her dear Wickham on every occasion, and no one could be compared to him. He was the best at everything in the world, and she was sure he would shoot more birds on the first day of September than anyone else in the country.

One morning, shortly after they arrived, while she was sitting with her two older sisters, she said to Elizabeth, "Lizzy, I don't think I ever gave you an account of my wedding. You weren't there when I told Mother and the others all about it. Aren't you curious to hear how it was managed?"

"No, not really," Elizabeth replied. "I don't think there can be too little said about the subject."

"Goodness! You're so strange! But I have to tell you how it went. We got married, you see, at St. Clement's because Wickham was lodging in that parish. It was arranged that we would all be there by eleven o'clock. My uncle, aunt, and I were going together, and the others were meeting us at the church. Well, Monday morning arrived, and I was in such a fuss! I was so afraid that something would happen to delay it, and then I would have gone completely mad. And there was my aunt, the whole time I was getting dressed, preaching and talking away as if she were reading a sermon. However, I only heard one word in ten because I was thinking about my dear Wickham. I wanted to know if he would be married in his blue coat.

"So, we had breakfast at 10 like always; it felt like it would never end. My uncle and aunt were so unpleasant the whole time I was there. I didn't even go outside for two weeks! No parties, no plans, nothing. London was pretty empty, but the theatre was still open. Just as the carriage arrived, my uncle was called away to meet with that awful man Mr. Stone. And, you know, once they get together, it's hard to get them apart. I was so scared I didn't know what to do as my uncle was supposed to give me away, and if we were late, we wouldn't be able to get married that day. Luckily, he came back in ten minutes and we set out. I realized afterwards that if he couldn't make it, the wedding wouldn't have to be postponed because Mr. Darcy could've done it instead."

"Mr. Darcy?" Elizabeth said in shock.

"Oh, yes! He was supposed to come with Wickham. Oh, no! I completely forgot! I promised them I wouldn't say anything. What will Wickham say? It was supposed to be a secret!"

"If it was supposed to be a secret," Jane said, "don't say another word about it. You can depend on me not asking any more questions."

"Oh, definitely," Elizabeth said, though she was dying to know more. "We won't ask you any questions."

"Thank you," Lydia said. "If you did, I'd probably tell you everything and then Wickham would be mad."

Elizabeth was so tempted to ask more questions, but she had to prevent herself from doing so by running away.

But it was impossible to remain in ignorance on such a point, so she had to try to find out more information. Mr. Darcy had been at her sister's wedding, even though it was a place and among people he had no reason to be. She thought of many explanations for his presence, but none of them felt right. She couldn't bear the suspense any longer, so she quickly wrote a letter to her aunt asking for an explanation of what Lydia had said, if it was possible to do so without breaking the secrecy Lydia seemed to think was necessary. She wrote,

"You can easily imagine how eager I am to know why someone who is not connected to us and is practically a stranger to our family was there at such a time. Please write back to me as soon as you can and let me know, unless there are very strong reasons for keeping it secret, in which case I will have to accept not knowing."

"Not that I will, though," she added to herself as she finished the letter.

"If you, my dear aunt, don't tell me in an honorable way, I'll certainly have to resort to tricks and stratagems to find out."

Jane's delicate sense of honor prevented her from speaking privately to Elizabeth about what Lydia had revealed. Elizabeth was pleased about it until it was known whether her inquiries would be answered. She would rather not have a confidant until then.

CHAPTER 52

Elizabeth was pleased to receive a response to her letter as soon as possible. As soon as she got hold of it, she hurried to the little grove where she was least likely to be disturbed. She sat down on one of the benches and prepared to be happy because the length of the letter convinced her that it did not contain a denial.

"*Gracechurch-street, Sept. 6.*
Dear Niece,
I have just read your letter and I'm going to spend the morning answering it since I think I need to explain a few things to you. I'm a bit taken aback by your request; I didn't expect you to ask this. Please don't think I'm mad, I just want you to know that I didn't think you would need to ask these questions. Your uncle is just as surprised as I am, and only his belief that you were involved would have caused him to act as he has done. If you are truly innocent and don't know what's going on, then I will have to be more explicit. On the day I returned home from Longbourn, your uncle had an unexpected visitor. Mr. Darcy called and was with him for a few hours. By the time I got back, it was all over, so I wasn't as frustrated as you seem to be. He had come to tell your uncle that he had found out where your sister and Mr. Wickham were and that he had seen and talked to them both - Wickham multiple times and Lydia once. As far as I can tell, he left Derbyshire one day after us, and came to town with the intention of searching for them. The reason he gave was that he felt responsible for not making it more widely known how untrustworthy Wickham was, which meant that a woman of good character could have been tricked into loving or trusting him. He said it was his pride that had stopped him from revealing his own actions to the public, and that his character should speak for itself. He said it was his duty to step up and try to fix a problem he had caused himself. If he had any other reasons, I'm sure they wouldn't be anything to

be ashamed of. He had been in town for a few days before he managed to track them down, but he had something to guide his search which we didn't have, and this made him more determined to follow us. There was a woman, Mrs. Younge, who had been governess to Miss Darcy and was dismissed from her post for some unknown reason. She took a big house in Edward Street and has since earned a living by renting out rooms. He knew that she was close to Wickham and so he went to her as soon as he arrived in town to try and get information about him. But it took him two or three days before he could get what he wanted out of her. I guess she wouldn't give up her friend's whereabouts without a bribe, because she did know where he was. In fact, Wickham had gone to her when they first arrived in London and if she had been able to take them in, they would have stayed with her. At last, our kind friend managed to get the desired directions and street name. He saw Wickham and afterwards insisted on seeing Lydia. He said his first goal with her was to try and convince her to leave her current disgraceful situation and go back to her family as soon as they were willing to accept her, offering his help as much as he could. But he found Lydia totally determined to stay where she was. She didn't care about any of her friends, she didn't need his help, she refused to consider leaving Wickham. She was convinced they would be married eventually, so it didn't really matter when. Since that was her opinion, he thought the only thing left to do was to arrange and speed up the marriage, which he quickly found out during his first conversation with Wickham, was never his intention. He admitted he had to leave the regiment due to some debts of honor that had to be paid immediately, and didn't hesitate to blame Lydia's elopement on her own recklessness. He planned to quit his job right away and had no clue what he would do next. He had no money and would need to go somewhere. Mr. Darcy asked him why he hadn't married your sister straight away. Even though Mr. Bennet wasn't particularly wealthy, he could have done something for Wickham and his situation would have been improved by marriage. But Wickham still had hopes of making his fortune by marrying someone in another country. Even so, he was not able to resist the temptation of an immediate solution. They met several times as there was much to be discussed. Wickham wanted more than what he was offered, but eventually he became reasonable. Once everything was settled, Mr. Darcy's next step was to tell your uncle and he did that the evening before I came home. But, Mr. Gardiner could not be found, so Mr. Darcy asked more questions and learned that your father was still with him, but would leave town the next morning. He thought it better to wait and speak to your uncle instead, so he postponed seeing your father until after he had left. He didn't leave his name and the next day people only knew that a gentleman had called. He came again on Saturday and by Monday it was all sorted out and the express was sent off to Longbourn. But Mr. Darcy was very stubborn. Elizabeth, I think that stubbornness is his real flaw. He has been accused of many things, but this is the real one. Nothing was to be done that he didn't do himself; though I'm sure (and I'm not saying this to be thanked, so don't mention it), your uncle would have been more than happy to take care of the whole situation. They argued about it for a long time, which was more than either the man or woman involved deserved. But in the end, your uncle had to give in, and instead of being able to help his niece, he was only given the credit for it, which he didn't like at all; and I think your letter this morning made him very happy, because it meant that he wouldn't have to take credit for something he hadn't done, and the praise would go to the right person. But Lizzy, you can't tell anyone else about this, not even Jane. You know what has been done for the young couple, right? His debts are going to be paid, which I think is more than a thousand pounds, another thousand will be added to what she already has, and his commission will be bought. The reason he had to do all this by himself was what I already mentioned. It was because of his shyness and lack of proper thought that Wickham's character was misunderstood and accepted as it was. This might be true, but I don't think his being shy could be blamed for what happened. Despite all this, Lizzy, you can be sure that your uncle would not have agreed to this if we had not made him believe there was another reason for it. Once this was all settled, he went back to his friends who were still at Pemberley, but it was agreed that he'd be back in London for the wedding and to finish all the financial matters. I think I've told you everything. I know this will come as a surprise to you, but I hope it won't upset you. Lydia came to us and Wickham had free access to the house. He was exactly the same as when I knew him in Hertfordshire, but I wouldn't tell you how unhappy I was with her behavior while she stayed with us, if I hadn't read Jane's letter last Wednesday which said her conduct when she returned home was the same. So what I'm telling you now *won't cause you any more pain. I spoke to her several times seriously, telling her how wrong and unhappy her actions had been. I don't think she was really listening to me, but I remembered Elizabeth and Jane and kept my patience. Mr. Darcy came back as Lydia told you and attended the wedding. He had dinner with us the next day and was due to leave town again on Wednesday or Thursday. Will you be very angry with me, my dear Lizzy, if I take this opportunity to tell you how much I like him? His behavior has been as pleasing as when we were in Derbyshire. I like his understanding and opinions; he just needs to be a bit more lively, and if he chooses his wife wisely, she can teach him that. I thought he was being quite sly, hardly ever mentioning your name, but that seems to be the trend. Please forgive me if I'm being presumptuous, or at least don't stop me from going to Pemberley. I won't be happy until I have been all around the park. A low phaeton with a nice pair of ponies would be perfect. But I must stop writing. The children have been looking for me for the past half hour.*

Yours very sincerely,
M. Gardiner."

The contents of this letter caused Elizabeth to feel both pleasure and pain, making it difficult to determine which emotion was stronger. She had vague suspicions about what Mr. Darcy might have done to help her sister's marriage, but was afraid to encourage them. However, it turned out that her suspicions were true! He had purposely followed them to town and had gone through all the trouble and embarrassment of finding out information about a woman he must abhor and despise. He had even been forced to frequently interact with, reason with, persuade, and finally bribe the man he had most wished to avoid, just for the sake of a girl whom he could not even like or respect. Elizabeth hoped that he had done it for her, but was quickly reminded of other considerations. Even her vanity was not enough to depend on his affection for a woman who had already rejected him and was related to Wickham. The very thought of being related to Wickham was enough to make any proud person revolt from the connection. Mr. Darcy had done a lot for them, and Elizabeth was ashamed of how much he had done. However, she knew that he had a reason for his interference, which was not hard to believe. It was reasonable for him to feel that he had been wrong and to want to fix it. He had the means to do it, and while she would not place herself as his main motivation, she could believe that his remaining partiality for her might have helped him in a cause where her peace of mind was at stake. It was painful to know that they were indebted to someone who could never receive a return. They owed everything, including the restoration of Lydia's character, to him. She felt regret over any ungracious feelings or actions she had directed towards him in the past, but was proud of him for his compassion and honor. She read her aunt's commendation of him again and again, finding some pleasure in it despite the mixed feelings of regret. She was even glad to see that both her uncle and aunt had been convinced of the affection and trust between Mr. Darcy and herself.

She was interrupted from her seat and her thoughts by someone coming up to her, and before she could move away, Wickham caught up with her.

"I'm sorry to interrupt your solitary walk, my dear sister?" he said as he joined her.

"You certainly do," she replied with a smile; "but that doesn't mean the interruption has to be unwelcome."

"I would be sorry if it was. We were always good friends and now we are better."

"That's true. Are the others coming out?"

"I don't know. Mrs. Bennet and Lydia are going to Meryton in the carriage. So, my dear sister, I hear from our uncle and aunt that you have actually seen Pemberley."

She replied in the affirmative.

"I almost wish I had gone too. I believe it would have been too much for me, but I could have gone if I was going to Newcastle. Did you see the old housekeeper, Reynolds? She always liked me. Of course, she wouldn't have mentioned my name to you."

"Actually, she did."

"Really? What did she say?"

"She said that you had gone into the army and she was afraid it hadn't worked out well."

"Of course," he replied, biting his lips.

Elizabeth hoped she had silenced him, but he then said,

"I was surprised to see Darcy in town last month. We passed each other a few times. I wonder what he was doing there."

"Maybe he was getting ready for his wedding with Miss de Bourgh," Elizabeth suggested. "It must have been something important to bring him there at this time of year."

"Definitely, did you see him when you were in Lambton? I thought I heard from the Gardiners that you did."

"Yes, he introduced us to his sister," she replied.

"And do you like her?" I asked.

"Very much," she said.

"I've heard that she's improved a lot in the last couple of years. When I last saw her, she wasn't very promising. I'm glad you like her. I hope she turns out well."

"I'm sure she will. She's past the most difficult age now," she replied.

"Did you go through the village of Kympton?"

"I don't remember, why do you ask?" she replied.

"I mention it because it's the living I should have had. It's an excellent parsonage house - it would have suited me perfectly."

"How would you have liked writing sermons?" she asked.

"I would have loved it. I would have considered it my duty and the effort wouldn't have been much. I shouldn't complain, but it would have been perfect for me. The quiet and seclusion of such a life would have been everything I wanted from happiness. But it wasn't meant to be. Have you ever heard the story of the parsonage house?"

"I heard from a reliable source that it was only given to you conditionally and at the will of the current patron."

"Yes, that was true. I told you that from the start, don't you remember?"

"I also heard that there was a time when preaching wasn't so enjoyable for you as it is now; that you actually said you would never take orders and that the issue was settled accordingly."

"You did! And it wasn't completely unfounded. You may remember what I told you about that when we first talked about it."

By this time they were almost at the door of the house, as she had walked quickly to get rid of him. Not wanting to upset her sister, she smiled good-naturedly and said,

"Come on, Mr. Wickham, we're brother and sister, you know. Let's not argue about the past. In the future, I hope we will always be in agreement."

She held out her hand; he kissed it with respectful politeness, though he wasn't sure how to look, and then they went inside.

CHAPTER 53

Mr. Wickham was so pleased with the conversation that he never brought it up again, and Elizabeth was glad that she had said enough to keep him quiet.

The day of his and Lydia's departure soon arrived, and Mrs. Bennet had to accept the separation, which was likely to continue for at least a year since her husband did not agree with her plan of them all going to Newcastle.

"Oh, my dear Lydia," she said, "when will we see each other again?"

"Oh, I don't know. Not for two or three years, probably."

"Write to me often, my dear."

"As often as I can. But you know married women don't have much time for writing. My sisters can write to me. They won't have anything else to do."

Mr. Wickham said goodbye with much more emotion than his wife. He smiled, looked handsome, and said many nice things.

"He's an impressive man," said Mr. Bennet as soon as they left the house. "I must say he has a way with people that I haven't seen in some time. I'm quite proud of him. I challenge even Sir William Lucas himself to produce a more valuable son-in-law."

The loss of her daughter made Mrs. Bennet very depressed for several days.

"I often think that there's nothing worse than having to say goodbye to friends. You feel so alone without them."

"Well, that's the consequence of marrying off a daughter, Madam," said Elizabeth. "At least you can take comfort in the fact that your other four daughters are still single."

"That's not the point. Lydia isn't leaving me because she's married, but only because her husband's regiment happens to be so far away. If they were stationed closer, she wouldn't have left so soon."

But the despondent state into which this event threw her was soon relieved, and her mind opened again to the excitement of hope, by a piece of news that began to circulate. The housekeeper at Netherfield had received orders to prepare for the arrival of her master, who was coming down in a day or two to shoot there for several weeks. Mrs. Bennet was very restless. She looked at Jane, and smiling and shaking her head.

"Well, well, so Mr. Bingley is coming down, sister," (for Mrs. Philips first brought her the news.) "Well, that's all the better. Not that I care about it, though. He is nothing to us, you know, and I'm sure I never want to see him again. But, however, he is very welcome to come to Netherfield if he likes. And who knows what might happen? But that's none of our business. You know, sister, we agreed long ago never to mention a word about it. So is it absolutely certain that he's coming?"

"You can be sure of it," replied the other. "Mrs. Nicholls was in Meryton last night; I saw her passing by and went out myself on purpose to find out the truth of it, and she told me that it was definitely true. He's coming down on Thursday at the latest, probably on Wednesday. She told me she was going to the butcher's on purpose to order some meat for Wednesday, and she's got three pairs of ducks, just right to be killed."

Miss Bennet had not been able to hear of his coming without changing color. It had been many months since she had mentioned his name to Elizabeth, but now, as soon as they were alone together, she said,

"I saw you look at me today, Lizzy, when my aunt told us about the current report, and I know I appeared distressed. But don't think it was because of any silly reason. I was only confused for the moment because I felt like I should be looked at. I assure you, the news doesn't affect me with either pleasure or pain. I'm glad of one thing, that he's coming alone; we'll see less of him. Not that I'm afraid of myself, but I dread other people's comments."

Elizabeth didn't know what to make of it. Had she not seen him in Derbyshire, she might have supposed him capable of coming there for no other purpose than what was known; but she still thought that he liked Jane, and she was uncertain if he was coming with his friend's approval or if he was daring enough to come without it.

"But it is unfair," she sometimes thought, "that this poor man cannot come to a house which he has legally rented without causing so much speculation! I will leave him to himself."

Despite what her sister said and truly believed to be her feelings in anticipation of his arrival, Elizabeth could easily see that her emotions were affected by it. They were more disturbed and inconsistent than she had ever seen them.

The matter which had been discussed so fervently between their parents about a year ago was now brought up again.

"As soon as Mr. Bingley comes, my dear," said Mrs. Bennet, "you will of course pay him a visit."

"No, no. You forced me to visit him last year, and promised that if I went to see him, he would marry one of my daughters. But nothing came of it and I will not be sent on a fool's errand again."

His wife pointed out to him how important it would be for all the neighboring gentlemen to greet him if he returned to Netherfield.

"It's an etiquette I despise," he replied. "If he wants our company, let him come and look for us. I'm not going to spend my time running after my neighbors every time they go and come back."

"Well, all I know is that it would be terribly rude of you if you don't visit him. But that won't stop me from inviting him to dinner here. We'll have to have Mrs. Long and the Gouldings soon. That'll make thirteen, including us, so there'll just be enough room for him at the table."

Feeling better after making this decision, she was able to bear her husband's rudeness, though it was very humiliating to think that their neighbors might see Mr. Bingley before they did. As the day of his arrival drew nearer, Jane said to her sister,

"I'm beginning to regret that he's coming at all. I could look at him without any emotion, but it's so hard to hear about it all the time. My mother means well, but she doesn't know, no one can know, how much I'm suffering from what she's saying. I'll be so relieved when his stay at Netherfield is over!"

"I really wish I could say something to make you feel better," Elizabeth responded. "But unfortunately, I can't. You have to experience and process these feelings yourself, and I can't just tell you to be patient like usual because you're already so good at that."

Mr. Bingley arrived and Mrs. Bennet was desperate to get news of him as soon as possible. She counted the days until they could send an invitation, not thinking she'd see him before then. But on the third morning after his arrival, she saw him from her window, entering the paddock and riding towards the house.

She called her daughters to share her joy. Jane resolutely stayed at the table, but Elizabeth, to appease her mother, went to the window. She looked out and saw Mr. Darcy with him. She went back to her seat by her sister.

"There's a man with him, Mama," said Kitty. "Who could it be?"

"It must be some acquaintance or other, my dear, I suppose. I don't know who it is," said her mother.

"Oh, it looks just like that man who used to be with him before. What's his name? That tall, proud man," said Kitty.

"Good gracious! It's Mr. Darcy! Well, any friend of Mr. Bingley's is always welcome here, of course. But I still don't like the sight of him," said their mother.

Jane looked at Elizabeth in surprise and concern. She knew little of their meeting in Derbyshire, so she felt embarrassed for Elizabeth, seeing him for the first time after getting his letter. Both sisters were very uncomfortable. Each felt for the other, and of course for themselves. Meanwhile, their mother kept talking about her dislike of Mr. Darcy, and her intention to be civil to him only as Mr. Bingley's friend, without either of them hearing. But Elizabeth had worries that Jane didn't know about; she hadn't yet had the courage to show Jane Mrs. Gardiner's letter or to tell her how her feelings towards him had changed. To Jane, he was just a man whose proposal she had refused and whose merits she had underestimated, but from what Elizabeth knew, he was the person who had done them an enormous favor, and she felt for him a reasonable and just interest, if not quite as strong as Jane felt for Bingley. She was extremely surprised when he arrived - not just coming to Netherfield, but to Longbourn, and specifically seeking her out again. Her shock was almost as great as when she first saw his changed behavior in Derbyshire.

The color that had drained from her face came back for half a minute, with an extra glow, and a smile of joy lit up her eyes. She thought for a moment that his love and wishes were still the same. But she refused to be sure.

"Let me first see how he behaves," she said. "Then I can start hoping."

She worked hard to stay calm, not daring to look up until her curiosity made her look at her sister as the servant was coming in. Jane looked a bit paler than usual, but more in control than Elizabeth had expected. When the gentlemen arrived, her color deepened. She greeted them politely, without any signs of anger or too much friendliness.

Elizabeth said as little as politeness allowed and went back to her work with more enthusiasm than usual. She had only risked a glance at Darcy. He looked serious, as usual, and she thought he looked more like he had in Hertfordshire than she had seen him at Pemberley. She guessed that he couldn't act the same way around her mother as he had around her uncle and aunt. It was a difficult thought to consider, but not an impossible one.

She had also caught a brief glimpse of Bingley, and in that short time he seemed both pleased and embarrassed. Mrs.

Bennet welcomed him with a politeness that made her two daughters embarrassed, especially when compared to the cold and formal politeness she showed to his friend.

Elizabeth was particularly hurt, as she knew her mother owed his friend the preservation of her favorite daughter from a terrible fate, and she felt the distinction was applied unfairly.

Darcy asked how Mr. and Mrs. Gardiner were doing, but didn't say much else. He wasn't sitting next to Elizabeth, which might have been why he was quiet, but that wasn't the case in Derbyshire where he had talked to her friends when he couldn't talk to her. However, several minutes went by without him speaking, and when Elizabeth looked up at him, she found him often looking at Jane or at the ground. He seemed more thoughtful and less concerned with pleasing her than the last time they met. Elizabeth was disappointed and annoyed with herself for feeling that way.

"Why did he even come, if this is how it's going to be?" she wondered to herself.

She didn't feel like talking to anyone else but Darcy, but was too nervous to speak to him directly. She asked about his sister and nothing more.

"It has been a while since you left, Mr. Bingley," said Mrs. Bennet.

He agreed with her.

"I began to be afraid you would never come back again. People did say, you meant to quit the place entirely at Michaelmas; but, however, I hope it is not true. A great many changes have happened in the neighborhood, since you went away. Miss Lucas is married and settled, and one of my own daughters. I'm sure you've heard about it; you must have seen it in the newspapers. It was in the Times and the Courier, I know; though it wasn't written in the way it should have been. It just said, 'Recently, George Wickham, Esq. to Miss Lydia Bennet,' without mentioning anything about her father, or where she lived, or anything else. It was written by my brother Gardiner too, and I wonder how he managed to make such a mess of it. Did you see it?"

Bingley replied that he did, and offered his congratulations. Elizabeth didn't dare to look up. She couldn't tell how Mr. Darcy was reacting.

"It's certainly wonderful to have a daughter who's well married," her mother continued, "but at the same time, Mr. Bingley, it's really hard to have her taken away from me like that. They've gone down to Newcastle, a place quite far north, it seems, and they're going to stay there, I don't know for how long. His regiment is there; I suppose you've heard that he's gone into the regulars."

Elizabeth, who knew that this was about Mr. Darcy, was so embarrassed that she could hardly stay in her seat. But it made her speak, which nothing else had done before; she asked Bingley if he was going to stay in the country for a while. He thought it would be a few weeks.

"When you have shot all the birds on your own land, Mr. Bingley," said her mother, "I hope you will come here and shoot as many as you want on Mr. Bennet's estate. I'm sure he will be more than happy to let you and he will keep the best of them for you."

Elizabeth was even more miserable at this unnecessary and kind attention! If the same good prospects that had cheered them a year ago were to arise now, she was sure that everything would end in the same annoying way. At that moment, she felt that no amount of years of happiness could make up for the pain of this moment.

"My first wish," she thought to herself, "is never to be in the company of either of them again. Their company can't give me any pleasure that could make up for this misery!"

But soon the misery was lessened when she saw how her sister's beauty had re-ignited her former lover's admiration. When he first came in, he had spoken to her only a little, but every five minutes he seemed to be paying more attention to her. He found her just as attractive as she had been last year, as kind-hearted and genuine, though not quite as talkative. Jane was determined that no one should notice any difference in her, and was sure that she was talking just as much as before. But her mind was so occupied that she didn't always realize when she was quiet.

When the gentlemen were getting ready to leave, Mrs. Bennet remembered her promise of hospitality and invited them to dinner at Longbourn in a few days.

"You owe us a visit, Mr. Bingley," she added, "because when you went to town last winter, you promised to take a family dinner with us as soon as you returned. I haven't forgotten, you see; and I was very disappointed that you didn't come back and keep your promise."

Bingley looked a bit embarrassed at this, and said something about being prevented by other commitments. Then they left.

Mrs. Bennet had been very keen to ask them to stay and have dinner that day, but even though she always kept a very good table, she didn't think anything less than two courses would be good enough for a man on whom she had such high expectations, or satisfy the appetite and pride of someone with an income of ten thousand pounds a year.

CHAPTER 54

As soon as they were gone, Elizabeth went out to try to cheer herself up, or in other words, to think uninterruptedly about things that would make her feel worse. Mr. Darcy's behavior shocked and frustrated her.

"If he only came here to be quiet, serious, and indifferent," she said, "why did he come at all?"

She couldn't think of any explanation that made sense to her.

"He can still be friendly and pleasant to my uncle and aunt when he's in town, so why not to me? If he's afraid of me, why did he come here? If he no longer cares for me, why is he so quiet? It's so irritating! I won't think about him anymore."

Her determination was briefly interrupted by the arrival of her sister, who had a cheerful look that showed she was more content with their visitors than Elizabeth.

"Now that this first meeting is over, I'm feeling much better," she said. "I know my own strength, and I won't be embarrassed when he comes again. I'm glad he's dining here on Tuesday. That way it will be obvious to everyone that we're just meeting as casual acquaintances."

"Yes, very casual indeed," Elizabeth said, laughing. "Oh, Jane, be careful."

"My dear Lizzy, you can't think I'm so weak that I'm in danger now," Jane replied.

"I think you're in very great danger of making him fall in love with you all over again," Elizabeth said.

They didn't see the gentlemen again until Tuesday and Mrs. Bennet was delighted by the good humor and politeness that Bingley had shown in his brief visit.

On Tuesday there was a big gathering at Longbourn and the two most eagerly anticipated guests, who arrived right on time, were Bingley and his friend. When they went into the dining room, Elizabeth looked to see if Bingley would take his usual seat next to Jane. Her mother, who was thinking the same thing, didn't invite him to sit next to her. When he came in, he seemed to hesitate, but then Jane looked round and smiled at him and he sat down next to her.

Elizabeth, feeling triumphant, looked over at his friend. He bore it with an impressive calmness, and she would have thought that Bingley had received permission to be happy, if she hadn't seen his eyes looking towards Mr. Darcy with a half-amused, half-worried expression.

His behavior towards her sister during dinner showed admiration for her that, while more restrained than before, convinced Elizabeth that if left to his own devices, Jane's and his own happiness would soon be secured. Even though she didn't dare count on it, she still felt joy from watching him. It gave her all the cheer her spirits could muster; she wasn't in a good mood. Mr. Darcy was as far away from her as the table could place them; he was on one side of her mother. She knew how little pleasure either of them would get from such a position, or how it would make either of them look good. She wasn't close enough to hear any of their conversations, but she could see how rarely they spoke to each other and how formal and cold their manner was when they did. Elizabeth's mother's lack of politeness made it more difficult for Elizabeth to accept all the kindness they owed the man.

She wished she could tell him that the whole family was aware of and appreciated his kindness. She hoped that the evening would give her a chance to get them talking together more than just exchanging polite greetings. She was so anxious and restless that the time in the drawing room before the men arrived was tedious and almost made her rude. She was looking forward to their arrival as the only thing that could make the evening enjoyable.

"If he doesn't come to me," she said, "then I'm giving up on him forever."

The men arrived and she thought he looked like he might respond to her hopes, but unfortunately the ladies had crowded around the table where Miss Bennet was making tea and Elizabeth was pouring out the coffee, so there wasn't a single seat near her. As the men approached, one of the girls moved even closer to her and said in a whisper,

"We don't want any of the men here, do we? They're not going to come and break us up, I'm sure of it."

Darcy had walked away to another part of the room. She watched him, envied anyone he talked to, and could barely manage to help someone get coffee. Then she got angry with herself for being so foolish.

"A man who has once been rejected! How could I have been so foolish as to expect him to love me again? Is there anyone of the opposite sex who wouldn't protest against such a weakness as making a second proposal to the same woman? There is no insult so abhorrent to their feelings!"

She was a little comforted, however, when he brought back his coffee cup himself; and she took the opportunity to ask,

"Is your sister still at Pemberley?"

"Yes, she will stay there until Christmas."

"And all alone? All her friends gone?"

"Mrs. Annesley is with her. The others have been gone to Scarborough for three weeks now."

She couldn't think of anything else to say; but if he wanted to talk to her, he could have had more success. He stayed by her side for a few minutes in silence; and finally, when the young lady whispered something to Elizabeth again, he walked away.

After finishing tea, the ladies all got up and the card tables were set out. Elizabeth hoped that Mr. Darcy would soon join her, but her hopes were shattered when she saw her mother pull him in to play whist. She no longer expected any enjoyment from the evening. They were separated into different tables and she had no hope except that his attention might be so much on her side of the room that he would play as badly as she did.

Mrs. Bennet had planned to keep the two gentlemen from Netherfield for supper, but unfortunately their carriage was ordered before the others, and she could not keep them.

"Well, girls," she said, as soon as they were alone, "What do you think of the day? I think everything went unusually well, I assure you. The dinner was as well prepared as any I've ever seen. The venison was cooked perfectly, and everyone said they'd never seen such a fat haunch before. The soup was fifty times better than what we had at the Lucas's last week, and even Mr. Darcy admitted that the partridges were exceptionally well done. I suppose he has two or three French cooks at least. And, my dear Jane, you looked more beautiful than ever. Mrs. Long said so too, and I asked her if you did. And do you know what she said? 'Ah! Mrs. Bennet, we will finally have her at Netherfield.' She really did say that. I do believe Mrs. Long is as good a person as ever lived, and her nieces are very well-behaved and not very pretty. I like them very much."

Mrs. Bennet was in very high spirits; she had seen enough of Bingley's behavior to Jane to be sure she would get him in the end; and her hopes of the good it would do her family when she was in a good mood were so unrealistic that she was very disappointed not to see him there again the next day to propose.

"It's been a very pleasant day," said Miss Bennet to Elizabeth. "The group seemed so well-matched and appropriate for each other. I hope we can meet again often."

Elizabeth smiled.

"Lizzy, you mustn't think that. You mustn't suspect me. It hurts me. I can assure you that I have now learned to enjoy his conversation as a pleasant and sensible young man without wanting anything more from it. I'm completely satisfied from his behavior now that he never had any intention of winning my affections. It's just that he's blessed with more charm and a greater desire to please than any other man."

"You are being very cruel," said her sister. "You won't let me smile and keep provoking me to do so."
She replied, "In some cases, it's difficult to be believed."
"And impossible in others!"
"But why would you want to make me believe I feel more than I'm saying?"

"That's a question I don't know how to answer. We all like to teach, even if it's something that isn't worth knowing. Please forgive me, and if you keep being uninterested, don't make me your confidante."

CHAPTER 55

A few days later, Mr. Bingley came back, this time alone. His friend had gone to London that morning but was coming back in ten days. He stayed with them for over an hour and was in a really good mood. Mrs. Bennet asked him to have dinner with them, but with many apologies, he said he had other plans.

"Next time you come," she said, "I hope we'll be luckier."

He said he'd be happy at any time, and so on.

"Can you come to-morrow?"

"Yes, I have no engagements," he replied eagerly.

The next day he arrived early and the ladies were not yet dressed. Mrs. Bennet ran into Jane's room in her dressing gown and with her hair half done, shouting,

"My dear Jane, hurry down. He is here. Mr. Bingley is here. Hurry, hurry! Sarah, come help Miss Bennet with her gown. Never mind Miss Lizzy's hair."

"We'll be down as soon as we can," Jane replied. "but I must say, Kitty is more forward than us, she went up to get ready a half hour ago."

"Oh, forget about Kitty. Come on, be quick. Where is your sash, my dear?"

When Mrs. Bennet left, Jane refused to go down without one of her sisters.

The same desire to have Elizabeth and Catherine alone was noticeable again in the evening. Mr. Bennet went to the library after tea, as he usually did, and Mary went upstairs to play her instrument. With two obstacles out of the way, Mrs. Bennet sat staring and winking at Elizabeth and Catherine for a while without getting a response from them. Elizabeth deliberately ignored her, and when Kitty finally noticed, she asked innocently, "What's wrong, Mama? Why do you keep winking at me? What am I supposed to do?"

"Nothing, sweetheart, nothing. I wasn't winking at you." She stayed there for another five minutes but then got up, saying to Kitty,

"Come here, my love, I need to talk to you," and took her out of the room. Jane gave Elizabeth a look that showed her distress at this plan and begged her not to go along with it. Not long after, Mrs. Bennet opened the door a bit and called out,

"Lizzy, my dear, I need to talk to you."

Elizabeth had to go.

"We might as well let them be by themselves, don't you think?" her mother said as soon as she was in the hallway. "Kitty and I are going up to my dressing room."

Elizabeth didn't bother trying to reason with her mother and just stayed in the hall until they were out of sight. Then she went back to the drawing room.

Mrs. Bennet's plans for the day didn't work out. Bingley was very charming, except for the fact that he wasn't interested in Jane. He was very easy to talk to and had a great patience for Mrs. Bennet's silly comments.

He didn't even need to be asked to stay for supper and before he left, he made plans to come back the next morning to go hunting with Mr. Bennet.

After that day, Jane stopped talking about not being interested in him. No words were exchanged between the sisters concerning Bingley; yet Elizabeth went to bed with a cheerful outlook as she was certain that everything would soon be settled, unless Mr. Darcy returned before the expected time. In reality, she was fairly sure that this had all been done with his approval.

Bingley arrived on time for the meeting and he and Mr. Bennet spent the morning as planned. Bingley was much more pleasant than his companion had anticipated. There was nothing in Bingley that could make him laugh sarcastically or make him stay quiet out of annoyance. He was more talkative and less strange than the other had ever seen him before. Bingley, of course, joined them for dinner and in the evening Mrs. Bennet tried to get everyone away from him and her daughter. Elizabeth, who had a letter to write, went to the breakfast room to do so shortly after tea as the others were going to play cards, so she was not needed to ruin her mother's plans.

When Elizabeth returned to the drawing room, she was shocked to see her sister and Bingley standing together by the fireplace, as if they had been having a serious conversation. Both of them quickly moved away from each other when they saw Elizabeth, and the situation was very awkward. Elizabeth was about to leave when Bingley suddenly got up, said a few words to Jane, and ran out of the room.

Jane had no reason to not tell Elizabeth what had happened and she immediately hugged her sister, expressing her joy and saying that she was the happiest person in the world.

"It's too much!" she exclaimed. "Far too much. I don't deserve it. Oh, why can't everyone be as happy?"

Elizabeth congratulated her with such sincerity, warmth, and joy that words could not fully express. Every kind word brought Jane even more happiness. However, she did not allow herself to stay with her sister or say everything that was left to be said at that moment.

"I must go instantly to my mother," she cried. "I would not on any account trifle with her affectionate solicitude; or allow her to hear it from anyone but myself. He is gone to my father already. Oh! Lizzy, to know that what I have to relate will give such pleasure to all my dear family! how shall I bear so much happiness!"

She then hurried away to her mother, who had intentionally broken up the card party, and was sitting upstairs with Kitty.

Elizabeth, who was left alone, now smiled at how quickly and easily the matter was finally resolved, after having caused them so many months of suspense and frustration.

"And this," she said, "is the end result of all the worry of his friend and all the deceit and planning of his sister! The happiest, wisest, and most sensible outcome!"

A few minutes later, Bingley joined her. He had been in a short and to-the-point conversation with her father.

"Where is your sister?" he asked quickly as he opened the door.

"She's with my mother upstairs. She'll be down soon, I'm sure," she replied.

He then closed the door and came up to her, asking for her heartfelt congratulations for their new relationship. Elizabeth was genuinely delighted and they shook hands warmly. Until her sister came down, she had to listen to all Bingley had to say about his own happiness and Jane's perfections. Despite being a lover, Elizabeth truly believed all his hopes for happiness were soundly based, because they were rooted in Jane's excellent understanding and superlative character, as well as their shared feelings and tastes.

It was an evening of great joy for everyone; Miss Bennet's happiness was so evident on her face that she looked even more beautiful than usual. Kitty smiled and hoped it would be her turn soon. Mrs. Bennet could not express her approval of the situation in enough enthusiastic terms, and spoke to Bingley about nothing else for half an hour. When Mr. Bennet joined them for supper, it was clear how pleased he was, though he didn't say a word about it until Bingley had left. As soon as he was gone, Mr. Bennet said to Jane,

"I congratulate you; you will be a very happy woman."

Jane went to him and kissed him, thanking him for his kindness. He replied,

"You are a good girl, and I am delighted that you will be so happily settled. I have no doubt that you and Bingley will do very well together, as your temperaments are so similar. You are both so agreeable that there will never be any disagreement. You are all so compliant that nothing is ever decided; so easygoing that every servant will take advantage of you; and so generous that you will always spend more than you make," said Mr. Bennet.

"I hope not, It would be unforgivable for me to be imprudent or careless with money."

"Exceed their income! My dear Mr. Bennet," exclaimed his wife, "what are you talking about? He has four or five thousand pounds a year, and probably more." Then turning to her daughter she said, "Oh, my dear, dear Jane, I'm so happy! I'm sure I won't get a wink of sleep tonight. I knew it would be like this. I always said it would turn out this way. I knew you couldn't be so beautiful for nothing! I remember when he first came to Hertfordshire last year, I thought it was likely you two would end up together. Oh, he is the most handsome young man ever seen!"

Wickham and Lydia were forgotten. Jane was her favorite child beyond comparison. At that moment, she didn't care about anyone else.

Mary asked to use the library at Netherfield, and Kitty begged for a few balls there every winter.

After this time, Bingley became a daily visitor at Longbourn, arriving frequently before breakfast and staying until after supper, except when he received an invitation to dinner from some detestable neighbor that he felt obligated to accept.

Elizabeth had little time for conversation with Jane in his presence, as Jane had no attention to spare for anyone else. However, Elizabeth found herself useful to both of them during those hours of separation that inevitably occurred. In Jane's absence, Bingley always sought out Elizabeth for the pleasure of talking about her, and when Bingley was gone, Jane constantly sought the same means of relief.

"He has made me so happy," she said one evening, "by telling me he had no idea I was in town last spring! I couldn't believe it."

"I suspected as much," Elizabeth replied. "But how did he explain it?"

"It must have been his sister's doing. They obviously weren't happy about his relationship with me, which I can understand since he could have chosen someone much better in many ways. But if they see that he's happy with me, they'll be content and we'll get along again, even if things will never be the same between us."

"That's the most unforgiving thing I've ever heard you say," Elizabeth said "Good girl! It would really bother me if you were to be fooled again by Miss Bingley's false affection."

"Can you believe it, Lizzy," Jane replied, "when he went to town last November, he actually loved me, and only the idea that I didn't care for him stopped him from coming back!"

"He made a little mistake, to be sure; but it is to the credit of his modesty."

This naturally led to Jane praising his diffidence and how he undervalues his own good qualities.

Elizabeth was pleased to see that he had not revealed the interference of his friend. Although Jane had the most generous and forgiving heart in the world, she knew it would bias her against him.

"I am certainly the luckiest person that ever existed!" cried Jane. "Oh, Lizzy, why am I the one singled out from my family to be blessed above them all? If only I could see you as happy! If there were only another man like him for you!"

"If you gave me forty men like him, I still couldn't be as happy as you. I can never have your happiness until I have your kindness and your good nature. No, no, I'll have to find my own way. Maybe, if I'm lucky, I'll find another Mr. Collins in time."

The situation of the Longbourn family could not be kept secret for long. Mrs. Bennet was allowed to tell Mrs. Philips, and she dared, without permission, to tell all her neighbors in Meryton.

The Bennets were soon seen to be the luckiest family in the world, though just a few weeks before, when Lydia had first run away, they had been generally thought to be destined for misfortune.

CHAPTER 56

One morning, about a week after Bingley and Jane's engagement had been established, he and the female members of the family were sitting together in the dining-room when they suddenly heard the sound of a carriage outside the window. They saw a chaise and four driving up the lawn, but it was too early for visitors, and the carriage and the livery of the servant who preceded it were not familiar to them. However, since someone was coming, Bingley immediately persuaded Miss Bennet to avoid the intrusion and walk with him into the shrubbery. They both left, and the remaining three continued to speculate, but with little satisfaction, until the door opened and their visitor entered. It was Lady Catherine de Bourgh.

They were all expecting to be surprised, but their astonishment was beyond their expectations; and for Mrs. Bennet and Kitty, who had never met her before, it was even greater than Elizabeth felt.

She entered the room with an air more than usually unfriendly, gave no other reply to Elizabeth's greeting than a slight nod of her head, and sat down without saying a word. Elizabeth had mentioned her name to her mother when she arrived, although no introduction had been requested.

Mrs. Bennet, in complete surprise, but flattered to have such an important guest, received her with the utmost politeness. After sitting in silence for a moment, she said to Elizabeth very formally,

"I hope you are doing well, Miss Bennet. Is that woman over there your mother?"

Elizabeth replied simply, "Yes, she is."

Lady Catherine then asked, "And is that one of your sisters?"

Mrs. Bennet eagerly responded, "Yes, she is my second youngest daughter. My youngest daughter recently got married and my oldest is walking around the grounds with a young man who I think will soon be part of the family."

After a short pause, Lady Catherine commented, "Your park is quite small." Mrs. Bennet replied,

"It's much bigger than Sir William Lucas's, but it's nothing compared to Rosings, of course."

"This must be an inconvenient room for the evening in the summer; the windows face west."

Mrs. Bennet assured her that they never sat there after dinner, and then asked,

"May I take the liberty of asking if you left Mr. and Mrs. Collins well?"

Lady Catherine replied, "Yes, they were very well. I saw them two nights ago."

Elizabeth now expected that Lady Catherine would produce a letter from Charlotte. But nothing appeared, leaving Elizabeth perplexed.

Mrs. Bennet politely asked Lady Catherine if she would like some refreshment, but she declined and said to Elizabeth,

"Miss Bennet, I noticed a small wilderness on one side of your lawn. Would you accompany me on a walk there?"

"Go, my dear," her mother said.

Elizabeth grabbed her parasol and accompanied her noble guest downstairs. As they passed through the hall, Lady Catherine opened the doors to the dining and drawing rooms, declaring them to be decent looking.

Her carriage waited at the door and Elizabeth saw her waiting woman was inside. They proceeded in silence along the gravel walk that led to the copse; Elizabeth was determined not to make any effort to talk to a woman who was even more insolent and unpleasant than usual.

"How could I ever have thought she was like her nephew?" she said, looking at her.

As soon as they entered the grove, Lady Catherine began speaking in the following manner:

"You must know why I have come here, Miss Bennet. Your own heart and conscience must tell you."

Elizabeth looked at her with genuine surprise.

"You are mistaken, Madam. I have no idea why you are here."

"Miss Bennet," Lady Catherine said angrily, "you should know that I am not to be trifled with. I am known for my sincerity and honesty, and in a matter as serious as this, I will not deviate from that. I heard a report two days ago that was extremely worrying. I was told that not only was your sister about to be married very advantageously, but that you, Miss Elizabeth Bennet, were likely to be married to my nephew, my own nephew, Mr. Darcy. Even though I know it must be a false and scandalous rumor, and I would never think it could be true, I decided immediately to come here to make my feelings known to you."

"If you thought it was impossible to be true," said Elizabeth, blushing with astonishment and indignation, "I'm surprised you took the trouble to come all this way. What did you hope to achieve?"

"To make sure the rumor was universally denied."

"Your visit to Longbourn, to see me and my family," said Elizabeth, calmly, "will only be confirming it; if, indeed, such a rumor exists."

"If? So you're pretending to not know about it? Haven't you been spreading it around? Don't you know it's being talked about?"

"I've never heard it."

"Can you tell me there's no truth to it?"

"I'm not as open as you are. You can ask questions, but I won't answer them."

"That's unacceptable. Miss Bennet, I demand an answer. Has my nephew proposed to you?"

"Your Ladyship said it was impossible."

"It should be, while he still has his senses. But you may have used your charms to make him forget what he owes himself and his family. You may have tricked him."

"If I have, I won't be the one to admit it".

"Miss Bennet, do you know who I am? I'm not used to this kind of talk. I'm almost his closest relative and I deserve to know his most personal matters."

"But you're not entitled to know about me; and this kind of behavior won't get me to be more open."

"Let me make myself clear. This match, which you have the nerve to try to make happen, will never happen. No, never. Mr. Darcy is engaged to my daughter. So what do you have to say now?"

"Only this; if that's true, you have no reason to think he'll make an offer to me."

Lady Catherine paused for a moment, then said,

"The engagement between them is special. We planned for them to be together since they were babies. And now, when both sisters' wishes would be fulfilled with their marriage, it's being blocked by a woman of a lower class, who has no power or influence in the world, and isn't related to the family! Don't you care about the wishes of his friends? About his unspoken engagement to Miss de Bourgh? Have you lost all sense of propriety and good manners? Haven't you heard me say that he was intended for his cousin from the beginning?"

"Yes, I had heard it before. But why should that matter to me? If there is no other reason why I cannot marry your nephew, then I will not be prevented from it by knowing that his mother and aunt wanted him to marry Miss De Bourgh. You both did all you could to plan the marriage, but its completion relied on other people. If Mr. Darcy is not bound to his cousin by honor or inclination, then why can't he make another choice? And if I am that choice, why can't I accept him?"

"Because honor, decency, wisdom, and even interest forbid it. Yes, Miss Bennet, interest; for do not expect to be respected by his family or friends if you deliberately go against the wishes of everyone. You will be criticized, ignored, and despised by all connected to him. Your union will be a disgrace and your name will never be mentioned by any of us."

"These are serious consequences," Elizabeth replied. "But the wife of Mr. Darcy would have such extraordinary advantages that she would have no cause to complain, overall."

"Stubborn, willful girl! I'm embarrassed for you! Is this how you show your appreciation for my kindness to you last spring? Don't I deserve anything in return?

"Let's sit down. You must understand Miss Bennet, I came here with a firm intention to do what I wanted and I won't be deterred. I'm not used to people controlling me or denying me what I want. That will make your current situation more unfortunate, but it won't affect me.

"Let me finish. My daughter and my nephew are perfect for each other. On their mother's side, they come from a noble line, and on their father's side, from respectable, honorable, and old, though un-titled, families. They have great fortunes. Everyone in their families wants them to be together. What could possibly separate them? The untitled and unconnected claims of a young woman with no family, connections, or money. Is that really acceptable? That won't do! If you were wise, you wouldn't want to leave the world you were brought up in."

"If I marry your nephew, I won't be leaving that world. He is a gentleman, and I am a gentleman's daughter, so we are equal in that respect."

"Yes, you are a gentleman's daughter. But who was your mother? Who are your uncles and aunts? Don't think I don't know what they are like."

"Whatever my connections may be, if your nephew doesn't mind them, they shouldn't be a problem for you."

"Just tell me, are you engaged to him?"

Elizabeth hesitated for a moment, but then said, "No, I am not."

Lady Catherine seemed pleased. "Will you promise me you won't get engaged to him?"

"I won't make any promises like that."

"Miss Bennet, I am surprised and shocked. I thought you would be more sensible. Don't deceive yourself into thinking I will ever leave. I won't go away until you give me the assurance I need."

"And I definitely won't give it. I won't be forced into something so unreasonable. Your Ladyship wants Mr. Darcy to marry your daughter, but would my giving you the desired promise make their marriage any more likely? Assuming he is attached to me, would my refusal to accept his hand make him want to give it to his cousin? Allow me to say, Lady Catherine, that the arguments you used to support this unusual request were as meaningless as the request was ill-advised. You have clearly misunderstood my character if you think I can be persuaded by such arguments. I can't say how your nephew would feel about your interference in his affairs, but you certainly have no right to interfere in mine. So, I must ask you not to pressure me any further on this subject."

"Not so fast, if you please. I'm not done yet. In addition to all the objections I've already made, I have one more. I know all the details of your youngest sister's disgraceful elopement. I know it was a hastily arranged affair at the expense of your father and uncles. Is such a girl going to be my nephew's sister? Are their nieces and the daughters of their late brother going to be associated with a family that has such an example of moral weakness before them?

"You have nothing else to say now," she replied angrily. "You have insulted me in every way. I must go back to the house."

As she said this, Lady Catherine also stood up and they began to walk back. She was very angry.

"So you have no regard for my nephew's honor and reputation? You heartless, selfish girl! Don't you realize that being connected to you would bring shame to him in the eyes of everyone?"

"Lady Catherine, I have nothing else to say. You know my feelings."

"So you are determined to have him?"

"I have not said that. I am only determined to do what I believe will make me happy, without taking into account you or anyone else who is not closely connected to me."

"It's fine. So you refuse to do me a favor. You refuse to comply with what duty, honor, and gratitude require. You're determined to ruin his reputation in the eyes of all his friends and make him the laughingstock of the world."

"Neither duty, honor, nor gratitude have any relevance to my situation now," replied Elizabeth. "My marrying Mr. Darcy would not violate any principle of these values. As for the resentment of his family or the world's indignation, if they were to arise from his marriage to me, I wouldn't be bothered by it for a moment. The world at large would have too much common sense to join in such scorn."

"So that's your real opinion? That's your final decision? Very well. Now I know what to do. Don't think your ambition will be fulfilled, Elizabeth. I came here to test you, I was hoping you'd be reasonable, but you can be sure I'll get my way."

Lady Catherine continued talking until they reached the carriage door, then turning quickly she added, "I won't say goodbye to you, Miss Bennet. I won't send any kind regards to your mother. You don't deserve that. I'm very angry."

Elizabeth didn't answer and without trying to persuade Lady Catherine to come back into the house, she walked in herself. As she went upstairs, she heard the carriage driving away. When she reached the door of the dressing room, her mother was there waiting impatiently to ask why Lady Catherine wouldn't come back in and rest.

"She didn't want to," said Elizabeth, "she wanted to leave."

"She is a very attractive woman! And it was so polite of her to come here! I suppose she just wanted to tell us that the Collins's are doing well. I suppose she was just passing through Meryton and thought she would call in to see you. I don't suppose she had anything particular to say to you, did she Lizzy?"

Elizabeth had to tell a little lie here, as it was impossible to admit what they had actually talked about.

CHAPTER 57

The shock of Lady Catherine de Bourgh's unexpected visit had left Elizabeth feeling extremely disturbed, and she couldn't stop thinking about it for hours. Lady Catherine had apparently journeyed from Rosings with the sole intention of putting an end to the supposed engagement between Elizabeth and Mr. Darcy. Elizabeth found it difficult to understand how such a rumor could have started in the first place, until she remembered that Mr. Darcy was a close friend of Bingley, and she herself was Jane's sister. This was enough for people to start speculating about a potential match. Elizabeth had also considered the possibility of being in closer contact with Mr. Darcy after her sister's marriage, and it seemed that the people at Lucas Lodge (who had probably heard of the rumor through their association with the Collinses) had taken that idea and turned it into a certainty.

In considering Lady Catherine's words, Elizabeth couldn't help but feel some unease about the potential consequences of her continued interference. Based on what Lady Catherine had said about her determination to prevent their marriage, Elizabeth suspected that she might plan to speak to her nephew, Mr. Darcy, and she couldn't predict how he would react to a similar warning about the dangers of a union with Elizabeth. Elizabeth didn't know the extent of Mr. Darcy's affection for his aunt or his reliance on her judgment, but it seemed likely that he held her in much higher esteem than Elizabeth did. Lady Catherine was sure to appeal to his sense of dignity and caution him against marrying someone whose family background was so inferior to his own. Though Elizabeth had found Lady Catherine's arguments weak and absurd, Mr. Darcy might consider them sensible and compelling.

If he was wavering before about what to do, which seemed likely, the advice and pleadings of such a close relative could settle any doubts and make him decide to be as happy as his pride would allow. In that case, he would not be coming back. Lady Catherine might see him on her way through town, and his promise to Bingley to return to Netherfield must be broken.

"If his friend comes up with an excuse for him not keeping his promise in the next few days," she said, "I'll know what it means. I'll give up on expecting him to stay faithful or hoping that he will keep his promise. If he's content with just regretting losing me, when he could have had my love and my hand in marriage, I'll stop regretting him altogether."

The rest of the family was very surprised to hear who their visitor had been, but they kindly satisfied their curiosity with the same kind of supposition that had appeased Mrs. Bennet's. Elizabeth was spared from much teasing on the subject. The next morning, as she was going downstairs, her father came out of his library with a letter in his hand.

"Lizzy," he said, "I was looking for you; come into my room."

She followed him in and her curiosity to know what he had to tell her was heightened by the thought that it might be from Lady Catherine. She dreaded what explanations might follow.

They both sat down by the fireplace and he said,

"I received a letter this morning that has astonished me greatly. As it mainly concerns you, you should know what it says. I didn't know before that I had two daughters on the verge of marriage. Let me congratulate you on a very important accomplishment."

Elizabeth's cheeks flushed as she realized the letter was from her nephew, not her aunt, and she was unsure if she should be pleased that he was explaining himself or offended that the letter wasn't addressed to her. Mr. Bennet continued,

"You look guilty. Young ladies usually have a good understanding of these matters, but I'm sure even your intelligence won't be able to guess who your admirer is. This letter is from Mr. Collins."

"From Mr. Collins? What could he have to say?" Elizabeth asked.

"It's obviously something important. He starts by congratulating me on the upcoming nuptials of my eldest daughter, which he must have heard about from the gossiping Lucases. I won't keep you in suspense. Here's what he says about you:

"' Having offered you and Mrs. Collins our sincere congratulations on this happy event, let me now add a brief comment on another, of which we have been informed by the same source. Your daughter Elizabeth, it is assumed, will not keep the name of Bennet for long after her elder sister has relinquished it, and the chosen partner of her fate can be expected to be one of the most distinguished people in the country.'

"Can you guess, Lizzy, who this is referring to?

"This young man is uniquely blessed with everything that mortal hearts could desire - splendid wealth, noble family connections, and extensive influence. Despite these temptations, let me warn you and our cousin Elizabeth of the potential pitfalls of hastily accepting his proposal, which you will surely be inclined to do.'

"Do you have any idea who this gentleman might be, Lizzy? Now we know.

"My reason for cautioning you is as follows: we have reason to believe that his aunt, Lady Catherine de Bourgh, does not view the match with a friendly eye.'

"Mr. Darcy is the man! I think I surprised you, Lizzy. Could they have chosen a man from our circle of acquaintances whose name would have been more effective in disproving what they said? Mr. Darcy, who never looks at a woman without seeing a flaw and probably never even looked at you! It's amazing!"

Elizabeth tried to join in her father's joke but could only manage a reluctant smile. His wit had never been used in such an unpleasant way before.

"Are you not amused?"

"Yes, please continue reading."

"After discussing the likelihood of this marriage with Lady Catherine last night, she immediately expressed her opinion, as she usually does. It became apparent that, due to some family objections on my cousin's part, she would never consent to what she called such a disgraceful match. It was my duty to inform my cousin of this news as soon as possible, so that she and her noble suitor are aware of what they are getting into, and do not rush into a marriage that has not been properly sanctioned.'

"Furthermore, Mr. Collins adds,

"I am truly pleased that my cousin Lydia's unfortunate situation has been so well hidden, and I am only concerned that their cohabitation before marriage has become so widely known. However, I must not neglect the duties of my position or refrain from expressing my surprise at hearing that you welcomed the newlywed couple into your home as soon as they were married. It was an encouragement of vice, and if I were the rector of Longbourn, I would have strongly opposed it. As a Christian, you should certainly forgive them, but never allow them to be seen in your presence or their names to be mentioned in your hearing.'

"That is his idea of Christian forgiveness! The rest of his letter only talks about his dear Charlotte's situation and his expectation of a new child. But, Lizzy, you seem unhappy. You are not going to be too sensitive and pretend to be offended by an idle rumor. After all, why do we live if not to entertain our neighbors and laugh at them in return?"

"Oh!" Elizabeth exclaimed, "I find this so amusing! But it's so strange!"

"Yes, that's what makes it so entertaining. If it had been about any other man it wouldn't have been so funny, but the fact that he's completely indifferent to you and you clearly don't like him makes it so absurdly amusing! I hate writing letters, but I wouldn't give up Mr. Collins' letters for anything. In fact, when I read one of his letters, I can't help but prefer him to Wickham, even though I value the impudence and hypocrisy of my son-in-law. And so, Lizzy, what did Lady Catherine say about this report? Did she call to refuse her consent?"

Elizabeth could only laugh in response to this question and, since it had been asked without any suspicion, she wasn't upset that he asked it again. Elizabeth had never been more uncomfortable trying to hide her true feelings. She wanted to cry, but she had to laugh. Her father had hurt her deeply by what he said about Mr. Darcy's lack of interest, and she couldn't help but be surprised at his lack of insight, or worry that instead of seeing too little, she might have imagined too much.

CHAPTER 58

Instead of receiving the expected letter of apology from Mr. Bingley, Elizabeth was pleasantly surprised to find that he brought Darcy with him to Longbourn just a few days after Lady Catherine's visit. The gentlemen arrived early, and before Mrs. Bennet had the chance to inform them that they had met with his aunt, Bingley suggested they all go for a walk, hoping for some alone time with Jane. Everyone agreed, although Mrs. Bennet did not usually walk and Mary was too busy to join them, leaving just the remaining five to set off together.

Bingley and Jane soon fell behind, allowing the others to continue ahead. Elizabeth, Kitty, and Darcy were left to entertain each other, but very little was said by anyone. Kitty was too intimidated to speak, and Elizabeth was secretly making a bold decision. Perhaps Darcy was doing the same.

As they walked towards the Lucases, Kitty expressed a desire to visit Maria. Since Elizabeth saw no need to involve everyone in this, she decided to continue alone with Darcy. This was the perfect opportunity to act on her decision, and while she was feeling brave, she spoke up:

"Mr. Darcy, I must confess I am a very selfish person. For the sake of easing my own feelings, I do not care how much I may be hurting yours. I cannot help thanking you for your unparalleled kindness to my poor sister. I have wanted to express my gratitude to you ever since I found out about it. If my family were aware of it, it would not only be my own gratitude that I would have to convey."

"I am very sorry, extremely sorry," replied Darcy, sounding surprised and emotional. "I regret that you have ever found out about something that may have caused you distress when viewed in the wrong light. I did not think Mrs. Gardiner could not be trusted."

"Do not blame my aunt. Lydia's carelessness was what first revealed to me that you had been involved in the matter, and of course, I could not rest until I knew all the details. I want to thank you again and again, on behalf of my entire family, for your generous kindness that led you to take so much trouble and endure so many humiliations in order to discover the truth."

"If you insist on thanking me," he replied, "let it be only for yourself. I won't deny that the desire to make you happy added to the other reasons that led me to act. But your *family* owes me nothing. As much as I respect them, I was only thinking of *you*."

Elizabeth was too embarrassed to say anything. After a short pause, her companion continued, "You're too kind to play games with me. If your feelings are still the same as they were last April, then tell me now. My affections and wishes haven't changed, but one word from you and I'll never mention this again."

Elizabeth was acutely aware of the awkwardness and anxiety of the situation, but she forced herself to speak. Although not very eloquently, she conveyed to him that her feelings had undergone such a significant change since the time he referred to, that she was now grateful and pleased to receive his current assurances. The happiness that her response brought him was likely something he had never experienced before, and he expressed himself as sensibly and warmly as a man deeply in love could be expected to do. If Elizabeth had been able to look at him, she would have seen how well the expression of heartfelt delight suited him. But even though she could not see him, she could hear him. He spoke of feelings that demonstrated how important she was to him, making his affection for her more valuable with each passing moment.

They continued to walk without knowing which direction they were headed. There was too much to think about, feel, and say for them to pay attention to anything else. She soon learned that their current good understanding was due to the efforts of his aunt, who did visit him on her way back through London and told him about her journey to Longbourn, its purpose, and the substance of her conversation with Elizabeth. Lady Catherine emphasized every expression of Elizabeth's that, in her estimation, demonstrated her stubbornness and boldness in believing that such a story would help her obtain a promise from her nephew that Lady Catherine herself had refused to give. Unfortunately for her ladyship, the effect was precisely the opposite.

"It made me dare to hope," he said, "in a way that I had never dared to hope before. I knew enough about your character to be certain that if you had truly and definitively rejected me, you would have acknowledged it to Lady Catherine honestly and openly."

Elizabeth blushed and laughed as she responded, "Yes, you know me well enough to believe that I would do that. After insulting you so terribly to your face, I would have no qualms about insulting you to all of your relatives."

"What did you say about me that I did not deserve? Even though your accusations were unfounded and based on mistaken assumptions, my behavior towards you at the time deserved the strongest rebuke. It was unforgivable. I cannot think about it without feeling disgust."

"We will not argue over who bears the greater blame for that evening," said Elizabeth. "If we examine our conduct closely, neither of us can be considered faultless. However, since then, I hope we have both become more civil."

"I cannot forgive myself so easily. The memory of what I said, my behavior, manners, and words throughout that night has been unbearably painful for me for many months now. Your criticism, which was well-deserved, still resonates with me: 'If only you had behaved more like a gentleman.' Those were your exact words. You cannot imagine how much they have tormented me - although I must admit, it took me some time to accept their validity."

"I did not expect my words to affect you so strongly. I had no idea that they would be taken so deeply to heart."

"I can believe it easily. At that time, you must have thought that I lacked all proper feelings. I am certain of it. I will never forget the expression on your face when you said that there was no possible way I could address you that would make you accept me."

"Oh, please don't repeat what I said then. These memories are too painful. I assure you, I have long been deeply ashamed of it."

Darcy brought up his letter. "Did it," he asked, "did it make you think better of me right away? Did you give any credence to its contents when you read it?"

She explained how the letter affected her and how her former prejudices gradually faded away.

"I knew," he said, "that what I wrote would cause you pain, but it was necessary. I hope you have destroyed the letter. There was one part, the beginning, in particular, that I dread you having the power to read again. I can remember some of the things I said that could make you hate me."

"The letter will definitely be burned if you believe it's necessary for me to keep your regard. However, although we both have reason to think that my opinions can change, they are not quite so easily altered as that implies."

"When I wrote that letter," replied Darcy, "I thought I was perfectly calm and collected, but I now realize that it was written with a terrible bitterness of spirit."

"The letter may have begun with bitterness, but it did not end that way. The farewell was the epitome of kindness. But let us not dwell on the letter anymore. The feelings of both the writer and the recipient have changed so much since then that every unpleasant aspect of it should be forgotten. You must learn some of my philosophy. Remember the past only if it brings you joy."

"I cannot credit you with any such philosophy. Your reflections must be completely free of blame for you to find contentment in them. That is not philosophy but rather ignorance, which is much better. However, it is not the case with me. Painful memories intrude that cannot and should not be pushed away. I have been selfish my entire life in practice, if not in principle. As a child, I was taught what was right, but not how to control my temper. I was given good values, but left to follow them with pride and conceit. Unfortunately, as an only son (for many years an only child), my parents spoiled me. Though they were good people, particularly my father, who was benevolent and kind, they allowed, encouraged, and even taught me to be selfish and domineering. I cared only for my family circle and thought little of the rest of the world. I even wished, or at least thought, poorly of others' intelligence and worth in comparison to my own. That was who I was from the age of eight until twenty-eight, and I might have remained that way were it not for you, my dearest and loveliest Elizabeth! What do I not owe you! You taught me a difficult but valuable lesson. You properly humbled me. I came to you with no doubt of my reception, but you showed me how inadequate all my attempts to please a woman worthy of being pleased truly were. Did you believe that I would propose to you then?"

"Yes, I did. What will you think of my conceit? I thought you wanted and expected me to make advances."

"It was my fault for not conveying my intentions properly. I never meant to mislead you, but sometimes my mood would get the best of me. You must have disliked me intensely after that evening."

"Dislike you? I may have been angry at first, but soon my anger gave way to more appropriate feelings."

"I'm almost afraid to ask what you thought of me when we met at Pemberley. Did you blame me for coming?"

"No, not at all. I was simply surprised."

"Your surprise could not have been greater than mine when I saw that you had noticed me. My conscience told me that I didn't deserve any special kindness, and I confess that I didn't expect to receive more than what was due to me."

"At that time," Darcy replied, "my objective was to show you, through every possible courtesy, that I wasn't petty enough to hold a grudge over the past. I hoped to obtain your forgiveness and improve your opinion of me by demonstrating that I had taken your criticisms to heart. I can hardly say when other feelings began to emerge, but I think it was about half an hour after I had seen you."

He then informed her of Georgiana's pleasure in their acquaintance and her disappointment at its abrupt ending. Naturally, this led to a discussion of the cause of the interruption, and she soon learned that he had decided to follow her sister from Derbyshire before he left the inn. His serious and contemplative demeanor there was the result of the inner turmoil he experienced when making such a decision.

She expressed her gratitude once more, but the subject was too painful for either of them to dwell on any further.

After walking for several miles at a leisurely pace, too preoccupied to notice the passing of time, they finally realized, upon checking their watches, that it was time to head home.

They began to wonder what could have happened to Mr. Bingley and Jane, which led to a discussion of their affairs. Darcy was thrilled to hear of their engagement, as his friend had informed him of it as soon as it happened.

"I have to ask, were you surprised?" Elizabeth inquired.

"Not at all. When I left, I had a feeling that it would happen soon."

"That means you had given your permission. I thought as much." Although he objected to the term, she realized that it was essentially true.

"On the evening before I went to London," he said, "I confessed to him what I should have confessed long ago. I told him about everything that had happened to make my past involvement in his affairs ridiculous and presumptuous. He was greatly surprised. He had never suspected anything. I also told him that I realized I was mistaken in assuming, as I did, that your sister was indifferent to him. Since I could see that his love for her had not diminished, I had no doubt that they would be happy together."

Elizabeth couldn't help but smile at his casual way of guiding his friend.

"Did you speak from your own observations," she asked, "when you told him that my sister loved him, or did you simply rely on my information from last spring?"

"From my own observations. I had closely observed her during my two recent visits to her here, and I was certain of her affection."

"And I suppose your assurance of it immediately convinced him?"

"It did. Bingley is genuinely modest. His own self-doubt had prevented him from relying on his own judgment in such an anxious matter, but his faith in me made everything easier. However, I was compelled to confess something that offended him for a while, and not without reason. I could not keep from him that your sister had been in town for three months last winter, that I had known about it, and that I had deliberately kept it from him. He was angry, but I believe his anger didn't last any longer than his doubt of your sister's feelings. He has fully forgiven me now."

Elizabeth wanted to say how delightful a friend Mr. Bingley had been, so easily guided and of such value, but she restrained herself. She remembered that he still had to learn to be teased, and it was a little too soon to start. Darcy continued the conversation, anticipating Bingley's happiness, which was sure to be second only to his own, until they reached the house. They parted ways in the hall.

CHAPTER 59

"My dear Lizzy, where have you been walking to?" Jane asked as soon as Elizabeth entered the room, and all the others at the table asked the same question. Elizabeth replied that they had wandered around until she lost track of where they were. She blushed as she spoke, but her embarrassment did not raise any suspicion of the truth.

The evening passed uneventfully. The acknowledged lovers talked and laughed while the unacknowledged were silent. Darcy was not the type to overflow with mirth when happy, and Elizabeth, feeling agitated and confused, knew she was happy more than she felt it. Besides the immediate embarrassment, there were other problems she anticipated. She feared the family's reaction when they found out about her situation, aware that no one liked Darcy except for Jane, and she even suspected that with others, it was a dislike that no amount of wealth or status could erase.

That night, Elizabeth confided in Jane, who, although not prone to suspicion, found it hard to believe what Elizabeth told her.

"You're joking, Lizzy. This can't be true! Engaged to Mr. Darcy? No, no, don't try to fool me. I know it's impossible."

"This is a terrible start! I relied solely on you, and if you don't believe me, I'm certain no one else will either. But I'm serious. I'm telling the truth. He still loves me, and we're engaged."

Jane looked at her skeptically. "Oh, Lizzy! It can't be true. You know how much you dislike him."

"You know nothing about it. That's all in the past. Perhaps I didn't love him as much back then as I do now. But in situations like this, having a good memory is unforgivable. This is the last time I'll ever think of it myself."

Miss Bennet still looked amazed. Elizabeth once again assured her, more seriously this time, that it was true.

"Good heavens! Can it really be true? But now I must believe you," exclaimed Jane. "My dear Lizzy, I would - I do congratulate you - but are you sure? Please forgive me for asking, but are you absolutely certain that you can be happy with him?"

"There's no doubt about it. We've already decided that we'll be the happiest couple in the world. But are you happy for me, Jane? Would you like to have him as a brother?"

"Very, very much. Nothing could give Bingley or myself more joy. But we thought it was impossible. And do you truly love him enough? Oh, Lizzy! Do anything but marry without love. Are you absolutely sure that you feel what you should?"

"Oh, yes! You'll only think that I feel even more than I should when I tell you everything."

"What do you mean?"

"Well, I must confess that I love him more than I do Bingley. I'm afraid you'll be angry."

"My dearest sister, now be serious. I want to talk seriously. Tell me everything I need to know right away. Will you tell me how long you've been in love with him?"

"It's been happening so gradually that I can't even remember when it started. But I think it was when I first saw his beautiful estate at Pemberley."

Another plea for her to be serious finally worked, and she was able to reassure Jane of her sincere feelings. Once Jane was convinced, she had nothing else to wish for.

"Now I'm completely happy," she said. "Because you'll be just as happy as I am. I always valued him. If it was just because of his love for you, I would always have held him in high regard. But now, as Bingley's friend and your husband, no one could be dearer to me than both of you. But Lizzy, you've been very sneaky, very secretive with me. You told me so little about what happened at Pemberley and Lambton! I only know what I do from someone else, not from you."

Elizabeth told her the reasons for her secrecy. She had been reluctant to mention Bingley, and her own uncertain feelings had made her equally avoid the name of his friend. But now she wouldn't hide from her his role in Lydia's marriage. Everything was acknowledged, and they spent half the night talking.

Mrs. Bennet exclaimed in surprise as she stood at the window the next morning, "Oh no! That annoying Mr. Darcy is here again with our dear Bingley! What does he mean by being so annoying and always coming here? I thought he would go hunting or something and not bother us with his presence. What shall we do with him? Lizzy, you must go for a walk with him again, so he won't be in Bingley's way."

Elizabeth couldn't help but laugh at the convenient suggestion, though she was annoyed that her mother kept calling him 'him'.

As soon as they entered, Bingley looked at Elizabeth so expressively and shook her hand with so much warmth that he must have been well informed. He then said loudly, "Mr. Bennet, do you have any more lanes around here that Lizzy can get lost in today?"

"I suggest that Mr. Darcy, Lizzy, and Kitty take a walk to Oakham Mount this morning. It's a nice long walk and Mr. Darcy has never seen the view."

"That might be alright for the others," said Mr. Bingley, "but I'm sure it will be too much for Kitty, won't it, Kitty?"

Kitty said that she'd rather stay at home. Darcy expressed a strong curiosity to see the view from the Mount and Elizabeth agreed silently. As she went upstairs to get ready, Mrs. Bennet followed her saying:"

"I'm really sorry, Lizzy, that you have to be stuck with that unpleasant man all by yourself. But I hope it won't bother you; it's all for Jane's sake, right? So there's no need to talk to him much, just a few times. Don't put yourself out."

During their walk, they decided that Mr. Bennet should be asked for his consent that evening. Elizabeth kept the task of asking her mother to herself. She couldn't predict how her mother would react; sometimes doubting if all his wealth and grandeur would be enough to make her forget her dislike of the man. But whether she was strongly against the match, or strongly in favor of it, it was certain that her behavior wouldn't reflect her good sense either way; and she couldn't bear the thought of Mr. Darcy hearing her initial joy or initial disapproval.

In the evening, soon after Mr. Bennet withdrew to the library, Elizabeth saw Mr. Darcy rise and follow him, and she was extremely agitated. She wasn't worried about her father's disapproval, but the thought of causing him distress by her choice, of being the one to make him unhappy by her decision to marry, was a terrible reflection, and she sat in misery until Mr. Darcy reappeared. When she looked at him, she was a little relieved by his smile. A few minutes later he came to the table where Elizabeth and Kitty were sitting; while pretending to admire her work, he whispered, "Go to your father, he wants you in the library." Elizabeth went right away.

Her father was walking around the room, looking serious and concerned. "Lizzy," he said, "what are you doing? Are you out of your mind, to be accepting this man? Haven't you always hated him?"

She then desperately wished that her earlier opinions had been more sensible and her words more restrained. But now she had to explain and prove her feelings for Mr. Darcy, which was very uncomfortable. She nervously assured him of her affection for Mr. Darcy.

"In other words, you're determined to marry him because he's wealthy and you'll have more fancy clothes and carriages than Jane. But will that make you happy?"

Elizabeth asked, "Do you have any other objections besides your belief that I don't care for him?"

"No objections at all," her father replied. "We all know he's a proud and unpleasant man, but that wouldn't matter if you really liked him."

"I do, I do like him," she said with tears in her eyes. "I love him. He doesn't have any improper pride. He's completely lovable. You don't know what he's really like, so please don't hurt me by talking about him like that."

"Lizzy," said her father, "I've given him my consent. He's the kind of man whom I could never refuse anything, if he deigned to ask. I'm giving my consent to *you*, if you're resolved to have him. But let me advise you to reconsider. I know you, Lizzy. I know that you couldn't be happy or respectable unless you truly respected your husband, unless you saw him as your superior. Your lively talents would put you in the greatest danger in an unequal marriage. You could hardly avoid disgrace and misery. My child, let me not have the pain of seeing *you* unable to respect your partner in life. You don't know what you're doing."

Elizabeth said, her emotions more heightened. She was earnest and solemn in her reply, and after repeatedly assuring her father that Mr. Darcy was her choice, she explained the gradual change in her opinion of him, assured him that his affections had been constant over many months, and enumerated his good qualities with energy. Her father was eventually convinced and said,

"Well, my dear, if that's the case, he deserves you. I couldn't have given you to anyone less worthy."

To further the positive impression, she then told him what Mr. Darcy had done for Lydia. He was astonished and said,

"This is an evening of wonders indeed! So Darcy did everything, made the match, gave the money, paid the fellow's debts, and got him his commission! That's even better. It'll save me a lot of trouble and money. If it had been your uncle's doing, I would have paid him, but these passionate young lovers do what they want. I'll offer to pay him tomorrow and he'll rant and rave about his love for you and that'll be the end of it."

He then remembered her embarrassment a few days before when he had read Mr. Collins's letter. After laughing at her for a while, he eventually allowed her to leave, saying as she exited the room, "If any young men come for Mary or Kitty, send them in, as I'm completely free."

Elizabeth felt a huge weight lifted off her shoulders and, after half an hour of quiet reflection in her own room, she was able to join the others. Although it was too soon for any real joy, the evening passed peacefully. There was nothing more to fear and comfort would come with time.

When her mother went up to her dressing-room at night, Elizabeth followed her and shared the important news. Its effect was most extraordinary; upon first hearing it, Mrs. Bennet sat completely still and was unable to utter a word. It took her many, many minutes to comprehend what she heard, even though she was usually eager to believe anything that would benefit her family or any lover who came their way. Eventually, she began to recover, fidget about in her chair, stand up, sit down again, wonder, and bless herself.

"Good gracious! Lord bless me! Can it be true? Mr. Darcy? Who would have thought it? Oh, my sweetest Lizzy! How rich and great you will be! Jane's is nothing compared to it. I'm so pleased, so happy. Such a charming man! So handsome, so tall! Oh, my dear Lizzy, please forgive me for not liking him before. I hope he'll forgive me. Dear, dear Lizzy. A house in town! Everything that's charming! Three daughters married! Ten thousand a year! Oh Lord, what will become of me? I'll go crazy!"

This was enough to prove that her mother's approval could not be questioned. Elizabeth, happy that only she had heard such an outburst, left soon afterwards. However, before she had been in her own room for three minutes, her mother followed her.

"My dearest child," she said, "I can't stop thinking about it! Ten thousand a year, and probably more! It's as good as a Lord! And a special license. You must and will get married with a special license. But my dearest love, tell me what dish Mr. Darcy likes particularly so I can make it tomorrow."

This was a worrying sign of what her mother's behavior towards the gentleman himself might be, and Elizabeth realized that even though she was certain of his strongest affection and had her family's consent, there was still something lacking. However, the following day went much better than she had anticipated. Mrs. Bennet was luckily so afraid of her future son-in-law that she didn't dare speak to him unless she could offer him any attention or show her respect for his opinion.

Elizabeth was pleased to see her father taking an effort to get to know Mr. Bennet and he assured her that he was growing more fond of him with each passing hour.

"I admire all my three sons-in-law very much," he said. "Wickham is probably my favorite, but I think I may like your husband just as much as Jane's."

CHAPTER 60

Elizabeth's spirits soon lifted and she wanted Mr. Darcy to explain why he had ever fallen in love with her. "How did it even start?" she asked. "I can understand why it kept going, but what sparked it in the first place?"

"I can't pinpoint the exact time, place, look, or words that started it. It was too long ago. I was already in love before I knew it had even begun."

"You rejected my beauty early on, and as for my manners - my behavior towards *you* was always almost rude, and I never spoke to you without wanting to hurt you rather than not. Now, be honest, did you admire me for my impoliteness?"

"I admired the liveliness of your mind."

"You might as well call it boldness. It was nearly that. The truth is, you were tired of politeness, respect, and people who were always speaking and looking for your approval. I got your attention because I was so different from them. If you weren't so nice, you would have hated me for it, but even though you tried to hide it, your feelings were always noble and you despised those who were always trying to please you. There, I saved you the trouble of explaining it and, when you think about it, it makes perfect sense. Of course, you didn't know anything good about me, but nobody thinks of that when they fall in love."

"Was there any good in the way you cared for Jane when she was sick at Netherfield?"

"My dearest Jane, who could have done less for her? But if you want to, you can make something good out of it. My good qualities are under your protection, and you should make them seem as great as possible; and, in return, it's my job to find excuses to tease and quarrel with you as often as I can; and I'll start right now by asking you why you were so reluctant to come to the point in the end. What made you so shy when you first called and then came to dinner here? Why, especially when you called, did you look like you didn't care about me?"

"Because you were serious and quiet, and didn't give me any encouragement."

"But I was embarrassed."

"And so was I."

"You could have talked to me more when you came to dinner."

"Someone who felt less than me might have."

"How unfortunate that you had an answer that made sense and that I was reasonable enough to accept it! But I'm curious to know how long you would have taken if I hadn't asked you! My decision to thank you for your kindness to Lydia certainly had a great effect. Too much, I'm afraid; what kind of lesson would that be if our happiness came from breaking a promise? That won't do."

"You needn't worry. The moral will be perfectly just. Lady Catherine's unjustifiable attempts to separate us were what ultimately removed all my doubts. I am not indebted for my present happiness to your eager desire to express your gratitude. I wasn't in the mood to wait for any sign from you. My aunt's information had given me hope, and I was determined to find out everything at once."

"Lady Catherine has been very helpful and that should make her happy since she loves to be useful. But tell me, why did you come to Netherfield? Was it just to ride to Longbourn and be embarrassed, or did you have something more serious in mind?"

"My real purpose was to see you and find out if I could ever make you love me. My goal, or what I had set out to do, was to find out if your sister still had feelings for Bingley and if she did, to tell him what I have since told him."

"Will you ever have the courage to tell Lady Catherine what will happen?"

"I need more time than courage, Elizabeth. But it needs to be done and if you give me some paper, I'll do it right away."

"And if I didn't have a letter to write, I could sit here and watch you write, just like another young lady once did. But I also have an aunt I can't ignore any longer."

Because she was unwilling to admit how much her closeness with Mr. Darcy had been exaggerated, Elizabeth had not yet replied to Mrs. Gardiner's long letter. But now, having something to share that she knew would be very welcome, she was almost embarrassed to discover that her uncle and aunt had already missed three days of happiness. She immediately wrote the following:

"I should have thanked you earlier, my dear aunt, as I should have done, for your lengthy, kind, satisfactory account of details. But to tell you the truth, I was too cross to write. You imagined more than actually existed. But now imagine as much as you please; give free rein to your imagination, indulge your fancy in every possible way that the subject will allow, and unless you believe me to be actually married, you cannot be far off. You must write again very soon and praise him even more than you did in your last letter. I thank you, again and again, for not going to the Lakes. How could I have been so foolish as to wish it! Your idea of the ponies is delightful. We will go around the park every day. I am the happiest person in the world. Perhaps others have said so before, but not one with such justification. I am even happier than Jane; she only smiles, I laugh. Mr. Darcy sends you all the love in the world that he can spare from me. You are all to come to Pemberley at Christmas.

Yours, etc."

Mr. Darcy's letter to Lady Catherine was in a different style. Mr. Bennet's reply to Mr. Collins was also different. He wrote:

"Dear Sir,
I must ask you once more for congratulations. Elizabeth will soon be Mr. Darcy's wife. Do your best to console Lady Catherine, but if I were you, I would stand by the nephew. He has more to give.
Yours sincerely, etc."

348

Miss Bingley's congratulations to her brother on his upcoming marriage were both warm and insincere. She even wrote to Jane to express her joy and repeat all her previous professions of affection. Jane was not fooled, but she was moved; and although she did not trust Miss Bingley, she could not help writing a much kinder reply than she knew was deserved.

The happiness that Miss Darcy showed upon receiving similar news was just as genuine as her brother's in sharing it. Four pages of paper were not enough to contain all her joy and her sincere desire to be loved by her new sister.

Before any response could arrive from Mr. Collins, or any congratulations from his wife to Elizabeth, the Longbourn family heard that the Collinses had come to Lucas Lodge themselves. The reason for this sudden move was soon clear. Lady Catherine had been so incensed by the contents of her nephew's letter that Charlotte, who was truly happy about the match, was eager to get away until the storm had passed. At such a moment, the arrival of her friend was a sincere pleasure to Elizabeth, although during their meetings she sometimes felt that the pleasure was dearly bought when she saw Mr. Darcy subjected to all the pompous and fawning civility of her husband. He bore it, however, with admirable composure. He could even listen to Sir William Lucas when he complimented him on winning the brightest jewel of the county and expressed his hopes that they would all meet frequently at St. James's, with great dignity. If he did shrug his shoulders, it was not until Sir William was out of sight.

Mrs. Philips' crudeness was another, and possibly an even greater test of his patience; and although Mrs. Philips, as well as her sister, was too intimidated by him to speak with the familiarity that Bingley's good nature encouraged, whenever she did speak, it was always crude. Nor was her respect for him, though it made her more quiet, in any way likely to make her more refined. Elizabeth did all she could to keep him away from the frequent attention of either of them, and was always eager to keep him to herself and to those of her family with whom he could converse without embarrassment; and though the uncomfortable feelings that arose from all this took away much of the pleasure of the courtship period, it added to the hope of the future; and she looked forward with joy to the time when they would be removed from a society that neither of them found pleasing, and to all the comfort and elegance of their family gathering at Pemberley.

CHAPTER 61

There was a day when Mrs. Bennet was happy to have gotten rid of her two most deserving daughters, and her maternal feelings were satisfied. She later visited Mrs. Bingley and talked proudly of Mrs. Darcy, showing off her accomplishments. It would be nice to say that the fulfillment of her earnest desire to establish so many of her children produced a positive effect, making her a sensible, amiable, and well-informed woman for the rest of her life, but unfortunately, this was not the case. Her occasional nervousness and consistent silliness may have been lucky for her husband, who may not have appreciated domestic bliss in such an unusual form.

Mr. Bennet missed his second daughter a great deal; his love for her drew him away from home more than anything else could. He loved going to Pemberley, especially when he was least expected.

Mr. Bingley and Jane only stayed at Netherfield for a year. Being so close to her mother and Meryton relations was not desirable to either his easy-going personality or her loving heart. His sisters' dearest wish was then fulfilled; he bought an estate in a neighboring county to Derbyshire and Jane and Elizabeth, in addition to all the other sources of joy, were within thirty miles of each other.

Kitty benefited greatly from spending most of her time with her two elder sisters. In a much better social circle than she was used to, she improved a lot. She wasn't as unruly as Lydia, and away from Lydia's influence, she became less irritable, less ignorant, and less boring with the proper attention and guidance. Her father wouldn't allow her to go and stay with Mrs. Wickham, even though she promised parties and young men.

Mary was the only daughter who stayed at home, and Mrs. Bennet's inability to be alone meant that Mary had to give up her pursuit of accomplishments. Mary had to interact more with society, but she still managed to moralize every morning visit. Since she was no longer hurt by comparisons between her sisters' beauty and her own, her father suspected that she accepted the change without much reluctance.

Regarding Wickham and Lydia, their personalities did not undergo any significant change due to the marriage of her sisters. Wickham accepted with a calm and rational mindset that Elizabeth must now become aware of any past ingratitude and deceitfulness on his part, which she had been previously unaware of. Despite everything, he still held on to the hope that Darcy might be persuaded to help him attain wealth.

Upon receiving a congratulatory letter from Lydia about her own marriage, Elizabeth learned that, at least according to Wickham's wife, if not Wickham himself, this hope was still being nurtured. The letter read as follows:

"Dear Lizzy,

I wish you joy. If you love Mr. Darcy as much as I love my dear Wickham, you must be very happy. It's a great relief to have you so wealthy, and if you have nothing else to do, I hope you'll think of us. I'm sure Wickham would love a job at court very much, and I don't think we'll have enough money to live on without some help. Any job with an income of about three or four hundred a year would do, but don't mention it to Mr. Darcy if you'd rather not."

"Your sincerely"

As Elizabeth would much rather not, she tried to put an end to any requests or expectations of help in her reply. However, she often sent them relief by being economical with her own money. It had always been clear to her that their income, with two people who were so careless about their spending, would not be enough to support them. Whenever they moved, either Jane or Elizabeth was sure to be asked for some help with their bills. Even after the peace returned and they had a home, their lifestyle was extremely unstable. They were constantly looking for a cheap place to live and always spending more than they should. His love for her soon faded to indifference, hers lasted a little longer, and despite her age and behavior, she kept the respectability her marriage had given her.

Though Darcy could never invite him to Pemberley, he still helped him with his job for Elizabeth's sake. Lydia sometimes visited Pemberley when her husband was away in London or Bath, and both she and the Bingleys would stay so long that even Bingley's good nature was tested and he talked about hinting for them to leave.

Miss Bingley was very upset by Darcy's marriage, but since she wanted to keep the right to visit Pemberley, she put aside her resentment and was even more fond of Georgiana than before, almost as attentive to Darcy as before, and was very polite to Elizabeth.

Pemberley was now Georgiana's home, and the sisters' attachment was exactly what Darcy had hoped for. They were able to love each other as much as they had intended. Georgiana had the highest opinion of Elizabeth, though at first she often listened with surprise bordering on fear at Elizabeth's lively, playful way of talking to her brother. He, who she had always held in high regard, was now the subject of jokes. She was learning something she had never known before. Through Elizabeth's teachings, she was beginning to understand that a wife can do things that a brother wouldn't necessarily allow a sister to do if she was more than ten years younger than him.

Lady Catherine was extremely angry when she heard of her nephew's marriage and, in her response to the letter that told her the news, she said such harsh things about Elizabeth that the two of them had no contact for a while. At last, Elizabeth convinced him to forgive the offense and move on, and after a bit more resistance from his aunt, she gave in, either out of her love for him or her curiosity to see how his wife behaved. She decided to visit them at Pemberley, even though it had been tainted by the presence of such a mistress, as well as visits from her uncle and aunt from the city.

Elizabeth and Darcy shared a deep bond with the Gardiners, often engaging with them in intimate conversations. Their fondness for the Gardiners was genuine, and they were immensely grateful to them for introducing Elizabeth to Derbyshire, thereby playing a significant role in bringing the couple together in matrimony.

PRIMARY CHARACTER SUMMARY

Mr. Fitzwilliam Darcy: A wealthy and proud gentleman, Mr. Darcy is initially seen as cold and aloof. However, his reserved nature hides a deep sense of loyalty and integrity, and his initial prejudices against Elizabeth Bennet give way to love and respect as he gets to know her better.

Miss Elizabeth Bennet: The second eldest daughter of the Bennet family, Elizabeth is witty, intelligent, and independent-minded. She initially dislikes Mr. Darcy due to his perceived arrogance, but over the course of the novel, she comes to appreciate his true character and falls in love with him.

Mr. Charles Bingley: A wealthy and amiable young man, Mr. Bingley quickly becomes enamored with Jane Bennet, Elizabeth's older sister. He is a close friend of Mr. Darcy and is initially persuaded by his friend's negative opinions of Jane and her family.

Miss Jane Bennet: The eldest Bennet daughter, Jane is kind-hearted and gentle. She falls in love with Mr. Bingley, but his sisters and Mr. Darcy conspire to keep them apart. Despite their interference, Jane remains steadfast in her affection for Bingley.

Miss Caroline Bingley: Mr. Bingley's snobbish and manipulative sister, Caroline disapproves of the Bennet family and tries to keep Bingley from pursuing Jane. She is also jealous of Elizabeth's growing closeness to Mr. Darcy.

Mr. George Wickham: A charming but unscrupulous young man, Wickham has a history with Mr. Darcy that eventually comes to light. He tries to seduce Elizabeth and elope with her, but his true character is eventually revealed.

Lydia Bennet: The youngest Bennet daughter, Lydia is flighty and impulsive. She elopes with Wickham, causing a scandal that threatens to ruin her family's reputation.

Mr. Bennet: Elizabeth's father, Mr. Bennet is intelligent but lazy. He is fond of his daughters but has a strained relationship with his wife.

Mrs. Bennet: Elizabeth's mother, Mrs. Bennet is obsessed with finding suitable husbands for her daughters. She is often silly and embarrassing but ultimately means well.

Mr. Gardiner: Elizabeth's uncle, Mr. Gardiner is a sensible and kind man who takes an interest in his nieces' lives. He helps to resolve the scandal surrounding Lydia's elopement.

Mrs. Gardiner: Elizabeth's aunt and Mr. Gardiner's wife, Mrs. Gardiner is a wise and compassionate woman who serves as a confidante to Elizabeth.

Charlotte Lucas: Elizabeth's best friend, Charlotte is practical and sensible. She marries the pompous Mr. Collins out of a sense of duty and security.

Mr. Collins: A distant cousin of the Bennet family, Mr. Collins is a pompous and obsequious man who is obsessed with social status. He proposes to Elizabeth but ends up marrying Charlotte instead.

Lady Catherine de Bourgh: Mr. Darcy's aunt, Lady Catherine is arrogant and domineering. She disapproves of Elizabeth and tries to prevent her from marrying Mr. Darcy

SECONDARY CHARACTER SUMMARY

Kitty Bennet: The second youngest Bennet daughter, Kitty is frivolous and prone to following the lead of her younger sister Lydia. She idolizes Wickham and is devastated by Lydia's elopement.

Mary Bennet: The third Bennet daughter, Mary is bookish and serious-minded. She is often overshadowed by her more outgoing sisters.

Sir William Lucas: A neighbor of the Bennet family, Sir William is a pompous but friendly man who values social status. He is the father of Charlotte and Maria Lucas.

Lady Lucas: The wife of Sir William Lucas and mother of Charlotte and Maria, Lady Lucas is a kind and sensible woman who serves as a confidante to Mrs. Bennet.

Maria Lucas: The youngest daughter of Sir William and Lady Lucas, Maria is a friend of Elizabeth's and serves as a companion to Charlotte.

Colonel Fitzwilliam: Mr. Darcy's cousin, Colonel Fitzwilliam is friendly and charming. He serves as a foil to Darcy and helps Elizabeth to see Darcy in a more favorable light.

Georgiana Darcy: Mr. Darcy's younger sister, Georgiana is shy and retiring. She is manipulated by Wickham but ultimately finds happiness with another man.

Miss Anne de Bourgh: Lady Catherine's sickly daughter, Miss de Bourgh is intended as a potential match for Mr. Darcy. She is not a major character in the novel.

Mrs. Hurst: Caroline Bingley's sister and Mr. Hurst's wife, Mrs. Hurst is snobbish and disapproving of the Bennet family.

Mr. Hurst: Caroline Bingley's brother-in-law and Mrs. Hurst's husband, Mr. Hurst is a genial but unremarkable man.

Mrs. Phillips: Mrs. Bennet's sister, Mrs. Phillips is a gossipy woman who enjoys meddling in the affairs of others.

Colonel Forster: The commanding officer of the regiment militia, Colonel Forster is a friend of Wickham's and ultimately helps to bring about his marriage to Lydia.

Mrs. Forster: The wife of Colonel Forster, Mrs. Forster is a friend of Lydia's and helps to facilitate her elopement.

Captain Carter and Lieutenant Denny: Two officers in the regiment militia who are briefly mentioned in the novel.

Mary King: A young woman who is briefly engaged to Wickham before he breaks it off and pursues a relationship with Georgiana Darcy.

Hill: The Bennet family's housekeeper, Hill is a loyal and efficient servant who helps to keep the household running smoothly.

Printed in Great Britain
by Amazon